## Matthew's Prize

Marcus Palliser gave up a successful career in corporate PR to work as a freelance business writer and pursue his passion for sailing. He recently spent three years living aboard a small yacht, sailing in the Mediterranean and crossing the Atlantic single-handed. He now lives in Truro, Cornwall, near some of the most dramatic sea coasts in the world.

*Matthew's Prize* is his first novel.

# Matthew's Prize

*Marcus Palliser*

ARROW

Published in the United Kingdom in 2000 by
Arrow Books

1 3 5 7 9 10 8 6 4 2

First published in the United Kingdom in 1999 by William Heinemann

Arrow Books Limited
The Random House Group Limited
20 Vauxhall Bridge Road, London, SW1V 2SA

Random House Australia (Pty) Limited
20 Alfred Street, Milsons Point, Sydney,
New South Wales 2061, Australia

Random House New Zealand Limited
18 Poland Road, Glenfield
Auckland 10, New Zealand

Random House (Pty) Limited
Endulini, 5a Jubilee Road, Parktown, 2193, South Africa

The Random House Group Limited Reg. No. 954009

A CIP catalogue record for this book
is available from the British Library

Papers used by Random House are natural,
recyclable products made from wood grown in sustainable forests.
The manufacturing processes conform to the environmental
regulations of the country of origin.

Typeset by Deltatype Limited, Birkenhead, Merseyside

Printed and bound in Denmark by Nørhaven A/S, Viborg

ISBN 0 09 928184 8

To Charles, an inspiration

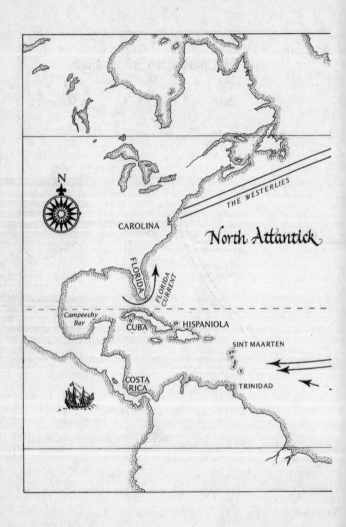

N

THE WESTERLIES

North Attantick

CAROLINA

FLORIDA

FLORIDA
CURRENT

Campeechy
Bay

CUBA

HISPANIOLA

SINT MAARTEN

COSTA
RICA

TRINIDAD

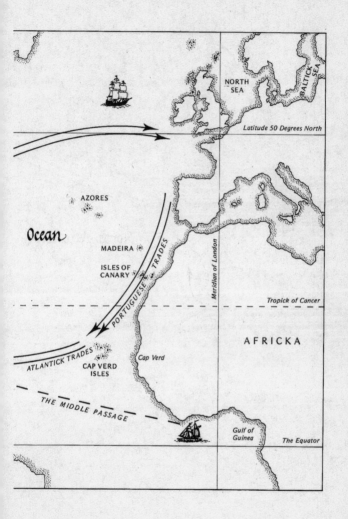

NORTH
SEA

BALTICK
SEA

*Latitude 50 Degrees North*

AZORES

Ocean

MADEIRA

ISLES OF
CANARY

PORTUGUESE TRADES

Meridian of London

*Tropick of Cancer*

AFRICKA

ATLANTICK TRADES

CAP VERD
ISLES

Cap Verd

THE MIDDLE PASSAGE

Gulf of
Guinea

*The Equator*

# 1

# *The Banks*

*The tenth winter of the reign of William, King of England, Prince of Orange, and his noble Queen, Mary.*

When dawn's wintry light revealed a seascape of frothing wave-tops and driven spray, the true plight of our ship came to me. Ugly rollers battered the Whitby collier-bark with bone-jarring thuds as I struggled alone, soaked and exhausted, at the bucking tiller. And I knew that the old man's madness had run us deep into the trap of the Essex shoals.

A wall of water reared up ahead and the *Prosperous Anne* plunged into it, shuddering as if the seventy tuns of Tyne sea-cole in her hold were more than her oaken frames could bear. At first she wallowed but then, with agonising reluctance, she lifted her broad bows and the wave hissed by, leaving her suspended above a dizzying trough. Rattling in protest, the topsails shed their wind, the sheets flogged and the tiller went light in my grasp. We were dead in the water.

Wrenching the tiller to bring her head round, I raged at the sea and the tempest of wind. We were so close – we had only to gain the Great Estuary to be safe.

'Let me get her to London!' I pleaded, but the waters were unheeding for, as any sailor knows, no prayer or promise ever swayed the sea.

Yet even as the words left my lips, the creaking collier plunged forward. Her sails bellied taut, the tiller trembled and she lifted gamely to the next sea. I swore softly at my own poor helming, for we had to keep her moving, we had to find a way through. Willing myself back to the task, I sent the bark surging through the gale-whipped sea and soon became so lost in the work that I fairly jumped at the sight of a tough, burly figure looming up at the hatchway.

Pulling the collar of his oiled-skin jacket closer, Walter Stalbone, my step-father and master of the *Prosperous Anne*, clambered like a drunk to the weather rail. Grizzled hair wetly astream, he glared about at the chaotic seas, all the time avoiding my eye.

'See – she's standing off,' he said, gesturing astern with an air of having been right all along. 'She'll not follow us in here.'

A league off our larboard quarter, barely visible through the wind-borne spray, lay a mighty ship, a sleek, well-armed three-master, moving slowly under reefed topsails. Night long, she had lurked nearby and now, in the grey morning, still she shadowed our poor lumbering bark.

'But she's Dutch!' I cried. 'She's no threat.'

The old man's mind had softened, whether in drink or fatigue, I no longer cared. Hours earlier, deluded, fighting the last wars, ignoring the peace and the trade – forgetting even the Dutch king on our throne – he had turned the *Prosperous Anne* inshore to escape an imagined enemy.

The master whirled on me. 'Then why is she keeping station with us?' he snapped.

Before I could gather myself to reply, a hard gust punched into the rigging and the sails rattled under the onslaught. I staggered, unfooted by the tiller-bar's kicks, and let the fore-topsail luff. The ship slowed.

'Fall off – bring her off the wind!' bellowed Stalbone.

I threw my weight on the tiller, but the *Prosperous Anne* refused to obey. The master reeled down the afterdeck and flung himself bodily on the bar, crushing my hands. Head to head, we struggled to keep the bark from going into stays.

'I said you were bad bluddy luck,' he spat between breaths, his face close. 'A curse is what you are, a curse on a ship.'

'You've lost your mind,' I panted, 'and you'll drown us all.'

'I'd watch you drown like a rat,' said the old man, and gave me a look of hatred.

The rudder blade bit at last, the ship's bows turned and, with reports like cannon shots, the sails snapped full of wind. As the bark picked up way, I managed to shove the old man clear and, regaining charge of the tiller-bar, steered quickly off to bring the wind freer. Salt showers streamed from my oiled-skin cap and stung me in the eyes, making

3

fresh tears spurt down my cheeks. In disgust, I wiped them away with my cuff.

'You're the one who's run us into the shoals,' I called above the din of the gale.

The old man's shout came back like the bellow of a madman.

'Dam' you! I should have fed you to the fishes two nights ago – soon as you showed yourself.'

I grimaced as we pitched into a trough. On the long, hard run down to London, he must have known the *Prosperous Anne* wanted three seamen to handle her, even without a gale of wind. I reckoned they should consider themselves fortunate I had stowed aboard.

'You and Barney would never have got this far,' I told him angrily.

'He's a sound hand, is Barney Goodhew,' the master said. 'Unlike some.'

'You may reckon that,' I said sharply, 'yet he's a-bed below and I'm still on deck steering.'

My step-father gave a snort of derision. 'By the blood of Christ, you're a proud bastard.'

'I'm proud of this ship, and I've a right.'

'O aye, Matthew and his bluddy ship.'

'You don't care about her – you never did.'

'I stopped caring,' snarled the master, advancing, 'the day you let my Thom die on her decks.'

'It was your fault – your fault!' I cried, bearing against the tiller and wishing I could as easily push away the horror of that day.

Stalbone's face was contorted with rage and pain like a baited bear. I saw the powerful fists clenched ready to lash out. But this time I met the master's eye. Rebellion surged into my every aching muscle.

'See what you can do, old man,' I said, half straightening. 'I'm not a boy any more.'

He faltered, then let his arms drop. The ship rolled as a beam sea passed under her keel, and he stumbled, saved only by stretching out a hand to steady himself. The fight was gone from him, and he turned away, clutching at the rail.

I steered on, my heart hammering like the flogging of a loose clew in a gale. At last, I thought, at last he has backed down. I shot a look at the old man and thought him diminished, bent and beaten.

Sheets of spray flew stinging into my face, and I squinted into the murk ahead, where the gale showed no signs of easing. Above the collier's tottering spars, the sky was massed with torn clouds rushing across the Narrow Seas towards the western horizon. Somewhere down the baying winds that flew on to batter the low coast of Essex the sandbanks lurked, ready to spring their trap, and I was tormented by the vision of a grounding. Don't dash away my dreams, I pleaded with my God, not now, when I'm so close.

As the cole-ship tore on through the thrashing seas, I sometimes resisted the tiller, sometimes obeyed its will, but still it pounded me with bruising blows. I glanced away up to the main-topsail's windward edge. The bulging canvas, ballooned with the power of the gale, stood out darkly against the morning's grey light and all my senses bore on the task of sailing the ship as hard and fast as she could go without tearing the masts out of her. We had

5

reamed in bar-taut every haulyard and sheet, and her yard-braces groaned under the load, yet the danger set me on edge and a part of me thrilled to it. The whole ship – her full-built hull, fifty five feet from stem to stern and of seventy tuns burthen, with her two stout masts carrying more weight of sail than they might stand – lay in my hands alone.

In a smooth patch of water, such as a helmsman finds in even the most troubled seas, the bark steadied, and for a brief moment the tiller trembled lightly under my grasp. Seizing this chance, I slipped a hand inside my stiff, salt-laden coat and felt under the sodden wool-jacket beneath it. The leather-bound pocket-book nestled there safely, and I fingered its shape to reassure myself, afraid the salt water might seep through and damage the precious documents.

The pocket-book's mere presence comforted me, for it had been sealed with Abigail's kiss in the very moment of our parting, when I had left her and stowed away unseen in the *Prosperous Anne*'s chain locker just before the collier cast off from the wharfside at Whitby. It held all my hopes for justice when I reached the Great Wen of London, not just the dream of regaining my rightful share in the bark, but of returning to save Abigail from marriage to the Justice's son. I could not endure the idea! I remembered her in my arms, her face alight with smiles as she had kissed me and promised –

A roaring sea tore in under the stern and struck at the rudder blade with a tun weight, sending a jarring shock along the tiller-bar. I blinked back to the present with a start and, casting my eye out over the waters, I could see at once that the *Prosperous Anne* was all but enclosed by white lines of breaking water where the running ebb-tide revealed the banks.

At the rail, the master seemed still intent only on the shadowing ship, ignoring the unmistakable danger we were careering towards. He waved his arm astern.

'That's not her, by Christ. Last night, there was a French bark, a bluddy man o' war, I tell you.'

'She's no Frenchman now,' I called back. 'Look at her lines – anyone can see she's a Dutchman. She's a flyer.'

A league to the east, in deeper waters, she stood off, biding her time, a powerful ship-rigged bark with the low forecastle and stern quarters of a new-built warship. Such a vessel could forge away with ease from our deep-loaded collier. Why had she slowed to stay with us?

'O aye, she's plain enough to see now – in broad bluddy daylight,' he said, and spat on the deck-boards. He brooded for half a minute, then spoke without turning. 'Anyways, for sure a private Dutchman might try to take us. Sea-cole fetches a fine price in Amsterdam.'

'So you steered us into the shoals to cheat them of their prize,' I said, bitterness edging into my voice. Fear for our poor vessel, ensnared in the shoals, was enveloping me.

'Got to keep ourselfs close in.' He was talking to himself. 'No Dutch or French can follow us here. I shall find our way through.'

'It's years since you sailed these waters!' I cried. 'Lord, you haven't even got pilots' charts on board.'

'Charts!' hissed Stalbone, turning towards me. 'Two years shy of twenty, and you tell me about charts – me, a master more than twenty three seasons. I know the shoals and channels well enough without any blasted charts.'

I struggled against an urge to fly at him. The master had never listened, never done anything but dismiss the Navigation as a tomfoolery. A seaman who knew his coast, he said, had no need of such angles and trickery.

'The banks are all around us,' I called as levelly as I could. 'I'll go aloft to spy a channel. You take the steering.'

'Keep her head up,' was all he said. 'We're safe on our course.'

It was useless arguing. Forcing myself to think back, I tried to remember my studies with the old Navigator, Jedediah Franklin, in the room behind Mistress Whistock's warm kitchen. I had the knack of picturing an entire folio page at a time, the contents laid out as if on a table before me. Now, as I struggled to recall the pilots' charts, shreds of an outline came to me, scraps of detail assembled themselves in my mind's eye. Gradually, the coast-line and the lie of the banks took shape, the Essex channels revealed themselves, and then I remembered it plain – the safe passage between Long Spit and the Great Middle, beckoning us to turn south-west and head into the Great Estuary of the Thames.

I called out to Stalbone's stubborn back. 'I

remember now – there's a gap at the end of Long Spit.'

'We're nowhere bluddy near Long Spit,' said the master with a dismissive wave. 'It's leagues behind.'

'We've got to bear off – I'm sure of it!' I shouted.

He made no response.

I looked out at the leaping seas. Was there a patch away to westward, calmer than the rest, a break in the shoals barring our way? On an impulse I called out towards the hatchway.

'Barney, Barney!' I shouted above the howl of the wind. 'On deck lively now.'

My step-father twisted round, angry. I met his eye, daring him to countermand the order, but he turned away, muttering a flood of oaths and pounding his fist on the rail.

I called again, and stamped on the deck-boards to rouse the slumbering seaman below. A minute later, Barney Goodhew appeared at the cabin hatch, looking lost and bewildered, darting apprehensive glances at the rough seascape. This was the lad who had bullied me when I was small, the lad who had grown to be a sailor who feared the sea. He gathered his oiled-skin coat against the freezing wind, his face drawn with tiredness as he hauled up from the narrow hatchway and gained the afterdeck, scrabbling for handgrips as the ship rolled and yawed. Though his terror had all but exhausted him, I knew he had the strength to handle the bark, if only he could keep his mind to it.

'Take her, Barney,' I shouted. 'I'm going aloft.'

He took over without a word and stared blankly ahead, working the tiller-bar to keep the collier's speed and course. At the rail, Stalbone fumed.

I went forward along the sloping deck to the mainmast ratlines, leapt onto the rail, gripped the tarred ropes and pulled myself aloft. The lines had a slimy feel as if they were icing up, but I climbed on, intent on each handhold, for the ship bucked like a sea-hog jumping. With aching arms, I gained the maintop, breathing hard. Thirty five feet below, the figures of Barney and the master seemed almost puny. I glanced up at the swaying topmast stretching high above, for I knew I had to go on.

I rubbed my hands in a blur to warm the cold-weakened fingers, swung myself into the ratlines once more and climbed without pause. Gaining height amongst the spreading canvas, I checked the gear out of sheer habit, despite the fatigue of my hours at the helm. In the night, we had shortened down to topsails and small jib, but the wind had risen and now we risked a breakage for the sake of speed. The sails thrummed, their edges lifting and snapping back taut, and the hempen ropes shed rainwater as they strained and slackened. Reaching the main-topsail yard, I flung an arm round the ratlines where they narrowed towards the truck, and held on, panting for air, to study the waves where they smashed into a white froth round the dark sandbanks. I reckoned the tide had turned to flood again. Soon, it would cover the shoals, but far too late to save us.

To the east, the Dutch flyer stood clear, but otherwise the sea was a desert. To the west, no land was to be seen, for the Essex coast, perhaps three leagues off to leeward, lay flat and low, lost in the rain and spray.

I stiffened. Six or seven cables off to steerboard there was a break in the pounding surf. It was surely the gap between the Great Middle and the Long Spit banks. With a shock, I saw, half a league ahead and directly on our course, another line of banks, curving to the south and east. If that's the Galloper's Knock, I thought, we'll sail headlong into the trap and be driven onto the stones. Scrambling back down on deck, I found Stalbone winding in the log line and counting the knots.

'Leave that!' I yelled above the gale. 'I've found the gap – we must steer off for it.'

'Hold your noise,' growled the master. He pointed at the steersman. 'Barney, mind to your task. Keep her head up.'

'Listen, old man, listen to me,' I pleaded. 'I can see it. Steer free, and we'll make the Fisherman's Gap.'

'Bollacks. We're two clear leagues from the Fisherman's.'

'No – it's to leeward. Look, look – it's there!'

He advanced and prodded me hard in the chest. 'I am master and I've sailed these waters before. Now get clear of the steering and let the seamen take her.'

In torment, I lunged at the tiller and tried to push it to larboard, shouting, 'Barney, he's wrong – steer off!'

Barney was torn. His eyes bulged as he searched first my face, then whirled back towards the master.

11

'Keep her to the wind!' bellowed my step-father.

Barney obeyed, pushing back against my efforts. All my weight bearing on the tiller, I wrestled with my shipmate for control, until Stalbone reeled over with a curse and shoved in Barney's favour. The *Prosperous Anne* lurched as if trying to throw us all into the sea, and I lost my footing, sliding down the deck to crash against the lee rail, winded.

My heart full of fear, I struggled to my knees and peered out at the sea.

'Breakers!' I cried.

From a froth of surf, an ugly dark bank of sand and stones reared up right off the steerboard bow. Shortly, there came a booming sound from below. The tiller jerked violently, throwing Barney and Stalbone flat onto the deck. The shock drove me down under the crook of the rail and, as I spread my arms to save myself, I felt the deck-boards tremble.

Slowly, fractured sound by fractured sound, the crash of the keel on the hard bank penetrated my disbelieving mind. I clawed at the rail as the deck tilted and the motion of the ship changed utterly in a fraction of a second. From her headlong canter she ground to a stop and heeled over, stricken. The sea heaved under her half-exposed keel, and she lay struggling on the bank like a wounded horse. Suddenly our ship seemed a fragile thing, and I imagined the hull splitting apart and spewing out black sea-cole, and the sea washing into her broken holds.

Even above the roaring surf, I heard the terrible sound of the hull grinding on the stones. The keel jarred cruelly on the hard bottom, her masts groaned in their steps. Sails and spars and gear flew about overhead smiting themselves to pieces. Torn from the mast as we struck, the twenty-foot mainyard crashed to the deck amid a welter of tangled gear, smashing a fathom length of the rail into splinters. Broken blocks and torn wet ropes followed, striking the boards around us as we lay prostrate. The mainmast whipped forward like a sapling in a breeze, straining the rigging lines to snapping point. I saw the haulyards and braces still attached to the fallen yard strewn everywhere in a cat's cradle. The belays were fouled, the sails ripped off her, and the spars and shrouds beyond repair. This, I thought dully, must be our end.

I sensed the ship shift beneath us. She was not stuck fast. There might yet be a chance of turning her head off the bank and driving into deeper water. But how could we get her moving before she broke her back? I glanced aloft. Though the main-topsail had split from top to bottom and flogged itself to shreds, the fore-topsail remained whole. It was aback and straining, ready to tear itself asunder, but I knew if we worked fast enough, we had a chance at least.

When Barney clambered to his feet, white-faced and stunned, I shouted to him. 'We must get the yard off her! I'll go up and cut it away – you clear the belays and throw everything over the side.'

As I made for the ratlines, my step-father staggered to the foremast where the ship's small cutter was stowed in chocks, lashed bottom up for weather. Drawing out a knife, he slashed at the ropes.

'Barney, give us a hand,' he called.

I had already climbed ten feet when I realised that Barney had gone to help the master. The two of them were heaving the little boat upright onto its keel and began to reeve the tackle for lowering it. They were abandoning the *Prosperous Anne*.

'Stop!' I cried, jumping down and running over. 'We must try to sail her off.'

I grasped Barney's arm and twisted him round. His face was as grey and unseeing as the lowering sky.

'We can save her,' I said. 'Help me cut the yard away.'

Stalbone whacked Barney between the shoulders.

'Get back to this bluddy work here,' he grunted.

Barney shook himself free and bent to untie the cutter's lashings. With a groan, the ship lurched and the cutter slid down the deck to leeward, taking Stalbone with it in a clatter of noise. It crashed to a stop at the rail and, swearing prodigiously, the master wrestled out from underneath it. When he looked up, it was to find me standing over him, driven into a fury.

'We can save her!' I roared.

He struggled awkwardly upright, shocked and deranged. A rivulet of blood crossed his temple and ran onto his cheek.

'There's nothing left in this old broken-back,' he snarled. 'She's finished.'

'She's my ship, my father's ship,' I began helplessly, 'I'll never leave her –'

'Your father,' said Stalbone, levering himself up

to the rail, 'were nothing more than a bluddy halfwit.'

Something in my mind snapped. He had no right. Enraged, I lunged at him. He struck out with bunched fists and I returned the blows with equal fury, catching him square on the jaw and sending him reeling away.

Just then, the *Prosperous Anne* in her agony lifted on a wave and fell back heavily onto the stone and pebble heaps. As the deck tilted, it drove Stalbone hard against the rail and his heavy upper body bent backwards, lifting his feet off the boards. In the second he realised what was happening, an awful fear crossed his face, the look of a seaman who knows how quickly death follows the kiss of the sea. Then, arms flailing, he was carried clean overboard.

I sprang to the rail, but he was gone. Peering down horrified, I saw the old man's grey head bobbing in the gap between the hull and the banks of stone as he was tossed about by the confused waves, his long hair floating free.

O Lord, not this, I heard myself say. I never meant to see him drowned.

'Barney – the ropes! Help me get ropes over!' I shouted in panic.

We threw ourselves at the coils of sisal stowed at the foot of the mainmast, tore at the light bindings and dragged the ropes to the side. I hurled a long bight over, but it was a slender hope. The old man was carried off by the wind and current past the bows of the ship and into clear water. Weighted down by the oiled-skin coat and seaman's boots, he struggled to stay above the waves but, like a sheep trapped in a bog, he only sank further. Weakly, he lifted both arms in the air as if to grasp a rescuing hand.

'The cutter!' I called. 'Barney – it's his only chance.'

Fumbling and cursing in our haste, falling over each other, we managed to get the cutter into the lifting tackle and hefted to the top of the rail. The oars were stowed inside, lashed tight. Drawing the knife from my belt, I sliced them free and they clattered into the bottom of the boat.

Springing in, balanced above the surging sea below, I called, 'Lower away, Barney – lower me down!'

He grasped the tackle lines, but the ship heaved and the boat swung out from the hull, only to crash back against the side. I lost my grip on the gunnels and thought I was about to be thrown out to join the master.

'Quickly, Barney!' I shouted in frustration, for he seemed frozen in fear and panic.

The old collier-bark rolled again, grinding the pebble banks beneath her. The cutter swung outwards, reached the end of its arc and then bore in against the rail a second time. It crashed to a stop so hard that I thought the planks would split asunder.

'Barney, you blasted –'

Dumbly, he let the hauling line run out free. I opened my mouth to shout a warning, but half a second later the end of the line passed through the top-block and the cutter dropped like a lead weight. It hit the water as though striking stone, and I was flung into the bottom of the boat, cracking my head on the thwart. The oars flew upwards and the rowlocks shot from their sockets and went overboard. Half-stunned by the blow, I grabbed frantically and caught one oar, but the other floated out of reach.

Barney leaned over the rail, mouth working like a landed fish. In the shock and confusion, he had let go of the painter line attaching the cutter to the ship. Panicking, I grasped the remaining oar and dug it into the water, but each time the force of the waves snatched the blade away.

'A line – throw me a line!' I screamed as the tossing boat surged free of the *Prosperous Anne*.

His face disappeared and a moment later a rope came snaking out over the rail. It fell short. The cutter was off, in the grip of the wind and tide and moving faster than a man could swim. The bulky shape of the *Prosperous Anne* receded as I was borne off, gazing in disbelief. O God save me, I am lost, I heard myself praying. For a wild moment, I considered diving over and striking out for the ship. But the strongest of men would drown before he had swum half the distance.

Tearing my eye from the bark, I tried to spot the collier-master. Once or twice I thought I saw the big, grey-haired head. But then a wave charged by, tipping the cutter and forcing me to hang on for life. When I squinted again through the streaming rain and salt-filled air, there was nothing.

The ship was by now three or four cables distant, upwind and – with the new flood – uptide of me, careened on the hard sandbanks. Even with two oars and two men's strong backs to row, it would not be humanly possible to regain her. I picked out the shadow of a figure standing at the rail, and glimpsed a white face turned my way. Dear God, I muttered, thinking of Barney left aboard alone, facing the sea's cold embrace.

It was icy in the tossing boat, and I huddled low, shivering in the bone-chilling wind as I clung to the gunnels. I raged at myself for getting separated from the ship, then tried again to scull by kneeling in the thwarts and dipping the oar. But I only succeeded in exhausting my remaining strength, and in the end I slumped down, all but defeated.

Suddenly, I wondered why my cutter itself had not been hurled onto the stones. I whirled round to trace the line of the banks from the way the seas were breaking. They curved away from the collier's bow, but just to the west was smoother, unbroken water – the gap I had wanted to steer for. With a few yards' grace, the *Prosperous Anne* could have cleared the shoal and sailed to safety.

So close, but those few yards had separated me not just from the ship but from all that mattered. In an agony of grief, I cursed the faceless wind and the unseeing waves, and shook my fist in rage and impotence until I was breathless from the effort. Then I stopped and fell silent. My quest for justice was over before it had started. When I thought of Abigail, it bore in on me that she would never know how it ended, and that I never would return to Whitby to take her in my arms. I despaired, abject, utterly heartsunk, bereft. Sitting alone and desolate, grasping the puny cutter's sides in the freezing seas,

I gazed about in shock. The moment the *Prosperous Anne* had run herself full tilt on the stony banks, everything I had ever hoped for had been dashed to matchwood.

After some minutes, during which a blackness filled my heart and shrouded my soul, I remembered the Dutch flyer. Heart leaping, I squinted into the wind. Where was she?

Seconds later, I spied her five or six cables off. With her foreyards backed and jibs flattened, she lay hove to, drifting past the now distant outline of the *Prosperous Anne*. She had swung south of the banks and on the tide's turn was being carried by the flood towards the mouth of the Great Estuary. My featherweight boat was driven by the wind at twice her speed, and I saw that if I could only push the cutter a few points to the east, there was a chance of closing on her. Grasping the oar and balancing on my knees, I dug the blade into the sea.

'Come about,' I urged my unwieldy little vessel, willing her onwards.

What strength I had left drained rapidly and my arms grew heavy, but after some minutes I looked again towards the flyer. The gap had narrowed by a good margin and the angle looked right. I was close enough to see her pennants and the lines of her standing rigging, and to pick out figures on the quarter-deck. I pressed on more urgently.

Suddenly, there were men aloft, unfurling the courses. Her gear clattered as the buntlines ran free and the canvas dropped from the yards. I caught snatches of voices in unison as the crew sweated the sheets home to a chanty. Lord, she was getting under way! In moments, she would pick up speed and be gone.

I was up on my feet in a flash, risking being sprung from the cutter and into the sea, but no matter. Frantically, I waved my oiled-skin cap high in the air.

'Here, here – help me!' I bellowed.

The great ship began to move blithely on her way, leaving me behind.

'Help me! Help me!' I screamed, waving demonically. My voice sounded weightless against the wind and the crash of the seas.

A row of heads appeared at the weather rail, above the closed gunports. I screamed again and staggered about, flailing my arms. But the ship was gathering way fast as the topsails were sheeted home.

Then a face on the quarter-deck turned. Arms were raised and pointing. Other heads spun my way. Was there a shout? Still the flyer picked up speed. I saw a froth of water at her bow and she began a wide turn, lifting to a sea and showing me her magnificent golden stern.

'Save me – O save me!' I yelled, losing heart.

Another cry went up. Figures ran about the quarter-deck, gesticulating. Still she sailed onwards, the gap between us opening wider. I sank down, exhausted and despairing. Then I realised I could see more of her larboard side. Was she swinging round? Sailors swarmed into the rigging once more. Her bows turned upwind. She was luffing! With a clatter and a rattle, the fore-topsail shed its wind and her jibsails shook. She slowed.

Not more than forty yards separated me from her. I paddled desperately, thrashing with the oar to make ground. Twenty yards from her, I heard a command.

'Get lines over.'

A rope snaked down from the big ship towering above me, her masts swaying and the dark hull dwarfing my puny boat. She had her fore-topsail brailed up now, and the jibsails shivered noisily as the gale rattled through them. More men appeared at the larboard rail and threw ropes. My cutter bumped alongside and I gasped as the ship rolled heavily, the great bulk of the hull toppling over, threatening to dash me to pieces against her massive topsides. Even at the low weather-deck, from the waterline to her rail was a man's height and half again.

'Tie the line to your boat!' came a shout.

I acted instinctively and looped the rope in a half-hitch around the cutter's thwart.

'Haul away, lads!' called a voice.

Instantly the cutter rose and I was jerked out of it and into the sea before I could save myself. Shocked by the icy immersion, I broke surface and saw the cutter lifted bodily out of the water.

'Help! Hoy, help me!' I cried weakly, knocked half insensible by the cold.

A new voice called out. 'Get rope here – save the sailor.'

A heavy knotted rope coiled down from the rail. I launched myself at it, kicking out madly, and clung to it with weak and frozen hands, afraid of being overwhelmed as the ship rolled yet again.

'Pull up, lads – Youssef say pull up!'

21

I was dragged rudely up and over the planked sides, knocking my limbs on her bulwarks. Strong hands grabbed my coat and swung me over the rail to slump on the smooth decks in a pool of seawater. I rested there, shuddering with cold, sobbing with fear and exhaustion, unable to move or speak, but sensing the solid weather-deck rising under me as the ship lifted to a sea. Spreading my arms out over the boards, I clawed at the firm decks and thanked God for this salvation.

'Bugger's alive – see to him directly,' boomed the voice of the big man who seemed to be in charge. 'Hoist that boat aboard here, lively now.'

'It's a fine little prize.'

'Ya – it's good zat ve stop.'

'We saved the seaman too – a brave seaman, sailing master!'

'Hold your crowing, Youssef,' said the resonant voice. 'For all I know, we've heaved us up a bag of trouble.'

Panting, retching seawater, I lay half under a blacked cannon that stood with its carriage lashed down to ring-bolts in the deck. Just beyond, the eager hands of a dozen men hauled the cutter over the rail, bringing it safe aboard. Dimly, I grew aware of the expanse of weather-deck stretching about, with gear and stores stacked high everywhere, and the crouching shapes of heavy guns along the rails. It was a greater ship than I had ever seen in Whitby, or even Hartlepool.

A high-boned, narrow, brown face bent down. 'Youssef has seen you safe, sailor.'

I wanted to show gratitude, but found I could not speak.

'To the braces! Sheet in jibsails!' called the commanding voice, and at once the brown face disappeared from view.

I listened to the sound of many feet running across the deck. Barked commands rang out, followed by the whoops and yells of men sweating up the braces and the creak of the sheets as they were hardened in. The motion changed to the easy swing of an ocean-going ship under way. Shutting out the bustle, I heartily wished the scene away. If only I would awaken and find myself back aboard the *Prosperous Anne*, heading into the Thames and sheltered waters, or even safe at home in Whitby once more. I shook without respite, as much from exposure to the elements as from the strange combination of remorse and terror that troubled me.

I was saved, but my shipmates were lost. My bark, the dear old *Prosperous Anne*, was wrecked on the Essex shoals, and with her, my future.

And what great vessel had I come aboard? Where would she take me?

## 2
## *Blood and Tears*

*Whitby Towne, County of Yorkshire, six winters earlier.*

In a dumb rage, my step-father slammed me bodily against the cottage wall, then his muscular hands gripped my coat, lifting me clean off the ground. He shook me so hard my joints creaked and neck-bones cracked. Walter Stalbone pushed his heavy features menacingly into my face, and a stench of ale-ridden breath enveloped me.

'I'll knock the fight from you, boy, you sniveller,' he breathed, dribbling spittle.

I heard myself wheezing for lack of air. He drew back a fist as if to strike another blow, and I shut my eyes. No punch came. Instead he dropped me, and I fell limply to the cold floor.

'Books!' I heard him say. 'Them cursed things are nothing but trouble.'

At his feet lay the remains of my only possessions of any value, my two books. One was the Good Book, a vellum-printed volume that was now no more than a crumpled, broken-backed heap of torn pages, scuffed by his boot into ragged, unreadable remnants. The other was my Book of Navigation, still almost whole, which he stooped to pick up. He opened it while muttering rapid phrases.

'Trouble, boy. That's what you've been ever since I married her.'

I lay quiet, my fingers clawing the earthen dampness of the cottage floor, hoping that the onslaught might end, that my book might yet be saved. My step-father slammed it shut and, with a snort of rage or derision, hurled it mightily against the wall of the low room. As it struck, it exploded into a blizzard of yellowing leaves that were still fluttering downwards when a face appeared in the doorway.

'Mister Stalbone, sir! For the Lord's sake, what occasions this?'

Into the dim room stepped the merchant, Mister Seth Jeffreys, dapper in a fancy long-coat and white hose, the commercial gentleman of the town. No one liked him, but just then I felt almost glad to hear his high, thin voice. Recovering from the book's near miss, he moved quickly towards me and bent down.

'What distress have you caused now, boy? You shall never strike a proper bargain with life until you learn to hold that tongue.'

He straightened and gazed for a second at the collier-master's drooping shoulders and swaying limbs. My step-father had once again taken too much drink, and the merchant sighed at the sight.

Involuntarily, I groaned and stirred at Mister Jeffreys' feet.

'Daughter! Abigail!' he called over his shoulder towards the half-open door. 'Leave your charge and bring a pail of water here.'

Warily, I lifted my head as Abigail entered the room, a girl of eleven, wearing a neat cotton dress with a woollen coat thrown over it and a bonnet tied under her chin. Holding her pail, she peered about, for the cottage room was lit only by a crooked window at one corner and furnished with nothing more than two straw palliasses and an empty candleholder sitting on an upturned fish-box. Catching sight of me prone on the floor, she came lightly over and let out a gasp.

I coughed harshly. Abigail bent down to help me into a sitting position.

'Just look what a state you've got yourself in,' she said, dabbing at my face with her piece of wet linen cloth, and wiping my streaming eyes.

'I – I only wanted to see her, Abby,' I croaked.

I tasted blood, and my ribs ached. I gazed at Abigail, trying to remember the last time I had been close enough to savour the sweet, clean smell of her clothes and skin.

'Take the dam' wastrel away!' bellowed my step-father coming towards us. 'By the Lord's breath, get him out of my house!'

The girl glared at the big man, putting up her hand protectively, and he hesitated.

Mister Jeffreys spoke sharply.

'Walter, do you forget this is a house of illness?' He shot a dark look at the collier-master. 'Your temper has control of your tongue, and not for the first time, neither.' He contemplated us, two children huddled together. 'Abigail, take him to the other room.'

The collier-master swung on the merchant with a blazing look.

'No! He'll not see her.'

'For pity's sake, he's entitled to see her for a last –' Mister Jeffreys stopped himself. 'He's entitled, Walter, and that's the end of it.' He turned to Abigail. 'Daughter, take the boy out. Quick now.'

With the girl's arm to lean on, I got up shakily and together we stumbled out of the room, down the passageway and into a cramped and stuffy chamber. A bed raised on wood blocks almost filled the darkened space, and a single candle burned on a crook-legged table. There was little air and I had to draw in hard for a breath. Fearfully I moved close to the bed where she lay quiet. I had not been allowed to see her for days.

Her chest lifted slightly, but otherwise she remained still. I tried to ignore the blotchy skin and dark rings under her eyes. There was a strange aroma about her, and none of the brightness and movement I remembered and longed to see again. I knelt beside the cot and gingerly took her pale hand in mine.

'Ma?' I said.

She stirred. Her eyelids flickered and she gazed toward the ceiling.

'Matthew?' It was a voice, low and cracked, quite unlike her own. 'I am glad to see you.'

I gave her an encouraging squeeze. She sighed and turned towards me sadly.

'Remember your father, Matthew. My Robert was a good man – wronged by the law.' Her face seemed to droop in weariness. 'The shares in the collier-bark – they are yours, so you shall remember him always. Do you understand, son?'

'Aye, Ma.' I gripped her wrist fiercely.

'And the lessons. He wanted you to learn the Nav – the Navig –' The effort was too much.

'The Navigation, Ma,' I said.

'See the oceans, he said, let the boy see the oceans.' Her gaze was past me and beyond to some place of her imagination. 'You shall do it, son – promise me?'

'I promise, Ma. As soon as I grow up a man, I shall learn the Navigator's arts. I shall sail the oceans as the best Navigator in all England.'

'Mind that pride of yours.' She breathed noisily. There was a long pause. 'I married Mister Stalbone to – to give you a chance make an honest seaman of yourself. It's what your Pa always said – plain trade for honest men.'

I felt her clutch my hand, a bony touch with little strength.

'See the oceans,' she murmured, and sucked in a painful breath. A shudder ran through her, then she seemed to fall asleep, her breast rising unevenly.

'Abby,' I whispered, swallowing audibly, 'please let her be well again. You can do that, can't you – make her well?'

Abigail made no reply. I studied my mother's face, wishing she would wake up and chase me out of the house for being naughty. I will never make you angry any more, Ma, I promised silently, but please get well.

At the sound of footsteps in the passage, Abigail tugged my arm.

'Matthew, come away!' she whispered urgently.

Seth Jeffreys entered the room scowling, and pointed a finger at me.

'I'm a fair man in all my dealings, whether of commerce or society,' he said in a low hiss, 'and I've allowed you a chance. But now – back to your work, boy.'

I laid my mother's hand on the bed and got to my feet. With a glance at Abigail, who looked away, I moved past Mister Jeffreys and into the passage. There was no sign or sound of anyone there. With careful steps, I crept towards the back room, and peered round the doorframe. My step-father was gone.

The floor was strewn with printed pages hurled down in his rage. The Bible looked quite beyond repair, so I left it where it was. Bending, I gathered up the pieces of the Book of Navigation from the floor, trying not to crush the papers any more than they already were. In the corner I found the leather cover, torn but not beyond saving. I smoothed the soft skin flat and with infinite care laid the papers inside, vowing to make the book as good as new and keep my promise to Ma. The word of saints and prophets hasn't helped me, I told myself, but the Navigation shall, and it's my escape from Mister Stalbone so I shall learn it as best I can. I tucked the book inside my weskit and headed for the door.

In the street, the freezing air made my bruised

face ache where it was tender from my step-father's blows. I spat bloodily onto the cobbles, wiping my wet cheeks with the back of one hand and then, taking a deep breath of raw, cold air, at which a stabbing pain shot through my ribcage, set off at a pace down the hill to the shipyard where the *Prosperous Anne* lay.

The yard in winter was muddy underfoot. I entered by the gate and picked my way down the slope, past the pit where two sawyers, one standing upon a great log of Baltick timber, the other in the pit below oblivious of the showering sawdust, worked from each end of their saw, making a long cut. I admired the three large colliers in build, with craftsmen crawling over them and woodchips flying as they worked, and the hulls and frames casting deep shadows across the ground. High above me, shipwrights planked up a big, fat-hulled collier-bark whose mighty spars lay in readiness beside her plump topsides. Forty-five foot on the lower main-mast alone, she must be, I reckoned, and the topmast would add another thirty, her truck half as high again as the *Prosperous Anne*'s. Dreaming of taking her to sea, where the air was clean and the day fresh, even in the heat of summer, I wished myself on passage – putting out to sea, heading off on a voyage, with a simple purpose and hard seaman's work to take my mind off my mother's illness.

But not with him. When I do at last cross the oceans, I muttered to myself, please the Lord it be with anyone but Mister Stalbone.

'Oy, little bastard!'

At the shout, I looked up to see Barney approaching. Not wanting to give him the satisfaction of seeing me run, I strode steadily across the stone wharf and up the tread-board onto the cole-ship lying peacefully alongside.

'Stop when I say,' he yelled, catching up but nearly losing his footing in the process. He grabbed the back of my coat. 'What's your bluddy haste?'

He was older than me and a size bigger, and took advantage of it to bully me. But even his own mother would not call him a good-looking lad, and the flattened brow and glassy-eyed stare reminded me of a hill-sheep. The dirty-arsed, stinking kind, I thought savagely, that would bleat loudest when the knife was at its throat.

Looking at me, he grinned with relish. My eyes must have showed a bit raw from my tears, and Barney had something on his mind.

'Your Ma dead yet, then?'

'She's not dying – don't talk about her!'

I flew at him, but he got his foot behind my legs and I crashed to the deck. He was on me in a flash, and it was only a firm shout that saved me.

'Barney – leave off!'

A tall, well-made young man stumbled up the gangway in a great hurry, and my heart leapt to see him.

'He's smaller than you,' said Thom Stalbone, wrenching Barney back by the shoulder.

'Aw, spit at the Devil,' said Barney, but he let his arms go slack at his sides and moved off across the deck.

'You all right, Matt?' said Thom, offering a hand

31

to lift me back to my feet. 'Trouble finds you, eh? I'll not always be around to help out, I've got me own work to see to.' He laughed in a brotherly way, then his face fell solemn. 'Who give you that bit of a red mouth, then?'

I fought back tears of gratitude, for Thom seemed to have an instinct for the right time to turn up. I jerked my head in Barney's direction.

'It wasn't that mule-head there,' I said, wiping a cuff across my lips.

'O aye, I know it,' said Thom, clapping me on the back. He became solemn. 'Reckon it were my Pa, then.'

I looked down.

'He's only upset, you know,' Thom said, brushing at my coat to clean off the mud stains and tarry marks, but the well-meant gesture spread the muck further over the already filthy garment. Then he asked, 'Have you seen your Ma now? How is she, lad?'

'I – I don't know.' In truth I did not, but I feared the way she seemed held in the creeping grip of illness. 'She's not very well, I think.'

Thom looked at me, then gazed around the collier's decks, strewn with tools, tubs of pitch and bundles of oakum for caulking, tar-buckets for the rigging, junk ends of rope and broken deadeyes, evidence of the work needed to keep her in one piece for the endless hard hauling of cole and ore up and down the coast between Newcastle and Whitby.

'Never mind,' he said, 'there's plenty on this old barrel to keep your mind off your troubles.'

'I want to go to sea, Thom,' I blurted through the

tears. 'As a Navigator. I promised her – I swore to my Ma!'

'All right, Matt,' he said, giving me a worried glance. 'But you'll have to stick to your prentice-ship with Pa first. Learn to be a seaman.'

My spirits fell, for I was always hoping Thom would say he'd take me aboard with him.

From forward at the windlass where he had gone to sulk, pretending to be smearing mutton grease on the shaft, Barney called out, 'Oy, tyke! Get up aloft for that topsail haulyard. I'll pay out the line.'

I caught Thom's eye and managed a rueful smile. He grinned back, banged me on the arm to say goodbye, and turned for the gangway, heading back towards his own collier-bark, where he was mate aboard.

I clambered heavy-hearted onto the rail by the main shrouds and hauled myself laboriously up the ratlines. My chest stabbed at every breath and my hands froze as they gripped the ropes. I thought my nose might be bleeding and stopped to touch it. There was blood on my fingers.

'Aloft, aloft!' called Barney from below. 'Or the master'll be up for you.'

I accelerated my climb, scrambled past the futtock shrouds and got onto the round-top. Not pausing, I grasped the ratlines and headed up again, reaching the truck of the topmast in one go. Gripping the spar with my legs, I steadied myself in position. Nearly fifty feet below, Barney grumpily paid out the line as I hauled it in hand over hand. The light messenger line soon ended in a join and when the heavier haulyard came up I rove it through the wooden block and let it pass downward for Barney.

How I yearned to be old enough to go voyaging, long and far away from Whitby. My step-brother's trading bark sailed across the North Sea to the Baltick lands, sometimes as far south as Holland. Even the *Prosperous Anne* herself had long ago worked all the way down to London with good Newcastle sea-cole for the gentry's fires, before I was born. That was proper passage-making, and I yearned to do more than coast up to Hartlepool or Newcastle with the filthy alum ore, and back again with eternal loads of cole.

The new haulyard line rattled freely through the block, but the sheave wobbled on its axle. It was badly worn and I knew the master would refuse to replace it, for he hated spending a copper. While Barney went to find scraps of used sisal to make up a downhaul, I fretted in silence at the masthead. The collier-master had hated me from the moment Ma had remarried, and now she was ill his temper had worsened. I bit my lip. It was an ague, Abigail had said. Did people get well after an ague?

I gazed around from my high vantage. Beyond the cluttered yard, with its sounds of trennels being hammered home and the screech of the sawyers' work, lay the harbour of Whitby. In the slanting light of a January afternoon, the Esk shone dully as the last of the sun from above the high hills in the west fell between the heads of the cliffs. Beyond them spread the flat expanse of a calm sea. The North Sea in this mood was resting between storms, gathering its strength for a fresh bout of fury. Then

34

it would lash the harbour and strain the lines of boats cowering at the wharves. I looked forward to summer, when the humour was more benign, and the anchorage between the narrow river and the outer heads would be crammed with fishing boats, whalers and tubby colliers, rafted up together and sighing as one when the tide lifted their keels. Then too we might sail the *Prosperous Anne* with a gentler wind and a warm sun on our backs. I loved to be at sea more than anything, almost as much as I loved my dear Ma.

'Oy, bastard.'

I was jerked back to the present by Barney's familiar hail.

'Heave that downhaul, tyke.'

I sighed deeply.

'Hauling now,' I called down.

The work progressed through the afternoon. I was glad of the diversion from my worries and so busy with a tricky lead of the mainbrace messenger's sewn join passing through the truck-block that I missed seeing Walter Stalbone arrive on board. His blunt tones carried upwards from the well-deck and quite made me jump.

'Boy! Get yourself down on deck.'

Anxious not to provoke another beating, I nipped monkey-like all the way down to join them. The collier-master stood, eyes cast down, fingering some repaired tackle blocks. He did not look up when he spoke.

'Get off to Mister Jeffreys' house. He's wanting to see you now.'

'Aye, sir,' I said, puzzled at his quiet manner,

such a change from his earlier temper. And what on earth would Mister Jeffreys want of me? I had stepped onto the gangway when my step-father spoke again.

'Matt. Wait, boy.'

I could not remember him ever having used my name, and I spun round, half expecting to see him lunging at me with his fist. But the collier-master stood where he was.

'Your Ma,' he said thickly. 'She's passed away just now. She's dead.'

For a fractional moment, he looked up and met my stare, then let his glance drop. My stunned mind was trying to take in the words, but I could not tear my gaze from the man's eyes. They were brimming full of wetness.

'Off! Get off to Mister Jeffreys'!' he shouted.

I sprang across the plank and pelted through the yard, past the sawing pit and under the massive, rounded shapes of the hulls in build. Slipping and sliding on the mud and churned tracks of the cartway, I reached the gate and turned into the road towards the town, dashing past a row of low cottages as far as the cobbled street of Sand-gate. I turned the blind corner at the bottom of Baxter-stair and ran straight into a stout figure. Powerful hands gripped the collar of my coat-jacket and spun me round.

'Blast it – look where you're going!' said the fellow who had hold of me.

I instantly recognised the man's coat as that of a warden from the Lynskill estate, and held my peace. With a start, I saw a familiar figure approaching, a pudgy lad my own age, his blond head of hair standing up like a wheatsheaf above a blue serge coat with a silk-trimmed collar.

'What have you there, Bowyer?' said the new-comer.

'John Lynskill!' I cried.

The blue-coated young lad squinted at me, his eye running over the torn and stained jacket, taking in the filthy rags that went for trousers and the flaxen sail-cloth remnants bound around my feet for shoes, blackened with cole-dust.

'Matthew Loftus?' Young John's face was a picture of disgust.

With a burning sense of shame, I fought to steady my voice. 'Aye, but I'm Matthew Stalbone now, John.'

His eyes narrowed, peeping out from pink flesh, dull and cold, like a pig's. I noticed how the puffy cheeks and full chin pushed the features of his face close together. John had grown fatter than ever I remembered.

'Master Lynskill to you, I think,' said the Justice's son.

'Master Lynskill – aye, I beg pardon. But you remember, it's not long past when we played together on the High Common.'

'Ratch Fields, you mean,' said John coldly. Then he opened his mouth and let out a braying noise, a sound that for me shrank the intervening years to nothing. It was the Lynskill laugh, mirthless and unforgettable. 'That's enclosed land now, you cole-jack, not commons. You shan't be roaming up near

Ratch Hall again, at play with me or anyone else. Nor shall your fellow villagers, neither.'

Lynskill pointed down the lane. Three forlorn figures sat on the stony road, huddled in the shadow of the wall with their hands tied behind their backs. I knew them as Whitby commoners, sheep-men from the high grounds.

'The penalty for grazing herd animals on a gentlemen's enclosed farming land,' said John Lynskill, 'is a whipping in the stocks.' He whirled on me. 'What cole-ship do you ply? Is it Stalbone's?'

'The *Prosperous Anne*, Master Lynskill,' I said at once. 'I am prentice aboard.'

'That rotten barge? Break her up for the good timber and burn the rest on the foreshore, I say.' John Lynskill stared hard into my face. 'Soon as the lending can't be paid, my father takes her back.'

I gasped. 'No – you can't – it's not fair!'

The Lynskill laugh echoed off the walls of the nearby cottages.

'You're stupid, Loftus – or Stalbone – or whatever you may call yourself,' said young John. 'Not fair? You inherited that notion from your father, I daresay. There's little else he left you, by the looks of it. Come along, Bowyer, we've the law to uphold.'

The warden gave me such a shove that I crashed to my knees, half-winded, and found myself on all fours staring at Master John's feet in their in fine buckskin boots for riding. I clutched at my coat for fear the precious Book of Navigation might fall out. The boy-gentleman pirouetted on his new boots and stalked off, brandishing the stock of his riding whip at the cowering sheep-men. Then he stopped and waited for the lumbering Bowyer to catch and pass him, and fell in again behind the protection of the big warden.

I patted the book to reassure myself it was safe and, with a nervous glance at Bowyer's broad back, set my jaw and walked off in the other direction, down towards Sand-gate. The second I turned the corner and was out of sight, I broke into a run. A woman in her doorway called out but I ran on, past the Restoration Arms and up the steep street where mules' hooves always scraped and grappled for purchase as they struggled up the hill with full sacks of alum strapped across their backs. In Prosperity-street I had hardly the air left in my lungs to go another pace, and I sank onto the steps of the drinking fount at the corner. I put my head under the spout and pumped the shockingly cold water over me until the tears mixed with the stream and the sound of water rushing in my ears drowned out my sobbing cries.

'Ma! My Ma's gone!' I wept.

The flow gushed over my head for minutes on end. At last I stopped pumping. Shaking the loose water from my hair, I used my fingers to wipe my eyes, and rubbed my hands dry on the legs of my pants.

I stood up and breathed deeply. There were no more tears.

'I shan't cry again,' I said out loud, startled at the hollow sound of my voice in the deserted street.

The cord holding up my frayed pants had worked

loose as I ran. Hitching them up around my waist, I pulled the jacket tighter and set off for Mister Jeffreys' house at a steady pace, looking neither right nor left.

# Rotten Prospects

A tall dwelling, four storeys from basement to attic, stood at the higher end of Prosperity-street, across the line of meaner houses leading up to it. The late sun, catching the panes of its front windows, reflected hard, golden flashes that made me flinch. Mister Jeffreys' was the handsomest house in all Whitby town.

I contemplated the stone steps lined with painted black railings up to the front door, where I had always come before. Now, though, I felt lost, as if I had been cast over the side of a ship and into the sea. There was no more Ma to run to, no Ma at home to keep my step-father off me. Fearful, not a little daunted by the big house's opulent prospect, I hesitated. Then, gathering my courage, I headed up the steps.

The brass knocker banged dully against its striking plate. Footsteps tapped in the vestibule and the door swung open to reveal an unsmiling Merchant Jeffreys, coatless and wigless.

'Inside, boy.'

I stepped in after and followed him into the receiving room. It was all in gloom, for the curtains had been drawn across the windows despite an hour still left in the day. A whale-oil lamp in the corner created little more than a glow that half-lit the room, but by the light of the flames from the grate I saw two high-backed armchairs. As Mister Jeffreys ensconced himself in the one, I saw in the other an immobile old gentleman I did not know.

'Step over here, boy,' said Mister Jeffreys, 'and let me have a look at you.'

Moving into the centre of the room, I grew hotly embarrassed. Compared with my own dwelling, the dank cottage my Ma had died in, it was so rich and comfortable. In the old days, when my station had been different and Abigail and I had played together, I had entered this private sanctuary only once or twice, for it was not a child's place. Now, with its furniture of polished wood, china pieces on the mantel, scrimshaw objects placed artfully on a small round table, the heavily padded chairs and even a red-patterned rug on the floorboards between the feet of the two gentlemen, it seemed impossibly luxurious. I felt awkward and out of place in the stuffy, unfamiliar surroundings, and could not tear my eyes from the fire. A pile of best sea-coles burned in a grate all of two foot wide, throwing out waves of heat. I had never before seen such a handsome, wasteful blaze. It reeked of a merchant's easy living and even as I wondered at it and the warmth crept over me, I shuddered involuntarily.

Mister Jeffreys cleared his throat. 'Condolences, boy, on the death of your poor mother.'

I stared at the grate, confused and shy in my rough, damp clothes, then glanced nervously across at the other gentleman. He looked a thin and bony old man, with sad eyes and a heavily lined face, who barely stirred except to rub his dry hands together, which he did often, each time with a little shiver.

'She shall be laid to rest in the morning,' said the merchant. 'It is best to get these matters settled soonest.'

There was a pause, during which I heard only the hissing of the coles on the fire.

'Now, Matthew Stalbone, how old are you?'

'Twelve years this month gone, sir.'

'And have you considered your future?'

'Sir – no, sir, I have not,' was all I could find to say.

'Your mother named me as your guardian,' said Mister Jeffreys. 'She felt that your step-father – ah – might not always act with your interests at heart. Thus I am responsible for your affairs until you reach majority, at twenty one.'

He crossed his ankles and I noticed the blacked and polished shoes on his feet, and how their buckles gleamed. Somehow, the merchant's foot-wear never became muddy and cracked like most people's.

'Your father left a letter to be read to you on your mother's passing.' Mister Jeffreys waved a piece of vellum covered in writing. At one corner, a blob of red wax had been pressed to the paper with a length of ribbon underneath it. He spoke very rapidly, without referring again to his document.

'Robert Loftus, your father, owned some thirty one of the sixty four shares in the collier-bark, the *Prosperous Anne*, as you may have known. It was his expressed wish that those shares should pass to you on his death. I have held them in trust for you, and shall continue so to do.'

'Is the *Prosperous Anne* to be mine, sir?' I asked.

The merchant clucked his tongue and uncrossed his ankles.

'Your father did not even own one half of her! And the ship may not be sold without the consent of the other owners.'

I tried to take this in, and brightened with a sudden thought. 'Shall I receive a little money from her earnings in the cole-hauling?'

The merchant put a hand delicately to his mouth and coughed. 'The plain fact is that the cole and alum hauling is less and less profitable in these days. After the King's outport taxes – which pay for harbour work – everything she makes goes on upkeep, meeting the debts and making the lending payments.'

'What lending is that, sir?'

The merchant looked up sharply. 'Why, Matthew, the sum your father borrowed against his shares. To buy a second share, you remember, in another collier, the *Blessing*. The one that was lost.'

I remembered the loss as if it had happened yesterday, for a terrible change had come over our house. Not long afterwards, we had moved into the miserable cottage.

'Your father not only misjudged his finances but his – ah – politicking as well.' The merchant fixed me with his eye. 'He was an intemperate man, and his rantings went against him. That nonsense about the Affrick trade. He failed to understand that a port

44

like Whitby needs all the commerce it can find. We had a chance for an overseas venture, an ocean trader. It would have made your father a rich man.'

I burned around the collar of my jacket, and longed to throw it off, for I hated hearing Mister Jeffreys speak about my father as if he had done wrong. If Ma were here, she would take the merchant on and tell him the truth, that Father was a good man.

'It was sad to see a clever man do himself down so, and that's an end to it.' He indicated the piece of vellum parchment. 'There are certain formalities. This gentleman is Mister Jedediah Franklin, a scholar of York who tutors Abigail. This document records my guardianship, and Mister Franklin shall be a witness to it.'

The merchant dipped a quill in an inkpot and handed it to the old gentleman, who signed it with a flourish, sniffed noisily and passed the parchment back. Mister Jeffreys dusted a pinch of powder over the wet ink, laid the document aside with care, put his fingers together and looked at me.

'You must remain with your stepfather and, under your apprenticeship to him, continue to work at his direction until you are seventeen.'

The news struck me like a blow. I had somehow supposed that with my Ma going, I might be free of Mister Stalbone.

'Your mother left in my keeping a small amount, to pay for tutoring. In token of my – ah – special regard for her, I am going to make you an offer both kind and generous, under the circumstances. You shall receive book-reading and hand-writing lessons, as you once attended with Daughter Abigail. What do you say, boy?'

Suddenly I remembered what I had vowed to my mother. 'Sir – my Ma promised me lessons in the Navigation. She said it was my father's wish, sir.'

'Do you think you deserve this, boy?'

'Why, sir, I only –'

'Mister Franklin is also going to teach it you.'

'The Navigation, sir?'

'Yes, yes, the Navigation, the Lord bless us. It is for your dear mother's sake, who wished it on her sick-bed.'

'I am most grateful to you, sir,' I said, and met the tutor's gaze. 'And to you, sir.'

Mister Franklin nodded, his head moving as if it were set in a bath of oil, like the card of a ship's compass.

'Now,' said the merchant, indicating a brown book lying on the round table, 'take up that volume from the stand there, boy. Open it and let us see what you remember of your reading.'

My heart thumped. I wondered if I could make any fist of it at all in front of these gentlemen. Opening the leather-bound book, I found the first page proper and began to read.

'*Intro–duct–ion.*' A sea of words swam on the page. I cleared my throat and read on. '*The volume you hold in your hand is but a – a scholar's attempt to lay before his fellow men, and equals in the world of – of pract–ical dis–covery, the soundest prin–ci-ples of modern sci–en–tif–ick thought, achieved by the method of*' – I was sorely hot and red by now, for this was a severe test – '– *ex–per–im–ent–ation and the precise recording of ob – serv – ations in order to attain the proof of a hy – a hypo – of a hypothesis of the true order of the motions of the heavenly or cel–est–ial bodies.*'

I rested a second and Jedediah Franklin spoke for the first time.

'Do you know what Book that is, young Fellow? Read me the Title.'

I turned back to find the page. '*The Principles of Natural Phil–os–ophy and Sci–en–ti–fick Knowledge,*' I read, '*by Isaac Newton.*' I looked up. 'Sir, these words are strange to me.'

Franklin spoke with deliberation. 'My young Sir, these Words are strange indeed even to certain Men of great Learning, and of high Position in the World, Men who, contradictorily, lack common Wisdom. They fear the Language of Scientifick Knowledge, or they fear the Ideas contained therein, for there is a new Way of interpreting the World which is bound, within the Confines of a short Space of Time, to –'

'Yes, yes, yes, yes, Franklin,' interrupted Mister Jeffreys. 'There is plenty of time to fuddle the boy's brain with your crank notions about the scientifick method, whatever that may be. The important thing is to discipline him in the Navigation so that he may go aboard trading vessels and make a commercial life of it.'

Franklin remained unperturbed. 'My dear Sir, I shall teach the Boy Everything known about Methods of Reckoning, the celestial Bodies, mathematickal Calculations and stellar Topography, to the

Point where he shall acquire more Learning than a Poopdeckful of the self-titled Navigators aboard His Majesty's Ships of the Royal Navy.'

'Good enough!' said the merchant, irritated. 'Do you understand, boy?'

'Aye, sir. I shall learn the Navigation, and go to sea on the poop of a merchantman. And I shall do my very best, sir, for my poor mother's sake. And in memory of my father.'

Mister Jeffreys fixed me with a lingering stare. His eyes were strangely small and bright-black, like a water-rat or certain small dogs, I thought, the kind that simpered to their keepers and bit innocent callers.

'Enough,' he said at last. 'Go down to the kitchen and let Mistress Whistock show you where the lessons shall be.'

I went out into the vestibule. The glazed street-door panels cast coloured rays onto the floorboards that reflected off the bright varnish. On the walls hung two framed engravings of ships, one of which was the *Prosperous Anne*. The other was a ship-rigged flyer, a Dutchman, going by her lines, but not a regular Whitby visitor that I had seen riding at anchor and could put a name to. Now, I thought, with the Navigation I shall go to sea aboard a great bark like her and see the world. I went to the stairs-door and descended.

'Laddie,' a woman's voice called out as I entered the warm kitchen. 'This way, in here.'

Mistress Whistock, a large woman in her middle years, ruddy-faced and pocky, stood framed in the doorway, smiling. My nostrils filled with the heady aromas of hot food, and mutton stews and bowls of pottage came to mind. I was as hungry as a badger.

'Here, and quick about it,' she said, grabbing my arm. 'Blame me if you don't look half starved.' She caught sight of my bruised face and bloody nose. 'My, us've been unlucky! Tripping over them ropes down on the wharves, I s'pose. Dangerous place to work. Better off inside, near a good, hot range like this one. Eh, Libby?'

The scullery girl scraped at a pile of metal bowls and dishes in a large pail of water as Mistress Whistock busied herself about, muttering all the while. Libby, three or four years my junior, looked up shyly but, catching my eye, glanced away and did not look up again.

'Your lesson shall be next door, where the old man sits of an evening,' declared Mistress Whistock. She cocked an ear towards the stair, then pulled me into the room, sat me down at a bench by the table and whispered loudly, 'Wait there, laddie, just wait.'

To my drooling astonishment, she put in front of me a generous wooden bowlful of soup, steaming hot, and half a hand of bread to slop it up with. Standing up from the rich brown liquid's surface was the knuckle of a real bone. I needed no urging to tuck in. Porage if I was lucky, or stale crusts dipped in small beer to soften them if not, was all I got since Ma had fallen into her last sickness. I attacked the vittles with vigour, burning the roof of my mouth and almost choking as I crammed the bread between my lips.

'My, my, my,' tutted Mistress Whistock thought-fully. 'My, my, my,' she said, and disappeared into the scullery shaking her head.

When I was done, and having carefully wiped a last morsel of bread around the bowl to make sure every tasty drop of stew was captured, I leaned back feeling the heat in my belly. I sighed and let my eyelids droop, thinking for a brief moment that I might never move my legs again and depart from that cosy haven.

'Stop dreaming, laddie,' called Mistress Whistock from behind the scullery door, making me wonder how she had noticed. 'Off and away! O, if Mister Jeffreys found out I'm feeding half of Whitby – I really don't know! Out by the back-door, and close it after.'

I had climbed the slate steps up to the street, when a sound made me turn in surprise. On the top step by the front door sat Abigail, in a pretty silken dress that rustled as she rose and took a few paces down.

'Abby!' I said, quite overjoyed. 'We are to have our lessons together again.'

'O no, Matthew!' She gave me her kindliest look. 'It is not for me to learn the Navigation or Mathematicks. Mister Franklin is to teach me book-keeping, so that I may assist my father, as none of the clerks in Whitby is to be trusted.'

I watched her expression. When she was speak-ing, or paused for a thought and tilted her head, her face was a painting, with its pink cheeks and smooth, clear skin. All of a sudden, I wanted to stay there forever. Unconsciously, she broke the spell.

'It upset me so when I came to your cottage today. That brute of a man. And your books! O poor, poor Matthew, I do fear for you.'

'I hoped there might be some money for me now, Abby,' I said, 'from my part of the *Prosperous Anne*.' I tried to brighten. 'But with my lessons in the Navigation, I shall go to sea – in the King's Navy! One day, I shall make my own fortune, with spoils and prize money.'

She seemed distracted. 'Why is there nothing for you? Have you not shares in the collier?'

'Your father has explained it. She cannot be sold, and there is the lending to pay. She shall be kept working.' I remembered what young John had said about breaking her up. 'Then the Lynskills shall never have her – never!'

Abigail's face crumpled. 'They own everything.' She gripped my hand. 'I think they must own all the people of Whitby.'

'They do not own me!' I said, hotly. 'I am not owned by anyone. The Lynskills shan't hurt me – or you.'

She hid her face and sniffled into a linen cloth. 'You shall know soon anyway, Matthew,' she said, her voice muffled until she put away the cloth and gazed at me sadly. 'I am to be betrothed. To John Lynskill.'

'Betrothed? To him? But – it can't be – why, it's too soon.'

'The marriage shall not be for a few years. It is for the best.' She chewed her lip. 'I shall be the wealthy wife of a young squire, think of that. And

51

my father – well, it shall be very good for both of us.'

I pulled her to me, hugging her tightly.

'Abby, but why must you – ?'

The front door swung open and Mister Jeffreys appeared. He seemed stupefied at seeing the pair of us standing on the steps, close together, holding each other.

'What in the Devil's name is this? Daughter, to your room at once!' he hissed, and turned to me as she fled. 'And you – away from this door! Lessons you may have, but you shall not speak to my daughter. Stay downstairs by the kitchen, and know your place.' He prodded me angrily in the back, sending me staggering down the steps. 'You're proving much like your father. Chasing idle dreams, thinking himself above his fellows. And see what good it did him!'

I stared back speechless.

'Don't try my temper, boy. I shall not remain a benefactor if you do. Away with you!'

He slammed the door so hard the panes of the front windows shook in their glazing bars.

I turned slowly and wandered off. It was the end of the day and almost dark, although the lingering glow of twilight lit the sky behind the hills. Their shadows cast an inky blackness over the river, which twisted away to the uptide staithes where the alum barges chafed at their lines on the flood tide, awaiting the next day's loading of their dusty cargo.

I began to walk briskly to keep warm, hands tucked inside my coat pockets. The events of the day were a jumble, and I caught myself thinking how I would tell Ma about Mister Jeffreys and Abigail when I got home. I dreaded the return to the cottage, with the fear of finding my step-father in a blind rage. With luck, the collier-master would be dead drunk and asleep by a heap of embers from the sea-cole that I got for him, on pain of a beating, by hoarding the leavings from the bark's hold, or thieving in the yard.

At least there was the Navigation to think of. I imagined a warship festooned with cannon and swarming with men, a mass of masts and rigging lines, and an acre of white canvas spread high above her decks. Or a trader on her way to Holland with woolsacks packed tight in the hold, like the Dutch ships that called into Whitby. Or a bark that crossed the sea to the North Lands and carried back timber for building the finest colliers in the land. Then I saw myself on a long voyage aboard a great merchantman, a white bone in her teeth as she forged south to the blue seas and the warm winds that carried ships away for years at a time to faraway places. The New World, the Spice Lands, the South Seas. The very names conjured adventure and riches into my imaginings.

How I longed to learn the secrets of crossing the wide, untracked oceans, far from sight of land. Without a bearing on the shore, or the lead-line to measure a depth, I knew voyagers must rely on the stars to find their way, the sights and angles and plots that combined into the art of Navigation and guided them through uncharted seas. I looked up and saw, in the eastern sky where all the light had gone and the night began in earnest, a gap in the passing clouds. A single star burned steadily there.

It made me think of my mother again, and a sudden wetness pricked at the corners of my eyes. I am alone now, I thought, with no-one to guide me. I have only myself and my dream of the sea.

Looking up at the lonely star, I tried to remember which celestial body it could be, for naming them somehow made them friends. I patted my jacket pocket, where the broken-backed Book of Navigation lay. In the morning light, I would try to read it.

The cloud thickened and the star disappeared from sight. I hunched my shoulders against the chill air and went down the hill to the cottage with my head full of dreams.

# 4

## The Wheeling Stars

In a tiny downstairs room off the kitchen of the Jeffreys house, I sat with my tutor in the Sciences of Mathematicks and Navigation, Jedediah Franklin. Between us stood a plain, deal counter, on which lay open several large and handsomely-bound volumes. The fearsome contents, once strange and terrifyingly unfamiliar, had begun to reveal their secrets a few at a time, in steps of agonising slowness. Sometimes my head reeled as I gazed at columns of predictions for the sun's declination, or tables of observations for the planets' movements, or dense pages of logarithmic sums. Yet I loved the treatise on measuring a ship's progress by doubling the angle on the bow, or finding a distance off the land by the cross-staff's angle to a headland's known height. This was the practical seaman's knowledge I so longed to apply at sea.

Although no fire burned near, a portion of the heat from the damped-down range in the kitchen seeped through the thick stone walls and crept around the door. I heard Mistress Whistock in her domain, banging empty pans and scolding Libby. Cooking smells lingered in the air, tantalising me with vivid images of food. As ever, Mister Stalbone was paying me no wage and gave me only the barest vittles, but being prenticed I had no say in anything. Now the hunger made it hard to concentrate on my lesson. The shapes of constellations I was trying to memorise dissolved before my eyes into sizzling mutton chops or haunches of roast venison. For a while, even the noon meridian altitude of the sun became inextricably linked in my thoughts with a midday feast of beef pie.

Wrapped though he was in his outer coat, with thick hose and leather slippers on to keep his feet warm, and a nightcap on his head, Mister Franklin was feeling the cold. A large drop of water hung from the end of his nose, until he snuffled it away with a kerchief which he fastidiously tucked back inside his cuff.

'It has been my hope, Matthew,' began the old Navigator with what might have been a glimmer of excitement in his eyes, 'that you would one not-too-distant Day be fit for Examination in the Art of Navigation by the Masters of Trinity House. For have we not completed two full Years of Lessons?'

He peered at me expectantly.

I said, 'I hope, sir, that I shall be able to do justice to your tutoring of me.'

There came a long pause, until Mister Franklin spoke again. 'Although you possess the Ability to learn, you neglect your Book.'

I squirmed. How could I explain to the old man that we worked the old collier from dawn to night-time with nothing more to eat all day than a plate of beans or a bowl of soup. I was so fatigued I could hardly read a word, and my step-father allowed me no candle to read by.

Franklin drummed his fingers on the table. 'You must put more Effort into the Tables, most particularly the Almanack of the Positions of the heavenly Bodies.' Old Jedediah shifted his limbs on the straight-backed chair and sighed. 'What is the average Angle of Rotation of Polaris about the polar Axis?'

I sucked my cheeks. I had not a clue. The silence hung in the air between us, as unbridgeable as the celestial void.

'What, then, of the Finding of the Longitude?'

My hollow stomach rumbled in a series of staccato bursts, and I coughed. But at least I knew this one.

'The longitude, sir, cannot be found at sea from celestial observations, and only inaccurately by means of deduced reckoning.'

'Your Answer is correct for the Time Being. But there is a theoretickal Means of finding the Longitude by the Lunar Distance Method.' Mister Franklin scratched his nose. 'However, there have never been calculated sufficient Tables of the requisite Accuracy for determining Predictions for the Moon's Course, but this Task the Restored King charged to the Astronomer Royal, and an Almanack may soon be completed. When it is done, the Longitude may be found at Sea.'

I found myself bursting with excitement about this important idea.

'Surely there must be many thousands of observations to be made to create such an almanack?' I said at once. 'And the moon moves so fast that sighting it is difficult for mariners. And will there not be too many calculations to be done at sea? But what is the Astronomer Royal?'

Mister Franklin made a noise that I thought was a chuckle. Outwardly, the old tutor's face remained impassive.

'Indeed, Matthew, the Calculation may be a large mathematickal Problem, but the Outcome shall be worth the Effort, for we shall lose many fewer Ships and Men strewn needlessly upon the Rocks than we do now in our Ignorance of the Longitude. And the Astronomer Royal is a Gentleman of Learning at the Royal Observatory in Greenwich.'

Another silence fell, and my thoughts were on the unsolved mysteries of sidereal time. Then I dreamed of standing on the deck of a ship in a Tropick latitude, taking a star-sight at dusk. Mister Franklin banged his arms against his sides to warm himself, and it occurred to me he was more likely thinking of Greenwich, wherever that was, and the comfort of a post there, perhaps with his own cell and a grate within it, a small pension and the means to buy a thicker coat.

Heavy footsteps sounded on the flagstones and we exchanged warning looks, knowing the pleasurable intimacy of our learning was at an end. Mistress Whistock burst from the kitchen and paddled into the little room.

'My, not still at it?' she cried. 'I shall never know what you see in those volumes, I never shall.' She rubbed her hands together with a rustling sound like a rat scrabbling in a hayloft.

58

'We have been discussing the finding of the longitude, Mistress Whistock,' I said in defence of Mister Franklin, for his nautical wisdom was wide and his patience boundless.

'Longi – ? Why, whatever is that, now?' wondered Mistress Whistock.

Franklin's face darkened, and he leaned towards me.

'This good Woman cares Nothing for the Navigation, dear Boy, yet she defends the Indefensible. I refer of course to the Lynskill Family.'

'Aye, sir!' I put in eagerly.

'There – see what nonsensickal notions you have put in the boy's thoughts.' The cook leaned down and wagged her finger in front of the old Navigator's nose. 'You'll get him in all varieties of nuisance, leading him along like that.'

I stood up, quite heated. 'No one's leading me along, Mistress. I know what their justice is. It's enclosing the common land – and hanging men who poach a gamecock or two!'

'My, my, my, what leavings of rubbish are inside your head,' Mistress Whistock said, shaking hers from side to side. 'Just because a few bellies are empty today, doesn't indicate that stealing from the squire is lawful, now does it?'

'It cannot be Justice of any Kind,' said Mister Franklin sternly, 'when a single Family enjoys Ownership of the Minerals, the Lands, the Transports and the Shipping, not to mention Control through the Courts of Prices and Wages –'

'Lord above!' cried the cook. 'We've no time in this world to worry about such things when there's a kitchen to be run and dinners to be cooked and pots to be cleaned. You show little care for the proper order of life.' She folded her arms and pushed her chin onto her chest, fixing the aged tutor with a look. 'Like going away to your beds in good time for a day's work in the morning.'

I heard loud gurgles from my stomach, and quickly gathered up the books on the table to cover the sounds. But Mister Franklin went on as if addressing an important gathering of learned men.

'My dear Woman, even our commercial Master at his Grate above our Heads is not immune from this encompassing Influence, for Money talks to Debt with a powerful Authority.'

'Enough!' cried Mistress Whistock. 'I believe you might carry on this way all night long, like idle women in the fishdock when the boats land no catch. Away to your sheets and candles.'

'Mistress, I take no Orders from a Cook who – '

'Orders! My, my, my, it's rich coming from you,' she said, triumphantly. 'For if you had learnt to take orders properly you might be aboard your precious Navy bark yet.' She folded her arms and waited.

I looked at the tutor. I knew nothing of Mister Franklin's past except that he had been in the Navy from its first days, after the Restored King founded it. He rose, clutching the coat about his lean frame.

'Mistress Whistock!' He seemed shocked. 'I thank you to refrain from raising Matters of which you have no Knowledge.'

'I know what I know. You were dismissed from the Navy for putting the King's bark on the rocks, that's what I know. The very idea! The King's own bark!'

I froze, staring in disbelief at Mister Franklin. But the Navigator simply blinked and sat down again without a word.

The housekeeper marched out of the door towards the stairway, and her voice reached us from there.

'Bed! Bedtime, if you please, or we shall never see the day's work done.'

And she was gone, banging the door behind her and hoofing noisily up the stairs.

Franklin looked beaten.

'Well – we must take no Notice of a Woman,' he said, after a long pause, and there was a quaver in his voice. But then he brightened a fraction. 'Mistress of her Kitchen she may be, but never Master of any Science!' He sighed and stood up as if in a hurry to leave. 'Good Night, young Matthew. Leave quietly and see the Door is properly closed after you.'

I nodded, and my belly struck another sonorous chord of emptiness.

'Good night, Mister Franklin, sir,' I said, dispirited, not least because before our dispute I had half hoped Mistress Whistock might give me a bowl of stew.

The old Navigator picked up the candle, which might have had a third of an hour left in it, and headed for the door to the stairs. Letting my eyes get used to the darkness, I made a fuss of collecting my little Book of Navigation. It was a sorry thing next to Mister Franklin's handsome morocco-bound volumes, which contained new celestial knowledge and methods. Nevertheless, I wrapped it in its leather cover before slipping it inside my weskit, as if I were about to depart the house. When I was sure the old man had shuffled upstairs, I cocked my ear and listened hard.

From somewhere above came low murmurs. Commercial men's talk at Mister Jeffreys' handsome fireplace, I decided. Abigail would be asleep in a front upper bedroom. Of Mistress Whistock there came now to my grateful ears the evidence of her absence from the waking world, for from a distant room in the back attic, a bass, rhythmical snoring seemed to shiver through the timbers of the house and resonate somewhere in the region of the cold cupboard behind the kitchen rooms. Libby would be sleeping as usual in a cot at the end of Mistress Whistock's bed, such a wan little thing who always fell into the deepest slumber the minute her peaky head hit the palliasse, as the housekeeper loved to tell.

I was heady from my hunger. Stealthily, I crept across the scullery and trod silently on the flags to gain the door to the cold cupboard. The latch was stiff and if jerked up too hard would cause a loud click. Where thunder and lightning, or a mayhem of overturned carts and mules in the street, or the irritable clanging of Mister Jeffreys' room bell, might leave the contented cook slumbering on in untroubled torpor, the very slightest strike of metal latch on metal hook would bring the woman gallumphing downstairs at a rate of knots to see who could be invading her cherished cupboard.

But I controlled the rise of the latch to perfection and, as I swung open the door, my nostrils filled with the siren scent of roasted chicken, boiled ham, cold turnips and leeks, even a sourdough loaf. Gingerly, I groped over the comestibles, terrified of disturbing some noisy dish or knocking over a goblet. At last, I came to the chicken. Using both hands, I separated a leg with the skill of a shipwright extracting a section of rotting timber from the delicate ribs of a rowing gig, slid the delicious item up my coat sleeve, closed the door with precision, and turned to retrace the ten steps to freedom. My head ran straight into a soft but unyielding form and a hand grasped my neck. I was dragged helpless back to the kitchen.

'Bring a light, Mistress W! I believe we have him.' It was Mister Jeffreys' voice.

I stumbled into the kitchen with the merchant's hand still clamped around my neck. Mistress Whistock thumped down the stairs and I saw her stockinged feet arrive in the uncertain light of the candle which she waved about in agitation.

'O my!' she said unoriginally. 'O my my my my my! And after all the titbits I've let you have too! My, O my, O my!'

'Give up your trophies, boy,' commanded the merchant, letting my head up. I shook the sleeve and the chicken leg dropped onto the table. The moment she saw it, Mistress Whistock began wailing possessively again. Mister Jeffreys snatched up the plump limb and pushed me into a chair, standing over me and pointing with the bone.

'I knew it! I knew it had to be you.' He shook his head angrily and straightened up.

'I am hungry, sir,' I said quietly. Even as I said it, I knew it would cut no ice with the merchant. 'A morsel of chicken is all I took –'

'Quiet, boy. You're lucky not to go before the Justice himself.' The merchant hustled me to the back-door and out into the little basement courtyard.

Perhaps it was the hunger that made me light-headed, or the tragedy written on Mistress Whistock's sad features, or Mister Jeffreys' triumphant tones. Perhaps I was just feeling sorry for myself because my belly would stay empty another night. But somehow a festering resentment in me boiled over and I could not stop myself.

'I've got nothing! Everything's been stolen from me!' I blurted out.

Mister Jeffreys halted in his tracks. The flickering light from inside the kitchen framed him against the doorway.

'What do you mean, boy?' His voice was ominously low.

'My wage – he takes my wage – and, I mean, there's my ship too,' I mumbled, conscious of his mean stare in the half light.

'You have brought your troubles on yourself, boy,' hissed the merchant, shaking me violently by the arm. 'Do you understand that?'

'No, Mister Jeffreys, I don't understand,' I said, pushing his hand away.

The merchant stared at me in disbelief. 'You steal food? You show disrespect in your guardian's house? Think on it, boy.'

I did. I thought hard about why I had to work for Stalbone, and about what my Ma had said about the shares, and Abigail too. I decided I had nothing left to lose.

'Then may I see my father's will, Mister Jeffreys? Perhaps I should have a paper or something, sir?'

I never saw the blow coming. The merchant let rip with the back of his hand and it struck me across the jaw. It did not have the weight of my step-father's punch, but it stunned me by its unexpected-ness, and the finger-rings cut the flesh of my cheek. Mister Jeffreys seized me and hustled me up the back steps and into the darkened Prosperity-street. He pushed his bony, sharp features right into mine.

'Worm! Ungrateful worm of a boy.' Mister Jeffreys' face was half an inch away. 'Say, just only say,' he spat, 'anything about that again, and I'll see it's the end of you. Understand?'

Mister Jeffreys shook me in a fury. I smelt the leather of the merchant's coat collar and the reek of food on his breath. I felt too bewildered and frightened to think.

'Yes, Mister Jeffreys, sir, I shall never say it again. Please let me go now!'

'You shall come to my house no more. Your lessons are finished – no more Navigation.'

With a shock, I realised it was the one thing left to me, and in the heat of the moment I had clean forgotten. And now it was too late.

'Sir – I – Mister Jeffreys, not the lessons,' I pleaded. 'I only meant –'

'No more lessons!' he screamed. 'Stay in the

work-yards the rest of your blasted life! Get out of my sight.'

The merchant gave me a shove in the chest, but for the first time and, to my amazement, instead of falling to the ground and taking a kicking, I managed to stand my ground. With an odd sensation of something having altered, I realised I was quite as tall as the merchant, just possibly a half an inch the better of him. I must have grown three good inches since my Ma died, and now Mister Jeffreys stood before me on a level footing, so to speak.

'Away, boy,' said the merchant, waving his hand.

In the silent street, I stood and listened to my own and the older man's breathing. We were alone in the darkness, and Mister Jeffreys appeared not to like it.

'Get off, you blasted nuisance!' he shouted, and with that, grabbing at the opportunity to break away, he turned and went down the steps, his heels tapping on the stones.

Just before the back door banged shut, I caught sight of the tall, stooping figure of Jedediah Franklin in the doorway, raised from the warmth of his bed by the commotion. He stood unmoving beside Mistress Whistock, watching and listening.

As the door slammed, the light went with it. My heart pumping hard, I strode off down the steep street to the bottom of Baxter-gate where the stone wharves lined the river's edge. I sat down on a bollard and gazed out over the black water. Everything felt odd. After a while, I understood it was anger that seethed inside me, rather than fear. I no longer felt like a little boy, flinching at every blow. I must get out of Whitby and away to sea, I thought.

Perhaps I should stow aboard a Dutchman one night and sail to Holland, where no one shall ever find me.

The river flowed swiftly by. The lights of one or two dying fires flickered in the shipyard, and a single vessel swung to her anchor in the roads, her riding light glimmering far off. She was the big Dutch flyer who had warped in earlier in the day. A fluyt-ship, she was called in that strange Hollandish tongue, and come up from the south to trade in whale-oil or fleeces or timbers or even sea-cole – whatever her captain and owners reckoned might turn a profit in Amsterdam. From the *Prosperous Anne*'s masthead, I had studied this sleek, beautiful bark and her powerful rig, with enormous mizen cross-jack and fore-and-aft staysails. I yearned to cross the seas aboard her and dreamed of standing on the quarter-deck as her Navigator, the back-staff raised, ready to shoot the sun. No sooner had I thought it than I dismissed it. How could I ever hope to Navigate now?

At a sharp rustling sound I squinted into the darkness of the lane. A figure came slowly forward and I tensed until the gloom revealed the stooping frame of Mister Franklin.

'Ah, young Matthew,' he said so softly his voice sounded far, far away. 'Your ready Tongue has lost you the Lessons.'

His sad old face seemed longer and more drawn than ever.

'I'm sorry, sir, I did not mean to disappoint you.'

'I too lost my Chance but it was the mere Fate of Storms and the Lack of a Longitude that divested me. You may choose to discard your Chance or not, as it lies in your own Hands. Do you desire to become a Navigator? Do you intend to voyage the Oceans? Or shall you let it remain your Dream unrealised?'

'O sir, I must go across the seas! I plan to stow away – I shall go this very night.'

'Wait, Boy,' said Franklin. 'Stowaways are surely thrown alive to Neptune, or if you depart by Road you shall starve before York. You must stay and with Diligence come to know the Navigation well, so that a Master may one Day take you aboard with a Wage and Vittles. On Sabbath Days, when the House and the Town are quiet, I shall find you and tutor you in Secret. For what Purpose have I left but to pass on my Knowledge? Until we are discovered by the Sabbatarians, your Lessons shall continue.'

'Sir, I thank you,' I said, grasping his dry hand in mine.

'Show me your Gratitude by your Willingness to learn,' he said and broke away to shuffle swiftly off into the night.

I sat there for a long time, forgetting my anger at Mister Jeffreys as well as my hunger. The night was crisp. Even in May, there might be a frost by dawn. After a while, during which I gazed at the sky and thought of my future aboard the great ships, I walked slowly back towards Grape-lane and the Stalbone cottage, with its dim prospects.

# 5

## *On a Dead Beat*

The *Prosperous Anne*, laden to the gunnels with seventy tuns of bagged alum, headed gamely northwards a league or two off the Yorkshire coast, bound for the Tyne. We had cast off from the snug wharves of Whitby harbour with the dawn tide, and now in the late afternoon the sun was bright overhead, with clumps of cloud picked out white against a clear sky. Her bows threw up showers of spray as she met the seas, for we were close-hauled and working our way against a stiff breeze.

I clung to the swinging mast by the parrels of the mainyard, high above the weather-deck as the ship lugged onwards. Trying to clear a snagged haulyard at the bull's-eye where it ran past the yard, I swore under my breath at the ragged condition of the rope. When I am a grown man, I promised myself, my own ship shall be the queen of Whitby, a vessel my father would have been proud to master. And one day, I shall take her away from the cold and treacherous Narrow Seas to where the Tropick waters are warm and endless.

Checking the mainyard's fittings out of sheer force of habit, my eye fell on the larboard jack-stay, which ran under the yard as a foot-rope for a man working the sail. A few feet out from the mast, it had frayed into wispy strands and looked as if it would barely take a boy's weight. I resolved, while the weather was fair, to tackle the collier-master over replacing it. After all, it was I, not he, who had to go out on the yard. My step-father was getting too stiff, he said, to run aloft like he used to, but I knew differently. Too drunk on ale was more like it, and the thought fretted me.

I scanned the sea around the *Prosperous Anne*. There was a swell building from the north, an unmistakable sign of heavy weather to come. Though for the time being the afternoon was bright enough, I made a bet it would blow hard before we ducked safe into the Tyne River's mouth next morning. Barney would bleat all night about it, and fancy a seaman being afraid of the sea! Glancing deckward, I saw him lying motionless, hands clasped over his middle and eyes shut tight, as he sheltered under the lee rail.

From the steering position aft, the master's voice boomed up at me.

'Oy, lad, enough of that bluddy dreaming.'

I heaved a sigh and scrambled down the tarry ratlines. Barney could doze, but there was no peace for me. I went quickly aft, stepping over the sleeper's outstretched feet, and reached the tiller, where my step-father stood gripping the long, oaken bar, feet planted apart to steady himself against the heaving of the deck.

'Take the steering, boy,' he said. 'Barney's got the watch. I'm going below for a bit of a rest.'

'Aye, sir.'

I stepped over and grasped the bar, feeling it twitch and jerk under my grip as the sea snatched at the rudder. The collier-master turned towards the hatchway and, as he did so, suddenly I gathered up my courage and determined to tackle him on the worn gear.

'Sir – sir, that jack-stay – on the mainyard. It's well worn out. Perhaps we ought to –'

'Ought to what?' He spun round and pushed his blunt face close. 'Ought to reeve up a new one, is that it? I can't pay for new bluddy ropes, but little Matthew always wants it done his way. I had enough of that from your father,' he said, glowering. 'I'm taking me a rest. Keep her headed up – and your mouth shut.'

He reached the cabin hatchway in two paces, turned to face the steps and paused to survey the sea before clambering down.

'Call me or Thom if it picks up. None of that hanging on to the canvas till it blows out. I'll wring your skinny neck if you break any gear.'

'Aye, sir.' I stared ahead until the old man had disappeared below, then breathed out with relief. It was hardly worth the argument.

I fell to steering, sending the collier smoothly over the swells, and when I had the feel of her, I relaxed and ran my eye over the rig. The bark carried all plain sail and the sheets groaned under the strain of making to weather, but the sails were asleep and nothing chafed. Satisfied, I settled back to enjoy the helming. The tiller-bar kicked in my hand and, looking down, I admired the smooth, worn grain of the wood. I loved the feel of guiding the ship as she ploughed purposefully along. And having Thom along for the trip lightened my heart. Barney and I and the master sailed her by custom, and we had no need of an extra hand, but I knew if the weather stayed quiet, I could look forward to hearing Thom's sea-tales through the night watches.

After a while, a thought struck me. There was a spare length of rope hidden in the anchor well, and I reckoned Mister Stalbone might have forgotten about it. It would be the work of a few minutes to change the jack-stay, but only if my reluctant crewmate would shift himself.

'Barney!' I shouted from the tiller-bar. 'Steer a minute while I nip aloft. She's going easy now.'

He did not stir.

'Come on, it'll only take a minute,' I pleaded.

Without looking up, he made a rude sign.

The sun continued to warm our faces even as it dipped lower. After a while it disappeared behind a towering cloud of ominous shape, and as darkness closed in the wind rose. Barney had the watch, after all, and must have known we would have to shorten canvas before long, but I steered on, thinking how I only ever got into trouble for opening my mouth. Let them work the ship any way they want. Yet still I fretted, trying to concentrate on the task in hand, squinting towards the gathering murk.

Soon, waves were breaking at the bow. One sent a froth of white water surging along the decks to catch the day-dreaming Barney unawares, drenching him where he dozed. He leapt up and shook his fist angrily at the sea, then came aft.

'Off the tiller, sheep-shit,' he said.

'You didn't come when I wanted you to,' I retorted.

Without warning, he whacked me so hard in the belly I sagged onto my knees, letting go of the bar. He grabbed it, steadied its movements and steered on, gazing ahead into the dusk, humming smugly.

'Just wait till I'm as big as you are!' I shouted in rage. I threw myself at him, pounding hard enough to make him drop the tiller. We fell to the deck, tearing at each other's hair and clothes, and landing half-blows that mostly missed.

The loose tiller shook along its length, then slammed against the stops as the *Prosperous Anne* turned into the wind in a clatter of protesting blocks and rattling sails, coming upright as she bore into the breeze. With my best heave, I pushed Barney away and fell on the tiller, hauling it amidships.

'Give me a hand here!' I yelled, expecting at any instant to hear the sound of tearing canvas from aloft.

Barney, red-faced, clambered dumbly to his feet, failing to see a head appear at the cabin hatch.

'Thom!' I shouted. 'I need a hand here!'

My step-brother, strong and tall, sprang from the hatchway and lent his weight to the tiller-bar. We soon brought the bark back on course and the sails snapped briskly taut as the wind refilled them. Barney staggered forward to his berth by the rail, pretending it was still a good place to rest, though now the spray was flying over the weather side.

Thom smiled, letting me have the tiller again.

'Barney getting at you, were he?' He gazed around at the sea. It had got much rougher. 'We'll have to shorten down in this – you might have called us sooner.'

I stared ahead. There was no point in dumping Barney in more trouble, for it would only come back to me later.

'Aye, it were his call,' Thom nodded. 'As much use as a barnacle in your belly button, that one.'

I smiled back.

'I'll go aloft and furl the forecourse, Thom, if you take the tiller.'

The courses were as much as I could handle on my own, but I wanted to show Thom I was up to it. With Barney reluctantly at the belays, I worked quickly, stopping the sail up on the yard in tight folds, eager to get back and talk to Thom, for it was so long since he had been aboard with us. He had embarked now for the ride to Newcastle to see an owner about a post as master. When I rejoined him, he was whistling a chanty tune.

'Shall you stay in Newcastle if the owner takes you on, Thom?' I asked.

He fixed me with a thoughtful gaze. 'Aye, it's my best chance, Matt – master of a collier instead of mate.' He turned his deep-set eyes full on me and smiled. 'You're fifteen, eh, lad? Two more years as prentice, then. But you shall come and crew for me. I'll get my Pa to release you.'

Speechless, I beamed back, bursting with joy and pride, for I had so longed to hear him say it. This would be my escape from Stalbone and my chance to practise what I had learnt of the Navigation, for I had confided in Thom about the lessons. My step-father held that logs and compasses and charts – let alone latitudes and almanacks and celestial positions – only got in the way of canny piloting by depth and by eye, and were a long way second best to knowing the coastline.

Thom looked pensive and spoke again. 'I plan to make a few sea passages in my time and I'll want more than coasting knowledge. That Navigation you're learning is what I'm after – and I'll see you keep it up when you're aboard with me.'

'Aye, Thom, I shall do as you say,' I said, excited at the sheer prospect of it.

'Watch your luff!' Thom said sharply.

Distracted, I had let the *Prosperous Anne* bear off a couple of points from our course. Quickly, I pulled her back, steadied the tiller and glanced nervously over. The smile had never left him.

'Don't worry, lad,' he said, 'I know you'll make the best seaman I can find, when you're full grown.'

We fell silent and thoughtful while the *Prosperous Anne* ploughed on, and I resolved to try all the harder with my books.

'I'm glad you came along this trip,' I said, after a while. 'Will you tell me again about your Baltick passages, before you were on the collier-barks?'

He chuckled, and began to describe his voyaging across the North Sea and into sheltered waters, and then further to where the mountains came down to the shore and a thousand rocky islets were scattered across a tideless inland sea. He told me of the strangers there with their sing-song language, and the bales of skins and bundles of horns that the seamen packed tight in the holds below, and how the little trading bark rolled her gunnels under on the way home, with the weight of timber balks lashed to her weather-deck.

I was dreaming of being free of my step-father at last, when of a sudden the *Prosperous Anne* slammed into a wave. The seas had built higher as we talked on.

'Shall I hand the maincourse, Thom?' I said.

'I'll go up, lad.' He stretched languidly and yawned. 'It'll give me something to do. Wake me up a bit.'

I inclined my head enquiringly towards the hatch.

Thom said, 'He's fast asleep, Matt. Leave him be, eh?'

It was more peaceful for us all if the master were left to slumber on, full of ale, and even his own son knew it. Thom worked his way forward and nudged the resting Barney in the ribs with his foot.

'Come on, bag of lazybones,' he encouraged. 'Work the belays while I go aloft and furl.'

Thom swung easily onto the ratlines and hauled himself hand over hand up to the maintop. He was agile enough on a boat to beat the lithest of lads up the shrouds, big-framed fellow though he was. I gazed out to windward and into the gloom of the gathering night. The sky ahead had turned black and heavy with rain, with the wind strong enough to whip spray from the wave-tops.

'Go careful, Thom!' I called. 'Squally weather coming.'

He heard the warning and gave a nod just as a hard gust of wind hit the rigging and shook the sails. A surge of weight came on the tiller-bar, unbalancing me as I struggled to keep the collier steady. A man aloft needs a good steersman, I told myself, concentrating hard and pushing with all my might.

Barney tended the belays in the waist of the ship, gripping the rail with one hand to keep stance. The clewlines flew clear and Thom, working his way out along the yard, reached the very outboard end of the spar and with both hands began the laborious task of hauling up the heavy, wet cloth.

With a pang that made my heart leap, I remembered the jack-stay.

'Thom!' I yelled. 'Watch that jack-stay!'

My words were snatched away by the risen wind, and Thom, busy with the folds of canvas, did not hear.

'Barney!' I called. 'For the Lord's sake, tell Thom – the jack-stay's no good!'

Barney might as well have been in St Hilda's Abbey for all the notice he took.

Above the shrieking wind, there came a crack from aloft and I jerked my head up to see the parted jack-stay snaking free of the yard. Thom's feet dangled in the air and he clung to the spar itself as the loosened sail flogged noisily, threatening to catch him a blow and fling him off. Just out of his reach was the flailing clewline. He made a grab for it but it struck him in the face and he almost lost his grip on the yard.

Grasping hold of the bucking tiller, I screamed at the top of my lungs, 'Barney – the clewline, belay the clewline, for the Lord's sake!'

Busy untangling the mass of ropes at the belays and oblivious to the drama above his head, Barney only scowled back.

I yelled again, in desperation, frantically pointing up at Thom. 'The clew, the clew! Take up on the clewline!'

At last, he craned up to see. Thom called out, but whatever he said was lost in the howling wind. With agonising slow-wittedness, Barney took up the bight of the clewline, passed it round a belay and started to haul in. The line tightened and Thom grasped it gratefully.

As the collier passed into the body of the squall, the wind buffeted her rig and the seas heaped up ahead. She dived into a trough, taking a tun weight of water over her bows, and a green sea coursed along the decks, knocking Barney back against the rail. At the same instant, the shock of the ship hitting the wave jerked Thom clean off the yard, leaving him swinging from the clewline.

I opened my mouth to scream at Barney to keep hold of the line, but even as I formed the words I saw it was too late. Saving himself from being dashed into the scuppers, Barney clawed at the nearest handhold and, fatally, let go of the clewline. As Thom's weight came onto it, the line ran out loose.

He fell crashing on the deck below without a cry, and broke his back on the lever of the deck capstan. He lay utterly still.

I stared in anguish, unable to take in the horror of what had happened. As the boarding sea surged away aft, gurgling through the scuppers, Barney struggled up in a daze, gaping at his crewmate's crumpled form. He looked from Thom Stalbone to the spar above and then down at the loose coils of rope by his feet. Suddenly, he leapt up and ran aft to the steering position.

'For the Lord's sake, see to him!' I yelled, hanging on to the kicking tiller-bar.

But he kept running aft and, reaching me, hurled me bodily away from my position.

'Get forward!' he screamed, waving me away, his eyes starting. He flung himself on the tiller-bar and clung to it like a frightened kitten clawing at its mother.

Dumbstruck, I staggered along the heaving deck to help my step-brother, hoping against all reason to find him sitting up and shaking his head. Don't die, not now, please don't die, I cried under my breath. But when I reached the inert figure and bent over him, I knew in an instant I was looking at the shattered skull and caved-in chest of a dead man.

The noise of the loose maincourse flogging on the yard brought the collier-master lurching from the cabin to stare around at the high waves. He looked aloft at the rig and saw the half-furled mainsail and dangling clewline.

'What the Devil?' he blazed. 'Why haven't you got her shortened down –'

He stopped, catching sight of Thom's lifeless form lying on the deck as I bent over him. With a bellow of pain, he staggered past Barney along the pitching boards until he reached his son's body.

Shaking him by the shoulders, he called out, 'Mercy of God, let him have another chance! Please God, another chance.'

But the master too could see he was dead, and he fell quiet, clasping and unclasping Thom's blue seaman's jacket. As the lashing rain and salt spray streamed down his wet cheeks, the collier-master bent and kissed his son's broken face.

Then he turned towards me. I knelt nearby, white-faced with shock, gripping the ship's rail. Mister Stalbone's eye fell upon the coils of rope at my feet, and the loose belay pin lying close by on the deck-boards.

'You bastard,' he said, softly at first. I saw a glint appear in his eye. 'Bastard! Bastard!' he shouted in a rising scream, and lunged.

I flung myself away and scrambled for the ratlines to escape. Grasping the wet ropes, I swung into the steps and ran a dozen feet up, when my limbs froze in fear. I could not face going aloft. I could not go on the spar where Thom had slipped and fallen to his death minutes before. My step-father was at the rail, struggling to heave himself up to the base of the ratlines, yet still I could not make my legs obey the command to climb.

The wind screamed across the decks and a beam sea thudded into the bark's topsides, throwing solid water over the rail. The collier-master went down on his knees, gasping for air and clutching a handhold. For a second, he twisted upwards and gazed in hatred at me. Then, in another instant, his seaman's instinct took over and he shouted back towards Barney.

'Steer away! We must get the cloth off her.' To me, he bellowed, 'I'll deal with you later. Get aloft and furl before we lose the whole blasted rig.'

I came to my senses and pulled myself rapidly upwards. I climbed and climbed as the collier-bark pitched into the steepening seas and seemed to be trying to throw me down to join my dear, dead step-brother. The master's curses floated up from below whenever the wind lulled for a second, but at last I reached the dreaded mainyard, high above the weather-deck.

The icy rain stung my face and the wind tore at my sodden oiled-skin coat. Numbed, I watched as Mister Stalbone dragged the body to the scuppers and put a lashing round it to prevent the sea taking away his son's mortal remains. Then he took the tiller from Barney and sent him forward to handle the belays. The ship had to be seen to, so with tears blinding me, I forced myself to crawl out along the yard. With the jack-stay gone, I used my belt to strap myself on, but it was laborious work moving the belt as I worked along the spar. For a while, I even managed without it, thinking it would be a relief if I were thrown down and killed too. I could not take my eye off Thom's shattered body where it lay broken far below, the Thom who would never again come and lay a kind hand on my shoulder and speak a word of comfort.

After a struggle, I managed to tame the sail by loosely lashing it to the yard with the clewline, until at last the bark was furled down with just her topsails set, and she sailed easier through the gale.

On the master's orders, we turned home for Whitby, easing the sheets to run off before the wind. Afraid to go aft to the shelter of the cabin, I stayed shivering on the foredeck, sheltered from the spray, all through the night. What did I fear more – facing the master or passing the ghastly sight of Thom's corpse where it lay in the scuppers?

The next morning in Whitby harbour, my step-father was lost in grief, silent and brooding as we made the ship fast at the wharfside. I kept out of his way until he left to get help, then I crept unseen into the cabin and crawled under a pile of sheepskin covers to find warmth. I lay trembling in the darkness and listened to the sounds of a crowd gathering on the wharf, come to examine the aftermath of a tragedy. Footsteps scraped on the deck-boards and I knew they were lifting Thom's body down the gangway. I rolled over, aching from the stiffness in my limbs and the chill seeping into my bones through salt-wet clothes. I did not want to come out and face the day. I truly wished I were dead myself.

I drifted into an exhausted half-slumber, but awoke at the sound of the collier-master's heavy tread on deck, followed by the sharp tap of leather shoes, which I knew must be the finickety step of the merchant-lender. Mister Jeffreys' nasal tones drifted into the enclosed cabin.

'Walter, what can I say? Such a terrible loss for you.'

The master's voice was thick. 'He did it – that miserable piece of a whale's turd.'

The door of the cabin was flung back and the light flooded in. I twisted away from the glare, but the big hands were round me in a moment, dragging me from the bunk and pushing me roughly up the steps. Blinking, my eyes cast down, afraid to look up and face anyone, I stood on the decks and waited.

'He let the bluddy line go!' said my step-father, his voice quavering.

He gathered the cheeks of his mouth and ejected a stream of foul gob, but I ducked and the spittle landed on the deck-boards with a splat. Half-crouched like an animal, I waited with my hands raised, braced for another onslaught. Out of the corner of my eye, I caught sight of Barney lurking by the rail, terrified.

Not caring any more, I shouted, 'The jack-stay was rotten!'

'He's a lying, spineless piece of rag!' bellowed my step-father.

'What about the broken jack-stay?' said the merchant. 'Were it not an unavoidable accident?'

Suddenly, I thought how it was the lending payments that forced the collier-men to skimp. In a way, it was Mister Jeffreys who was to blame too, but he'd find any excuse.

'It was never my fault!' I half sobbed. 'You're all to blame – all of you!'

Mister Jeffreys' eyes, narrow and mean, bore into me. 'Still a troublemaker, aren't you, my lad?' he said quietly.

My step-father's face was ruddy with fury. 'He's a curse on a ship – I should have thrown him over the side!' he raged. 'Off my bluddy ship, boy! You're going down on the barges.'

I stared back dully. It was enough that Thom was dead and they were making me the cause of it. Not this too, I pleaded silently, not the barges.

'The dust'll choke your throat,' the collier-master was saying. 'I'll see you spend your life in the hold of a bluddy river barge.'

I heard the words through a distant roaring in my brain. To think I would no longer go to sea, never fill my lungs with salty air and steer a ship along her course, but instead scrape and shovel in the filthy alum on the river barges crushed me. I fought to stop it, but I knew my chin trembled like a stupid little boy's.

'Daniel Goodhew, he's needing a bargehand,' said Walter Stalbone at last, eyes vacant as they turned to me. 'You'll stay there till the Lord shakes hands with the Devil.'

He pushed me so hard I went sprawling across the deck. I lay there, hoping I might never have to get up.

'Walter,' I heard the merchant say, 'he costs you nothing to keep, you know.'

'To Hell with it. He's signed on to me and if I say he's going on the barges, that's an end to it.' The master held out his paw towards me. 'Boy, give up your seaman's knife.'

Instinctively, I touched the handle at the belt of my pants, but they were on me in a second, Mister Stalbone pinning my arms while Barney whipped out the precious blade.

'Only a proper seamen wants a knife like that,' said the master. He held out his hand and reluctantly Barney handed over the instrument. 'You'll not be needing it on a bluddy river barge.'

'I shan't stay there!'

'O aye – you shall that!' he shouted. 'Take your

foul carcass off my ship and down to Daniel. If I see your face aboard here again, I'll break you in half.'

I looked at my guardian, Mister Jeffreys, but he gave the slightest shrug of his shoulders as if to say, there's nothing to be done. Defeated, I sloped to the ship's rail, clambered over and dropped down to the wharfside. I passed through the busy shipyard as if it were not there, its noise and bustle muffled to me, as though a blanket of coarse sheep's wool had enveloped me. Now, I thought, I am truly alone. Thom's gone, and my future with him.

Something deep in my guts balled into the hardness of stone. By the Good Lord's own blood, I breathed, I must not give in. The ships and the sea are gone from me for now, but I shall find a way back.

Without another glance backward at the old *Prosperous Anne*, I departed the shipyard and all the other tubby colliers and the stout-masted trading barks that I so loved to be amongst. Instead, I trudged along the narrow riverbank path towards the dust and filth of the alum wharves, to find Daniel Goodhew and beg for work on the low barges.

# 6

# *Dust and Ashes*

The deep-laden barge swung sharply to steerboard as the current caught it by the bow. I pushed the tiller-bar hard over to correct the drift, waited, then hauled it to centre again. Right forward stood Daniel Goodhew, a coiled head-rope in his hand, ready to catch fast a stake as we came alongside the piling of the wharfside. The dirt-encrusted lugsail had been lowered from the stubby mast and lay slumped on the deck amongst its slackened ropes. The sail had done its work, and the barge's headway would carry us alongside if I had judged it right.

A gust of wind fanned across the river, chasing a swirl of alum dust from the high-piled open hold and into my face. I spat harshly, dumping a mouthful of greyish spittle on the boards, and wiped a sleeve across my eyes.

'Ready to swing in!' called out Goodhew from the bow.

I levered the tiller to port and the barge began its slow turn into the current. The riverside floated across the bow as the barge swung round to face upriver and then crabbed its way towards the shore. As the gap closed, Goodhew jumped onto the bank and made the headrope fast. Scrambling aft to reach the stern line, I heaved it shoreside to him, then leapt onto the wharf. Together, we shortened the lines until the barge lay snug to the riverbank.

'Not bad, Matt, for a bluddy collier-hand,' grinned Goodhew, straightening up.

I smiled back, a touch grimly, I suppose. Daniel was a fair fellow, a trait he had failed to pass on to his goat-featured son, but there was a twinge of pain in the jibe, for he had been a collier-master himself until increases in the lending payments had lost him his seagoing trade.

'Now begins the best part,' said the bargeman.

He laughed ruefully at his own joke, and we set to on the three-hour stint of shovelling the alum into sacks, raising choking clouds of dust and working deep in the hold until it was swept bare. Load by backbreaking load, we barrowed the sacks ashore, stacking them on the wharf ready to be stowed aboard barks for shipping out, or put onto mule trains heading inland for the fleece works. Tomorrow would be the same again, ten hours a day, until the relief of the Sabbath.

In the two winters since I last sailed aboard my old bark, not a day had passed that I did not yearn for my seventeenth year to come. Now, with my prenticeship to Stalbone almost ended, I would soon be free to go to sea with another master.

With half the load shovelled out and run into the stacks, I straightened my tortured back and glanced downriver to seaward.

A couple of hundred yards off, down by the cole wharves, a two-masted collier-bark was being poled from her berth and pushed out into the current. A skiff with four oarsmen stood off at the bow and rowed her away from the quay with measured pulls of the sweeps. A figure ran up the ratlines and out on the fore-topyard, while another on the collier's deck moved about at the belays. The fore-topsail unfurled, bellying and slacking until it caught air enough to stretch out full. The forecourse below it soon followed, filling instantly with a wind off the bluffs. The collier gathered way, the waters swirling at her stern. A break in the clouds let a shaft of sun fall onto her stout shape, catching the spread of tan sails against the darker sea horizon. The main-topsail and maincourse now dropped away from the yards and were sheeted home. Under all plain sail, the bark picked up speed, a brave little vessel standing out towards the open sea.

I gripped my shovel fiercely. She was the *Prosperous Anne*, bound for Hartlepool, her hold packed full of alum sacks, and then for the Tyne to take on cole. How bold she looks, I thought, as she bends her solid shape to the purpose. One day, I swore, I shall go with her again.

A hail of grit and small stones fell on the back of my neck. Startled, I spun round. Daniel Goodhew let out a laugh, and dissolved into a fit of coughing.

'Oy, sheep's brain, there's alum enough to clear,' he gasped. 'You can dream after.'

In my filthy clothes and dust-matted hair, I resigned myself to the labour, rhythmically scraping with the shovel, lifting the ore, bagging it and hefting the sacks to the bank, my mind filled with bitterness. Tottering across the wharfside with a loaded barrow, quite lost in my own misery, I heard the rattle of a carriage approaching fast from along the York Road. I looked up to see a rig pounding towards me with its two good horses in a sweat, being driven hard by the Lynskill man at the reins.

'Clear the bluddy way!' shouted the driver, waving his whip from side to side.

Heaving the stubborn barrow over a rutted part of the road, I overbalanced and the load fell on my legs. As the carriage bore onwards, I lay pinned by the weight of the alum sacks. With a vicious tug at the reins, the driver swerved clear, cursing volubly, and the carriage flew by with its tackle jangling, the over-driven horses white-eyed and grinding their bits. Inches from my face, the iron-rimmed wheels spun past, scrunching the gravelly dirt into the air and sending grit flying into my eyes.

When the whirlwind had passed, I lay on the ground, stunned and spitting dirt, enraged by the humiliation. The fresh-painted black carriage was the good Justice Lynskill's best one, though the judge might not appreciate the treatment it was receiving today. Seated in it was the young gentlemen I knew straightaway as Master Lynskill, dandified and arrogant as ever. Opposite, encased in a black dress with a severe cap on her head, was Mistress Elizabeth Lynskill, the Justice's Puritan wife, and beside her, demure in a pale shift and fair-day bonnet, sat Abigail, out riding with her betrothed and his mother. Her white face was turned backwards in shock, and I heard her girlish voice carry above the clatter of the rig.

'Stop – stop the horses!'

The carriage slewed to an abrupt halt, and the

horses stamped their hooves and shook their heads, breathing noisily. Abigail was out of the carriage and hurrying back towards me when a sharp command stopped her short. She caught my eye, then twisted round in alarm.

'Miss Jeffreys – come back at once!' It was John Lynskill. He jumped down and strode over, grabbing her arm.

'Let me go!' she cried, trying to break away.

Master John dragged her back to the carriage.

'I must see to him, he is hurt,' I heard her protest, but he was too strong.

I managed to half-rise, dazed. A flying stone had caught me a blow to the temple and a warm streak of blood dribbled from the wound. I tried to focus, but saw no more than a blur. Nor could I wet my tongue to speak, for the dust filled my throat.

There came an older woman's voice.

'You transgress the will of the Lord, girl,' said Mistress Lynskill gravely. 'He punishes those who would dare cross the natural divide between our stations.'

'But it's Matthew – I only wanted to help him,' wailed Abigail as they pushed her inside the carriage.

'Be silent! Such intransigent pride,' said Mistress Lynskill, 'cannot go unpunished. Drive on, Bowyer, and don't spare the whip.'

As the horses jerked into forward motion and the carriage moved off, Daniel Goodhew came running over with Jem Wiggate, a bargehand about my own age.

'Are you hurt, lad?' asked Daniel, as they helped me up.

'O aye, I'm dam' fine, I am,' I said, wondering unkindly if the fellow had any idea at all.

Young Jem watched the Lynskill carriage hurtling off, the driver swinging his whip this way and that. 'Bluddy Lynskills, charging around the town as if they owned it.' He grinned, but the joke fell flat.

The receding carriage left us standing in a swirl of alum dust as it sped off. I surveyed the desolate wharf, with a dozen burst sacks strewn about beside the barrow. It would take an hour of unpaid work just to refill them.

'Dam' you in Hell!' I cried, jumping a foot in the air and waving my fists as the carriage rounded the bend and was gone from sight. 'Be damm'd,' I muttered, and set to work like a stoat after a rabbit, scooping the hated alum up bare-handed and filling the sacks at a rate.

'Them Lynskills,' said Wiggate, squinting into the fog of dust hanging in the roadway. 'There'll be trouble soon at this rate of things.'

The only reply I could give was a grunt. I laboured on in a pure fury for the rest of the afternoon, my mind working like a capstan winch. There must be a way, I told myself, to get back to sea and escape the confines of Whitby. And to help dear Abigail, who at sixteen has grown so pretty. As the day ended, I marched away without a word and spent the last hour before dark alone, trying to study my Navigation, but could not keep my mind on it.

Passing Market-place that evening after dark, I

was surprised to find a few souls lingering there, until I remembered it was a quarter-day. Country folk had travelled the width of the county of Yorkshire to reach Whitby for the fair, and the crier had announced a bear-bait, a visiting band of minstrels, and the Revenue Troop newly arrived from York to fire off muskets in a volley, just for show. In better times, the town would have been crowded with revellers until late. This eve, there was a limp air about the place, like an emptied sack.

Catching a whiff of mutton chops cooking somewhere, I felt a pang of hunger bite into me and decided to head round to Sand-gate towards old Mistress Portenshaw's shop to see if she might give me a bit of cold, left-over turnip pot-soup, or a hand off yesterday's loaf. As I turned from the square into Benson-yard, shrieks of coarse laughter rose from the alleyway at Tate-hill, where the great urine vases stood. Folk were trying to unbalance a fellow as he stood on the edge of one vase and pissed copiously into it.

'Keep your stance, man,' his friends shouted as they sought to unfoot him.

'You'll not be in my bed tonight if you go in,' called a portly woman, cackling.

The fellow, wobbling and giggling as they grabbed his ankles, sprayed them and sent them into gales of laughter. The piss in there was weeks old, ready to be carted off to the fleece works. One way or another, it's a dirty business, this wool trade, I said to myself, turning down the hill. From that filthy alum ore to the piss-vases, it's a hard way to finish a few fleeces that only make a profit for the wool merchants.

The sound of the laughter receded and, stepping into the narrow passage down to Mistress Portenshaw's, I saw lanterns moving about near the bottom, and the shadowy outlines of figures. All at once, the crowd surged forward and I heard voices raised in anger.

'Let's 'ave a bluddy go at 'em, lads!' said one.

'Aye, put 'em in the river,' called another.

'Throw the Lynskills in the piss-vases!'

A chorus of cheers went up. In the lanterns' light, I caught sight of Daniel Goodhew and ran up to him, joining the throng as it moved off towards the Restoration Arms.

'What's happened?' I said breathlessly.

'A penny cut!' said Daniel. 'Another bluddy penny cut in our wage, all for Justice Lynskill's tax. And it's our wage that gets cut to pay for it. Come along, Matt, we're going to have ourselfs some ale and make plans. Things'll have to change.'

The Lynskills again, I thought. The cole trade was falling off and the alum hauling was slow, but while the town went short of food and everyone wanted for a fire in their winter grates, the only hardship the Lynskills and their ilk suffered was the absence of French wines or brandy to wash down their roasted pig and mutton cutlets, for the King had banned the wine trade. My mouth watered at the mere thought of a table laden with meat, and through the rags of my coat I rubbed my stomach, feeling its spare, hard flatness.

'Aye, come on, Matt,' said Jem Wiggate, coming up. 'A pint mug of ale'll help.'

'I haven't got a coin for any ale,' I told him glumly.

'Why, can you not ask that guardian of yours for a farthing?'

'He says he owes me nothing, Jem,' I said.

'That Seth Jeffreys,' said Goodhew, 'is nothing more than a liar and a bluddy cheat.'

'It's taken you long enough to figure it, Daniel,' said Jem, laughing.

Goodhew ignored him and got into his stride. 'Merchant Jeffreys is like a little terrier dog, sniffing after them Lynskills. He's at their calling for commerce, and hides his own dealings, and all the time puts coin in his pocket.' He laughed without mirth.

'Aye, but there's that pretty maid of his betrothed,' said Jem. 'Uniting the money and the lender, there's craft in that. I saw her go by again in the carriage this eve. Red-eyed, she were. The Lynskills don't just beat men with the whip, and between the Justice's son and the Justice's wife, I reckon she's getting a right hard time of it. And she's not even wed yet.'

I felt my face grow hot.

'Still soft on little Missie Abby?' said Jem, digging me in the ribs. 'Fancy yourself between the sheets with her, instead of that fat boar? She'll be bearing some big-arsed youngsters for him in no time.'

In a flash, I lost control. I flung myself on him and we crashed to the cobblestones, Jem swinging his fists in defence. It took all Goodhew's strength to drag me off.

'Matt, lad – ease up there, for the Lord's sake,' he said, one hand on my chest and the other pushing Jem away.

'You've no right to even say her name!' I bawled at Wiggate.

Of a sudden, he knew he'd gone too far, and began to look abashed. 'I'm sorry, Matt, lad. I know you're moonstruck on her.' He held out his hand. 'It's not worth us falling out over them dam' Lynskills.'

I slowly took his proffered handshake. He was right – we had to stay combined.

Daniel looked solemn and said, 'Forget about the lass, lad. You're a bluddy alum man, lucky to have a sixpenny wage at all.' He squeezed my arm and grinned. 'But you're hot in your head, Matt. All heated up about such things as you'll never change, just like your Pa.'

For the first time in an age, I thought about my father, and something Mister Jeffreys had said years ago popped into my mind.

'Daniel,' I said slowly, 'what did my Pa say about the Africk trade?'

'The Africk trade?' He was puzzled for a moment, until a memory seemed to return. 'Cause of all his trouble, it were. A bad business, he said, and he'd have nowt to do with it. Long time ago now, but it were a pity he ever went to York to speak out. Best forget it, lad. It's gone, it's past.'

'And forget about the Jeffreys wench,' said Jem, but not unkindly. 'She'll marry quality and wear

95

fine clothes and fancy hats and ride in carriages. You can never give her that.' He clapped me across the shoulders. 'My last couple of coins'll buy us both a mug. There'll be talk of what to do.'

We were outside the inn now, where the men had gone to douse their anger. Jem Wiggate stooped to lift the latch, and disappeared with Goodhew through the door. I hung back, imagining Abigail on her marriage day, that pasty slug mauling her, claiming what he would call his husbandly rights.

Worse, I began to remember Barney's taunts from the time when my father never came back from York. He'd swung for it, said Barney. For shouting his mouth off about the stupid Africk trade, he'd gasped to death on the gibbet in the public square, and the people had clapped.

I pushed the door open and followed Daniel and Jem into the noisy interior.

At the sound of massed tramping feet, I glanced up from where I sat on the stacked alum bags by the road that ran along the wharfside. Making their way up from the slips of the shipyard were fifty men or more, some wearing the loose, undyed working slops of labourers, others clad in the tooled-leather aprons of time-served shipwrights or craftsmen-joiners.

Leading the shipyard men up the rise marched Josiah Heslam, with his five sons and his two brothers, and behind them followed the shipworkers of Whitby – every carpenter, smith, rigger and sawyer that ever adzed out an oaken keelson, or laid a plank against a rib, or hammered home a copper fastening into one of the wooden hulls that rose from the slips beside the River Esk.

'Ahoy, Daniel Goodhew,' called shipwright Heslam. 'Today we are joined in our cause.'

'Right enough,' cried Goodhew, and shouted to the assembled men behind him. 'We march against the tax on the carrying trade – and we call for protection of the seas, as the King promised.'

A chorus of support went up and I cheered with the rest of them. In the months since we had talked that night in the Restoration Arms, the French had sunk ships off the Yorkshire coast, and the King in return had banned all trade with France. But he put no Navy cruzer on station to protect our trade with the Hollandish and Baltick lands, so no cloths, no ales, no fleeces went away on the barks that once crossed the Narrow Seas in their legions. Timbers and oils and continental goods were no longer brought in return to English ports. The coastal trade in cole had withered and died and the alum barges were laid up. Now the wharves were crowded with Whitby's unused collier-barks and small traders, their yards lowered and canvas packed away, the ships rafted up together in silence, waiting for trade to return, while their hulls rotted and the worms attacked their keels.

The old alum barger Zachary Duck joined in the speech-making.

'We demand a Navy cruzer! Justice Lynskill must make representation to the Crown.'

'Rid us of the bluddy Lynskills!' said someone. Everyone chorused in agreement.

'Aye, no more night curfews.'

97

'Give us back our fair-days!'

'All right, lads,' said Daniel, trying to keep things on an even keel. 'We carry no staves nor any axes nor arms of any kind, for we are peaceful men.'

I seethed. Goodhew could keep his timidity.

'If John Lynskill raises a hand against anyone,' I shouted, 'I shall be ready to fight back!'

A huge roar rose from the crowd, and old Zachary caught me a hefty clap across the shoulders.

'Now there's the spirit of your father,' he said.

Just then a voice called out, and we all turned in surprise to see the merchant Jeffreys. With the long grey wig and black top-coat he wore on collecting days, he stood atop a pile of alum sacks, flanked by three or four Lynskill wardens, as if to make an address.

'Good men of Whitby,' he called. 'I have commercial news.'

'Go on, Mister Merchant,' someone cried, 'tell us how much money you've made today!'

He patted the air in front of him with the flat of his hand, as if he were feeling the spring in a bale of fleeces.

'Men – I beg you to hear me out. The trade is bad, but I have good tidings – news of commerce.' The merchant-lender tried a smile. 'A Baltick venture, our most established and traditional trade. A bark is to be brought round from the Tyne for a refit, putting work in the shipyard. Woolsacks and cloth shall be loaded for the northern ports.'

'What of the Whitby farthing?' Josiah Heslam shook his fist. 'It's a tax for the King's Hollandish wars – where's the benefit to hungry folk? Lift it, and let the trade come back!'

The merchant glanced around nervously. 'Only commerce and venture can bring a return of the trade. Now hear this, men. I have another venture in mind, if the good Justice sanctions the monies. A vessel shall be purchased to ship manufactures for the Guinea Coast and take a cargo across to the New World, returning from there with produce.' He raised his voice to a higher pitch. 'She too shall be fitted out in the yard here, and there'll be work aboard for Whitby sailing men. And if she makes good of her Africk trade, other barks may follow after.'

An Africk venture! Now, without prompting, a sharp memory returned, of my father speaking of the trade in people with black skins, who wore no clothes and folk whispered they were Devils. What had Pa said? They were men too. Before their God, he had told me, they were men like us.

'Look – in the river!' A shipwright stood pointing to seawards.

All of us craned to see a two-masted bark hoving into the harbour, the first ship for many days to pass between the heads. With her canvas all furled up, she progressed slowly under a long tow from a Revenue cutter, with twelve Troopers pulling at the sweeps, bringing her up with the flood tide under her keel.

I gaped. She was the *Prosperous Anne*. How had I failed to notice she was away from her usual berth, rafted on the outside of her sisters? Now the old collier progressed steadily upriver, with Stalbone at the helm while Barney nipped about the decks readying the mooring lines. Another figure stood beside the collier-master, luminous in a bright green Amsterdammer coat, his legs planted apart and a riding crop in his hand.

'The Lord's blood,' breathed Jem Wiggate, who had wormed his way next to me. 'It's that damm'd John Lynskill. Looks like he's taking her up to Salt Quay.'

My heart rang inside my chest like a carpenter's hammer on a trennel as I understood what was happening.

'She's smuggling!' I shouted, turning to the mob. 'When we're going hungry!'

I ran to pick up an axe-handle, and lofted it so everyone could see. As one, the crowd picked up their own axe-handles and staves, and we streamed upriver. From the corner of my eye, I spotted Mister Jeffreys sloping away into town, shielded by the burly wardens.

We easily reached Salt Quay ahead of the *Prosperous Anne*. The flood had an hour of rise left in it, so the cutter pulled the bark in a wide circle to bring her head to tide, and she slowed, committed now to her chosen berth. As the collier closed the stone quay, we saw her deck spaces were crammed with barrels of French brandy, casks of wine and sacks of Mediterranean fruits, dried in the southerly sun.

'Fancy goods!' I shouted. 'They smuggle for profit while we starve!'

'Reckon they've loaded her from a bark off-shore,' said old Zachary, 'like we did years ago, under the Lord Protector. And she'll be packed below with jean cottons and Frenchy cloths.'

Jem Wiggate began to strike his stave rhythmically against the stone walls and, with a roar of approval the Whitby men stamped their feet and rattled their wooden weapons in time.

Standing on the collier's after-deck, John Lynskill waved his arms.

'Keep away there, you fellows!' he bawled. 'Clear the wharf or pay the consequences.'

'To Hell with you, Lynskill,' shouted Josiah Heslam. 'We're ready for you this time.'

The Whitby men raised up a cheer behind me and we leaned eagerly forward to grasp the bark's gunnels and draw her in for our assault on her bounty of wealth, bent on depriving the Justice and his family of at least one valued cargo.

John Lynskill's voice rose again above the hubbub.

'Troop! Show yourselves!' He pointed over our heads. 'Musketmen – step forward there!'

Alarmed, we turned, following his pudgy arm, to see springing from behind the bond-house twelve Troopers of the Revenue armed with long muskets. Ten more leapt out from the other side in a clatter of gun barrels and a jangle of swords. The presence of better than twenty fully armed men utterly changed the balance of the confrontation and we shrank instinctively into a huddle.

'Muskets!' I muttered to Jem. 'He's armed them with muskets, for the Lord's sake, while we carry staves.'

'Arrest these two ringleaders,' commanded Lynskill, pointing at Heslam and Goodhew, 'and hold them in the name of the Court.'

In confusion, the crowd fell back as half a dozen musketmen pushed their way to the quay's edge and took hold of the two men.

I could stand it no longer. They were getting the better of us again.

'No!' I bellowed. 'Free them!' As the *Prosperous Anne* bumped alongside, the Port Controller staggered but kept his footing and stared open-mouthed at me.

'You cheat us!' I bawled down from the wharf. 'You try to break our spirits and blame the French for it. You live off our backs and train your muskets on our heads.' I waved a fist at him, a surge of hatred overwhelming my reason. 'You pay men to betray their own – you steal our common lands! There is no justice in Lynskill justice!'

A huge cheer went up and the crowd surged forward.

Lynskill's face registered disbelief as he gazed around.

'Who is this fellow? Has he lost his head?' He pointed his fleshy finger at me. 'You speak like a traitor. Your fellows are not with you. One word more and you shall hang, by the love of Justice.'

'Free our friends!' I shouted. 'Justice for all!'

Everyone cheered and the mob surged forward.

'Release them!'

'Free those men!'

'Free them! Free them!' the crowd chanted in unison.

Lynskill blinked, for a fatal moment unsure of his next move. The crowd bayed their demands, and at the front we made a rush towards our captive fellows. With a sharp explosion, a musket discharged, its report crashing off the stone walls of the bond-house. The hubbub of oaths and cries ceased instantaneously, and the men fell away. I stood stunned by the noise, thinking I must have been shot.

Lynskill looked madly around. 'Hold your fire, for God's sake!' he cried. 'Arrest that Trooper.'

There was a momentary commotion at the rear of the crowd where a puff of whitish smoke hung in the air, and one of the Troopers was hustled away. The crowd cleared back, leaving me standing alone, the tang of flash-powder seeping into my nostrils. I looked down and saw Jem Wiggate slumped on the stones, clutching his belly and groaning.

Lynskill pulled himself together and leapt from the *Prosperous Anne* onto the quayside, shouting commands.

'Lower your muskets! Pikemen, I want this quayside cleared.'

The twelve Revenue men in the cutter snatched up their pikes and leapt onto the quay with their weapons on guard. As everyone stared at Wiggate's bloody body, the white-faced men of Whitby recovered their wits and a low, angry murmur arose. Jem groaned at my feet, and his blood oozed onto the stones, spreading into a dark pool. In another second, I knew the men's wrath would explode. The Troopers and pikemen would dissolve into a panic and in an instant we would be wallowing in a bloodbath. Standing rooted by the fallen man, I was horrified at what my outburst had unleashed.

'Away, lads!' I cried. 'Clear away in peace before there's more blood spilled.'

I knelt and cradled my friend's head. It felt loosened from the neck, and Jem's cheeks were bereft of colour. The crowd was motionless, gazing at me and Jem. Then their shoulders drooped and they lowered their wooden weapons. Gradually, they backed off, falling away into knots of twos and threes, casting their staves on the ground, and the pikemen retook the quayside.

I bent over Jem. His face had gone a ghostly white, as if the life were draining from him. I wept but I could not speak.

'Arrest that man,' I heard Port Controller Lynskill say. 'He's a rabble-rouser.'

Six pairs of arms enclosed me and bundled me to the ground.

'Manacle the prisoners,' said Lynskill. 'Take them to the courthouse.'

The Revenue Troop officer hoisted me upright and shoved me forward. Four Troopers stooped to pick up Jem, flinging him carelessly onto their shoulders. His head rolled backwards and his eyes were white blanks, veined with red.

As we were marched off, the blood banged in my ears. If only I had held my peace, the poor fellow would be walking alongside me and laughing even now. I could not look at the crumpled body, the shirtfront wet with blood, being lugged along as if it were the carcass of a sheep.

After a little, Josiah Heslam, manacled alongside me, managed to talk.

'You stood bravely, lad,' he puffed. 'We needed someone to speak out for us.'

'But it was my fault, all my fault!' I cried.

Daniel Goodhew, borne swiftly along two paces in front, twisted painfully round.

'O aye, well said today, Matt.' His mouth contorted into a bitter grimace. 'You always know what's right – and dam' the bluddy hurt for anyone else.'

The Revenue officer came up and cracked a gloved fist across the back of Daniel's head.

'Face forward and hold your peace, man,' he said. 'By my lights, you should hang. Face what's coming to you.'

# 7

## *False Deeds*

Heaving myself painfully up on my elbows, and
scrunching out of shape the straw palliasse under
me, I scowled at the scullery girl in the darkness.

'Libby – you must tell me what you saw.'

Perhaps my tone was harsh, for she shrank back
in confusion, dropping her linen rags. The dim room
in the Stalbone cottage smelled of balm-oil and
camomile. An end of a candle, brought inside her
apron to help her see to nurse me, flickered on the
box-top beside the cot.

'Libby, I'm not angry. I just want to know.'

The girl bent to pick her cloth from the floor and
her eyes came level with mine for a second. She
looked like a squirrel, disturbed by a crackle of
twigs in the woods and caught stock still, poised on
the point of flight. I shot out one hand and took her
wrist.

'O – Matthew!' she gasped.

I smiled and let her go, allowing myself to fall
back onto on the rough mattress.

'Libby, you know I love you,' I said, tenderly.
'You are so kind to me, and what a gentle touch you
have.'

I closed my eyes and listened to the dipping and

wringing of her cloth into the pail, and waited for the soothing dab-dab-dab of her ministrations to resume. The whip-cuts on my back were closing well, she'd said, and cleanly too, showing no sign of the flesh-rot. Yet even after twelve days, it was agonising when I tried to move. The thirty lashes struck on me, stocked and manacled in the court-house square, had nearly killed me, and I wondered how I might ever have survived all two hundred lashes of Justice Lynskill's sentence. But the crowd had rebelled before the sentence could be fully delivered, and carried me off, along with poor Josiah Heslam, who now lay near death in his own cottage. I remembered, as I was bounced and jiggled away in agony, slung in the coats of my fellow Whitby men, how I caught a last glimpse of the arena of punishment. I knew the sight would remain with me till my final breath, for what I saw was the silhouette of a corpse swinging lazily from the gibbet, its head hung brokenly forward onto its chest, a pool of piss and muck discolouring the stones beneath it. It was my friend, Daniel Good-hew, hanged for sedition.

I had spent each and every hour, since being brought to the cottage that morning, lying on my stomach and soothed only by the balmy caresses of Libby. I levered myself half off the palliasse again and turned to see the girl. Pretty was not the right word, for her face was too rounded and her body stocky, like a moors pony, but she was kind and dependable, and when she wed, she would make sturdy children. Perhaps that's the best way, I thought wistfully, admiring her ruddy skin and the thickness of her arms. Just be content to raise a fine family with strong bones and good backs, and make a life of that.

'This is Miss Abigail's doing, you tending me like this,' I told her. When I thought of how Abigail had come to the courthouse square to petition her future father-in-law, Justice Henry Lynskill, and plead for clemency for the rebels, I clenched my fists. I was sure she had done it for love.

'O no, you're quite wrong,' said Libby. 'It is Mistress Whistock sends me down, and tells me not to be seen by anyone, most of all Mister Jeffreys.'

'Have it your way. But tell me what you saw, for the Good Lord's peace of mind.'

'You know she is kept indoors.'

'Yes, Libby. Aye.'

'And though I saw her just once or twice the whole of last week, her eyes were quite red from crying.'

'Aye, you told me.' I sighed.

'Last evening, me and Mistress Whistock took her up a pail for her bathing.'

I let my eyelids drop, collapsing into the sumptuous thought of Abigail's bared body before me, soaping herself with a washcloth.

'Well, Mistress Whistock did not let me in to her room, and when she come out, she pushed me back downstairs all the way to the kitchen in one rush. She was tutting to herself all evening and saying "my, my" like she does.'

'Yes, she does.'

'Bruises, she said. Terrible black and red bruises she seen all over her buttocks and –'

'That bastard – ooooow!'

'Look now, there's blood again. Quiet down, Matthew,' said Libby, dabbing at the split scabbiness that criss-crossed my back.

'As soon as I can walk, I shall go to the house and challenge him.'

'O no! You must not. It'll be a great deal the worse for her if you act so stupid. And it's beyond anyone to stop the marriage.'

I groaned. I almost wished, rather than live to see that joining take place, that I had been hanged along with poor Daniel.

'And think of Justice Lynskill too, just look what trouble there'll be if you cause any more upset.'

'To Hell with the Justice!' I shouted, startling Libby into dropping her cloth yet again.

'You mustn't speak like that,' said Libby, bending to pick it up. 'The Justice shows a mercy, and you say –' She stopped, fearful. 'O, I'll not repeat the Devil's words.'

'We only got away because the Justice feared a riot,' I said angrily, 'and now he says as soon as I can walk, he'll put me in gaol.'

She dabbed on in silence, a little harder, to make me understand she was annoyed.

'I shall go to Prosperity-street and take Abigail in my arms. And see off that John Lynskill in a bare-knuckle fight.'

'O, you're dreaming as ever.' She straightened and drew my shirt down to cover the injuries. 'I must go, before Mister Jeffreys notices I've been away.'

'Libby, thank you. Leave the candle for me.'

She wrapped her cloths and oils in a neat bundle, and tamped it into the bottom of her empty pail. There came a loud knocking on the street door. Libby jumped, tipping the bundle from her pail. She scrabbled around, trying to recompose her things.

'Libby, see who it is. Let them in.'

She skipped away and I held my breath. If the Troopers were coming for me now, well, I would make the most tremendous fight of it before the manacles were on and they dragged me to those cells of death. I heard low whispers, then the street door closed and there came footfalls in the passage. The steps shuffled into the doorway.

'Well, who is it?' I said, with the strongest voice I could manage.

'Ah, ah, Matthew Stalbone. This Cottage makes a most dark and confined Place.'

'Mister Franklin, sir!' I cried, overjoyed at hearing the old tutor's voice and trying to turn and greet him as he quickly crossed the room to my bed. I beamed up at him. 'I'm sorry I cannot offer you more than a box to sit on.'

'No Matter, it suffices. I trust the Girl's Nursing of you has improved your Condition.'

'I'm healing well, sir, but I fear going back to the gaol.'

'Nevertheless, it was a famous Victory. The good Justice was discomposed by the Townsfolk's Antipathy. With the Arrival of a new Troop from York, such a State of Affairs cannot last and there is no Good in making Rebellion against superior Forces.'

I drew in a long breath, filling my lungs and wincing as the tightened skin pulled at my cuts.

110

'I have more News,' said Franklin. 'Indeed, I come from the House of Mister Jeffreys himself with Information directed to your Future.'

Franklin scratched his nose and skithered his hands together rapidly. There came the familiar audible shuddering, and I glanced at my Book of Navigation on the box beside me, thinking of our secret lessons.

'Mister Jeffreys, as your Guardian, begs me to inform you the Collier-Bark, the *Prosperous Anne*, is to be sold –'

'Sold?' My head spun.

'Indeed. Mister Jeffreys is to instruct Mister Stalbone, on his Return from Hartlepool, to fit the Bark for hauling a Burthen of best Sea-Cole to London, whereupon the Cargo shall be disposed of (and at a fine Price too, it may be reckoned, in Consideration of the Risk of French Attack in carrying cole down the Coast and through Waters infested with Foreigners). The Bark herself shall then be auctioned to the highest Bidder, under the Direction of Mister Jeffreys, who is to journey to the Capital by Road, the Proceeds of these Sales being set against the outstanding Debts on the Bark, and to this End he has instructed me to say, as you have a Form of Interest in her in Terms of your Shareholding held in Trust, that he expects there to be no residual Equity for Distribution amongst the Shareholders.'

'He's a liar and a crook!' I cried in anguish. 'He said she can't be sold – he's trying to take her away from me.'

Jedediah Franklin shifted uncomfortably on the box.

'Mister Jeffreys further instructs me to inform you he has obtained a Relief on your Behalf from Justice Lynskill. He advises that you may depart from Whitby and, unless and until you return, your Incarceration is suspended.'

I thought for a moment. 'He wants me out of Whitby forever.'

Franklin coughed, sounding like a sheep with poor chest. 'That seems indeed to be the Case, by Mister Jeffreys' Account. But it is a Chance, Matthew, for you to embark upon a new Life elsewhere. We both know you make a fine Hand aboard any Bark, and in Hartlepool you may happen upon a Captain who requires your Understanding of the Navigation. The Pity of it is that your proper Lessons ceased before you could achieve Qualification by Trinity House Examination, yet nonetheless the Navy expands and the ocean carrying Trade enters upon new Ventures so you must have a great Chance before you.'

'He wants me gone because he knows she loves me,' I murmured, thinking I could not escape to sea while Abigail needed me.

Franklin sniffled. 'Well, Matthew –'

'She must love me, she truly must,' I muttered, hardly hearing the old tutor.

'Ahem. Matthew.' Jedediah Franklin shivered and drew the coat around him. The candle flickered on the box-top, its light faltering, and there was a rustle of paper as he pulled a parchment from his pocket. 'Before the Light dies, I wish you to see this

Document, which forms Part of my extra Purpose here that Mister Jeffreys knows Nothing of.'

I nodded absently, concentrating on remembering Abigail's face, for I had an awful fear now of never seeing her again.

'I discovered this Paper by Chance while searching for Something of relevance to – ah – naval History. Records of a Court-Martial, in Fact, resulting in a Discharge from the Navy for the most specious Allegations concerning a Navigator's supposed Deficiency of his Duties, which need not trouble us now. Mister Jeffreys retained certain Documents as an Incentive for me to continue in his Employ and as a Reason for keeping my annual Remuneration at a Minimum, and thus I consider Recovery of these Documents for my own Use justified.'

I thought I understood the gist of this, but my head was full of thoughts of Abigail.

'It called for only a minor Adjustment to the locking Mechanism on the Merchant's Escritoire to cause it to give up its Contents. In locating the Parchments I desired for Myself, I also happened upon this Bundle.' The papers rustled as Franklin held them up for view, but I did not bother to look. 'The Bundle contains your Father's Will and a Certificate of Share Ownership.'

I twisted round too quickly and let out a gasp of pain.

'I examined many other Papers in that Desk,' he continued, 'and I was forced to the Conclusion that you were defrauded.'

'I knew it! Mister Jeffreys is a cheat.'

'From my Examination of the Documents, it seems so, yet the Fraud he perpetrated was on behalf of the Lynskills, who appear to hold him in their thrall. The Papers in Mister Jeffreys' Desk indicate that there are in Truth no Debts on the Collier, but that Jeffreys and Justice Lynskill over a Period of Years created false Owings upon her, through accruing unfair Charges on her trading Activities. Thus the original Owners – your Father and your Step-father – were forced to forfeit their Shares against Losses which have never in Reality existed, and against Charges which have been improperly applied. Your Guardian has broken your Father's solemn Trust.' Franklin paused, and I heard the rapid rubbing of his dry palms. 'It is as much a Deception of Mister Stalbone as of your Family, and I believe he is no more aware of it, either. Where in your Case deliberate Subterfuge misled you, in your Step-father's Instance I believe the larger Measure of Blame may be apportioned to Stupidity.'

'Does it mean I shall get my shares now?'

'Not by any Certainty,' said Franklin. 'But I have written a Letter declaring what I swear to be the true and legal Position.' He waved a paper. 'I urge you to follow my Advice. Journey to London, and find this Lawyer, whose Name and Directions for his Premises I have enscripted upon the same Letter, and make a legal Claim upon the Bark. He has particular Expertise in maritime Law, and he shall take his Fees from the Gains of the Action, if any. You have Nothing to lose, dear Boy, and much to win. The Collier may realise five or six Hundred Guineas by London Prices, for the King demands more Ships for the Navy and for the Protection of the carrying Trade, and prices are high.'

Five or six hundred guineas – and, as Mister Jeffreys had told me when my Ma died, I rightly owned thirty one shares, almost half of her. Why, I could not earn ten guineas in a year as a seaman, half that as an alum labourer. I decided immediately I would spend it on a share in a new ship, and become her master. And if I captained my own vessel, I could win Abigail over and take her away.

The old Navigator coughed.

'There is Something more, Matthew.'

I waited.

'Mister Jeffreys did not hold your Father in high Regard, I understand. Yet he appears to have been more commercially-minded than Mister Jeffreys is ready to admit. According to these Papers, your Father owned sixty three of the sixty four Shares in the *Prosperous Anne*, your Step-father owning the remaining One.'

My heart almost stopped beating.

'If you can succeed in winning your legal Case, dear Boy, the Collier is as good as yours from her Keel to her Truck, barring, let us say, her Bower. You shall be a young Man of Means indeed.'

Lying on the palliasse, I closed my eyes and let the news wash over me. I knew she was mine, all along I knew she was mine, I said to myself, over and over. I hoped desperately that when I looked again Mister Franklin would still be there, sitting in the gloom, to show me I had not dreamt the whole exchange.

'Dear Boy?' said Franklin.

I was adrift on a sea of hope and could not speak. At last, I swallowed noisily and found my voice.

'Mister Franklin, sir, shall I really get what's mine now?'

'You must pursue your Case with Vigour, and there are many Pitfalls. I have no Wish to excite in you an impossible Hope, Matthew, but this Intelligence and these Papers might help to put right the Wrong done to you, in which I unwittingly played a Part, to my eternal Regret. You must now take hold of these Papers and keep them safe until you reach London.'

London, I mused. It seemed as far away and impossible to reach as the ends of the earth. Then I realised I knew a bark going that way, for had Mister Franklin not just told me the *Prosperous Anne* was bound for the Great Wen? I had only to be aboard her when she cast off, and to lie undiscovered until we were far offshore.

Franklin put his documents carefully on the mattress. I stretched out to pick them up, then reached for my Book of Navigation, which lay on the box by the candle, and cradled it in my hand.

'I read my book still, sir. There is a leather pouch in here where I shall keep the documents safe.'

I opened Deverill's *The Science of Celestial Navigation* and took out a slim wallet, into which I folded the papers, then gratefully fell forward onto my chest again.

Franklin cleared his throat, and there was something particular about the way he did it. Then, with a tremor of excitement, I remembered what was coming.

'What,' the old Navigator began slowly, 'is the average Angle of polar Rotation of –'

'Of Polaris, sir? Two and one half degrees by the back-staff.'

'Precisely so. And if your Vessel were at the Isles of Canary, what would be your first Necessity for continued Navigation westward?'

I did not have to think for a second. 'To determine the deviation of the compass by means of comparing it with the sun's azimuth and declination while at a known longitude, sir.'

'Indeed. And what further Adjustment of the Reading of the Compass would a Ship require if running its Westing down to the New World?'

'Sir, the magnetick variation of the needle, as indicated in the Genovese Tables and the English Pilot. About one degree of the card for each hundred leagues of westing.' I paused, then remembered more. 'And there must be a correction for its annual change too, which may be found in the tables of the Nautical Almanack for the Royal Navy.'

'Very good Work. Remarkable, in all Truth.' Franklin raised a bony finger and pointed it at me. 'You have learned your Navigation properly, I see, dear Boy.'

I smiled up at the old Navigator, feeling that I had at last rewarded his patience with me.

'Mister Franklin,' I said carefully, 'shall you see Miss Abigail?'

'Ah.' He sat quite still. 'She keeps to her Room of late, but it may be possible to find an Opportunity of speaking to her.'

'Will you ask her to meet me? Please, Mister

Franklin – she may tell Libby a time and a place. I shall be walking in two or three days.'

'Matthew,' said the old Navigator, 'it pleases me to do this for you.'

'Thank you, Mister Franklin. You have given me hope.'

'Hope! Indeed, dear Boy,' said the tutor, standing up. His kneebones cracked loudly. 'Hope gives Life.'

Jedediah Franklin sniffed and thrust his hands deep into his pockets in preparation for the chilly walk back to Prosperity-street and his solitary chamber at the top on the house. As he shuffled off down the passageway and into the lane outside, the wick of the candle-stub doused itself in the pool of melted wax and the cottage was plunged into night. I hardly noticed the darkness, for already I was dreaming of winning back my collier-bark. But first, I resolved, I shall see Abigail.

It was late afternoon and the shadows were long as I fretted in the shipyard where, from my hiding place by the upturned hulk that had lain for years in the top corner of the yard, I had a clear view of the gate and the wharves.

The *Prosperous Anne* lay alongside the stone quay in her usual place, made ready by the master and Barney for what was planned to be her last departure southwards from Whitby. My pulse quickened at the thought of the hundred leagues of voyaging, past a coastline beset by gales and fogs, and through the shifting sandbanks, graveyard of a thousand ships. The threat of French attack was present every inch of the way, until she could turn west into the mouth of the Great Estuary, picking her way into the deep channels between the shoals that barred the entrance to the River Thames. What dangers my dear old *Prosperous Anne* faced! But she would not face them without me.

The afternoon's wind blew in from the east, bitterly chilling. I had waited for two hours, watching as Stalbone and Barney trudged homewards for a good supper of stew in readiness for setting sail on the evening tide. I had no such supper, for I had managed to hoard only a few pieces of hard cheese and a hand off a loaf to sustain me in my escape, but hunger hardly troubled me now, and I waited in excitement that I could barely contain.

Fiddling with my coat collar to close a gap where the wind fingered down my neck, I cast a glance over Whitby harbour. In the anchorage bobbed the masts of a handful of sheltering fishing boats, but the shipyards were empty and silent. The whalers had long gone and the colliers had been sold off in the south. The *Prosperous Anne* was alone at the quayside. St Wystan's bells across the river struck six of the evening. I hope she comes before I freeze to death, I said to myself. And before Stalbone and Barney return.

I saw a girlish figure enter at the gate and make her way across the yard, carefully avoiding the discarded timbers, ropes and trestles strewn haphazardly about. She wore a familiar dull-coloured, washed-out cotton dress with a pinafore, a cap on her head and a shawl drawn about her shoulders.

My spirits drooped, for it was Libby. But she might bring a message.

'Libby!' I called as she neared. 'Quickly – round here where no one can see us.'

The girl looked up and broke into a run. When she was a few feet off, I saw it was not Libby after all, but Abigail. Of course – the dear girl had dressed in the scullery maid's clothes to make her dangerous adventure here. With a rush of pleasure, I stepped forward smiling. To my distress, she backed away.

'Abigail –' I stopped in confusion. She wore such a fearful look that I checked myself from trying to take her hand. 'I'm – I'm glad to see you,' I said at last. How limp it sounded. She looked so tired, worn out, frightened.

'Shall we be seen here, Matthew?' she said, glancing about. 'Don't come too close.'

'Round this side,' I said gently drawing her near. 'The yard is quiet, and Stalbone is up in the cottage. Abigail –' There was a bluish mark on her temple, and my anger flared. 'Who beats you – Lynskill? Your father?'

She shook her head but did not meet my eye.

'Matthew, are your wounds healed?' she said, speaking so low I had to bend to hear her speak.

'Aye, well enough,' I said, touched that she worried on my behalf. 'But it's not my troubles that concern me.'

She wrung her hands nervously. 'I came only to say goodbye, Matthew.'

I reached out, wanting to enfold her sweet,

delicate form, but she drew away and peered edgily around the yard.

'Abigail, I shall become a rich man,' I told her firmly. 'I am stowing aboard the collier to seek my rights. I shall return a man of some property – the rightful property your father has tried to steal from me.'

She shot me a dull look, and I felt hope withering. In desperation, I took both her hands in mine, expecting her to struggle and break free. But she stayed unmoving, and her palms felt dead to my touch.

'God, Abigail, they are breaking you. Listen – when I come back, I shall marry you and take you away with me. On a ship. I love you, and I believe you love me. Just tell me you do. Please!'

At last she looked straight at me, her beautiful face framed by the plain shawl.

'Matthew, you live in dreams. I wish I could enter into your world.'

'You can! You poor girl, you're not well.'

'Perhaps I am more practical than you think.' She smiled a little, and squeezed me. 'You're wrong about my father. He has helped you.'

'But he's forcing you to marry Lynskill!'

'I'm sure he wants the marriage for me, not for himself,' she said, and wiped a tear from her eye. 'You must see that the dowry might ruin him.'

'Delay the marriage,' I urged her. 'Find a reason, but just delay it till I return. Abigail, promise me only that.'

'My father wishes it settled soon. Before we leave for America.'

121

'America!' The news was a nightmare. I gripped her hands. 'What is this?'

'He plans a venture in the New World, with my – my future husband. We shall voyage there soon.'

'How soon?' I was in an agony.

'As soon as Father has settled his affairs.'

'When he's sold my ship, you mean – you'll go to the New World on my inheritance!'

She cast her eyes down, and instantly I wished had swallowed the remark.

'Abigail – at least give me some prospect for my return. My love for you is everything in my life.'

'O, Matthew.' There were more tears starting in her eyes. 'I wish it could be.'

'There, you do wish it,' I said, a flicker of hope rekindling in me. 'Now, I will not let you go until you promise to wait.'

Abigail sniffled back her tears.

'All right, I promise. If you want, then I promise.'

I stroked her soft skin, wiping away the streaks of wet on her cheek. She blinked and smiled up at me.

'I do believe you really love me, Matthew.'

I bent my head and our lips brushed in a sweet, brief meeting. The touch of her mouth thrilled me. Then she pushed me back and turned and ran off up the yard. Caught off-balance as she dashed away, I stood with my arms still outstretched.

The distant figure slipped through the gateway at the top of the yard and was gone. I stood without moving for a minute on end, believing I could still feel the warm touch of her mouth on mine.

Then I stepped out from cover. Looking left and right in the growing gloom of the evening, I dodged rapidly across the yard and arrived at the *Prosperous Anne*'s gangway certain that no one could have seen me. I knew just the place, the box-like space of the chain-locker right forward in the very bows. There, I could hide undisturbed, and after a day's sail out to sea it would be too late for the master to turn her back.

As I crept on deck and sloped forward to stow away, the wind off the dreary wastes of the North Sea flapped at my worn jacket. Icy gusts whistled through the shrouds of the old collier, and the lonely little ship at the empty wharfside shifted on her mooring lines like a disgruntled old horse. I knew it would be hard to endure the long and freezing stow. But Abigail had kissed me. She had promised to wait.

Despite the wind, and the cold prospect of the voyage ahead, I burned inside.

# 8

# *The Catch*

*Aboard a Dutch flyer, not far from the mouth of the Great Estuary.*

Now, after all my efforts, it had come to this. I lay exhausted and speechless on the weather-deck of the great Dutch bark, thinking of my drowned step-father, my abandoned shipmate Barney, and the doomed *Prosperous Anne* stuck fast on the shoals.

Footsteps approached. Standing over me was the large fellow I remembered hearing addressed as the sailing-master. A thick red-brown beard sprouted from his chin, and beneath an oiled-skin coat he wore the whitest seaman's slops I had ever seen. Our eyes met.

'We shall find out in due course, my handsome,' he said slowly, 'whether I'd have been better off leaving you to the fishes.' Before I could make any reply to this, he shouted, 'You sailors – take this man to the quarter!'

'Aye, aye, Mister Pengarth!' came the cry, and two sailors dragged me stumbling across the wide deck and up onto the quarter, planting me in a heap at the base of the mizen. I reached out to steady myself against the fat spar. There was a spoked wheel here, with a sailor at work steering, and a great compass binnacle of a size I had never seen before. Overhead was an expanse of fore-and-aft canvas on a lateen yard, hauled in amidships. The ship was heeled hard, and going fast to weather.

I stood up with difficulty and scanned the sea. A league off, I spied the collier-bark, masts a-tilt, stuck fast. I turned to the big man with a despairing look.

'Sir, c-can we turn back?' The freezing cold had numbed my tongue. 'We must go back!'

'Tell it to the captain. It was him that hove up the ship for you.'

Pengarth gestured towards a tall, broad-shouldered gentleman, bareheaded and wigless, wearing a heavy-weather coat, under which flashed a brocaded silken jacket, with green pantaloons and calf sea-boots. It resembled the garb of the Dutch masters who touched at Whitby with their flyers. The captain, braced against the taff-rail, ranged the sea aft of the ship with a long spy-glass, examining the *Prosperous Anne*. After a minute, he slid the instrument into itself, pocketed it and fixed his eye on me.

'Let him come here, Mister Pengarth.' He pronounced it 'Pingarss' and the Hollandish accent confirmed my guess. Obediently, I lurched over, eager to tell the captain of our plight.

'Sir, p-please help save our bark –'

'Silence. Nothing can be done,' said the captain, the Low Countries accent revealing itself again. He appraised my bedraggled figure. 'You should be

125

grateful to be aboard my ship, what so? What is your name?'

'M-M-Matthew St-Stalbone, sir.'

'Why did you abandon ship?'

'I did not, sir! She's on the b-banks. The master went over, and I went after him.'

'Indeed? A brave seaman. Perhaps you admired him very much.'

'He's drowning – we must find him!'

The captain took a step closer. 'When did this man fall in the water?'

'Not more than half a g-glass ago. We can put down the cutter, and your boats too, and search –'

'The water is near ice. And with such a sea running, this action is entirely pointless.' The captain gazed away to larboard. 'What vessel is she, sailor?'

'A c-collier-bark, sir, the *Prosperous Anne*, seventy t-tuns. Three d-days out of Whitby.'

'Ah – Whitby.' The Dutchman pronounced it 'Vittbay'. 'And where bound?'

'For the Estuary – for London, with sea-cole, sir.' What use were such questions? In anger and frustration, realising that with every minute we were sailing further and further from the *Prosperous Anne*, I blurted out, 'By the Lord's mercy, what can be the matter with this ship? Why won't you help?'

The captain's face went dark. Grabbing me fiercely, he steered me to the far rail and pointed to the south and west.

'There is your answer, sailor.'

To my amazement, I saw another sail had appeared, a league astern. A powerfully built three-master, close-hauled and heeling hard, she creamed out of the Estuary headed our way.

'An English cruzer,' said the Dutchman, 'and thus we fly away to sea.'

'But why, why?' I whimpered like a child, unwilling to believe that we would abandon my stricken vessel. But for the captain, the matter was done.

'You are to know,' he said brusquely, 'that you have been brought aboard the Dutch fluyt-schip – flyer, to you – the *Cornelius*, out of Vlissingen, Captain Josua Brogel her master. Mister Pengarth here is my sailing-master. We are clearing the waters of England, bound westward.' It sounded like 'vessvadd'.

'But when can I get to land?' I stuttered, only to be cut off by a laugh.

'Land, he says!' boomed the sailing-master. 'My handsome, us are leaving the land behind, the captain's just told you. Now, he's a sentimental man and he wanted you plucked up, but by my log-book, a jack-tar that leaves his ship is a no-good jack-tar. And you'd best take on board my meaning.'

I did not care a dam' for this Pengarth and his meanings, for the depths of my plight seemed quite beyond him. My whole world was slipping away.

'What about my ship?' I pleaded to the captain, but his back was to me and he had raised the spy-glass once more.

'This here,' said Pengarth, stabbing a finger at the deck-boards, 'this is your ship now.'

'You should count yourself lucky, man,' said the captain, lowering his glass to examine me briefly.

Lucky? I shuddered involuntarily, for surely the cold had seeped into my bones.

'Have him taken forward for hot broth and dry slops, Mister Pengarth,' ordered Captain Brogel. 'And then work him in your usual manner.'

'Hard labours do keep a sailor's mind off his troubles, captain.'

'Thank you, Mister Pengarth.' The captain lost interest and resumed studying the English cruzer's approach.

Pengarth grinned at me. 'Aye, my little fish,' he said, 'I shall work you till your heart bursts.'

'One moment!' said the captain, pointing. 'Look, sailor. Perhaps they seek a salvage prize.'

I followed the captain's arm. The English cruzer had luffed up to make a slow turn towards the *Prosperous Anne*.

The captain grunted. 'Your bark appears an easy prospect for salvage, I believe. Unless her back is broke, she may lift on the tide.'

I stared at the old collier-bark and the cruzer. Might she yet be saved, and Barney – and even poor Stalbone? But I would not be there to see it.

The sailing-master delivered me a punch between the shoulder blades.

'To the foc'sle, Mister Stallyboon,' ordered Pengarth, issuing a kick. 'And double it like the seaman you says you are.'

I woke from a fathomless sleep. Someone tugged at my leg.

'Wake up! You come on deck.'

In pitch darkness, I found myself swinging in a

rough hammock, cloaked in a thick woollen cover under which my salty clothes were clammy in the suffocating dampness. Water rushed past the hull inches from my ear and, half asleep, I believed I was aboard the *Prosperous Anne*. I groaned, stretching stiff and aching muscles, thinking it must be Barney.

'Wake up – turn to!' said the voice, but this time I knew it was not my shipmate.

'O Lord, where am I?' I mumbled thickly.

'Aboard *Cornelius*. I am Youssef. Some call me the Barbar.' He laughed.

I was in an enclosed tween-decks space, and the atmosphere was foetid. Still confused, I slid down from the gyrating hammock.

Youssef spoke from the gloom. 'I am second mate, larboard watch. You are Mattoo, yes?'

I nodded, squinting at him as my eyes adjusted to the gloom. The fellow was about twenty, short and wiry, with a long, bony face and a prominent, curving nose. He spoke rapidly in a high-pitched tone, his strange speech shot through with throaty coughs.

'On deck, sailor!' he whooped.

The Barbar shoved me up the steps, towards the square-shaped block of light at the top and a breath of fresh sea air. Blinking in the daylight, poised in the hatchway, I halted in sheer astonishment.

I was at the raised foc'sle deck of the vessel, looking sternwards along her length. Before me spread the weather-deck, with four gleaming black guns either side by the rails, bolted down and facing closed gunports. Between the fore and the main were two animal pens, one thronged with chickens, the other jammed full of pigs. Above these was lashed a massive launch, thirty foot long, upturned and roped down to spare booms and yards. The decks were crammed with gear right down to the rise of the poop – sacks, barrels, boxes, timber in stacks, coils of rope, all of it stowed for heavy weather. Just before the poop was a massive capstan winch for bracing the yards. The only clear spaces were at the shrouds, where the men could work the belays and reach the ratlines, and by the capstan. Behind the big guns, there was just room enough to run the pieces back.

'O Lord, what a sailing bark,' I breathed.

The foremast was twice thicker round than the mainmast on the *Prosperous Anne*. Above soared a towering spread of thousands of square feet of light-coloured canvas. She carried three courses of squaresails, bulging with wind – the lower courses, the topsails and then topgallants too and a huge mizen sail on a cross-jack, with a lateen yard for a fore-and-aft sail. Whirling round to look forward, I marvelled at her great beak, and the massive iron bowers stowed in the catheads. Between them was the barrel of a heavy anchor windlass. Two swivel guns were at the rail, and the bowsprit stretched forward and upward, with a spritsail yard halfway along its length. The ship yawed heavily as she surged downwind, a white froth of foam streaming away either side. Bending again to look far aft, I saw a broad wake creaming out behind across the broken, grey-green seas. She creaked as she rolled, the wind moaned low through her forest of rigging and the bow wave hissed busily as she cut the water with her stem. She was moving faster than any ship I knew.

Youssef's grinning face was close, dark-skinned and with his bright black eyes dancing.

'Now you learn the ropes on *Cornelius*. Aloft!'

He dashed to the mainmast shrouds, launched himself at the ratlines and climbed like a cat. Following, I swung awkwardly over the unfamiliar layout at the futtock shrouds, finally catching up with him at the roundtop. Where the mainmast met the topmast was a platform large enough for three or four men. There were six fellows already out on the jack-stays of the mainyard, unfurling the course.

'Out on the yard, Mattoo.'

Youssef grinned and started up a chanty new to me, but the others joined in. Working my way along the yard, I noticed everything was new and freshly tarred, with not a frayed rope or a worn sheave-block in sight. When the great maincourse was fully unfurled and sheeted home, I stared above into the cloud of canvas. Where the mast broke clear of the topgallant yard, a clear hundred feet above the deck, was a lookout perched on an open step, with a rope run around his waist to keep him on station while he used a long spy-glass to rake the horizon.

A ray of sunlight broke weakly through the cloud cover and I saw a distant land, no more than an undulating line of smudged white shapes perhaps three or four leagues off.

'English coast of Dover!' called Youssef cheerily.

I glanced up at the sun. With the Cinque Ports coast to the north of us, I knew we were in the

English Channel heading west, many leagues from the Great Estuary. Running fast before an east wind, the *Cornelius* was rushing me headlong out to sea, and far away from the Thames and London. And there was nothing I could do.

Our work finished, I scrambled deckwards with the other seamen. They were dressed in a variety of seaman's slops and shore clothes, some with blue coats and calico trousers, others with striped weskits and jump jackets, a few with leather shoes and the rest barefooted. They were all ages, one a youngster of twelve or thirteen, another an ancient fellow who grinned and smacked his toothless mouth and reeked of baccy. Amongst the English voices I heard snatches of a tongue I took to be Dutch. There were twenty fellows in each watch, and the ship's company must have counted fifty all told, including idlers like the surgeon, the sail-maker and the quarter-deck officers. It was a strange thing to be aboard so crowded a vessel, for I had never sailed with more than half a dozen hands. Yet the seamen took little notice of me, for it seemed that to men who had sailed the world, I was yesterday's wonder.

When Youssef gave me a set of sailor's slops from the bosun, to replace my torn pants and jacket, I became just another crewman. But I held onto my precious weskit, and as soon as I was alone for a second, I fumbled inside its sodden, salt-encrusted pocket. Still sewn in tight was the leather wallet carrying my letters. I could not bear to open the pouch, for what use were these papers to me now?

Aft, Mister Pengarth strode about the poop deck watching the binnacle and the steersman. The captain stood at the taff-rail, sweeping the horizon with his spy-glass. Why should they care for the plight of the poor seaman they had fished aboard? Dispirited, I sloped off towards the foc'sle hatch to swallow some broth with my fellows.

In the afternoon, the captain ordered the *Cornelius* steered up to bring the wind from dead aft onto her steerboard quarter. We braced up her fore and mainyards and then piled aft to heave in the mizen cross-jack. With growing excitement, I calculated that the new course, north of west, would set us towards the coast. Any port in England, I said to myself.

I sat in the lee of a deck-gun with Quaker John, a small-built Englishman of about thirty five. The guns rested on half-wheeled carriages, their pulling tackles rigged but the gunports closed up weather-tight with hardwood wedges knocked through the eyes.

'You run about that rig like you were weaned on it,' said John, chewing on a baccy plug.

'I've seen many a flyer that's hove into Whitby, so I know the rig,' I said. 'And working aloft takes my mind off my troubles. What's our next port of call?'

'Could be Dartmouth.'

I knew of it as a safe little harbour in the West Country. I resolved to jump ship ahead of even the mooring lines being shot ashore. But before I left her, I had something to settle about the *Cornelius*.

'Were you chasing us that night – you know, off the shoals?' I asked.

'O aye,' said John brightly. 'The captain reckoned your collier for a plump little bounty – just put a prize crew aboard and sail her back to Holland.'

By the Lord, I thought, with more than a twinge of shame, Walter Stalbone was right after all. Perhaps I should have listened. I shifted uncomfortably, thinking of another matter that troubled me.

'The sailing-master said he did not want the ship hove up for me.'

Quaker John snorted. 'Gilly Pengarth can't never see that risking the ship for one jack-tar is worth it. Live to fight another day is his motto. He was all stoked up about Brogel going in for your collier. We came close enough to those banks to scrape the pitch off her bottom. It was Gilly steered her off in the end.'

'Mister Pengarth,' I muttered, 'must be a first-rate sailing-master.'

'O aye, Gilly Pengarth's two or three foreign prize trips under his belt. Mind you, Brogel had the pick of the best in Amsterdam. Not easy to get aboard the *Cornelius*.' Quaker John smiled and dug me in the ribs. Then he fell thoughtful. 'As a captain, Brogel's sharp like a whetted blade. Believes in the calculations – instruments and books, all such stuff. I don't fathom it myself.'

I sat up. 'The Navigation, do you mean?'

'Aye, that's the thing,' said the Quaker. 'Now Pengarth, he's more for what a seaman understands. The log, the lead-line, the lookout – and the lash. He's no mind for books and studies.'

He lapsed into silence, eyes shut, basking in the tentative warmth of the afternoon sun, but all I could think of now was the harbour. I nudged him and he blinked awake.

'Shall we unload at Dartmouth?' I said. 'There must be a wharf there.'

Quaker John coughed, sat up suddenly as if surprised, and spat into the scuppers. Then he laughed, shoulders wobbling and face screwed up in what looked like pain.

'Unload!' The Quaker wiped his eyes, chuckling. 'That's the wrong notion about this bark. The *Cornelius* don't plan to haul around any sea-cole like your old collier.'

The ship sped onwards, rolling a little easier now with the quartering wind. I waited for more, my irritation mounting, but John volunteered nothing.

'Why can't someone just tell me,' I demanded rudely, 'what we are doing and where are we going?'

'I'll tell you all right.' John looked from side to side as if he feared being overheard, but no one was within earshot. 'We haven't got an inch of room for cargo. We are block-loaded with stores – barrels of small beer and water, bags of flour, sacks and sacks of peas and beans, sails of every shape and size, dozens of bolts of flax and canvas, lengths of good timber, spare spars lashed on a boom-gallows, coil on coil of sisal and hemp, good manila too, anchors and cables, and ironwork and hoggers. Anything we need for repair and rebuild, we have it stowed. This is going to be my longest voyage ever. Two, three years, maybe more.'

Shocked, I let my mouth hang open. 'Years?' I said, slumping back in dismay.

Quaker John grinned. 'O aye. And every locker, every corner below decks is crammed to the deckheads with muskets, pistols and sabres, a tun or two of ball, sacks of wad, half a hundred pole-axes, and half-pikes in their dozens. There's mortars, gun tackles and field carriages. We got round shot and chain shot and stone shot and partridge shot. Tun on tun of powder, too. We got powder for the swivels, powder for the muskets, powder for the mortars, powder for our pistols. There's enough saltpetre down there to blow your Whitby Towne clear into Lancashire. And you may not have seen yet, but bowsed down in the holds she carries eight more guns – six-pounders, they are, culverins. When we hoist them up on the tween-deck, I reckon we can sink a ship-rigged four-decker. Makes us a veritable floating fort.'

'Then she is a cruzer!' I said.

'Too light for a cruzer, too fast for a schooner, too big for a bomb ketch and she's armed like a Navy fighting ship. Anything her size or smaller, she can sink it. Anything heavier, she can outrun it.'

'John, tell me,' I said slowly, 'she is a privateer, then?'

'Private ship, Dutch letters of commission for taking unfriendly vessels in the Main, and a fair gaggle of eagle-eyed owners waiting in Amsterdam for her to return and make them rich. That's about it.'

Quaker John looked pleased with himself, but his news devastated me. If the *Cornelius* were a privateer heading west, and might be gone for years, then I had to get off her. Dartmouth must be my only chance.

An hour later the coast appeared out of a haze. I was kept busy aloft and alow, altering trim as the ship came under a craggy stretch of shore where cliffs loomed above a white line of surf. To the west lay a wide bay fringed by a beach curving south to a distant rocky headland. As we closed, the entrance to Dartmouth still did not show itself, and I guessed only a sailor who knew it could find the way in.

Or, I thought, a Navigator in possession of proper chartings and the skills to read them. As I was not to be long aboard, I cast about for what I could learn. I had seen the heavy main compass mounted in a wooden binnacle on the quarter-deck. I had obseved Pengarth spinning out the log from the taff-rail with one eye on the minute-glass, and counting the knots back in. Yet I had seen no back-staff used nor sunsights taken, so I guessed they were reckoning the ship by the log and the line, as she was still in soundings.

In soundings! I had never sailed anywhere but within soundings. I was forced to confess to myself that it thrilled me to be aboard this magnificent voyager headed for the unplumbed, unfathomable oceans. The *Cornelius* was going where even the longest lead-line at its fullest extent – three hundred fathoms on an ocean-going Navy cruzer – would dangle above the abyss of the deeps, out in the great wastes of the sea where storms raged unhindered and the swells roamed free around the globe.

A hand fell on my shoulder, breaking my wistful

imagining. Youssef had seen me gaping at the horizon.

'The *Cornelius* goes that way, my friend,' he said softly.

'If we go into the ocean,' I said tentatively, 'when shall we see land again?'

'Not for weeks. We go south. Near to my country.' He peered at the horizon, narrowing his eyes on the distant line. 'My country is in Africka, the land of the Barbars.'

'Your home – how long since you saw it?'

'Many years, my friend. A sailor must forget home.' He studied me for a moment, as if trying to read my mind. 'The *Cornelius* can make you rich and content.'

I gripped the rail and resisted the urge to shout and rant, saying I cared not a tub of tar for riches and contentment but wanted only to be free again.

The Barbar became very solemn.

'What do you do before, sailor – load cole? Dirty hard work. Now you see blue oceans, green islands, warm days, pretty girls, plenty rum. And money, and gold. And prizes.'

There came the rattle of a luffing sail and irritable shouts from Pengarth.

'Brace up! Mainsheet there!' called the sailing-master.

Youssef raced off and I sloped after.

The *Cornelius* closed the coast to within five cables and at last I saw an entrance, a keyhole in a cleft between two cliffs. We brailed up the courses and dropped the jibsails, slowing her to no more than a knot of speed. Pengarth paced about the quarter-deck, watching the sails and ordering the lead-line cast time and again.

Quaker John stood idling at the rail, and I joined him. 'Shall we be towed in, John?'

'We shan't go in there – nor drop the hook neither.' He grinned. 'The *Cornelius* likes to be ready to fly.'

Pengarth called an order and two men went right aft to the taff-rail, where there stood a swivel gun. After a minute, a signalling shot rang out, its echo crashing against the cliffs. The sailing-master ordered signal flags run up at the cross-trees, and it was plain we were waiting for boats to come off to us. I realised I had to abandon my plan of jumping off at the wharf and get off another way.

The ship crept towards the shore with agonising slowness, for the day's wind had died and the breeze off the land was light. She gurgled unhurriedly along until Pengarth had her brought round and hove-to. She lost way and lay beam on to the shore with her courses stopped up and foresails backed, rolling on the ground swell, two or three cables off the narrow entrance. I reckoned I could just stroke the distance. I sneaked a look over the ship's side at the dark sea slopping at the waterline. It looked calm, but cold.

There was a shout from the lookout aloft and we saw a pulling gig appear from the entrance and head our way. The sailors crowded as one at the landward rail. Pengarth was busy with boarding ropes at the waist, and Brogel had his spy-glass to his eye. Youssef gazed at the shore. Quaker John rested beneath a cannon with his eyes closed.

I went quickly to the steerboard side, grasped the shrouds and launched myself off the rail. As I hit the water, eight feet below, a shout of alarm went up. I entered the sea awkwardly, but kept my head and stroked underwater to the stern before breaking surface. I passed clear of the rudder at the decorated quarters and headed for the shore. The splashing in my ears and my own sharp breathing rhythms failed to drown out the sound of shouts from the ship. I paced myself carefully, confident of gaining the shore. They have no reason to pursue me, I thought, for I am not of their crew, and I am going back to England.

After a few minutes, during which the shoreline stubbornly refused to get any closer, I trod water to recover, my chest aching and the breath coming in forced gasps. For all my efforts, I had covered no more than a cable.

I heard cries and saw the pulling gig alter course towards me. With four long sweeps each side, dipping cleanly, it clawed along so fast there was a bow wave. With dread in my heart, I turned and swam onwards. My strokes slowed as the strength drained away, and a minute later the gig was on me. I twisted round, fighting the drag of my clothes. The bow loomed, and men leaned down with ropes at the ready.

'Leave me be!' I shouted.

'Get a bight round the bugger,' said a voice, right above.

In no time the loop of a running bowline went over me, trapping my arms. Many hands reached down and dragged me from the sea, dumping me amongst the feet and legs of the rowers, along with some gallons of icy water. With a rattle of oarlocks, the gig pulled off towards the ship. I sprawled there shivering, my limbs stiff and frozen, knowing that I would have drowned long before gaining the shore. They have rescued me again, I thought dully, yet I despise and hate them for it.

When the gig drew alongside, they dragged me up to the rail by pulling on the bowline from above and urging me on from below with kicks and shoves. I lay panting on the decks for the second time in two days, frozen half to death after a sea soaking, desperate to get away yet thankful just to be alive.

'Let the bastard freeze,' said Pengarth angrily, turning away. He shouted, 'Bring the messenger to the captain!'

I saw someone in a gentleman's land garb – buckle shoes, silk hose, brocaded coat, bewigged and hatted – scramble aboard from the gig and head aft. Then hands were lifting me and I was propelled stumbling along the deck.

'You blamed idiot.' It was Quaker John.

'Youssef must talk to you,' said the Barbar, not hiding his anger.

They bundled me down the steps to my hammock and tied my hands and feet, lashing them to a ring-bolt in the deck-head. They threw a woollen blanket at me and disappeared up the steps. Seconds later, Youssef returned and crouched low.

'Madman!' he hissed into my ear. 'Why do we pull you out again? I do not know, but Youssef says to Pengarth, we must save him. Pengarth is angry

141

and maybe Youssef is a fool.' He thumped me hard in the back, not in a friendly way. 'Idiot! Sailors give half an arm to be aboard *Cornelius*.'

I raised myself half up and, despite my chattering teeth and shaking bones, with all the power remaining to me I bawled at the Barbar.

'I must go back – I shall go back! I love her, I love Abigail!'

Youssef looked astonished. 'All this is for a girl? Plenty of girls where we go. Why jump in the cold sea for just one girl?'

'She is the girl I love.' I tried to jerk free of the ropes. 'Have you never loved a woman, Youssef?'

'Many, many times Youssef has loved girls.'

I groaned in misery. 'You don't understand.'

He examined me for a long moment, then shrugged. 'Mattoo is right – Youssef cannot understand.'

'Let me go,' I pleaded, 'just let me go free.'

'Aye! When the *Cornelius* has left England far astern,' said the Barbar, 'and we are in the ocean many, many leagues from here, then you are free. Free to go anywhere on board ship.'

He rested his hand fleetingly on my bedraggled shoulder and then, with a cackle, dashed up the companion steps, leaving me to tug at my bonds in desolate misery.

# 9

## Foreign Exchange

Under a blazing sun, the sea all around the *Cornelius* lay bright and sparkling, the wind-whipped wave-caps frothing and boisterous. Thirteen days and nights we had headed southwards, the weather growing warmer and the seas ever more regular, for beneath our keel, the blue-black water was deeper than any lead-line could plumb. The sun climbed higher and puffy white clouds marched in ranks across the dome of the sky, and when I saw them I knew we had entered the region of the hot tradewinds that breathe forever across the great blue expanse.

The ship surged down the rolling swells, the wind on her larboard quarter, all sails set and drawing. A brave breeze, Quaker John called the northeaster which blew steadier than any English wind, but Youssef said it was the Portuguese trade, and said it would carry us south until the hard cheeses in the cook's store softened and the beef lard melted in its barrels.

'Land! Spy land on the steerboard bow!'

The lookout's shout brought us off our knees and running to the rail, except the oldest seaman aboard, who carried on sanding the decks without an upward glance. Eli Savary must have seen it all before, I thought with a smile.

I carefully laid aside my bible – the precious piece of holystone that Pengarth had handed me saying if it came back broken, so would I – and joined the others at the rail, grateful for the relief. Holystoning the decks – or at least those parts that could be reached under the mess of barrels, jars and boxes packed on the weather-deck – was the Devil's work, on our knees all day in the scorching southern sun scraping off the pitch and oil and tar that made the boards lethally slippery in rain or spray. Though I sweated profusely, I refused to remove my weskit for a second, guarding the only link I had left with my past.

The lookouts were a hundred feet up, and from the rail no land could be seen, yet we crowded there nonetheless in our excitement.

Youssef waved at the horizon.

'Look! The great white land in the clouds – the mountain summit, where the Guanchy men say the gods dwell.'

Sure enough, soaring high into the clouds was a cone of white, seemingly floating disconnected from any land below it, a trick of the sea and the sky.

'Half a league high and white with snow – the Peak of Tenereefy,' said Youssef, grinning. He pointed away to the east. 'The coast of Africka lies there, twenty, thirty leagues off, and the land of the Barbars is to the north.'

'What is Tenereefy, Youssef?' I asked him.

'Where we find water – the Islands of Canary.'

Instantly, I was transported back to my lessons

with old Jedediah Franklin, and I remembered a
chart with England at the top, Portugal under, and
below that the great bulge of Africa down to the
Cape of Verd. West of the unknown continent was
the island archipelago called Canary, in the latitude
around twenty five or thirty degrees north, the
longitude centred around fifteen degrees west. For
voyagers, I knew, these islands were the last point
of near certain longitude before the ocean itself was
breached. From the Canaries, ships rarely turned
back for Europe, but stood out to sea with fresh-
filled casks to brave the long Atlantic crossing,
counting off the days to the New World.

'Aloft and furl the main course,' called Youssef,
and I raced up the ratlines with the others. Balancing out on the yard, I wondered why we furled, for
the wind was steady and the sky clear. Eli Savary
was up there too, pulling his weight with the rest,
though he was all of sixty.

'Why are we taking sail off?' I asked the old
fellow.

'You get a vile flaw off that mount,' he called
over. 'Wind screams straight down. Can bust a sail
from tack to clew.'

Now I spied the land itself, dark and low on the
horizon, and paused to study it. Then, furthest out
by the end of the yardarm, I busied myself hauling
up armfuls of canvas and was tying it off when to
my surprise I found the brace-line block had split.
Everything on the *Cornelius* seemed in such good
trim, unlike the poor old *Prosperous Anne*, where
between them Stalbone with his penny-pinching and
Jeffreys with his lending payments had made sure

her gear always wanted seeing to. I knew only too well how a brace-line block could shatter under load, leaving the boat with her mainyard jammed aback, so I turned to speak to Eli. But there was not a man left on the yard. While I had gawped at the island, everyone had gone – swarmed down the ratlines and disappeared below for a ration of small beer. Keen to let someone in charge know, I dropped down to the deck looking for Youssef, but he was occupied right forward at the catheads, surveying the anchors with the mate of steerboard watch. The weather-deck was deserted but, spotting figures on the poop, I went aft to the break. Apart from the steersman at the wheel, the sailing-master was alone on the quarter-deck.

'Mister Pengarth, sir,' I called out.

Pengarth spun round from examining the swing of the compass card. 'What the Hell is it, Stally-boon? Get back to your post.'

'Sir – I found a – there's a split block and –'

'Blast your eyes – where?'

'At the mainyard brace, sir – larboard side,' I replied, heartily wishing I had waited to tell Youssef.

Pengarth eyed me mockingly. 'Think you know ships, do you? "Yes captain, sir, I'm a collierman, sir." To Hell with your colliers! This is no tub of scrapwood full of cole – it's a proper ship.'

'Aye aye, sir,' I said, watching the sailing-master's big fists and taking a step back. 'But I never asked to be aboard here.'

'Makes you the odd man out, don't it? We should have left you in the water like a junk-end.'

'Sir, I'm only reporting a damaged –'

'Close up your hatch! I said I'd see to it.' Pengarth's face was redder than his beard. 'One more bleat out of you and I'll flog and flay you raw. It's best to pay me some regard, my handsome. Dismissed. Go on!'

I needed no second telling, and took off forward. Seven bells rang and I joined the starving throng by the galley furnace below for a bowl of soup and a hand of biscuit-bread. I was more incensed than ever with the *Cornelius* now, for I had thought only of the good running of the ship and had missed my beer just for a telling-off. Next time I would hold back and let Gilly Pengarth run things the way he wanted.

At noon the next day, the *Cornelius* crept cautiously into the place called Santa Cruze of Tenereefy, under the cool shadow of the high mountain, where the shores rose steeply from the water's edge. Brogel had sent no fewer than six lookouts aloft, for the island chain was reckoned to be infested with French ships. We ran up signal flags to tell the town, little more than a handful of wooden houses, that we wanted water, but launches were already making off from shore. The inhabitants must have long since seen our sails, and were ever ready to restock a bark with pure Tenereefy water barrels, whatever nation she hailed from.

Mister Pengarth once more had the ship hove-to, and the anchor windlass stayed unused. Close under the lee of the high land, the breeze all but died and we hardly moved.

147

'Ready for sea any time,' called Youssef.

Quaker John spat disgustedly. 'The bloody French! Everywhere, they are these days.'

The launches bumped alongside, jammed with what Youssef called the Guanchy men, brown-skinned, stocky fellows with beards and darting eyes. We slung their fresh barrels aboard with tackles and sent away the empty, stinking ones that had held small beer. The second mates were arguing with the Guanchies over the price when the bargaining was interrupted by a cry from the lookout.

'Sail ahoy! Spy a sail away north.'

Captain Brogel clambered quickly onto the rail, balancing himself with a hand on the mizen shrouds, and lifted his spy-glass. He spoke rapidly to Pengarth, then the order came from the quarter-deck.

'Clear those launches – get them away!' bellowed the sailing-master.

We pushed off the boats against the protests of the Guanchy men.

'It's a Frenchman, so jump to it!' cried Pengarth, and instantly we ran to our tasks. 'Loose out the courses – set topsails – brace up the yards steer-board side!'

'To the sheets, lads!' called Youssef, and we scrambled for the belays.

Soon the *Cornelius* was close-hauled, six points into the wind and barrelling out of the Bay of Santa Cruze. The breeze filled in as she cleared the land, and the captain eased her onto a beam reach, when she picked up yet more speed. When I looked up from my work, I spotted the shape of the French sail

148

bearing down with the wind on her quarter, little more than a league off our larboard bow.

I watched as Captain Brogel spoke to his sailing-master, then Pengarth strode forward to the break of the poop.

'To the guns,' he cried. 'Clear for action and run back the deck pieces. Gunners to the stores for chain-shot and round-shot. Charge up your garlands.'

I was too busy to think what it all meant. Youssef and his fellow second mate Jan Hilsum, of steerboard watch, assigned three of us to each of the eight guns, leaving a dozen able crew ready at the belays.

'Watch me, mate,' said Eli, seeing the bewildered look on my face. 'You'll soon see how it's done. Here.' He spat out an enormous plug of baccy and rolled it between his palms to squeeze the moisture from it, then broke it in half and offered a piece to me. 'In your ears – like this.'

He rounded it between finger and thumb and pushed it into his ear-hole, and I did the same.

'Gun tackles!' called Pengarth.

Working quickly, we set up the pulley system on our gun, and Eli showed me how, when the gun was run out, the tackle should be sweated in hard as a recoil preventer. He nipped away below, only to reappear carrying a couple of large ramrods, one with a sponge at the end, a leather bucket and a hessian bag, whose contents he laid out carefully – a mess of spare sponges, wads and horns. Others staggered up carrying iron balls of round-shot and foot-lengths of chain, bucketloads of bent iron nails and short pieces of thick rope. They dragged garland racks behind the guns and stacked the round-shot in them.

Quaker John poked his head over the rail. 'She's coming up fast on our larboard bow, a frigate of about twenty. We're a poor match for this one.'

I watched a couple of men busy at the *Cornelius*'s stern-chase and craned round to see the forward swivels similarly being made ready.

John chewed furiously at his baccy plug. 'Pity our big culverins are bowsed down in the hold.'

'Ah, we may not have the weight of shot,' put in Eli, 'but she's a fast one, the *Cornelius*.'

John spat a brown gob of juice onto the decks. His hands shook so violently he could barely keep them under control. My heart was racing and I felt short of breath. Holding out my own hands, I was surprised to find they were shaking too.

'John, have you fought at sea?' I said in a low voice.

The Quaker glowered. 'I have, though it's against my religion.' He gave out a loud honk that might have been meant as a laugh. 'Look at me now. I tremble before my God, I do.'

He dissolved into a fit of coughing, and Eli chuckled quietly, but I saw the old man's eyes showing white in their sockets.

Youssef came over, wearing a belt with tapers, flints and linstocks jammed into pouches that hung from it, accompanied by the young sailor Gaspar, his powder boy, who dumped a small tub of firing powder next to Eli, and from a bag meticulously

150

doled out flash powder into a horn the old sailor held out.

'Keep dry, lads!' called the Barbar, and dashed away to powder up the three remaining larboard-side four-pounders, Gaspar lugging his tubs along behind.

Pengarth's voice rang out. 'Gunners, load chain-shot. Ready for either chain or round-shot after. All deck pieces primed and charged – jump to it!'

We hauled at the traversing tackle and ran the gun back. Eli scooped handfuls from the powder tub and crammed them into the barrel, followed by a thick piece of wadding cut to fit the gun's bore.

'Rammer,' he said, pointing at the rod.

Picking it up, I pushed it into the mouth of the gun and vigorously tamped in and out.

'Chain-shot,' said Eli, and John brought over several pounds' weight of chain, nails and rope from the assemblage by the garlands. We pushed it all into the barrel's mouth and I tamped it in with another wad. Eli bent over the touch-hole and horned in a small measure of fine powder, pressing it in with a finger, then stepped clear. A pull on the tackle brought the gun to the rail, its mouth pointing at the port, which remained wedged shut. I craned over to see whether the others had been raised.

'We haven't been told to open those yet,' said John, looking nervously about. 'Reckon Brogel's hoping to get away without shooting if we don't run out the guns.'

He faced me directly.

'This, my friend, is the part I do not like. The sailing's fine, the warm days and the rum I don't mind at all. The prize money, well, that's what we're here for. But when them guns are going off and that hot stuff is coming at us and here we are sitting on a couple of tuns of powder in the magazine right below our arses, and only three-inches thickness of oak to keep us from being blasted to Kingdom Come, that's what I don't care for.'

'No one cares for it, John,' said Eli, without looking at him. 'Not one of us.'

As the *Cornelius* reached along on her larboard tack, I sneaked a look over the rail and saw the French ship running dead downwind only a few cables off our bow, bent on interception. On our quarter-deck, Brogel ordered a large standard hoisted at the jack-staff and as the flag billowed out from the pole it revealed itself as the colours of France.

'I don't think our Frenchman'll fall for that one,' said the Quaker, rolling his eyes heavenward. 'But it might give us a chance to get in close so we –'

A sharp report came from upwind and at the same time a hail of objects whistled between the main and foremasts, punching holes in the topsails and partially severing the larboard ratlines.

'Spoke too soon,' said Quaker John. 'Now she'll turn and give us her bloody broadside.'

Youssef came dancing over, excited. 'When the Frenchy turns, we go about double quick and chain-shot the rigging. Good plan!' He dashed away shouting, 'Ready at the belays!'

John's face was grey with fear.

Pengarth bellowed, 'Gunners! Knock out the wedges, raise ports.'

We ran to obey, and I struggled to work out what the captain intended. If we were out-gunned, I guessed our tactic rested on being able to make a quick turn, dodge under the Frenchman's heavy broadside and loose off our own. I thought it must make good sense, but what did I know of battles?

'Run out the guns!' ordered Pengarth, and we heaved on the tackles. With a mighty rumble, the eight heavy pieces wheeled and slid forward along the deck boards until their muzzles poked out through the ports. This is it, I thought, I am about to fight a sea battle. I almost laughed when I realised I was already on my knees beside the massive gun, but not for praying.

Then I remembered the split block. Craning up in alarm, I straightaway saw the lazy brace-line dangling. Pengarth had forgotten it after all, and now the block was bust. When the ship went about, we would be unable to brace the mainyard. The maincourse would go aback and leave the *Cornelius* dead in the water.

'Youssef – Youssef!' I yelled, scrambling up. 'The larboard brace-line!'

Youssef swung round in surprise, uncomprehending.

There was a bang as another hail of chain-shot crashed into the rigging, and I ducked for my life. Bits of ironmongery struck the foreyard, sending wood splintering in the air, and pieces of smashed gear and lengths of chain fell to the decks, driving the occupants of the pig pen into a frenzy of squeals.

Youssef slumped forward with blood oozing from his temple. I ran to him and with Eli's help dragged him to the foot of the main, where he sat dazed and dumbstruck.

'Youssef!' I patted him urgently on the cheek, but his head lolled like a drunkard's.

I went to the rail and saw the French frigate bearing down on our bow at top speed. The time was past waiting for an officer's order. I broke out a spare coil of line stowed by the main, and sprang towards the ratlines. Eli followed, moving like a man half his age, and tugged at my shirt.

'You can't go aloft.' He held my arm.

'Look – the larboard brace-block!'

He squinted up, and swore. 'By the blood of Mary!'

A third collection of old French chain and nails blasted the rigging, striking the forecourse. With a terrible ripping sound, the sail tore a seam from luff to leech and the ship shuddered and slowed percept-ibly.

'Pay out the line behind me, Eli,' I told him, and sprang for the shrouds. There were shouts from below, but I ignored them and quickly gained the main-roundtop. From the corner of my eye, I saw the huge cloud of French sail approaching from upwind, and tried to put it out of my mind. I worked rapidly along the yard, hands shaking. Up here, the breeze was stronger and ripped pieces of canvas cloth flew about, and loose lines whipped and threatened to strike me. The brace-block was fixed at the very end of the mainyard, outboard of the decks and above the sea. Now, as I scrambled along, slipping in my haste and missing my footing in the jack-stay, it seemed further out than ever before.

The French frigate was two cables off when she raised her ports and the black snouts of her guns appeared all along her topsides. If her chain-shot did this much damage, I thought, those heavy guns can reduce us to matchwood. Puffs of smoke rose from her forward swivels – the only guns she could yet bring to bear – and another hail of metal and chain hurtled into the rigging. It missed me, whirring by far too close. One of the three mizen shrouds parted on the larboard side and I saw the mast flex under the altered loading.

Fumbling, I tried to reeve the brace-line through the hard-eye, bypassing the useless block. The rope would come under strain the instant the yard was braced up, and without the block the load would be doubled. But it had only to last a tack or two. My fingers continually disobeyed, but at last I got the rough sisal rove through, and paid the line out to Eli. Fifty feet below, the old sailor ran with it to a belay.

At the sound of flogging sails, I twisted round to see the French frigate turning with infinite sedateness, like a Royal barge, designing to come steerboard-side to our larboard, run with the *Cornelius* and bring her main guns to bear. There was another report and more chain-shot whistled into the rigging above my head, sending wood splinters buzzing past.

'Tack ship!' came Pengarth's cry, oblivious that he had a man on the yardarm.

On the quarter-deck, the helmsman sent the wheel spinning. The weather-deck came alive with seamen running to the belays and taking the larboard brace-line to the capstan winch. I had no chance to get back along the yard to the relative safety of the roundtop. With my feet in the jack-stay rope, and gripping the yard as though it were a fat pig, I clung on.

The *Cornelius* bore up to the wind and shook herself upright with all sails luffing. The steerboard braces were let go, and the mainyard swung free. I closed my eyes and prayed. The yardarm swept an arc of ninety degrees and crashed to a stop so hard I was all but thrown off. Winded by the violent movement, I held on as the spar steadied, quivering. I tasted blood in my mouth, and believed I must have bit my tongue at the impact.

The sailors rushed to brace up on the new tack, all unaware of the precarious condition of the brace-line, or of their crewmate aloft. They sweated round the capstan and the line began to take the strain. As it came slowly home, the huge main-course filled again with wind. Agonised, I watched the brace-line. It groaned under the enormous load as the yard came home. Still they sweated up below, chantying round the capstan winch, their bare feet scrabbling on the roughened deck-boards for grip as they put their mighty backs into the work. The line cracked and creaked at the yardarm end inches from my face. Just hold, I pleaded, just hold this one time.

The brace-line held and the big sail bulged out,

driving the *Cornelius* forward on her new tack. I felt her pick up speed, and she charged off fully braced up and going well. In sheer relief, I let my head fall on the yard for a second. Then, grabbing my chance, I swarmed the length of the yard to reach the roundtop and held on there, amazed by what I saw.

The *Cornelius*'s sudden tack had confounded the French ship. She was in disarray, her broadside now aimed at her rival's bows. Having come part-way round onto her beam, she attempted to fall off downwind on her original course with her main-yards awkwardly braced up for a reach. Shouts rang out from her across the half a cable of water separating us, and men ran this way and that, some to ease the yards, others to brace up. Her gear banged, the sails shook and she visibly staggered, badly off-balanced.

But the *Cornelius*, close-hauled and heeled over with her sheets in hard, cantered up, aiming to run alongside close in under her main guns. As we closed and drew level with the frigate, it seemed I could almost reach out and touch her yardarms.

We came abeam and our steerboard guns loosed off their shot. The violence of the recoil shook our ship from her keel to the truck of her main, springing the great mast like a longbow. I clung to it, and the shots spewed their chain and ironmongery into the Frenchman's rigging, striking high in the rig and raking it from end to end. Her fore-topgallant yard shattered. The maincourse split asunder with a ripping sound that carried above the mayhem. In seconds, the *Cornelius* had creamed

157

clear, leaving the frigate wallowing and feebly loosening off a stern-chase. The shot seared past and dropped into the sea off our bow.

'Tack ship!' bellowed Pengarth, in charge of quarter-deck battle tactics.

The ship was brought up yet again amidst a cacophony of clattering gear and slamming yards. As she held the wind's eye, I made a leap for freedom and started down the ratlines. The yards crashed over once more, and the *Cornelius* heeled on the opposite tack just as my feet gratefully touched the deck.

'Ease braces!' called the sailing-master, standing behind the helmsman and watching his every move. We came momentarily onto a reach, and then swung off the wind to close the enemy. With our yards near squared off on a quartering run, the *Cornelius* bore towards the stern of the half-disabled Frenchman.

I found John crouched by the gun carriage, staring fixedly. Eli solemnly shook his head and gazed at me.

'My eyes tell me I saw you do it,' said the old salt, 'but by Christ's palms, my mind denies it.'

Pengarth's voice boomed out from aft. 'Steerboard guns, reload with chain-shot! Larboard, ready with chain-shot and your levels raised!'

Quaker John muttered, 'No more, please God.'

The *Cornelius* rolled down towards the floundering Frenchman as she tried to regain composure and turn for a broadside. As the stern of the frigate loomed up dead ahead, I saw Pengarth speak in Captain Brogel's ear. The captain nodded.

'Fire as we come under her guns,' ordered the sailing-master.

Suddenly, at every golden window of her decorated quarters, French musketeers poked out their weapons and, as one man, they loosed off a volley. Balls spattered onto the *Cornelius*'s weather-deck and the penned animals squealed in mortal fear. A pig lost its entire haunch to a musket ball and fell bloody and twitching, while the others trampled it in panic.

As the storm of musketry savaged the ship, Eli Savary sank down, clutching his face.

'John!' I cried. The Quaker pulled himself up, darted over head down, and helped me drag him behind the mainmast, leaving a trail of bloody droplets on the deck-boards.

Youssef came over looking like a wild-eyed demon, a lather of sweat and blood caking his face. He had recovered enough to lay a dozen curses on French heads before shoving a smouldering linstock into my hand and dashing off. I gaped at the lighted taper, then at the gun.

'Come on, pirate,' said John with a grim chuckle. 'The gun's ready.'

The frigate's hull loomed above the rail as the *Cornelius* overtook her not thirty feet away, so close I could read the fear on the white faces of her crew.

'Fire!' boomed Pengarth's command above the noise.

I stood to one side of the gun and shoved the linstock into the touch-hole. A thunderous detonation rang out as the four-pounder belched flames from its mouth. It leapt backwards, clear off the deck, snapping back against the chains and ropes of its tackle. The noise dinned in my ears and the heat of the discharge glowed on my skin. I swear the deck-boards bowed before the tun-weight of the gun crashed to a stop and stilled itself.

The rigging shots again struck home on the Frenchman with terrible effect. This time the entire fore-topyard and topgallant, sails and all, went down by the board and dragged in the sea alongside the ship. Her main-topyard split with a bang and sagged downwards. A sailor, crouched at her main-roundtop with a musket in his hand, was struck by a length of flailing chain and arched backwards in a spray of dark stuff, dropping like a ragged doll to the deck.

The Frenchman all too tardily loosed off her heavy broadside. A roar of sound and pressure knocked me flat to the deck as the fiery blast sent eight huge balls into the air. A wave of heat and choking smoke passed overhead, accompanied by an outlandish whistling like a mermaid's scream. But the Frenchman's levels were set for a greater distance and the round-shots flew fifteen or twenty feet too high. If those heavy balls struck our topsides, we would have been crippled. Striking below our waterline, they would have sunk us in minutes.

Even so, the *Cornelius*'s cross-jack took the full force of an eight-pound ball and shattered into a hundred flying splinters. The lateen came sagging onto the quarter-deck, unsighting the helmsman, and the officers struggled to heave it clear. Another ball took a six-inch curved bite out of the mizenmast, but the remainder whizzed past and dropped hissing into the sea five or six cables distant, sending up plumes of spray.

The *Cornelius*'s stern-chase bellowed once and then we were away like the flyer she was cracked up to be. Brogel's gamble had worked, and we had disabled the Frenchman's rig yet dodged the weight of her broadside. He ordered the ship steered off to keep under the frigate's bows, and sure enough the Frenchman's forward swivels fired, but the shots dropped in the sea to one side out of harm's way. The enemy wallowed under her shattered rig, men running pell-mell about her decks as the gear crashed on their heads. Before she could turn, reload or collect herself for the chase, the *Cornelius* had sailed clear out of range.

Brogel had the bark brought onto a beam reach for an extra knot of speed. We raced away, and soon were a league from the French guns. Lustily, we men of the *Cornelius* set to cutting away and salvaging the broken gear, then trimmed up the sails until she made her best speed. Youssef came over and grabbed me with both hands, swinging me round in a gleeful dance.

'See, the *Cornelius* is a very good ship with a wise captain,' he cried. 'And Mattoo is a brave fellow!'

We sped off southwards, with the northeaster on our larboard quarter, shaping to run between Tenereefy and Grand Canary. As the Frenchman's sails grew smaller, it was clear she could give no chase.

We had to lift the remains of the cross-jack yard from the quarter-deck and sling the broken pieces aside. The mizenmast swayed dangerously, with half its shrouds gone, so we quickly furled its sails and strapped a baulk of timber to the damaged part where the ball had bitten. Needing every inch of canvas, we sent down the tattered forecourse and at once bent on a spare sail. It took hours to double the mizen shrouds, replace the ratlines and reset the mizen staysail. We even broke out a spare boom and rigged it as a cross-jack. By the time our work was done, the sun had dipped low into the west. The darkening mass of the island of Tenereefy lay no more than a league off the steerboard beam, and we plunged across the empty sea as the breeze freshened and the *Cornelius* pointed her bows into the ocean.

At last I regained the weather-deck to find Quaker John sitting quietly with a pipe. His hands had stopped shaking, but he had a drawn look and his voice seemed slurred.

'How is poor Eli?' I asked.

'Below with Surgeon Petty pitching and stitching him, and half his jaw off,' reported John. 'But he'll live.'

Relieved, I sank down beside him, weary beyond exhaustion. Yet a strange excitement thrilled inside me. After the gore of combat and death, I somehow felt more alive than ever before. I breathed the warm, damp air of the ocean, reliving the exhilaration of those intense minutes of battle. With the sounds of the guns and the crash of musketry still ringing in my ears, I drifted into a half-doze for a minute. I woke with a jump to see the Quaker cutting a baccy plug.

'The sailing-master and the captain handled the ship wonderfully,' I mused, yawning and stretching. 'We sailed in rings around that Frenchy.'

'You risked your life up there,' said John. 'It's beyond understanding.'

I was only half listening. 'Could we have taken her, John?'

'What!' cried the Quaker, horrified. 'We was lucky to get away.' He eyed me suspiciously. 'You quite look as if you relished it.'

I sat up quickly, ready to make a dispute of it. But looking back, I remembered only the intensity of the moment. The confrontation with death, risking all and getting away with it, had seared me to the core, despite the terror – or because of it. After that, it dawned on me, nothing mattered in quite the same way. Not my own life, not perhaps even Abigail. If you could be an instant from death, yet live, then by comparison every other moment was a fleeting grey shadow.

'No, John, relish it I did not,' I said haltingly. 'But the way the ship moved, and the noise of the guns, and – and just that we're alive and others aren't. We did it, by God, and we got away. What a sailing ship the *Cornelius* is!'

'O Christ save us all,' groaned John. 'There's no sense in a youngster. Live quick, die early.'

We fell quiet, and the ship's company crowded the decks, enjoying the cool of the day's end. They chattered excitedly, waving pipes in the air, quaffing small beer and reworking the manoeuvres of the day. Someone brought out a whistle and played jigs, while the gorgeous smell of roasting meat wafted up from the galley-furnace below. Youssef came over, eyes shining.

'The pig has given us the gift of his life and tonight Youssef eats pork,' he said, rubbing his hands in anticipation. The wound at his temple had scabbed, but his arms showed nicks from wood splinters and powder burns. He turned to me.

'You see the captain in the morning.' He smiled. 'Now the Barbar's happy he pulled Mattoo aboard.'

I smiled back, remembering his wild demeanour and enthusiasm for the fight. The smell of cooking filled our nostrils, and everyone drifted towards the foc'sle for the feast.

'We eat the pig now!' Youssef yelled at me before disappearing into the forehatch.

But though my belly rumbled with hunger, I lingered at the rail, listening to the gush of the bow wave as the ship sped onwards, my head full of dreams and swirling excitement. This *Cornelius*, I mused, is bent on taking me away, but to what places I hardly know. Nor am I any more her prisoner, for today I am set free. Or have I been captured again?

I watched the sun dip its lower limb in the sea, flame orange-red, and extinguish itself in the sea-horizon. Night, close and damp, settled on the Atlantic ocean, empty save for the flyer heading purposefully due west, carving a path over the curve of the globe.

164

# 10

# *On a Dead Run*

'The *Cornelius* has good reason to thank you, Matthew Stalbone.'

Captain Josua Brogel sat in the Great Cabin with his back to the stern lights, one arm over the seatback to steady himself against the rolling motion. The morning sun streamed in through the windows and, astern of the ship, Atlantic swells marched up to overhaul her, hissing by with their tops foaming. At each wave, the *Cornelius*'s stern lifted, then she yawed, her braces creaked and she plunged her bows into a froth of blue sea, pausing in the trough before the next roller thrust her forward. After her escape from danger, it seemed to me as if the bark revelled in her speed, running free in the boisterous trades.

Youssef, balancing himself by holding on to the deep fiddle rail that ran around the table, on which were strewn the vital clutter of Navigation – pilots, sea-charts, almanacks and dividers – directed a wide grin at me. Gilly Pengarth sat facing the captain and, out of the corner of my eye, I saw the big fellow watching me closely.

Captain Brogel tapped his fingers on the chart

table. 'When did you see the block was broken, Stalbone?'

The sailing-master uncrossed his legs and stiffened. I could see no gain in telling the plain truth, that Mister Pengarth might be the finest sailing-master afloat, but he had forgotten to fix the split block. That would remain forever between him and me.

'Just before we tacked, sir, when I glanced aloft by habit. On board my old collier, the gear was always breaking.'

'Ah – of course! Aboard your old collier,' said Brogel, nodding sagely.

'Aye, sir,' I said. 'Constant wear and tear, and we couldn't pay for new gear.'

The captain chuckled, smiling at Pengarth. 'We pulled a fine fish out of that cold sea. Sailing-master, pass me my private box.'

Pengarth's mean eyes were small as he reached behind the outboard seating. He slid back a panel, lifted out a miniature seaman's chest, of a size to carry a couple of four-pound balls, and handed it over. Brogel took out a key and unlocked the box, flicking back the hasps of the lid and throwing it open. He rummaged inside and brought out some small objects.

'Four Spanish dollars, the chief coin of the Main. Each is worth an English crown.'

I took the silver, feeling their weight and reckoning them the most money I had ever held, the better part of a whole sovereign. These precious coins would go inside my leather pouch for safe keeping.

'Thank you, sir.'

Although I sensed Pengarth glowering at me, my eyes were on the table and its treasure trove of instruments and sea-charts. Thinking I might never be in the Great Cabin again with such a chance, I spoke without leave.

'Sir, I think you have the Davis Quadrant here.' I indicated a wooden instrument on the table. 'It appears to have reflectors – does this improve the Navigator's ability to take a sighting for latitude?'

Brogel's mouth dropped open. 'What do you know of quadrants and latitudes? You are a common seaman!'

'I was taught the Navigation in Whitby, sir.'

The captain's eyes were wide. Youssef stood half twisted round, staring in amazement. I took a lungful of air and bore on.

'I know the science of all practical Navigation, sir. Sun latitude, north-star latitude, lunar distance, celestial positions, the azimuth, the swing of the compass and the variation of the needle. I am practised in the use of the tables, the methods of calculation and the plotting for position. I am familiar with the quadrant – the cross-staff and the back-staff – as well as the reading of sea-charts and pilots.'

'Good God, what so!' cried Brogel. 'You have experience of Navigation at sea?'

I hesitated. 'We sailed by pilotage, sir, in soundings. In home waters.' Now it sounded lame, and I almost pleaded for my chance. 'But might I practise the celestial work now, sir? Under your direction and tutoring?'

Pengarth sat bolt upright, while Brogel seemed

only amused. 'Well, by God, you shall indeed. In truth, it relieves me of a burden. Our Navigator died as soon as we left Amsterdam. The pox and blindness.' He beamed at the sailing-master. 'Mister Pengarth, we have been more fortunate with our catch than ever I thought.'

The sailing-master grunted, stony-faced.

'Come aft to the quarter at six bells of the noon watch, Stalbone,' said Brogel. 'Let us see how you fare with the new reflecting Davis instrument.'

Youssef and I left the cabin, reeling as the *Cornelius* careened down a wave and gave a flick of her tail to the sea. Pengarth followed into the dark passageway, closing the door behind him as the Barbar sprinted up the companionway and disappeared onto the sunlit deck.

'Stallyboon!' The sailing-master's voice hissed from between clenched teeth. I halted abruptly. Gilly Pengarth's figure loomed close, his ginger beard and hair seeming to glow in the half-light.

'You're a cocky jack-tar,' he said in a low growl, and jabbed me in the chest. 'And your course is crossing mine.'

'Sir, I'll make no trouble –'

'You were trouble from the first. Leave the bugger in the water, says I, I've got her well under way. Put up the helm, says Brogel. Now Captain Pious plants you on my quarter-deck. Thirty years at sea, and I'll get along well enough without your dam' Navigation.'

I held my peace. All I wanted was the chance to put my knowledge to work.

Still, he gave me an evil look.

'You've stuck yourself on the captain's sea-briches like a cursed goose-barnacle.' He leaned so close I felt the spittle flecking onto my face. 'If you're alone with me on a dark watch, best not stray close to the rail. Get my meaning? Dismissed!'

Without another word, I swung onto the steps and launched myself upwards into the dazzle of the day. Youssef sent me aloft and I went gladly, working high in the rigging where the air was fresh and the empty ocean spread in all directions. I'll be damm'd if I let the sailing-master frighten me off, I resolved. To Hell with Gilly Pengarth.


'Seventy five degrees and four minutes, sir,' I called, standing on the quarter-deck with my back to the sun as I shot its angle.

Captain Brogel had ordered a chair brought up and lashed to the rails. Each day he sat there by habit, puffing at a long clay while I busied with the noon sight-taking.

It was nearing midday as far as could be told by the captain's time-piece, a first-class pocket-clock that he kept on a chain, safe from any thieving seaman's hands, for such a piece was as common as a sea-hog sitting in a basket, and twice as notable. Yet it gave no help in the Navigation for, although by custom it lost no more than three or four minutes in the twenty four hours, it was useless for timing the sunsights. And its accuracy had begun to vary more widely in the heat and salty damp of the Tropick latitudes we had entered.

We sought the sun's zenith, so again I raised the unwieldy back-staff to my shoulder, one foot planted firmly in the scupper, and braced against the taff-rail trying to catch the high sun in the reflectors as it climbed along its arc. Running dead downwind, the *Cornelius* rolled merrily, careless of the difficulties of the Navigator's art. The reflectors were unfamiliar to me, for the instrument old Jedediah had allowed me to practise on had relied on a shadow cast on the engraved scale. But on Captain Brogel's magnificent quadrant, I could only marvel at the new mirror-glasses. They were green and clear and easy to adjust, so I soon found a knack for using them. Yet each time I caught the sun on the sighting end, the ship swayed and the image jumped. Keeping the end of the six-foot-long staff sighted on the horizon with my one eye, and the dancing reflection in the other, was a tricky balancing act, calling for a quick hand on the instrument's sliding transom.

At last, when the shadow froze for an instant, I adjusted the arm a notch, brought it level with the horizon and captured the angle. Lowering the quadrant, I examined the register and read off the sun's angular height.

'Seventy five and six minutes, sir.'

'You have an aptitude for this art,' said Josua Brogel, watching the minute-glass fixed in gimbals to the taff-rail. At the instant of its emptying he flipped it over. 'Minute,' he called.

It was not essential to mark the passing of each minute, and I suspected it was an excuse for him to watch over my work. But by a stroke of luck, I stilled the sun a second later and caught a reading.

'Seventy five degrees and nine minutes,' I sang out.

The sun arced inexorably up to its daily zenith, and the readings steadied.

'Again, seventy five degrees and nine minutes, sir.'

The next sight showed the sun on its descent to the horizon once more.

'Seventy five and seven minutes, sir.'

'Good so, Stalbone. The previous minute shall be the ship's noon time for deck-watches,' said the captain, fiddling with the pocket-clock. 'Go and make the calculation.'

I folded the quadrant and, under Brogel's watchful eye, worked across the deck from one handhold to the next, taking care not to strike or knock the prized instrument. Pengarth stood at the break of the poop gazing aloft and watching the sails, giving me not so much as a glance.

Entering the gloom below, I lurched along the now familiar passageway and into the Great Cabin, eager to work the sight and plot the ship's new position. I had become versed at consulting the tables to find a declination of the sun, making an adjustment for the instrument's errors, an allowance for the instrument being more than double a man's height above sea level, and thus finding an answer for the noon latitude. Plotting the deduced position was harder, for it meant taking the distance run in leagues – found by the reckoning of Pengarth's preciously-guarded log – and our presumed course by the compass, both procedures having errors.

The main compass aboard the *Cornelius* was as

fine a piece of craftsmanship as I had seen, yet the globe's magnetick variation could confound it as we progressed westwards. I made sure to sight an azimuth each evening at the dip of the sun's lower limb to find how much variation to allow for. Yet errors remained, and if a poor helmsman allowed the ship to wander about her proper course, even by a quarter of a point, my deductions might prove worthless. Then too, inattentive running out of the log-line, or a tardy flip of the minute-glass as the chip was streamed, would render the log of the ship's speed inaccurate, and introduce yet another error into the art. And both course and log were out of my hands, and in the sailing-master's.

Thinking about all this, I sighed, took up the dividers, stepped off the day's run on the chart, then made a cross where I calculated the ship to be. Dipping a quill in the ink-pot let into the table, I wrote the observed latitude and the deduced longitude in the captain's daily log-book. I sat back, allowing myself to be a little pleased with this work, for with habit and Captain Brogel's guidance, I reckoned to have taken the first, admittedly uncertain, steps towards mastering the finely wrought art.

I scratched my nose, trying to assess the cumulative error. Today's position would put the island of Sint Maarten in the Leewards two and a half or three days away, but I fretted about this forecast, and guessed our landfall could be as much as three or even four days off. What a weighty task I am charged with, I mused, thinking that if I miscalculated and the bark tumbled on the shore one black night, the captain would surely hang his Navigator. I leaned back and stretched, contemplating the chart. We had crossed eight hundred leagues since leaving Santa Cruze. How could we know to within forty leagues when we might strike land?

Strike land! An unhappy phrase, I thought. I shall say 'Sight land' or 'Make landfall' in future, now I am responsible for it. I picked up the chart to stow it safe in the drawer under the table until noontime tomorrow.

To my surprise, for I had found Brogel a man of a tidy nature, I saw underneath the chart some papers carelessly left out. A word on the topmost leaf caught my eye, jumping out at me – 'Wittbay', the Dutch way of writing Whitby, which I recognised from Franklin's old pilot books. Scanning quickly, I saw 'Daartmoote' scrawled in the corner in what I recognised as Brogel's hand, and the title 'Hubert Waspik, Agent of Shippes, Sint Maarten'. The papers were fair copies made by a professional scribe, such as legal documents of the ship's business might appear, I thought. With a twitch of frustration, I realised the text was in Dutch, but on the next page I picked out 'Cornelius'. With a pounding heart, I rushed onwards and found a second half-recognisable word leaping out from the unintelligible text. It was the name 'Linskyl'.

What the Devil was this? I searched for more that I could make some meaning of, but heard a step in the passageway. Quickly, I unrolled the sea-chart across the papers and bent over as if studying it.

The captain entered the cabin and waved his pipe. 'What are you doing?'

'Sir, I – er – I have plotted our position, captain.'

'Good so. Let me see.'

Brogel stood sucking at the clay, one hand gripping the sturdy fiddle rail of the table. I wondered if the captain could hear the thud of the blood in my ears. To me, it drowned out the surge and slop of the sea as the *Cornelius* forged blindly on towards the land that lay somewhere ahead.

'Well,' said Brogel at last, 'twenty two days out of Santa Cruze.' He smiled. 'Tonight we double the watch aloft and furl our courses.'

'Surely, sir, there is no need for such caution. We have two and a half more days sailing – perhaps even three?'

He sat down and stared out of the stern window at the rocking horizon and the gushing swirl of blue and white sea.

'Navigation is the most uncertain of all our arts, Mister Stalbone. We do not know where we are, nor what land we have reached until we arrive there. Nor shall we until – as I believe, though some yet dispute it – we have an accurate time-piece, workable at sea, that keeps a time constant from a known longitude.'

'Sir, what of the Method by Lunar Distance?' I said. 'The Astronomer Royal is making an alma-nack for a hundred stars or more.'

Brogel's eyebrows lifted.

'I see my Navigator is abreast of the science,' he smiled. 'For sure, the heavenly bodies appear to work like a miraculous clock, which is one of the greatest works of the Lord. But at sea, the mariner cannot shoot the Moon and a star together when the ocean heaves, nor can he work the sums. And nor can the Astronomer Royal,' he said, leaning forward and wagging finger at my nose, 'calculate and tabulate the celestial motions with the necessary degree of accuracy. If the heavens are a clock, we know not what time they keep to. No, Mister Navigator, we need a clock of the Lord's own design, but what clock do we have to compare? A piece that falters by one minute in a sailor's watch of just four hours, a piece now fast and now slow? Where is the clock that stays true? Answer me that.'

'We have clocks for the time of day, sir, good enough for seamen to know to change the watch, and for landlubbers to go a-bed by.'

Brogel chuckled, enjoying the joke.

'Good so, but you get my argument. God may have a clock that keeps perfect time, but he has yet to show it to us. The sun rises each day, but beyond that we have no certainties. The paths of the moon and the planets are all but impossible to follow, and only the sun itself, the planets and a few stars may be calculated for with any proof. The compass swings, the magnetism varies with distance, the quadrant warps in the sun, the tables are a vale of scribes' errors, the knots on the log-line may be short or long, the angle of leeway is a mystery to judge – error piles on error, Mister Navigator, and no mariner at sea can know for sure where his ship lies.'

Brogel's eyes gleamed with a passion. Suddenly it struck me that the captain loved the study of science as much as the old shore-bound Jedediah Franklin.

'Aye, sir!' I cried, and thumped the table with enthusiasm.

The captain laughed and put down his clay.

'Aye, sir! Or nay, sir! Yet I know we are within a hundred leagues from land, for at dawn I saw a pair of pure white birds, with red bills to set off their long tail-feathers – the so-called Tropick birds. Our ship must be a strange sight for them indeed. But when a Navigator spies such creatures, he knows the land looms below the sea's horizon whatever his calculations may indicate. So when we stream the log, we shall keep our knots a thumbnail short. Lest we come ashore before we expect to, as a wise sailor has it.'

Brogel stood, lifted the sea-chart from the table and rolled it up. He glanced in surprise at the papers beneath, then gathered them quickly into a bundle.

'Away to your seaman's duties. Only an officer may idle his time in the Great Cabin.' The captain took out his private box and folded the papers into it, locking it carefully afterwards. 'You are a jack-tar, aloft and alow, until I decide otherwise. Dismissed.'

I sprang up and left the cabin, heading for the foc'sle and a few hours' sleep before my next deck-watch. My mind reeled with possibilities. There are no certainties, the captain had said.

Crossing the weather-deck, where the watchmen lay quietly dozing under the rails with little work to do as the ship ran her tradewind westing down, I forgot scientifick thought and puzzled instead on the riddle of Brogel's papers. What connection had the *Cornelius* with 'Wittbay' and 'Linskyl'? God's clock of the universe be damm'd, I thought, clambering down into the foc'sle and hauling into the swinging cradle of my hammock. If God knows what's going on, I wish he would tell me.

'Hey, Navigator!' It was Quaker John, stirring awake. 'What's our position, my friend?' He coughed a wheezing laugh.

'I wish I knew for sure,' I said, and closed my eyes.

Only two days and half a watch later, at least twelve hours before my earliest estimation, the lookouts spied land. An island hove up dead ahead, a smear of grey at the bottom of the sky. Dumbfounded, I went straight to the quarter-deck.

Brogel's eye twinkled. 'A touch earlier, Mister Stalbone, than your expectation?'

'Aye, sir, beg permission to go below and –'

'The current at this season may give a league or two of westing,' said the captain. 'Permission granted, Navigator.'

'Aye, sir!' As I rushed to the hatchway, it came to me the captain knew all along. I re-worked the sightings and calculations and emerged hours later blinking into the sunlight, resolving to take more note of the currents in future.

The anchorage at Great Bay, by Phillipsburg, was a drab and desolate place to come upon after a month at sea. The *Cornelius* dug her bower into the sandy bottom of a wide bay that swept round in a curve of glassy blue water which, close to the shore's edge, turned green and opaque. A border of bleached sand fringed the anchorage, and behind it straggled a line of bare-trunked trees with foliated tops bearing large brown nuts. Their fronds hung limply in the thick, still air.

I longed for a sight of the homely coast of England, with its sudden changes of weather and slanting sunlight. In Sint Maarten, the Tropick sun rose high into a washed-out sky and roasted the earth until, in the late afternoon, it plunged downwards in crudely red and orange hues, when flocks of sea birds roosted noisily amid a chorus of trills and croaks from a million hidden creatures on the land. Then the suffocating night enveloped the ship and the sailors lay cursing in their hammocks, swatting mosquitoes.

In the sticky, warm water the crew swam under the ship's cool shadow, caulking her seams and scraping growth off her bottom. A forest of goose-barnacles, their trumpets four inches long, dangled from the hull, though the planks had been scrubbed bare and pitched in Amsterdam. The barnacles were so well fixed it was hard to shift them even with the blade of a knife. Eli held that they floated in the ocean and clung to the planks as a ship passed by, but who could believe such a tale?

The *Cornelius* had the bay to herself until a second ship-rigged Dutch bark hove in with an exchange of friendly signals and anchored half a cable off. Late in the day, as our work ended, we rested under a deck awning pulling junk-ends of rope apart for baggy-wrinkle to wrap around the shrouds, to save our precious flaxen sails from the worst of chafe in the rolling Tropicks.

I slapped at a mosquito screaming in my ear.

178

'Brogel's onions might do for scurvy but they can't keep these off,' I said, rasping irritatedly at the red weals.

Eli started to chuckle, then stopped himself, wincing in pain. The old man's jaw sprouted stiff spines of gut-thread where the surgeon had stitched together the hanging pieces of his cheek.

Quaker John glanced up. 'Prefer that sower-crowt from Brogel's own barrels, even if it is a Hollandish poison, to them onions any day. Pity there's none left.' He spat pointedly on the deck-boards and contemplated the gob as it evaporated in the sun. 'Last time out, half of us was scurvy-sick at the Canary Isles. Onions may be foul on the tongue, but I'll eat them watch and watch about to stop the black-gum.'

I peered over the rail towards the new arrival in the anchorage, and wrinkled my nose.

'Lord, that's a foul smell,' I said.

'Aye, with them onions we must stink like the Thames,' said the Quaker, leaning back with his eyes closed and mistaking my meaning.

'No, I meant that bark – there's a reek off her strong enough to knock over a hill-sheep,' I said, squinting to see better in the sun.

'Blagger-muss,' mumbled Eli through the remains of his jawbone.

I was bemused.

'Blackamoors,' cut in John, opening one eye. 'She's a slaver by the looks, just in from Guinea. Cut off my nose if that's not the worst of whiffs.'

'The Africk people smell like that?' I said in wonder.

'You'd smell as bad, chained below weeks on end in your own filth,' said Quaker John. 'Packed in with no air and left to rot. A bad business, but good money.'

I felt as though a spirit of pure evil had crept up behind and had its bony hands around my neck. I was beginning to see what the Africk trade meant.

'But they are men like us. Why are they kept as animals?'

'Get a fine price for a strong Negro-man,' the Quaker said, by way of explanation. 'Good pay for a seaman on a slaver, but no prize money. Less risky.'

'Than what?' I thought sailing aboard a slaver must be the worst voyage a seaman could make.

'Than being on the bloody *Cornelius*!' cried Quaker John. He sat up and blinked. 'Still think we're going hauling cargoes? We're after the yellow stuff, my friend – gold.'

'What gold – whose gold?' I said, disturbed by the Quaker's sudden, unnatural glee.

'Anybody's blasted gold,' said John, and rolled over to sleep.

With the day's work over, I left them and headed aft for an hour to read. On the captain's shelves was a volume, *Practical Navigation*, by an Englishman, John Sellers, newly published and expounding the use of the quadrant more fully than Franklin's books. Brogel forbade the book's removal from the Great Cabin, so I studied it there while the captain went ashore on business. Absorbed in the possibilities of calculating running fixes by the stars, I failed to hear a party arrive on deck until there were footsteps in the passageway outside and the door burst open.

Captain Brogel entered, followed by two gentlemen. I got up in confusion, and let the book drop.

'Careful, Stalbone,' Brogel said sternly. 'It is unlike you to handle books roughly. Leave us, we have private affairs.'

Embarrassed, I replaced the Sellers on a shelf that had a half-bar across it to keep books in place as the ship rolled, and moved to the door. The first stranger, stout-framed with a broad-brimmed feathered hat on, clutching a leather satchel and sweating like a team of horses pulling up a hill, touched me on the arm.

'Is this your Navigator, Brogel?' He spoke with a heavy Dutch accent. 'I see he studies the subject.'

'Yes, yes, Mijnheer Waspik,' said the captain absently, unlocking his private drawer and rummaging for documents. 'He is the Navigator I told you of.'

'Then he is a fortuitous find,' said the be-hatted stranger, smiling at me. 'The Tropick fevers and the flesh-rot kill men off like weevils. By Gott, I could make my fortune shipping out qualified men. Craftsmen and guildsmen –'

'Hands off, Waspik,' snapped the captain, straightening up.

The corpulent Dutchman laughed, mopping the sweat from his brow with a vast square of lace cloth.

'I shan't steal him, captain,' he laughed, with a nod in my direction.

But my attention was elsewhere, on the sheaf of

documents that the captain held. With a start, I had recognised them as the 'Linskyl' papers.

'Navigator,' said Waspik conversationally, 'where did you learn the art?'

'In Whitby, sir, in England.' I could not tear my gaze from the papers that Brogel now put on the table and, as he laid out the documents, the names 'Wittbay' and 'Linskyl' seemed to glow on the pages.

'These are the bundles we took aboard in Dartmouth, Mijnheer,' said the captain. 'Perhaps we could get on with our business –'

'In Whitby – is that so?' said Waspik, leaning forward to gather up the papers. 'My company once had interests in that town. I am agent, you see, for a venture company in Amsterdam that deals in English capital. Did you pass examination at the King's establishment?'

'Trinity House, sir? No, my lessons were ended before –'

I trailed off, for Waspik was absently scanning the Dartmouth papers. Somehow I had to get his interest in my plight.

'Sir, beg pardon, but did you know the Lynskills of Whitby? Justice Henry Lynskill, John Lynskill? Perhaps they –'

'Linskyl?' Waspik took his eye off the papers and fixed me with his gaze. I knew at once he must have seen the name on those papers by now. 'What do these Linskyls mean to you, young sir?'

I could not prevent myself blurting out the whole story. 'There was a Mister Jeffreys in Whitby who was agent for the Lynskills and I believe I have been cheated by him and I shouldn't be here on this ship and I must get back home as soon as I am able –'

Waspik's hammy hands went up in front of my face.

'Wait, wait! Let us have this from the beginning, please!' He stroked his chins. 'I do not know of these Linskyls, so you had better tell me what is on your mind.'

I knew I had his full attention, so I took a deep breath.

'I am a seaman of Whitby Town. The merchant Mister Jeffreys – who arranged for my lessons in the Navigation – held my shares in a collier-bark which were left me by my father and –'

I stopped as Waspik's eye travelled over my clothes, from the tattered slops to my blackened, bare feet.

'You do not look like a fellow who owns shares in a collier-bark,' he said, raising an eyebrow. 'Is she sound? What tunnage?'

'Seventy tuns burthen, sir, and sound enough,' I retorted. 'But she went on the shoals – I think she floated off on the tide. And I owe my life to Captain Brogel.'

The captain made a face and shook his head dismissively, as if it mattered little.

'Mijnheer Waspik, this is a diversion of no importance,' he said. 'We have a deal of business here and I would like to make a start.'

'My dear Brogel, I must examine these papers a little,' said Waspik, and Brogel, to my surprise, deferred to him. The agent fished inside the satchel

183

and brought out a pair of gold-rimmed lenses, which he stuck on his nose. 'I enjoy a mystery. Indeed. Ah!'

Waspik scanned the documents, making grunts of surprise every so often, while we waited in silence. Brogel leaned back and closed his eyes, impatient at the delay, while the other gentleman who had come in with Waspik, a powerfully-built man of sixty or so, his long white hair gathered at the neck with an ebony clasp, fixed his look on me. The eyes were blue and unblinking, and I found them unsettling, so I focused instead on Mijnheer Waspik's spectacles.

At last, Waspik finished reading.

'You should understand that I am agent here for all Dutch shipping interests,' he began, 'and for many English interests, as our trade is now so closely organised. These papers concern a venture by a Henry Linskyl of Wittbay. One Seth Jeffreys is the agent. Interesting, is it not?'

'What do the papers say, sir?' I said eagerly. Whitby had followed me across the Atlantic, it seemed, and I felt I had the right to know everything.

'You held shares in this collier?' said Waspik, heaving himself down into a seat.

'Sir, I owned sixty three of the shares but Mister Jeffreys told me –'

'Sixty three? So you as good as owned the bark?'

'Aye, sir, and I have proof she was mine. I was going to London to get my rights.'

'A most dramatic tale!' said Waspik with glee. He took out a pocket-book with a brown morocco-bound cover and picked up a quill, dipping it in

Brogel's ink. 'You want to know the bark's fate and recover your interests, is that not so? What was her name?'

'The *Prosperous Anne*, sir.' Now I am getting somewhere, I thought.

Waspik stroked his bulbous face. 'A seventy-tun bark, and Wittbay-built. What's she worth, de Vliegel?'

The lugubrious gentleman, who had remained motionless throughout, kept his eye unnervingly on me as he spoke in flat tone.

'An English-built collier-bark of seventy tuns is a fine little vessel although too small for an ocean trader in these times when we require a greater carrying ability most particularly for the Middle Passage –'

'But what of her value?' said Waspik. He shrugged at me as though to excuse his companion. 'Mijnheer de Vliegel owns the saltings on this Godforsaken island and has great knowledge of all commercial aspects of the Africk trade.'

De Vliegel continued as if there had been no interruption. '– the Middle Passage which requires a greater burthen to make the venture pay although upstart English West Country merchants send small barks to trade overseas despite misunderstanding the necessities and thus they make poor purchases and lose half of the Negroes along the way but nevertheless the ten percenters are greedy for ships to service the Royal Africkan Company so if they chose to acquire such a vessel she might fetch better than five or even six hundred guineas dependent upon –'

'A price at last!' cried Waspik, beaming. 'His interest in the subject diverts him so.' He concentrated on his book, squinting as he scratched the name and some numbers on a page. 'At least five hundred guineas, and shall we say a quarter of her worth for pulling her from her stranding? That is, if she floated.' Waspik peered over his lenses. 'Expenses to scribes and clerks, but say, upwards of three hundred and fifty guineas nett worth. Is that not so, Mister Stalbone?'

'Aye, sir, if you say it.'

'And you possess proof of ownership? A will, perhaps, of your father?'

I nodded. The will and the letter from Jedediah Franklin were hidden in a crack in the *Cornelius*'s planks not sixty feet from where we stood. The vellum had survived its soaking, although the ink was smudged in places.

'Good. Bring the papers to me before I leave.' Waspik smiled ingratiatingly. 'Now, what is it worth to you, Mister Stalbone?'

I blinked. 'I am not sure I understand, sir.'

'Let us imagine that an agent could find this bark and that he recovered your share. What is this worth?'

In truth, I had no idea. 'Five guineas, sir?' I said tentatively. It was a great deal of money to a poor sailor, I thought, and guineas sound better than sovereigns.

'Ha!' cried Waspik. 'Five English guineas do not tempt me. You are unused to dealing with money.'

'I have had none to deal with, sir,' I said in all honesty.

'In the world of men and commerce, Mister Stalbone, this is a small sum. There are at stake here three or four hundred guineas nett. Let us try again. One half and we have agreed upon it.'

I looked in disbelief at Brogel, who gave a minute shake of the head.

'One fifth,' I said, believing myself dreaming.

'One third,' replied the agent, quick as silver.

I turned wide-eyed again to the captain, dizzy at bargaining away a fortune I might never see. He had to help me.

'You are on the horns of a dilemma, Stalbone,' the captain said wearily. 'Allow Mijnheer Waspik a third against the uncertain prospect of any gain, or refuse the offer and get nothing for sure. The choice is yours.'

'Sir, I am only a seaman,' I cried helplessly to the Dutch agent. 'But if you find my ship, and recover my shares, then I shall give you one quarter of the value. No more.'

'One quarter!' Waspik stared back as if insulted, then shrugged, smacked his lips together and grinned at de Vliegel. 'Ah, such work a poor agent must do for less than a hundred guineas.'

'Have we agreed upon it, sir?' I said, offering my hand.

Waspik grasped it with a fleshy, damp palm.

'You are quite a bidder, Mister Stalbone,' he said, showing sharp teeth. 'I shall have news when you return to Sint Maarten.'

I looked at Brogel. 'Why, sir, where are we bound?'

'Enough so!' exclaimed the captain, rising and

slamming the flat of his hand on the table. 'Too many impertinent questions for my liking, Stalbone. My patience has gone so I thank you to be gone likewise.'

I made for the door, and stopped. 'Sir, thank you for –'

'Go!' bawled the captain, and I dodged out and away to the foc'sle, intensely excited at the prospect of finding my old ship – and perhaps going home.

# 11
## *Gainful Trade*

With a small gale filling her sails, the *Cornelius* bowled downwind on a fast passage from Sint Maarten, the vessel in full fighting trim and her crew's spirits buoyed up. On the dawn of the third day, the lookouts sighted the mountains of Hispaniola and the bark bore away to cruise along the southern shore. As she entered the Bahia del Sol where the breeze faltered and the rollers flattened off, we sprang to hand her sails, readying her to come to. Eagerly, we scanned the shore's rim for the way in to the hidden lagoon where our prospects lay. We were after what the Quaker called the yellow stuff, but more than that, we were to relieve a settlement of Spanish repression.

'Furl courses and main-topsail,' called Gilly Pengarth, and sent the leadsman to sound depths from the beak.

'Ten fathom!' came back the cry.

When I scrambled aloft with the others, I was astonished at the seawater's clarity. The ship floated in sixty feet of water, yet from the height of the foretop I could see clear down to the bottom, past shoals of fishes moving silently through the glassy prism. With the sun over our shoulders, the sea-bed was laid out for us to read as if on a perfectly detailed chart.

'It's like looking through a clear glass!' I cried, gathering armfuls of canvas up to the yard.

Quaker John spoke from further along the yard-arm.

'No better way to see the world, than through the bottom of a glass.'

Eli cackled merrily and sang up a chanty until we all joined in.

Captain Brogel ordered the Great Launch lowered. From its upturned stow on the weather-deck, where at sea it doubled as a shelter and stowage for spare sails, it was hoisted over the side by the capstan winch and a tackle. Ten men took up the long sweeps, with second mate Jan Hilsum of steerboard watch steering at the tiller. The tow line came taut and the ship crept forward under oar power, all canvas furled and her yards squared off.

Youssef sent me out in the cutter that once belonged to the *Prosperous Anne* to sound the way in, and I stood in its bow swinging the lead-line as we pulled into the narrow-necked entrance. The sun burned through my thin slop-shirt, and I wore a soft cap with a neck-flap, tied at the forehead with a piece of red cloth.

In between casts of the lead-line, I gazed at the scene. In the Great Launch and at the *Cornelius*'s bowsprit, every seaman sported a cap with a coloured band, giving us something of a naval aspect. Down each planked side of the flyer's hull gaped four open gunports on the lower deck, and from every one a fat, black barrel poked out like the nose of an animal sniffing the air at its burrow. Limber enough with the culverins stowed low in the holds, the *Cornelius* had shown on the run from Sint Maarten that with the heavy pieces moved up, she could roll her gunnels under. Yet, with her eight four-pounders ranged on the weather-deck, the half-pound swivels fore and aft, and now the eight culverins ranged on the tween-deck, she had transformed herself into a formidable two-decker of eighteen guns. I sensed that a great adventure was under way.

The channel opened into a broad, sheltered stretch, edged all round with the twisted roots of mangrove trees growing right out of the water. Further inshore, the ground rose steeply to the east to form the blue mountain we had seen from ten leagues out at sea. At Youssef's signal, the bower was let go. The Great Launch took a line off the *Cornelius*'s stern and pulled until the cable came taut, digging the anchor's flukes into the sandy bottom. At last she was secure, lying to a steady east wind, and Gilly Pengarth called for a muster on deck of all hands.

We assembled like a dutiful congregation, squatting cross-legged under awnings or hunched by the rail for shade. With the sailing-master on the quarter-deck stood the captain and a gentleman-landsman brought aboard in Sint Maarten, a blond-haired young fellow who had never been seen to smile. Pengarth looked bored, for I had learnt that he despised the captain's habit of assembling the crew for discourse and votes.

'Seamen of the *Cornelius*,' began Captain Brogel,

'the committee of the ship, that is myself, Mister Pengarth, and Supernumerary Sorenson here, who is the owners' appointee from Sint Maarten, proposes that the action determined upon by ourselves at Phillipsburg now be carried out. Namely to –' He consulted a parchment. 'To relieve the Settlement of Barlovento, on Hispaniola, of the Imposition of the unjust and harsh Catholick Law of Spain upon the Souls who occupy that Place, the Relief being carried out on behalf of His Majesty King William of England, Prince of Orange.'

I had discovered that the crew voted on major actions – destinations, reliefs, prize-sharing and the like – and in Sint Maarten I had raised my 'Aye' for the Hispaniola venture with the rest of them. For our loyal service to the Crown, said Youssef, we'd be rewarded with gold and whatever booty we could take.

'Thus,' continued Brogel, folding the parchment away, 'at dusk, we go ashore to redress the wrongs at Barlovento. Mister Pengarth?'

Gilly Pengarth stood, legs planted apart and hands on hips. A cutlass gleamed at his side, and two pistols were stuck into the red band at his waist.

'Thirty five men are to take up muskets and half-pikes,' he boomed, 'and a watch of a dozen remains to guard ship. Two field-guns and one mortar shall be fitted to the field-carriages. I take the mortar detachment, and the second mates are field-gunners. Any seaman unfamiliar with the musket shall remedy that case now.'

He surveyed the assembly, and we shifted restlessly under his gaze.

'Any man who does not enter the fight with a will – fifty on the grating.'

I saw the captain dart a glance at the sailing-master. Brogel was for reason and the custom of the seamen's court, but Gilly Pengarth preferred to rely on the lash, the cat and a keel-hauling.

'I shall have my eye on all of you tonight, my handsomes,' Pengarth went on. 'Now – get to your work.'

There was a buzz of excited chatter. I was handed a long flintlock musket from the armoury stores below. Eli saw my puzzlement, for I had never before handled one.

'Like them deck-guns,' he mumbled. His injury had left him with a one-sided biscuit-chewing action. 'Powder, tamp. Wad, tamp. Ball, tamp. Powder to the flashpan, flintlock cocked back. All correct? Raise the piece, hold steady and trigger the lock. Now sponge out your hot barrel with the other end of the tamping rod. Clear pan. Check flint. Repeat.' He sniffed and spat. 'That's it, youngster.'

I tamped and wadded enthusiastically. To get the feel of the thing, I lifted the weapon and squinted down the unwieldy barrel.

'Eli, I can't aim it steady.'

'Don't try to pick a mark,' he said. 'We just send in a volley of balls. Have to get close in, though – more than a hundred paces off, ball's too slow to drop your man. Down like this, see.' He dropped to one knee and raised his own musket. 'Point ahead, breathe out and squeeze for the shot.'

The flintlock clicked loudly and I flinched.

Eli grinned. 'Jumpy, lad?'

I had to admit I was as nervous as a poacher in court.

As dusk fell, our party climbed into the Great Launch, muskets and half-pikes clattering together in the hugger-mugger of boarding. The oarsmen could barely pull at the sweeps, what with the armour pieces squatting on the centre line, and powder bags and shot-boxes all about the bottom of the boat. As we gained the quiet shore, the night closed around us and the tree frogs chirped in a frantic chorus. The vegetation gave way to a ghost of a track that led off into the hinterland, and we formed into a ragged file. For two full hours, in pitch dark, we wheeled and dragged the armour pieces along on their field-carriages until Brogel raised an arm and the column halted. He spoke in a low voice as we crowded close to hear in the still of the thick night.

'Now we must move forward with stealth,' said the captain. 'From the high ground, we shall direct a round of shot and mortar into the target. If fighting men appear in strength, we offer to parley. If we cannot come to terms, we attack the garrison, fire the fortifications, relieve the settlers and retrieve what the Spaniards have stolen. Understood?'

A murmur of 'Ayes' and 'Yas' went round.

The night was moonless, but in the Tropick starlight I distinguished an open space, surrounded by low buildings like a garrison. Flat, cleared croplands lay between us, the attackers, and the settlement below. When we got the mortars and four-pounders in place, the crews primed and charged them. As we loaded our muskets, the weapons clattering and tamping rods thumping, the officers urged us to silence.

Quaker John and I stood fiddling nervously with our muskets.

'The captain said we are going to put a shot or two in first,' I said, 'as a sort of warning.'

'Set afire to the place,' said the Quaker. 'Then a musket volley and we charge them with our half-pikes. That's their blasted warning.'

'But the captain –'

'Field-guns – fire!'

An instant after Pengarth's bellowed order, the guns discharged in unison, sending out from their belching muzzles brilliant flashes that illuminated the sailors' startled faces. A violent pressure shock enveloped me, and a booming thunder rumbled into the night air. The round-shots arced away, glowing dimly red from the heat of the charge, then seemed to flatten and drive straight into the buildings below, with sparks bursting in all directions and flames lighting the dark sky. The crash of splintering wood reached our ears and, moments after, I thought I heard a woman's scream.

'Mortar – fire!'

The mortar, a hundred feet forward of the guns, belched out roaring smoke and flames. A mass of livid sparks around a glowing spherical core shot straight upwards as if about to fall back on our own heads and then arced down towards the enflamed area where the shots had landed. The mortar shell exploded amongst the buildings in a balloon of flames, spraying liquid limbs of fire on all sides. Its muffled report dinned in our ears. My God, I breathed, this is a spectacle, and the gunners' aim is good tonight.

'Gunners, reload. Musketmen, hold where you are,' called Pengarth.

Down in the compound there was movement. Men ran about, apparently without organisation. If these are the defending troops, I thought, they are slow to get off the mark.

The gunners worked furiously to recharge.

'Ready? Fire!' cried Pengarth.

The armour roared into explosive life once more, and two round shots and a mortar bomb hurtled into the smoking buildings in showers of burning debris. I saw the figure of a man engulfed in flames, rolling on the ground. But of armed troops resisting the attack, there came no sign. A third barrage of round-shot and a mortar bomb crashed into the village and then came the order.

'Musketmen – forward!' cried Gilly Pengarth.

Weapons clanging, we scrambled off the bluff, following the tall figure of Pengarth in those distinctive white slops. As we headed towards the blazing scene, I stumbled with the awkward musket, but we covered the distance easily in a minute, halting within a hundred feet of the flaming houses. Men and women staggered about between the buildings, shouting and screaming in confusion. I saw no soldiers, nor – I realised with a shock – had there been any fire returned, neither musket ball nor pistol shot, let alone gunnery.

'Muskets,' called Pengarth. 'Raise your weapons. Aim your volley ahead.'

With Quaker John on one side and Eli Savary on

the other, I put the musket to my shoulder, levered back the flintlock and aimed the barrel level at the gaps between the buildings, brightly lit by flames, where human figures moved about.

'Let go volley!'

I squeezed the trigger at the instant of Pengarth's command. The lock snapped down and ignited the pan in a blinding flash. As the musket bucked, a long tongue of flame burst from its muzzle end and a rush of noise and heat engulfed my head. I staggered a step or two before I could regain balance. My nostrils filled with the sharpness of burnt powder, and sparks flew from the flashpan, stinging my hands. All around, muskets discharged with dazzling flares and loud cracks, and the balls seared angrily away into the mayhem in front. The rounds spattered into their targets, sending aloft splinters of wood, and thudding into softer objects. Human screams rose from the cluster of houses. The settlement now presented a scene of utter devastation, with dimly discernible figures fleeing or crawling from blazing houses and huts.

'Come on, Mattoo!'

Youssef dashed past, waving a pistol and a half-pike, and a surge of men drew their hand weapons and charged forward. I shouldered the musket, hefted my half-pike and followed into the mêlée.

Within the settlement itself, amongst the burning buildings, the world closed in. The smoke and confusion was disorienting. I stepped over the figures of men and women slumped on the ground or huddled under the shattered dwellings, some crying out in pain, others as still as dead fish. Pieces of broken wood from the shattered dwellings crashed to the ground as I stumbled hither and thither, and my leather-shoed feet landed on charcoals of blazing timber. I tried to follow Youssef's figure scurrying ahead, but suddenly the Barbar was gone and I was alone. I stopped short, panting, half-pike at the ready, and tried to get my bearings.

An anguished cry sounded behind. I turned to see a man running at me, hand upraised with a cutlass silhouetted against the billowing flames. Reacting instinctively, I dropped to one knee and held the half-pike outwards. The figure pelted onwards, mouth opening in a shriek. With a strength born of fear, I thrust the pike upwards and the attacker ran pell-mell onto its blade. My end of the pole embedded itself in the ground and the assailant was levered clear over me, tearing the pike from my grasp. The fellow landed heavily, cutlass clattering to the ground, and let out what sounded like a sigh of regret.

'*Madre de Dios!*' he gasped, and slumped down with the pike deep in his chest. In the disturbed light of the flame-engulfed houses, I saw his eyes bulge and his arms thrash.

I scrambled up, blinded with panic, and my empty musket fell to the ground. Unarmed and vulnerable, I looked around in terror and saw the attacker's cutlass, with a blade a foot and a half long, glinting on the ground. I picked it up and brandished it at the fallen man in case he leapt up and attacked. But the fellow, groaning fearfully with the half-pike standing up from his breast like a sentinel, was in no condition to harm me. Moving cautiously over, I lay down the cutlass and grasped the pike with both hands, trying to lever it out. From the wounded man's throat came a gurgling sound and he gripped the half-pike as if trying to pull me down. Seized with an overwhelming horror and a desperate will to free the pike, I put my foot on the man's chest and worked the blade back and forth. Bones cracked and something bubbled, then I wrenched the blade free and held the pike upright. I felt the handle grow stickily wet.

Another figure came running out of the night. In a blind reaction, I snatched up the cutlass and crouched like an animal. At the last second, the running figure pulled up. It was Quaker John.

'What made you go off like that?' he said, breathing raggedly. 'Let Youssef and the other idiots do the fighting, I say.'

He saw the man lying nearby, legs and arms waving like an insect on its back, and looked at me, white-faced.

'Poor bastard.'

I hung my head, feeling sick.

'By the Lord's Grace,' I mumbled, 'I – I didn't intend –'

John hissed into my face.

'You're the poor bloody bastard – you've killed a man.' The Quaker's teeth gleamed in the flickering light of the fires all round us and his eyes shone fiercely. 'Now you know what's inside you.'

He leapt away, heading off towards the shouts and cries of battle. I shook myself to my senses and, with a last fearful glance at the fallen man, who lay still now, gathered up my musket and dismally loped after the Quaker.

When we reached the centre of the hamlet – for it was no more than that – it was clear the fighting was over. Dead and wounded lay in every alleyway, men and women alike. There had been no military opposition. In the open space were gathered the victorious crew of the *Cornelius*, who had come to relieve the settlers of Catholick tyranny. As the fear of immediate death drained away from my pumping heart, a sickening dread took its place.

In the middle of the simple square were twenty or thirty men and women, a few children amongst them, huddled on the ground and roped by their hands and feet. Half were white Europeans, the men in rough cotton shirts and broadcloth briches, the women in loose smocks, some with cotton caps, others bareheaded. The rest were a short and stocky race, dark-skinned with flat faces, wearing nothing more than bands of cloth wound around their bodies. The children and the women wept, and the men squatted in silence, their heads bent, while the houses – made only of wood and bark and leaves – burned on. Their weapons had been collected, a forlorn pile of broken cutlasses and one or two hand-pikes, and many hoes and digging tools. There was not a single musket or pistol to be seen amongst them.

I was aghast. 'These men and women were barely armed,' I said wonderingly, but no one was listening.

Numbed, I sat down at the side of the square.

Where were the Spanish troops and Papist conquerors who were said to rule the place in a reign of terror? These people looked like farmers or peasants, tillers of fields, tenders of animals. The laments of the prisoners rose in a wail and drowned out the ringing din the gunnery had left in my ears, but at the sound of Brogel's voice, I looked up.

'Well fought, men,' said the captain, addressing the throng. 'The armour did our work for us. Report on the wounded, Mister Pengarth.'

'Jan Hilsum, second mate, cutlass wound to left arm,' said Pengarth. 'One man with powder burns, one finger severed. Nothing more.'

'Good so.' Captain Brogel faced the huddle of captives. 'Bring me the chief of these people. *Capitan! Duce!*'

A man of European features, though even in the half-light of the flames he appeared dark-skinned, was pushed sprawling before the captain.

'Who amongst us speaks Spanish? Youssef – step here and speak in this man's tongue.'

The Barbar translated as Brogel pressed the prisoner.

'Disclose where the gold is hidden and you go free.'

The leader lifted his head to meet the captain's eye, then spat sideways on the ground. Pengarth spoke in Brogel's ear and a white woman prisoner, her loose dress torn and her hands bound behind her, was led out and made to kneel. The sailing-master raised his pike as if to drive it into her neck. The Spaniard became very agitated.

'No, no, no, no!' he cried, and spoke rapidly.

201

'The gold is buried in the near field, sir,' said Youssef. 'And he says Spanish troops shall return and kill us, for we have offended their God.'

'Nonsense, there are no troops,' said Brogel with a dismissive wave, and detailed four men to take up spades and go with the village leader to find the spot. 'Booty may be taken, but discipline maintained. Mister Pengarth, see to it.' The captain followed the gold hunters out of the square.

'Leave this place to burn,' ordered the sailing-master with a wave of his hand. 'Let the prisoners remain here under guard until we are done. Musketmen, recharge your weapons. Gunners, make the pieces ready for transport.' I could see his grinning teeth in the midst of the ginger beard. 'And take whatever you want, boys!'

Fatigue overwhelmed me as I sat in the desolate little clearing. Our night's action repelled me, and the deaths of these poor farmers crushed my soul. I imagined the villagers, now beaten and captive, in their unmolested lives tending crops and sharing food. What I had taken part in was no heroic salvation of an enslaved people, but repression itself. And I had killed a man in its name.

After a few minutes, during which I dazedly cleaned and reloaded my musket, I glanced up to see Youssef holding a young half-white girl by the arm. She was not more than fifteen or sixteen, and her large eyes shone in the flames that lit the night. She trembled with fear.

'Mattoo, you are second mate just for a little minute or two.'

The Barbar put his pistol down beside me. I

supposed my thoughts were plain to see, but Youssef misunderstood.

'She's safe with me!' he cried merrily and, laughing, pulled her away and disappeared into the darkness.

I breathed deeply, but found the atmosphere in the village stifling and longed for a fresh breeze of sea air. I could not rid my mind of the girl's terrified face. She was pretty even though her skin was browned from the sun. With a pang, I remembered Abigail had spoken of a settlement in America. What if, one day, she became a prize for a sailor after a raid like this?

I wandered out of the square, heading for a dark part of the village, where no fires burned. With my musket slung aback, I held the half-pike and my newly acquired cutlass at the ready. I was determined not to let myself be surprised again. If I am attacked, I decided, I shall disarm or wound without killing.

As the hubbub of the square receded, I heard muffled moans from a shack nearby. It sounded like a child's crying. There came low grunts and women's voices protesting, then a man cursed in Dutch. The sound of a blow, like a stave on a face, reached me where I stood outside hardly breathing. In the still air, a coarse laugh rang out amidst wails of distress. Enough, I raged, there has been enough killing and destruction and evil here. Bracing the half-pike at my hip, cutlass in my right hand, I charged the doorway and hurled aside its flimsy barrier of woven reeds.

Inside was a mean, dim space lit by a wick in a

bowl of palm oil. Two native women lay sobbing on the floor, faces turned upwards as if pleading. Beside them, three half-grown children, a young boy and two girls, cowered in their nakedness. A sailor called Boxsmeer stood over them with a pike raised, his grinning features lit by the uncertain light. On a rough straw mattress knelt another seaman, Jack Taggart, slops round his ankles, grunting and pushing at a small body under him.

Boxsmeer's smile vanished at the crash of the door and I stepped into the room with my pike held out.

'Dam' you – they're children! Leave them be.'

'Get out of here, Yorkie,' snarled Boxsmeer.

He lunged, but I brought the cutlass's heavy handle up under his chin with such force I heard the crunch of a gristly tongue caught between teeth. With a groan, he crumpled to the floor, clutching his mouth. Taking a pace forward, I stabbed the pike's point into Taggart's bare arse.

'Christ be damm'd!' bellowed the sailor and rolled off his victim, who scrambled away to her mother's side, whimpering and trying to cover her body. I poked the blade at Jack Taggart's neck, puckering the skin.

'On your feet. I've killed once tonight and I'm ready to kill you. Get up!'

Taggart slowly gathered himself, pulling up his briches.

'What's this?' he said. 'What's the matter with you?'

'May your God forgive you,' I said, backing warily away.

Boxsmeer was on all fours on the ground, shaking his head. I kicked his fallen half-pike clear.

'You too, Boxsmeer. We're going to an officer.'

The women and children clung to each other, flinching even as I half turned towards them. Ashamed, I could not meet their eyes. I prodded my pike-end in Boxsmeer's back to get the vile man moving.

'Let's see what our captain says,' I said grimly. 'Move!'

Boxsmeer and Taggart reluctantly dragged themselves out of the house and into the lane outside.

'No harm in it,' grunted Taggart. 'They're only half-caste Dago natives.'

'Hold up, or you'll find my pike where you don't want it,' I growled. Suddenly, a figure appeared from the shadows. I was on my guard until I saw, with great relief, that it was Youssef.

'Thank God!' I cried. 'Listen – these two were in that house. They were – they had children in there.'

Youssef examined their faces in the gloom.

'Ah, Taggart and Boxsmeer. These bloody men, with children again?' He cocked his head at me. 'But they break no law of the ship. You must let them go.'

'What they've done is a crime! I'm taking them to Captain Brogel.'

Taggart spread his hands. 'Aw, see now, Youssef – he's gone off his head.'

'Yes, Mattoo – let them go, my friend.'

'Not a chance, Youssef, I'm going to –'

With sudden swiftness, the Barbar grabbed my

205

half-pike, slamming me backwards and pinning me against the wall. His grip was like iron.

'Go! Taggart, Boxsmeer – go!' he hissed over his shoulder, and they ran off laughing. Youssef relaxed and slowly let me away from the wall. 'Calm yourself, my friend, this is just the sailor's way.'

I shook my head, thinking I had been led halfway into Hell.

'I can't believe it – we've burnt their houses, killed their men, violated their children. This is worse than –' My mind whirled back to Whitby days, where I had thought to have seen enough of death and injustices. I stared pleadingly at the Barbar. 'Youssef, what's it for? What are we doing?'

'Mattoo,' said Youssef evenly, 'these are only natives and Papist people – Spanish!' He spat on the ground. 'We sailors are a long time at sea. There's no harm.'

'But what those two did – the Lord save their souls!' I blazed at Youssef. 'Captain Brogel must hear. He is a fair man.'

The Barbar looked helplessly at me.

'Telling Brogel shall be very bad for you. Not good to make enemies on board ship.'

I glared back, but his look was almost pitying.

'I tell you, Mattoo, you will be killed. You cannot be sailor aboard *Cornelius* and make trouble for your fellows. This is just the sailor's life.' He punched me gently on the arm. 'You must understand.'

'Never!' I said hotly, but in my guts I knew he was right about making trouble on board. Lord, I

206

thought bitterly, all I ever wanted was to go to sea. Hardly realising it, I began to shout, my anger pent up inside. 'It's wrong – can't you see it? I wish I never had to come ashore to – to –' Helplessly, I cast around for the words. 'To this stinking evil.'

I spat vehemently on the ground and marched off. Youssef followed slowly. When we regained the square, the captain had returned and the men were clustered round to hear his news.

'The gold is found!' the captain cried.

Wild cheering broke out as I watched in silence, dry-mouthed, my blood still at boiling pitch. The field party returned carrying a litter between them on which lay two heavy bags. Brogel opened one and lifted out objects like small, dull coins.

'Bring a light,' he ordered.

A sailor held up a torch and the captain raised a handful for us all to see. The sailors jostled closer. The captain rubbed the coins with his sleeve, and they glinted yellow in the flame's light. Gasps of admiration grew into a prolonged buzz of excited chatter. Quaker John and Eli pushed to the front and, despite myself, I moved forward too, the dull glow of the money drawing me on, eager as the rest now to see the gold that men lusted for so badly they would dishonour themselves just to seize it in their fingers.

'See this!' cried Brogel. 'This is gold the Spanish steal from the native peoples. We return it to King William, the Good Lord bless his honoured person. When we are at sea, there shall be a prize-sharing – dollars and pieces of eight and crowns for every man jack of you!'

The tars waved their half-pikes in the air, linking arms and jigging around. On the edge of the mob, Jack Taggart and the Dutchman Boxsmeer broke off their huddled conversation and glowered in my direction before moving in to inspect the booty. Oddly, I knew the lust for gold had entered my blood too, for Youssef was right. I could not take what I wanted from the *Cornelius* and ignore the rest – I could not take the ocean voyages and the Navigation as if they were apart from this. The yellow stuff was what we had come for, and I could not detach myself from the winning of it.

The victorious raiding party departed the farming village, leaving its men dead or dying, its women tearfully bathing wounds that might never heal in the stinking sultriness of the Tropicks, its children weeping in fear and shame, and the embers of its houses smouldering in ashes.

The return march was a raucous affair, although I walked alone. Soon the party reached the lagoon and we began loading the Great Launch. The moon had risen full in the night sky, and at the shore's edge, where the water lapped at the sand, I stood, drained, and listened as the tree frogs and *cucarachas* sang their love songs.

The *Cornelius* lay in the middle of a glassy pool, a light burning at her stern and the reflection shimmering on the blackness of the water. She sat motionless, a proud sailing vessel, powerful, elegant and calm. For the first time, I saw her anew, and a surge of disgust rose in me. She had brought me willy-nilly to this place and, from all her grace and beauty, disgorged only death and plunder and violation. Instead of honest trade, she sought only to enrich herself at terrible cost to others. The *Cornelius* puzzled and angered me more than I could account for.

'Hey, Stallyboon!' Pengarth's taunting tones shattered my reverie. 'Over here to help with this gold.'

There was no choice. Reluctantly I dragged myself over.

'You're a troublesome jack-tar,' Pengarth sneered. 'You never pulled your weight all night. Loading this stuff's heavy work, so put your dam' back into it, or I'll have you flogged.'

Back aboard at last, I grabbed a pot of rum from Quaker John and drained it without pause. He made as if to fight over the matter, but, perhaps catching my black countenance, thought better of it. As for me, I found the rum dulled the memories of the night.

When dawn crept in from the east, we weighed anchor and towed our bark from the lagoon. With an angry flash, the sun burst above the horizon and drove the darkness away. We loosed out canvas and headed into the open sea, with a breeze at our backs and the gold in our grasp.

# 12

## *Spoiled Goods*

Deep in the recesses of the pump-well, I touched the taper to the oil in the pan. As the light flared, it illuminated the soaked sidewalls dripping slime and ringed with scums of grease and worse.

'Filthy tars,' I muttered, gagging as the cloth round my mouth moved and I caught half a breath of the foulest air on God's earth. The chain pump-well was where the noisome excretions of sailors and animals mixed with the swirling bilge-water at the very arsehole of the hull. After our twelvemonth in the Main, we had worked back to windward, almost four hundred leagues from the Coast of Riches, to reach Phillipsburg once more. By now, the *Cornelius* had loosened her seams, and water seeped in at a thousand places. We had to send men over the side with oakum and mallets to re-caulk her planking tight before we could even pump the well clear.

By the lamp's glow, I groped in the slime for the sulphur piece in the well's bottom. Grasping the slippery object, I flipped it into the whale-oil, which burned hot and clean, and bent to see whether the sulphur block would catch alight. There was a hiss and an intense yellowish glow appeared.

I tore off the gag.

'Haul me up, boys!' I yelled into the echoing chamber.

The bosun's chair jerked under me and the rope creaked. From nearly twenty feet above came the muffled sound of the men's chain-pump chanty. I watched the faraway square of light from the manhole grow, and near the top caught a draught of fresh air. At last I burst into the sunlight, shouldered clear of the manhole and sprawled on deck at the feet of the pump-men.

The boy sailor called Gaspar Rittel slammed on the cover and dogged it down. From the underside of the lid came a wisp of yellow-orange smoke. Everyone shrank back out of its way.

I coughed and wiped my streaming eyes.

'Water,' I croaked. 'A drink.'

Gaspar turned to the barrel and dipped a ladle. I slurped the contents noisily down and held out the ladle for more, scowling at him.

'Call yourself a seaman? You can't keep hold of a gatepost, let alone a line.'

'I never meant to drop the sulphur, sir,' wailed Gaspar. 'And you had no need.'

'Aye, I know you were ready to go down,' I said, with a forgiving clap on his back, 'but I had to see the step for myself.'

Only days earlier, we had parted a back-stay in a squall, straining the step of the mainmast.

'Any movement, second mate?' said Carpenter Sedgewick, a round-faced fellow with enormous hands.

211

'It's still nice,' I told him. 'Tighter than a tar with a rum-pot.'

I looked around at my watchmen. Like a bag of nails, I thought, some straight and strong, but others were bent even before you tested them with a mallet. Still, they sprang to when asked and were a tribute to Jan Hilsum's discipline as second mate of steerboard watch. Even after so long, I marvelled at what a simple cut-wound might do to a man in the Tropick lands if he was unlucky with its healing. After being wounded in Hispaniola, Hilsum had endured weeks of suffering as the surgeon hacked at the arm to stem the green-rot's spread, until at last the poor fellow had died in a lingering agony, little relieved by laudanum.

We left the sulphur in the pump-well to do its work on the stinks. Even we tars on the *Cornelius* could stand the stench no longer, though our habits were the cause in the first place. We eased our bowels in the pissdale or squatted in the holds, just because it was sometimes too bumpy and wet to perch out over the bow.

'Main hold next, lads,' I called, and sent them off to clear it and scrub it with vinegar.

Youssef came over and we sat together under the deck awning, chewing sugar-cane sticks.

'*Cornelius* must refit and resupply,' he said thoughtfully.

'In England, preferably,' I joked. 'What's Brogel's next move?'

'Clean her bottom again,' said the Barbar. 'For speed.'

A raven-haired girl of about eighteen or twenty, a

212

clean-limbed and feline figure, appeared from the quarter-deck companionway and headed for the break of the poop. She was barefooted, in a bright red shift dress of soft cloth gathered in at the waist. Spanish blood showed in her mass of dark hair and the hip-swinging walk, but somewhere in there – it struck me – was a quarter or an eighth from the Dark Continent. It gave the Cuban girl her smooth tanned skin, and the long limbs she carried so elegantly.

Neeta made her way onto the weather-deck towards us. A soft yellow chain glinted at her neck, following the curves of her breastbone. Gold was Brogel's way of keeping her sweet.

'Hello, Cubanita,' I said, smiling up at her. She radiated back with a display of pearly teeth and dancing eyes, and when she smiled her top lip curled pertly upwards. She ignored Youssef, whose face registered uncut lust.

'The capitan wants you. Come to the Great Cabin.'

She billowed back to the poop with her hair flying and skirts flouncing, and I trailed after her like a barge towed by a schooner. At the foot of the companionway, Neeta squeezed my hand, flashed her smile and left. I breathed in the air laden with the scent of her body. Then I went to the door of the Great Cabin and knocked.

'Enter,' came the captain's voice.

Brogel was seated at the table, while Supernumerary Sorenson stood, blond and unsmiling, with his back to the sternlights. Since coming aboard on behalf of the Amsterdam owners, Sorenson had made his presence felt by pushing the *Cornelius* into increasingly risky ventures solely for the benefit, as he insisted, of filling the prize coffers and advantaging the seamen, though we still had taken no great Spanish prize. No one could like the fellow for himself, and being a landsman condemned him utterly in the eyes of all aboard.

The captain was sweating and drawn, and he caught my look.

'Ah, second mate. Yes, the guts again. Blasted Tropick lands, what so?'

On the table was a blue apotheckary's bottle for laudanum, empty. Surgeon Petty swore it was an excellent binder of the bowels.

'This letter for you was brought by Waspik's man,' said the captain, holding out a folded paper with a red wax seal closing it.

I broke the seal and unfolded the paper. I had had plenty of time to resent the cut-throat deal the Dutch agent had engineered over the *Prosperous Anne*, but at the prospect of news, I forgot it in a second.

'Mijnheer Waspik wishes me to see him at Simpson Bay,' I said, fumbling to refold the parchment. At last, I thought, I shall hear something. 'Captain, permission to go across the island.'

'Granted, so long as your watch has idling tasks enough to busy them,' said Brogel, wagging an admonishing finger. 'Remember Taggart, the dam' jump-ship.'

'We were well rid of him, sir. And steerboard watch are vinegaring the main hold.'

The captain smiled, though a touch painfully, and massaged his belly.

214

'A clean ship, what so?' He let out a deep breath. 'We've kept more men in good health this voyage. The pity is our supply of sower-crowt is done. We'll get onions again when we can, and perhaps some man-joes for –'

'Captain,' broke in Supernumerary Sorenson. 'This talk of vegetables interrupts ship's business. The second mate should remain aboard, after the delay when we broke that stay-back.'

'Back-stay,' cried Brogel, thumping the table. 'And Sorenson, no orders can reach us for weeks. A ship cannot take the Tropick passage at this season for fear of crossing with a hurry-cane.' He snorted. 'Even a landsman should know that.'

'Very well, Captain, have it your way,' said Sorenson, with rapid blinks.

Brogel glanced at me. 'Hand your watch to Youssef. Dismissed.'

I left the Great Cabin smartly and within half a glass had set off to find Waspik. At my belt was the pistol I had inherited from the dead second mate along with his post. I had charged it with ball and powder and wrapped spare balls and a horn in cloth before setting out. At my side was still the old cutlass from the very first Hispaniola raid.

The track from Phillipsburg to Simpson Bay led through the flat salt-pans where gangs of Africkan men and women worked, spreading the drying salt in the sun with broad-bladed wooden shovels. I passed close enough to see their skin glistening with sweat and hear them singing sadly in a strange language. Overseers stood by with their whips and pistols at the ready. Everywhere in the Spanish

215

Main, I had found, people feared the Negroes, for they outnumbered many times the Europeans who ran the plantations. On this island, though hundreds of indentured white labourers had been shipped out for five or six years to work, yet still there were more Affrickans than anyone. No wonder the overseers glanced up warily as I walked by.

Reaching Simpson Bay, I found the town sported a handsome brick building for commerce such as, I supposed, salt trading and the slave market. It fronted an open square of wooden houses with streets radiating off, but the settlement was quiet in the afternoon sun and I walked through not encountering a soul.

I sought the *Tryall*, a two-masted English merchantman. Gazing over the lagoon, I saw a dozen vessels riding at anchor on the flat waters. One, a broad-beamed carrier, not fast but built to haul loads, caught my eye. She had every inch the lines of an English-built ship, not unlike a collier, with her bluff bows and undecorated stern. Five deck guns were ranged each side, but as the gunports were of new wood I guessed she had been a Narrow Seas trader until her conversion into armed merchantman. Somehow, she had a hang-dog air about her, I thought, studying the slung-about yards and slackened shrouds. On her stern was the name *Tryall*.

I found a dark man asleep under a rowing boat at the lagoon's edge, and for the round trip gave him a piece of Dutch metal worth less than half a farthing. As the blackamoor sculled me slowly out, I saw thick weed growing round the *Tryall*'s waterline.

There was a strong smell of rotting, and she appeared bereft of life. No watchman spied our boat as we approached.

'Ahoy *Tryall*!' I called when we fetched up alongside.

A broad feathered hat appeared at the stern rail, and beneath it was Mijnheer Waspik's face.

'Mister Stalbone! Come aboard.'

I scrambled up a rope ladder and stepped into the waist of the ship. Broken gear and half-mended work was strewn about without care. The deckboards badly wanted benefit of holystoning, her stays hung slack and the ratlines were frayed. Beneath awnings, men dozed and rested, their legs sticking out from under – white men with burned skins, and some showed the blackened toes of long-time scurvy. The air was foul all around, and more than scorbutic. It was rancid.

'By Gott, Mister Stalbone,' said the Dutchman, smiling, 'just to stay alive in this Tropick Hell is an admirable feat.'

We clambered down into the gloom of the stern quarters and Waspik, breathing noisily, led the way into the Great Cabin. It had small stern windows, the deadlights propped open in the vain hope of any movement of air, and was a mean space against that of the *Cornelius*. The agent plumped down, took off his hat and fanned himself, a dribble of sweat running down his temple. He waved me to a seat and nodded toward the two gentlemen already in the room. One I recognised as the fish-eyed slave owner who had been with Waspik on the *Cornelius*. I looked at Waspik in surprise and he caught my meaning.

'I have taken the liberty, Mister Stalbone, of inviting you to this vessel in the presence of these two gentlemen who may be able to illuminate aspects of your affairs. I trust you have no mind about allowing them to hear the matter out?'

I bowed my head minutely. 'If they can assist, I am honoured,' I said.

'You may remember Mijnheer Simon de Vliegel?' puffed Waspik.

I nodded with what I hoped was courtesy enough, for the man unnerved me still, with his unblinking stare.

'And this is Captain James Gould, of the *Tryall*. Mister Matthew Stalbone, of the *Cornelius* out of Vlissingen.'

'Honoured, Stalbone,' said Gould, nodding but not rising or offering a hand. He was a tired-looking Englishman of around forty, thin and hollow-eyed, who spoke with a West Country burr like Gilly Pengarth's.

'Are you a westcountryman, Captain Gould?' I said. 'You may know Mister Pengarth, of Plymouth.'

At the mention of the name, Gould smirked in a way that made me uneasy.

'I know him. Big fellow, gingery hair and beard, eh? Wears white stuff and a red cloth at his waist. A good master.'

I shrugged. 'He is sailing-master of the fastest and finest flyer in the Main.'

218

Gould shot me a dark look, then laughed with exaggeration.

'Mister Stalbone, let us celebrate that grudging testimonial of yours with a tot of de Vliegel's finest. He has the Negroes grow cane behind his great house and press it into a fine rum.'

The salt owner's long, sad face registered nothing in response. Gould reached into a locker and brought out a black bottle and four pewter tumblers. We each drank a tot and took some water after from a carafe on the table. Gould, I noticed, downed two tots to everyone else's one, while de Vliegel watched him carefully.

'I daresay you cast a sailor's eye over my ship, Stalbone,' the captain said.

'Have you been in the Main many years?' I enquired.

'Why? Think we look it, do you?' Gould's tone was unpleasant.

'I thought I might learn something of your experience,' I said mildly.

He grimaced. 'We left Fowey Harbour, let me see, a year and half ago, trawled the Guinea Coast – fever-ridden Hades of a place – then brought a cargo here, doubled back via the Azores and Madeira, took on another cargo and made the Middle Passage a second damm'd time. Never again. Lost fully a third of my men. Fever, scurvy, pus-wounds, guts awry, the Lord knows. In all my Balticks, I never lost a man to disease,'

'What cargo?'

'Slaves I purchased from the Guinea traders, the

219

caboceers. The most Devilish damm'd thing I ever did.'

'Transporting slaves?' I said. The Africk trade has caught up with me at last, I thought grimly, and here I sit aboard a slaver, drinking rum and talking business. I wonder if, just below our feet, chained to the deck-heads, and that terrible stench – it was too much, and I tried to put it from my head.

'No, the whole misbegotten venture.' He smacked his lips disgustedly. 'I never relished a Tropick voyage, but the owners want the ten percent trade.' He slugged down another tot of sugar-rum. 'The caboceers in Guinea and Sao Tome are thieves, curse their white teeth and black skins, and I paid too dear for my blackamoors.'

'The ten percent, Mister Stalbone,' cut in Waspik, 'goes to the Royal Africkan Company, whose monopoly the King has ended.'

'Can't you smell it? Doesn't it curdle the inside of your nostrils?' Gould was letting the drink get hold of his tongue. 'Those stinking pieces of black flesh – lost half of 'em – half!'

'There is something of a bad air about the vessel,' I said uneasily, ignoring a dark glance from the Englishman. 'Can't you turn them out into the breeze? Wash them?' How calmly we discuss such an evil, I thought.

Gould laughed harshly. 'They'd attack us. They are chained – let me see, now – two hundred and thirty four or five –'

'On this ship?' I cried. 'Why, she's too small!'

'Do you want to see my log, dammit?' said

Captain Gould touchily. 'We left the Guinea Coast with all of four hundred and fifty.'

'Ah, such a credit to your abilities, Captain,' said Waspik, shooting a warning look at me. 'Mister Stalbone is, I am sure, impressed at your ingenuity in arranging the stowage and transportation of such valuable cargo.'

'It is beyond my wit to see how it can be done,' I said in irritated disbelief. 'Why do you not sell the blackamoors at once? Why keep them in these conditions?'

Gould, the pewter mug to his mouth, choked on the liquid and gasped.

'Be damm'd, sir, if I don't object to your manner!' He slammed down the tumbler in anger. 'Who the Hell do you think you are, Stalbone?' He tried to go on but choked again, eyes watering, and he fell to gasping once more. Before he gathered himself, Simon de Vliegel cut in.

'Let me answer your question,' said the slave owner slowly, in a voice as colourless as a saltpan, 'for my trade is in Negroes and while I have bought the best few of the good captain's there are now available at market many better examples of the species which glut is due to the appearance of venturesome vessels such as this one applying themselves to the late freeing of trade but without understanding that while the best of Negroes may always be sold those not of the first quality are unwanted.'

'Surely you cannot keep them forever,' I said, 'as if they were bales of cotton.'

Gould groaned and shook his head pityingly. He reached for the bottle.

'The good captain here has unfortunately acquired only males,' continued de Vliegel, 'but we landowners after many years perfecting our use of slaves prefer to purchase a mix of the sexes for the men become more compliant at their work and less rebellious if they are allowed women and in addition to this benefit they breed with the happy result that we achieve a degree of self-replication and if you care to visit my saltings you may see the slave-huts and other arrangements and discover that I have a fine house with a stables and a dining hall with a decorated ceiling and a court for the pastime of real-tennis.'

I smiled coolly. 'I thank you, sir, but I must return to my ship today,' I said, thinking de Vliegel was welcome to that fine house and his real-tennis. I had no desire to admire what the profits of enslavement could buy. Instead, I tackled the captain. 'What becomes of your ship now, Captain Gould?'

'The upshot, if you cannot see it,' he said, glaring, 'is that I am in a fix. I cannot return to Fowey without profits. I may sail north to America. The settlers demand slaves for their new plantations in Carolina. If any are left alive by the time I get there.' He snickered, as if to say he cared nothing for the death of his Negroes except the loss of their value, and lifted the bottle. 'O, and we are using fire, by the way.'

'Fire?' I said, having lost a thread somewhere.

'The smell, dammit. For the bad air you spoke

of.' Gould poured out two good fingers and tossed back the sugar-rum. 'We are burning pitch in the bottom-holds where all the turd and piss and pieces of rotten shark-meat collect and cause the stink.' He looked up. 'Have to feed the slaves something, and we are good at catching shark, if nothing else.' He grinned evilly. 'Now, Mister Stalbone, you appear so interested in the niceties of the Negro trade, do you know what is the best bait for sharks?'

I shook my head, sure that I would not like to hear it, and nor did I like the idea of pitch fires in the hold of any ship, however well arranged.

'The best bait for sharks – remember this, it shall be useful to you one day – is human flesh. When a black one dies, we cut off a limb for bait, catch a shark and feed the cargo. Something efficient about that, gentlemen.'

Gould laughed mirthlessly, but I wanted to change the subject.

'How do you control the fire?'

'Pour pitch down, fire it all up and douse it with buckets of seawater if it goes too strong. Clears the smell for a seven-night or better.' Gould held the black bottle as if it afraid it would fall over. 'Another?' he asked, and refilled his own tumbler without waiting for a reply.

There was a brief silence between us as the rum gurgled into the captain's tumbler. Waspik spoke.

'Gentlemen, Mister Stalbone and I have affairs to discuss.' He brought out a soft leather bag and extracted a bundle of papers. 'Our agreement.'

Wrenching myself from thoughts of Gould and his God-forsaken ship and its gruesome cargo, I sat bolt upright. The agreement! Now I was to find out if I had given away a quarter of the old collier for no good purpose – nothing for nothing.

'Letters at last from London,' Waspik went on, unfolding papers and smiling ingratiatingly around the room. 'And this is what they tell. In March of two years ago, an English cruzer on patrol in the approaches to the Great Estuary took under tow a stranded vessel and brought her safe into Gravesend, the pump barely keeping her afloat.'

'It must be her!' I said, sitting forward in my eagerness.

Waspik beamed, enjoying the moment of revelation. 'Ya – the vessel was the collier-bark, the *Prosperous Anne*.'

I was beside myself. 'She is safe – good old *Prosperous Anne*! I told you she was sound. But what news is there of Barney and my step-father?'

Waspik looked puzzled. 'I have no news of these.'

I sighed. 'Please go on, if there is more.'

'She was beached and the sea-cole shovelled out so that she could be repaired and refloated. The cole was taken into wherries and landed at Billingsgate, where it was sold at the cole-market there by direction of the owner, a Mister Seth Jeffreys, of Wittbay. The collier-bark fetched five hundred and twenty pounds at auction at Petts' Yard, by Wapping. After deductions for salvage and towing, and repairs to her hull, rudder and spars, the nett sum realised amounted to four hundred and twenty pounds.'

Can it be true, I thought, that at last I may

become a rich man with my own bark? Waspik coughed and took a generous finger of sugar-rum, savouring the unfolding of this story. In irritation, I rubbed my nose which itched as though someone had lit a pipe. I wished the agent would get to the heart of the matter.

'I have caused a search to be done of the bark's papers, and confirmed from the Registry of Lloyd's in Mincing Lane, St Paul's, that sixty three shares were held by the owner, Richard Loftus, but on his death they passed into the creditor, Mister Jeffreys.'

'Creditor?' I cried. 'The shares were my father's – he left them in trust for me!'

Mijnheer Waspik patted the air in front of him.

'Yes, yes – as the papers you kept in your possession clearly show. I forwarded them to lawyers in London, who agree they make a reasonable case that your father was cheated, and thus yourself.'

Waspik offered a finger of sugar-rum, which I accepted and swallowed down.

'But Jeffreys has sold the collier and taken the money anyway,' I said.

'We can find your Mister Jeffreys and pursue a claim.' Waspik crossed his plump legs. 'In conjunction with Henry Linskyl, he transferred a great deal of capital – some of it your capital – into a new venture. A Baltick.'

My head swam as a flood of memories washed into my mind. 'Lord, he did speak about investing in such a venture, that day at Salt Quay. Can I lay claim upon it?'

'That is precisely the case.'

'Why, that's – splendid,' I cried, and coughed, for there was something in this stifling cabin that caught in my throat. 'Mijnheer Waspik, when can I get my money? Shall you go to London? Or shall I go there to make my claim?'

Waspik laughed heartily. 'No, no, no – we make the claim by letters from here – and we wait for news. Mister Stalbone, like it or not, your money is tied up, invested in a ship which may make profit, or lose money on her trading, or disappear at sea, or be taken for a prize or – whatever. Unwittingly, you are now a merchant venturer, and you must be patient until your ship comes home.'

I smiled. It really did seem as though I might get a rightful share of the money from the old *Prosperous Anne*. Despite Waspik, I immediately resolved to get back to London somehow, to wait for news there. The Lord knew when the *Cornelius* might head homewards, but I had a little gold in my pocket now, and perhaps could jump ship for a passage to Europe. I swigged back more rum, and revelled in the idea of coming into my wealth, imagining myself bringing home my own proud ship, with a cargo of timber or skins or horn or cloth from the North Lands, and Abigail waiting to throw her arms around me as I stepped onto the wharf.

Gould coughed and spat into a dish on the table.

'Beg leave, gentlemen,' he said, getting up unsteadily. 'I must see about that blasted smell.' He lurched to the door and out into the passageway, calling for the mates and ship's carpenter.

I snapped out of my reverie. Something was wrong.

'Ah, it's a pity he has had to go,' said Waspik, rubbing his eyes, 'because –'

'Wait,' I cut in. 'There's smoke in here.'

The cabin was filling with a greyish haze. There was a commotion on deck, men running about and shouting. Waspik looked at the deck-head, as if he could see through it to tell what the upset was.

'There is some alarm up there,' said de Vliegel, unnecessarily, 'and I trust the captain is in command of the case.'

'I hope the fires are under control in the holds,' said the ship agent uncertainly.

'This is more than smoking the holds to freshen them,' I said. 'Look!'

Billows of treacly black smoke streamed up through gaps between the boards and filled the cabin. I stood up, sweating.

'For the Lord's sake, the ship is on fire!'

De Vliegel struggled to rise, blue eyes darting from side to side, seeking escape.

Waspik said, 'Calm yourselves. I am sure Captain Gould has it under control. Let us have another drink, gentlemen. I want to tell you –'

'We must see to the ship first,' I said in alarm.

The cabin door burst open. It was Gould, looking distraught.

'I – we need hands to help with buckets. The fire is gaining on us. Come quickly.'

He headed for the steps and de Vliegel followed, stumbling on to the deck. I took a pace to the door and swayed lightheadedly. Too much dam' rum. Where are the pumps? Save the ship, I thought foggily, and what about the Negroes below? I clambered up to the quarter-deck with Waspik lumbering after.

The scene that greeted me was out of my worst shipboard nightmares. From two large gratings let into the weather-deck, one before the mainmast and one aft of it, poured thick grey-black smoke, boiling upwards into the still air, where it formed a column rising hundreds of feet above. Men ran about with sea-buckets, shouting and splashing water down the gratings. There was a continuous wailing sound, like the noise a multitude of chickens crammed in their pens might make when something frightened them, and they would begin to peck and pluck and trample on each other in agitation.

'The pumps!' I cried, grabbing a seamen who rushed by. 'Get everyone to the pumps and we can haul water.'

'Only one pump bloody works,' said the sailor and lurched off.

'Captain!' I yelled, spotting Gould at the rail, handing buckets in a chain. 'You must organise the men at the pump. Come on, man – you can't fight such a fire with buckets.'

Gould looked at me savagely. 'Neither pump is any good, you interfering idiot. The chain-pump is busted and we haven't money for repairs. The forward pump's brake just sheared. Get a bucket if you want to help.'

We had to bring up water by the tun to have any hopes of dealing with a fire this strong. I ran to the chain-pump head. It was dismantled, the lifting gear lying about in pieces. With a growing sense of doom, I went forward to see if the fore-pump were truly irreparable. In doing so, I stepped across the main grating, chained and bowsed down, that stretched almost the width of the deck. It belched smoke from the belly of the ship. Glancing down, I stopped in horror.

Underneath the hardwood slats of the heavy grating was a mass of seething humanity, the Negroes chained and locked below. Some had managed to get free enough to put their fingers through the grating and I realised I had stepped on their hands even as it dawned on me what I was looking at. The faces were jammed at the slats of the hatch-cover, pressed hard against it, their tongues lolling, a sea of black round heads with white eyes wide with terror and red mouths screaming for their lives. Smoke billowed around them. I could see no more than a few inches into the Hell that must lie right below.

'O, the Lord save us,' I muttered, taking a step back.

Next second, I was down on my knees tugging at the grating, trying to lift it. The fingers beneath it grabbed at mine, and I yanked away my hands in disgust. The fingers fluttered near my feet, trying to grip them. The uncanny wailing sound had become a high scream which, I now understood with a creeping prickle along the back of my spine, was the agony of the hundreds of human beings just under the decks, choking and roasting to death as they tried to free themselves from their chains.

I stood up and looked wildly around.

'An axe here!' I screamed. 'Get axes, for Christ's sake!'

Seamen were running about in a chaotic manner, some with buckets, others aimlessly going through the motions of dealing with the fire. One group was busy lowering boats over the side, and Captain Gould was nowhere to be seen. A loud crack rang out and instinctively I ducked, expecting a spar to crash down. Nothing fell. O God, I thought with a shudder, the crack came from below. Her hull is opening with the heat.

I ran to the nearest seaman and grabbed him. 'Help me! Where are the axes?'

The seaman had panic in his eyes. He shook his head and wrenched free, dodging away in the smoke. I could hardly see more than a few feet, and fumbled back to the quarter-deck, searching for Gould or Waspik or de Vliegel or an officer of the ship. I found the agent leaning over the taff-rail, gasping and trying to find clear air to breathe.

'Where is Gould?' I shouted.

Waspik, red-faced and choking, waved his big head from side to side and retched over the rail. I turned in despair and my eye fell on an axe lashed by the wheel. Thank God, I thought, pulling out my knife and slashing at the bindings in a fury. Wrenching the axe free, I dived into the smoke and followed the rail to guide me back to the weather-deck. The screams were louder again here. At the grating, the fingers still waved like worms, dozens, tens of dozens of them now. They must be tearing themselves free of their manacles down there.

'Get your fingers clear!' I screamed. 'Move your hands away!'

It was such a stupid thing to say, I realised,

choking back the smoke. Salty water streamed from my eyes. I have to cut their fingers to save their lives.

I planted my feet apart and swung the axe high, bringing it down with a strength born of terror. The axe blade clanged on the hardwood, jarring my arms and sending sharp splinters flying into the air. The blade hardly made a chip in the solid oaken grate, so I swung the axe again and this time it bit into the wood, sticking tight. As I worked it free, red stains seeped into the broken grain around the cuts I had made. I swung the axe yet again, and levered it free and swung it once more like a demon. The wood rang dully and the axe blade made small impressions, yet I swung it time after time, and the splinters flew about and the bloody stains grew and spread across the fresh, white wounds of the cut wood.

The smoke streaming from the grating turned black and thick as treacle. It was all I could do to avoid slicing my own feet with the blade. I heard only the clunk and ring of the axe and the howls of agony and the rasp of breath in my chest as I struggled to find strength for another swing and break open the stubborn grating. The deck shivered beneath me as I brought down the blade, yet still the grating would not yield. A second crack rang from the depths of the hull. The ship was burning her timbers through, and splitting herself open below the waterline.

Breathless and choking, I thought I would die from lack of air. I staggered clear of the grating and reeled to the rail, groping blindly, tripping on tools

231

and jars and barrels scattered around the deck. I found a space free of smoke and gasped a dozen clean breaths, my raw throat in agony. I turned to see flames shooting high into the boiling smoke as it burst from the grating. They were gone, doomed, all those people in their chains.

I sank to the deck, sobbing in rage and helplessness. The deck was warm – hot, even – under me. Perhaps I should get off her while I still could. It struck me I might be the last seaman on board. But I found it contemptible to rise up and save myself while hundreds died within an arm's reach. To leave now seemed too terrible a thing, not while I had breath left in my body.

I staggered to my feet and picked up the axe. It felt enormously heavy. I wiped the smoke and tears from my eyes and fought back into the flames. The heat seared my clothes and scorched my feet. Still I beat at the smoke and tried to go forward, waving the axe in fury at the great gouts of flame in front of me, as if I could push it aside. The bare flesh on my arms burned, and my hands were balls of pain. With a wail that came shuddering out of the depths of my soul, I dropped the axe and stumbled away, at last finding clear air. I was blinded by the hot smoke, and it choked me. My hands seemed soft and pulpy as I gripped the rail. I felt heat around my head and knew my hair was ablaze.

Willing my muscles to respond, I hauled myself to the top of the rail and threw myself over. I landed in the water to a sizzling sound as my flaming clothes and skin were doused. It was cool. I floated face down for a long time just beneath the surface, suspended in the great, calm, silent pool of sea-water. Blinking open my eyes, I found myself gazing at the clean sandy bottom of the lagoon, and saw a school of small fishes swimming below me. After a time, I saw the brooding dark shape of the *Tryall*'s hull nearby, still and quiet in the clear green water, showing no sign of the torment within her wooden walls.

I broke surface and sucked air painfully into my scorched lungs. Shouts reached me and a boat appeared. Eager arms stretched down to haul me upwards, and I passed gratefully into unconsciousness.

# 13
## *Venture Bound*

*I sensed an awakening. The core of my being rose sluggishly from the depths, like a bubble in a barrel of viscous, boiling pitch. As the globule burst at the surface, death relinquished its grip. I still lived, though where and in what condition I could not tell. I struggled for relief from the sticky heat of sickness that bathed me in sweat. Sodden, filthy covers clung like a winding sheet to my dampened skin.*

*The ship moved, her timbers creaked. I heard the gurgle of water as she lifted her stern to the slightest of swells and – ah! a shiver of relief shot into me. I am at least aboard a ship. She is on an even keel, and anchored. Sheltered. Calm. Hot. But where? And what ship? I fought to remember, but again the fog closed in.*

*I was surrounded by night. I tried to cry out but my tongue stuck against the dryness of my mouth, and only a cracked whimper broke the silence. I gathered what strength was left, and shifted for respite from the heaviness of my limbs. A pain of flaming intensity engulfed me, gripping like the bite of a great white shark. I fell back, agonised, and waited for the beat of the rhythms of pain to subside.*

*There came a sound – irregular, drawn out, a*

scraping sound. I dreamed of a skeletal figure laboriously holystoning a ship's decks. The deathly apparition knelt on the planks, its face hidden, scraping back and forth, grinding and polishing until the wood gleamed like bones whitened in the sun. I longed to see its countenance, but even more I feared the horror of it.

After a long while, I understood that the sound was my own breathing. The rasp became a rattle. Panic rose, and blood roared through the chambers of my skull. I was borne along as if by a boarding wave that swept me into the scuppers. I submitted to its overwhelming strength. The pounding subsided, and my breathing resumed its ragged, limping gait.

A voice came nearby, soft and murmuring. Someone lifted my head and put water to my lips. It flowed coolly over the cracked, dry tongue. My muscles tensed like pincers so I could not swallow, but then my gorge relaxed and the delicious liquid passed into the gullet. A woman's face swam before me, and I saw my mother bent close, her lips moving in silent words of comfort. But the vision faded the moment I reached out to touch her. Desperate, I tried to speak but what burst forth was no more than a broken gasp and a spasm that racked me from end to end.

Then came a moaning like a winter wind whining through a ruined abbey lost on the empty moors. I dreamed I was aboard a ship in hard weather in the cold and lashing dark, then I was enveloped in a nightmare of choking dust. From this blackness, I heard the sounds of fighting, men crying out, the

235

discharge of muskets, cutlasses clashing. As suddenly as they had come, the sounds faded and I lay beached upon a sandy shore, bathed in the sun of a Tropick day. I rose and walked into the warm surf and swam, then drifted across an endlessly blue and vast expanse of ocean until I saw a fine, proud ship. I yearned for her, longed to gain her. By moving in the water, I closed on the great bark, and was lifted aboard by unseen hands.

Becalmed, the ship rolled like a dead whale, sails slatting and the gear crashing aloft. Broken spars littered the decks, the sails hung torn and lifeless in the flaccid air, blood spattered her boards. The abandoned bark's hatches lay thrown open, and a banshee wail rose from up them. Drawn forward, resisting, I was pulled towards the black holes. An intolerable stench of corruption emanated from their yawning mouths. I gagged at the sickly sweet smell of open wounds, the cloying stench of excrement, the foulness of scorbutic breath that suffocated me. Yet I stumbled on towards the miasma of corruption pouring from the gaping blackness of the ship's hatches. As I drew fatally near, something moved below. Without warning, swarms of emaciated figures burst from the openings, running at me, their flesh on fire, iron anklets glowing red at their feet, neck-bracelets clanking, bony arms outstretched, their faces blank and grinning –

I awoke screaming. I tore at the bonds and thrashed from side to side. In the darkness, I wept for mercy. Strong hands forced me down, soothing words were spoken. A bottle at my lips sent a bitter *draught searing down. I slept again, deep in the oblivion of a nether world.*

Alone in the cramped surgeon's bay in the *Cornelius*'s stern quarters, I gave thanks to my God for deliverance from the delirium, and rested my healing body. I rolled over, half awake, and winced. The skin on my hands and face had healed without pus, but still it pained me to move. Brogel insisted I remain in the sick room and be washed, to deter the putridity that all too terribly made wounds mortal.

In the absolute stillness of the Tropick night, I heard a movement in the passage outside. It was just enough to wake me fully, now that I slept more lightly and swallowed fewer laudanum draughts. It was the dead watches of the night, and I remembered hearing six bells struck not long since. Or had I fallen asleep and awoken much later?

The door opened with the rustle of a dress. It sounded like the Cuban girl, who had bathed me since I was brought from the *Tryall*.

Her voice whispered, 'Mazzew.'

Neeta fumbled for a flint and lit the candle beside my bunk. She had brought a fresh bowl of water and oil.

'I come to wash your wounds,' she said softly.

'Neeta – but you came last night. Why are you not asleep?'

She smiled in the yellow light.

'The capitan takes much laudanum. He is in big fever. Too hot to be with him.'

She touched my tender forehead with her cool hand. In the light of the flame, her eyes glowed and the gold shone at her neck where the heat of the night had put a silken sheen on her skin. I longed to touch her. She moved over me, dabbing at the crusty scabs over my eyes and murmuring in a voice like a warm night breeze off the land. Her breath was as sweet as sea air, and soothing.

'Neeta can make the hurt go away,' she whispered.

The loose shift hung free of her smooth brown breasts as she bent over me, and I reached out to feel their roundness, stroking her through the cloth. She kissed my mouth with soft butterfly touches, and I pulled her closer. She smiled, and parted the front of her shift to reveal the innocent nakedness beneath. My mouth fell open, but she put her fingers to my lips.

'Mazzew stay quiet now,' she said huskily, and moved onto the bunk, sitting astride me and running her hands over my chest. She pulled aside the seaman's slops I wore around my loins and brought my nakedness against hers. It was as if I were being led to a cavern of pleasure where heady scents filled my nostrils and the rhythms of music washed over me.

'Neeta,' I said hoarsely.

'Sshh.' She bent towards me and joined our mouths at the same time as our bodies became one.

But when I awoke, she was gone. Only her scents remained to tell me I had not dreamed her.

The *Cornelius* had been in harbour too long, and wanted a sea passage to wash off the weed and slime that clung to her waterline. In the stuffy and crowded Great Cabin, I stood by the table, perspiring in the afternoon's cloying heat, waiting for the captain and the cool, fair-skinned Supernumerary Sorenson to begin. It had been an uncomfortable shock to find Captain Gould with them, seated a little apart, nursing a black bottle.

'Are you ready to work?' said Brogel, surveying me. I noticed a yellowish tinge at the corners of his tired eyes.

'Aye, sir, I am that.'

'Good. Our commercial transactions are done here.' He fingered some document rolls on the table in front of him and nodded at Sorenson.

The Super picked up a roll of papers, bound together with a length of green ribbon. He fixed his blue eyes on me.

'When the body of Hubert Waspik was dragged from the lagoon,' said Sorenson, 'tied to its wrist was a leather bag containing papers. This packet would appear to be yours.' He held it out as if it contained the vilest substances known to the bilges of an ocean-going ship.

I snatched the bundle from him and peered at it. My name was scratched in ink on the outside, and there were several papers rolled inside the outermost one.

Brogel embarked on a prolonged bout of coughing, and put a cloth up to cover his mouth. When he it took away it showed dirty red stains. At last he was able to speak.

'We need bigger prizes.' Captain Brogel sounded unsure, and continued hesitatingly. 'Here in the Main, we have taken gold and a few spoils. The men have lived a rummy life. Warm nights and easy women.' He shot me a look.

Supernumerary Sorenson snorted. 'These indolent sailors enjoy too little work and too much rum.'

'The owners are dissatisfied, Sorenson tells us,' continued Brogel, 'and the committee brings our sojourn to an end. We are to turn north in hopes of taking one of the Spanish gold-ships that ply homeward along the Florida coast.'

North towards America, I thought, and perhaps a return to Europe, the prize I longed for most. I became aware I was standing there with my mouth hung slackly open, and quickly closed it up, but neither the captain nor the Super had noticed. As for the Englishman, he appeared to have lost interest in all matters bar the bottle he cradled so protectively.

'Moreover, we are to meet on the American coast with an English warship,' continued Brogel, 'and join together for an attack on the French patrols.' He heaved a sigh. 'It must of course go to the vote. Stalbone, I want something of the mind of the foc'sle.'

I stiffened. There was nothing to be gained from telling tales on the crew.

'On behalf of steerboard watch, sir, I say we are ready and willing.' I was on the point of saying more, for I was as sure of their loyalty as I was sure the *Cornelius*'s planks were caulked up tight. But I managed to stop, for the least said the better. Keep your sea battles and raiding parties, I thought, this is territory just as dangerous.

'Go on, second mate,' said the Supernumerary, leaning forward.

Gould belched and grasped the rum bottle.

I addressed the captain. 'I have nothing more to report, sir.'

'Very well.' Brogel coughed. 'You should know – and tell the Barbar Youssef – that Captain Gould accompanies us on passage and shall assist me in the running of the ship. Dismissed.'

Crossing the weather-deck, I went right forward to the beak and sat on the bowsprit by the spritsail yard, over the green waters of Great Bay, where I untied the ribbon from Waspik's packet.

I found the original paper on which the agent had scratched the name of the *Prosperous Anne* when we had first met in the Great Cabin. This paper was folded around letters from agents in London whose dates showed they had arrived in Sint Maarten more than a year earlier, aboard an English warship, the *Success*, out of Portsmouth. She had voyaged via the established southerly route to the Canaries and the Windwards, taking the favourable winds and current, and called at the island with mail and packets.

There was a sealed letter, with my name on the outside. The letter, folded and rumpled, and a touch salt-stained, was of vellum parchment, and I peered in surprise at its seal. With a shock, I recognised it as Mister Jeffreys' own mark, the one he used for commercial business. I broke the wax and smoothed the paper flat on my thigh. My heart leapt when I saw the handwriting. It was Abigail's.

*My Dearest Matthew!*' I read, almost in disbelief. '*I have learnt from the Dutch agent that you are alive! It is a miracle of the Lord and fills my heart with joy! We had given you up for lost, but the Good Lord was by your side that terrible day aboard the collier-bark. The pity is He could not save your step-father, but we have His Mercy to thank for sparing the Goodhew boy.*

*Mister Waspik wrote my father on business matters but I see his correspondences, as I am his only trusted scribe. The agent told us of your claim and my father was most angry, but Mister Waspik bargained with him and he allowed that your share of the money was put into the Baltick venture. I suppose the agent has told you this.*

*My father does not know that I write to you. Whitby is in straits and the people dispirited. I waited for you, Matthew, I longed for you to return. We have taken passage on an English naval ship, the* Success, *for the colony of Carolina, and I am to marry John Lynskill when we arrive at Jamestown, where he purchases blackamoors for a plantation, and we shall grow tobacco.*

*Are you well? How do you live? Waspik told us little. I wonder what cargoes your ship carries, and where.*

*Dearest Heart, I say this now, knowing my future is without you. I shall never forget that day we kissed on board the collier. I have carried the memory with me close to my breast since we were parted. Now I fear we shall not see each other again.*

*Always know that I shall remember you.*

*With all my womanly love, Abigail.*

For minutes, I stared at the letter, and read it over and again. How her face came alive in my memory after our long separation! I closed my eyes against the fierce Tropick sun and wished myself back in the damp, grey Whitby streets, listening for her footsteps on the cobblestones, waiting for her to appear with a smile.

She was not married yet. But the letter was more than a year old, so by now she must be wedded to Lynskill after all. Yet, I thought, hardly daring to allow myself the pleasure of it, what if she is not? And the *Cornelius* is bound north, perhaps for America itself. If we touched the coast, I could jump ship and find Jamestown. I pressed the vellum to my chest and held it there, my heart filled with longing. I shall see you again, Abigail, I said quietly. Soon, somehow.

There came a movement from behind, and Gaspar Rittel's anxious head appeared in the beak.

'Second mate, steerboard watch begs your presence in the foc'sle.'

They would not leave me with my luxurious dreams for a second. With an unjustified scowl at the poor lad, I hurriedly folded the letter and, together with Waspik's bundle, tied the ribbon tightly round and tucked it inside my weskit. I followed Rittel to the foc'sle hatchway where conversation ceased when I clambered down the steps into the gloom of the seamen's quarters. As my sight adjusted to the dimness, I saw the shadowy outlines of the men of steerboard watch, and a few of Youssef's larboard, ranged around squatting on the sole, swinging their legs from hammocks or seated on the edge of bunks, some whittling at sticks or working with rope-ends.

Quaker John moved close. 'Is it true the captain plans to leave the Main and go to America?'

'There is to be a vote,' I said warily. 'The captain shall let you have the choice.'

'Brogel is finished. There are plenty aboard for Pengarth – or Gould.'

So this was it, there was rebellion brewing.

'I am not of that opinion, John,' I said, eyeing the fellows in their bunks.

'You'll have to choose in the end,' said the Quaker.

'Between what?'

'Must you have it carved on the deck-head? Drop Brogel now, and Pengarth might let you alone.'

'That is mutinous talk, John.' I wondered how far it was the Quaker himself who stirred the brew. Then my temper snapped. 'Get a light here – Gaspar, a candle!'

The sharpness of my command made the young sailor jump up and fumble nervously with a flint till a candle glowed. The whittlers and fiddlers stopped and cocked their ears. I took a deep breath.

'Hear me. Brogel may be in a fever, but he is the only man to captain this bark to success. Gould is a drunk who burnt his own ship without a care for the seamen or the Negroes aboard.'

A few men grunted in acknowledgement.

'Pengarth would make us a renegade – pursued by the Navy, a legal prize for any damm'd Spaniard or Frenchman.'

The silence was impenetrable. I knew the risk of

it getting back to the sailing-master, but the rot had to be cut from this festering mutiny.

'What should we stay in the Main for? Rum and women, while the ship-worm softens the timbers under your feet? What have you got from it but a few paltry pieces of eight and a pox on your pricks? Such Spanish leavings are not enough for me – I want a great sea prize.'

The men shifted and sat up in their bunks, and I knew I had them. They were seamen far from home, the shore life and all things of the land left far behind to go aboard a privateer and grow rich – or dead. They were natural men like every one of us, I thought, reckless and greedy, like fat bonitos with their mouths wide open, chasing the flying fish down the swells.

'We are as fine a flyer as ever sailed these waters. Faster than the Spanish, better seamen than the English, abler gunners than the French – aye! We can fight them, sail rings around them, and fly away to the horizon. We can take richer prizes than Gilly Pengarth's petty spoils. What about a Spanish galleon for our prize?'

I banged my fist into my palm.

'Gaspar – Eli – Jakob – Hannes – Henry! With Gilly Pengarth, you'll die in drink and leave your carcass rotting in some Tropick Hell. Or you'll hang for a pirate in London or Amsterdam. With Brogel, we shall capture a prize with gold enough in her to sink us. Gold enough to dine on roasted meat forever, and make women claw at your briches. Gold enough to buy your own ship, to win a free pardon, to live your lives as kings or princes!'

The men murmured amongst themselves, half saying aye softly under their breaths, the others shaking their heads and cursing in whispers. But I had sown doubt.

'Truck to keel, I am for Brogel,' I said. 'He'll take us to the richest prizes. I fight for Josua Brogel till the day he dies. Who is with me?'

There was a sound from the hatch and Youssef came down the steps. He must have been listening. I smiled, for I was sure the Barbar would back me.

'You are loyal to your captain, Mattoo,' he said slowly, eyes glinting in the candle's glow. 'But if Brogel dies, then I am loyal only to myself.'

I fought an urge to fall on him with my fists and make him pledge for our good captain. But there were low grunts of agreement from the seamen. This was harder than I had reckoned.

'That's enough of this talk,' I said, clapping my hands. 'Back to work, fellows. We are nothing unless we keep our ship in proper trim.'

With that, I headed for the companionway to let my anger cool in the breeze. Youssef followed and drew me aside to the rail.

'Pengarth wants an easy life in the Main,' he said. 'Gilly is stupid. But Gould – this is an evil man, Mattoo. He is our danger.'

'How can we stop them? Pengarth controls the armoury.'

'There's more than one armoury on the *Cornelius*, Mattoo,' said the Barbar in a low voice. 'Youssef has collected many weapons in raiding, and none knows but old Eli – and you. We can arm a dozen, maybe fifteen, with pistols and cutlasses.'

'You're planning your own dam' mutiny!' I cursed bitterly for not seeing it sooner.

'Not until – unless – Brogel dies.'

'Then you'll take the *Cornelius* for yourself,' I said fiercely. Lord, I thought, why have I been so unprepared for this?

'The men choose in the end,' said the Barbar, 'And Youssef is not the only one they respect, Mattoo.'

Grinning broadly, he gave me a friendly punch and leapt away, shouting to muster the larboard watch for their deck work. But the Barbar's reckless spirit left me uneasy to a degree, for what I feared most – above any sea battle or bloody raid ashore – was a mutiny in the confines of our bark.

The *Cornelius* ticked off the leagues through the days and nights, heading northwards under all plain sail, eager to see America. In a breeze from southeast, her yards were eased just shy of square and a merry wake creamed from her stern as she bowled along on a broad reach with the sails bulging full of a warm wind. But the sailors were less settled than the vessel beneath their feet. Fearing idle thoughts, I busied them working the ship into what Brogel called 'Vlissingen fashion', to keep their minds from brewing mutiny.

Noon approached and, as the sun rose towards its zenith, I went with Gaspar Rittel on the quarter-deck to shoot the angle for a latitude. On the lee side stood Captain Gould, sheltering under the mizen sail from the heat of the sun and looking unsettled in the guts. He was in close discussion with Supernumerary Sorenson, who leaned coolly with one hand on the rail, unconcerned by the ship's motion, but sombre faced.

As I sighted along the back-staff, the ship rolled awkwardly and the instrument struck the rail. I put out a hand to steady myself and caught a wearied look from Captain Brogel. Though the wind held and the ship's speed was admirable, he was as leery as a seaman behind an ox-plough. Scowling, he stumped across the quarter-deck to the sailing-master.

'Stream the log again, Mister Pengarth, if you will,' the captain ordered.

With a dismissive smirk at me and my back-staff, the sailing-master flipped the minute glass, cast the log-chip and freed the reel. The line ran out whirring as the log-chip trailed from the stern.

'Seven and a half by the log,' he sang out as the glass ran empty.

'Again,' said Brogel, standing with his back to me and studying the wake. When the knots were counted again, he walked unsteadily back to the chair lashed to the rail and slumped into it, eyes closed.

I raised the back-staff once more and concentrated on getting an angle. Taking the paper on which Gaspar had noted down the figures and recorded the noon meridian, I crossed to the sailing-master's log-book. With surprising swiftness, Pengarth moved to block my way.

'Hands off, Stallyboon,' growled the big man.

'I'll give you permission to examine the sailing-master's log, and no one else.'

I knew he was baiting, so I spoke levelly. 'Sir, permission to –'

'Granted, my handsome.' Pengarth's grin showed through the fronds of his ginger beard, and he stepped aside. 'Just for the time being, until we have no more need of your Almanacks and Science.'

As calmly as I could, I copied out the readings showing the distance run since the previous day's noonsight. I was determined to do nothing to give him cause to punish or confine me.

'And when shall that be, sir?' I asked, straightening and meeting his eye.

'When we go a-coasting again,' said Pengarth. He lowered his voice. 'But if I had my way, I'd dispense with your calculations here and now.'

'Then we might lose our way at sea, sir,' I said, but I knew very well what dispensing with my calculations truly meant, especially on a lonely night-watch.

'We'd get on well enough, my sea bird,' said Gilly Pengarth heartily, 'with Captain Gould's fine nautical skills.'

'Navigator!' It was Brogel, calling with undisguised irritation. 'Go and work the sight.' His appearance was haggard, perhaps from the dark suspicions haunting him since our narrow vote, perhaps from the debilitation of fever. 'When you have made the plot, I shall review your calculations myself.'

'Aye sir, but I am sure that –'

'That's enough, Stalbone.'

The yellow skin was drawn tight over the captain's cheekbones, and the dullness in his gaze showed the sickness gaining control. As I turned to go, I noticed Pengarth grinning and I was tempted to approach the captain and lance the rising boil there and then.

'Stalbone, I said get below to work your plots!'

Brogel's angry shout drove me off and I slunk down the steps to the Great Cabin. With something like relief, I engrossed myself in working the position. The charts showed the American coastline illustrated with mangrove trees, swamps and great-jawed monsters like caymans. Lingering over the inlet marked 'King James's Town', I fell to wondering, and failed to hear Neeta enter the room. She put her hand on my shoulder and I spun round.

'Neeta!' I cried. 'Don't let the captain find you with me, for the Lord's sake.'

'Capitan is sick, Mazzew,' said Neeta sadly.

'Dear Neeta,' I said, thinking how poorly she looked herself. The glow of vitality had diminished and even the luxuriant hair fell limply over her brown shoulders. But her eyes had not lost their sparkle.

'With rest and fresh supplies we shall all be restored,' I told her, taking her hand. 'We shall be in harbour soon enough.'

She moved close. 'Which harbour?'

'We are heading north for Carolina waters.'

'Capitan is in danger, I think. I see this Gould, how he looks at him. You help capitan.'

My heart went out to her. 'Aye, Neeta. But sometimes he doubts those who are for him.'

There came footsteps on the companion.

'Away now!' I urged, and the Cuban girl was gone in a flurry of skirts. When Brogel entered the cabin, I was hunched over the chart.

'Well, Stalbone?'

'Sir, I – I believe this is our position.' Covering my confusion, I twisted the sea-chart round, offering it to him.

'You believe this is the ship's position, what so.'

Brogel threw himself into the seat and stared through the sternlight at the zigzagging wake frothing behind. The ship must be doing eight knots now, I reckoned. For a moment, Pengarth and Gould were driven from my mind by the Navigational concern that greatly troubled me.

'Sir, if I may – the latitudes seem to show we progress north faster than the log records. What of the great sea-river?'

'You pester me with this obstinate question,' said the captain impatiently.

'But we must try to reckon it, sir. Can you not say how the sea looks when we are in the Florida current?'

Brogel sighed hugely. 'Some say the colour of the water changes, and the shape of the waves, too, when there's north in the wind.' His eyelids drooped as if he were imagining an insurmountable difficulty. 'The American coast when we close it lies low and flat for hundreds of leagues. There are shoals offshore. We shall have little warning before we go into soundings.' He focused on me with difficulty. 'Navigator, our position is perilous.'

'Aye, sir. But I am certain enough of these sights –'

'I did not refer to that.' The captain leaned forward. 'What do the men say now?'

His breath stank of putrefaction and I shifted uncomfortably.

'Sir,' I began hesitantly, 'the vote was close. The men are – unsettled. Some listen to those who call for our return to the Main.'

'Aye!' snorted Brogel. 'The sailing-master, what so? He says Carolina means the worse for them and they believe it.' He leaned forward, head in hands, as if about to weep. 'And no sight of a damm'd prize ship.'

There was a long silence, which I broke by clearing my throat.

'The position, sir.'

Brogel brought himself back to the present reality with a struggle. He studied the sea-chart for an age. With the dividers he picked off a distance to the land, and I craned forward to see where on the coast our intended landfall might be.

'The ship's position is about one hundred leagues from Carolina,' said Brogel, 'according to your findings, Stalbone.'

'Aye, sir.'

'We shall lay our course for the King's colony of Charlestown,' the captain said without looking up. 'Draw the new track.'

The blood pounded in my skull. I knew Charlestown to be an established colonial settlement on the Carolina coast. It was less than fifty leagues south of Jamestown. I took up the chart and the rule, trying

252

to steady my hands, which I am sure shook visibly as I marked a line from the *Cornelius*'s position to a river bay on the coast.

'You, I hope, are loyal, Stalbone, for I need your help to Navigate this coast,' said Brogel in a tremulous voice. 'And I need relief from the fiendish Tropick heat. Thank the good Lord in His mercy, the nights are cooler as we press north.' The captain passed a hand across his brow. 'Are you done? Dismissed, then.'

Crossing the quarter-deck, I watched Pengarth standing possessively by the log-reel, but avoided his eye and stepped quickly up to the foc'sle for an hour's rest. In the hammock, stripped but for my slops, I lay swaying gently in time with the *Cornelius*'s movements. The bark held nothing for me now, it seemed, but the prospect of some awful strife.

Instead, I longed for America. From Charlestown, could I reach Jamestown, perhaps aboard a coasting vessel? Or was there a passage by land? As soon as the bark made harbour, I would jump ship and go in search of Abigail.

# 14

# A Long Reach

'I tell you, I must see the captain.'

Exasperated, I was at the quarter-deck companionway, fizzing like the touch-hole of a culverin on the point of its discharge. The Supernumerary held me back with a raised hand.

'The captain is feverish and cannot be disturbed.'

'Sir, I have been disbarred from plotting our position since we turned west-northwest. We are closing a dangerous coast.'

'Raise your concerns, if you must, with the sailing-master. He is due on deck in –'

'Aye – in two more hours! I know full well when the sailing-master is due on watch, Mister Sorenson.'

I stalked across the quarter-deck and stood by the steersman, seething. I glared at the compass and glanced aloft to scrutinise the set of the sails. All's well as far as any bow-legged landsman can tell, I muttered to myself, but the Navigation's out of kilter. We cannot trust the dead reckoning if we are in the Florida current. I must plot the sun-sights.

'Steer small,' I told the helmsman, Jakob Tosher, taking his trick at the wheel.

'Aye aye, sir.'

Why did Gould and Pengarth keep me from the Great Cabin? Was the captain sick to the point of dying? They might be doubling the surgeon's draughts, or preventing Neeta from tending him, anything to hasten his end. I had to find a way in, before we ran on too far.

I stumped to the lee rail and gazed over the side. Brogel was right at least about the look of the sea. No one could tell if the sea-river flowed here, nor judge its rate. All I knew was that it flowed northwards, often with great strength, and just two knots of current would add eight or nine leagues to our logged distance, each and every day. The current was said to run sometimes at twice that speed. The *Cornelius* might be twenty, even thirty leagues, further north than we knew.

I raked the horizon off the larboard bow, fretting that the low coast would give no indication of dangerous shoals. The lookout might be vigilant, yet he was there to spy a sail, for everyone had convinced themselves the land was far off.

After a while, Captain Gould joined me at the rail.

'Hey, Mister Second Mate,' he said breezily, 'don't you stream the log?'

I stuck to what I knew.

'Twice of the watch and at the change of the watch is the captain's order and it suffices. The log hardly gives an accurate reading here.'

'O, how's that?' said Gould, with a leering grin.

'The current. The latitude can show it but I am not allowed –'

'Bollacks,' said Gould. 'There's no current. You

should learn respect for those who have Navigated hereabouts.'

'I believe we must swing the lead, Captain Gould, rather than stream the log.'

'O do you? The senior –' he stressed the word '– officers disagree. I think it best you hold your noise, second mate.'

'Aye, sir,' I said, and buttoned my lip. The Lord forbid, I thought, that our ship should fall into the hands of this Gould.

Gilly Pengarth appeared at the change of the watch, and I hesitated before quitting the quarter-deck.

'What concerns you, Stallyboon?' said Pengarth. 'Worms eating your guts? Get off to the foc'sle.'

'Sir,' I said cautiously, thinking it futile and perilous even to broach the matter, 'we must post a leadsman and find the depth –'

'We're leagues offshore, man!' cried the sailing-master, incredulous.

'There's the current, sir, and my latitudes –'

'To Hell with latitudes. There's no current. Captain Gould knows these waters.' Pengarth took a heavy step forward, shivering the boards, and grasped my loose shirt. 'I'm at the bitter end with you. Brogel's man you were from the first, a boot-licker who grovels and flatters in the Great Cabin.'

I struggled but the big man held me effortlessly. Something smooth and cold touched my ear.

'You get the point, my handsome,' rasped the sailing-master. 'Things are on the change, and if you don't tread careful, you'll be feeding the sharks.'

He shoved hard enough to send me reeling backwards against the mizenmast. I saw the glint of his knife as he sheathed it.

'Dismissed the quarter-deck!' came his shout.

Fear for our fate brimmed inside me. I had to act. Going right forward to the foc'sle, I found Eli Savary.

'Eli, I am idling you and Jakob off the watches,' I told him. 'Do two and two about at the beak of the ship, and keep low out of Gilly's sight.'

The old fellow rarely missed a nuance. 'An extra pair of eyes to spy a shoaling shore, sir?'

'Aye,' I said sombrely. 'What do you think, old man? How strong is the current?'

He rubbed his bristly chin. 'I reckon we're in the sea-river for sure. I trailed a hook with a bit of pork-rind on it this afternoon, and caught me a fine big kingfish. They love a current.' He gave a gappy grin. 'We'll have fish steaks for a supper tonight, second mate.'

I smiled. 'You and your sea lore, old man! Up on the beak now, for any sign of a sea-change, or a sight of your scaly monsters.'

'It's a poor place for a lookout.'

'If I put you on the foretop, Pengarth shall have you off again and charge me with an insubordination. There's no choice. I'll let Jakob relieve you at four bells.'

'Aye aye, second mate.' He sprang away and I went to tell Tosher.

Two hours later, a growing unease woke me from a troubled sleep. I crawled stealthily from my hammock and stuck my head above the foc'sle hatchway. Darkness had fallen, bequeathing a night sky of radiant clarity. A million starry pinpricks cast a faint illumination across the decks as the ship rushed on, oblivious. The quartering breeze had stiffened, yet the *Cornelius* held on to all plain sail, though her braces groaned and creaked in protest. Pengarth and Gould seemed demented in their haste to reach Charlestown.

Checking aft, I saw Youssef with the steersman on the quarter-deck, and the watchmen asleep by the weather-deck rail. All was peaceful. I kept low as I crept forward to find Eli crouched at the base of the bowsprit and staring fixedly ahead.

'How goes it, old friend?'

I touched him on the shoulder and he jumped in alarm. The whites of his eyes showed faintly in the starlight.

'Look at the waves!' he cried, hoarse with fear. 'It's shoaling up!'

'Quickly, let me up, old man.' I levered up onto the bowsprit and searched the waves ahead of the bounding spritsail. It was hard enough to judge in the full light of day, let alone half awake and squinting out over a dark sea. The train of the waves had foreshortened. They were steeper and closer together, the rollers piling up one atop the other. We had met shallow ground.

'Give the order, sir – turn her about!' Eli's voice shook. 'If we strike, we're going so fast she'll break in half.'

I scanned the distance but the sea-horizon gave no sign of land. If I turned the ship now and was proved wrong, I would be at the mercy of a crowing

Pengarth. But even as I dithered at the bowsprit, I sensed she was hurtling into destruction.

'It's an onshore wind,' said Eli agitatedly. 'If we ground, she'll never come off again.'

The breeze on our larboard quarter was a stiff one, a small gale of wind. The wave train heaped up awkwardly now, confused and broken. For a second, the blackness of the water's surface gave way to an impression of it lightening, reflecting something other than the deeps. It was enough. I remembered the awful tearing sound of hull planks on stone and sand. The sea gave no second chances.

Leaping from the bowsprit, I dashed to the foc'sle hatchway.

'All hands! Steerboard watch – rouse up there!' I shouted down the steps, banging the side of the hatch. I ran on into the waist, beating the legs of the dozing men and shouting for them to get to the belays.

'Brace up on the larboard tack – make ready to tack ship!' As I gained the poop almost out of breath, I saw Youssef's face whirl round at the commotion.

'Youssef, swing the lead, for the sake of the Lord – we're in shoal water!'

The Barbar stood rooted to the decks, amazed.

'I beg you – I'll explain later,' I pleaded, turning to the wheel. 'Bring the wind abeam, steersman.'

The seaman gazed back in disbelief, and held his course.

'Shall I do it myself?' I shouted in a fury. 'Bring the wind abeam, dammit!'

The poor fellow flinched and spun the spokes.

The *Cornelius* swung her bows to larboard in an instant and heeled as she came onto a beam reach.

The sheets loosened and flogged noisily.

'Sheets there – sheet home hard!' I cried and the men ran to the belays. 'Now bring the wind a point ahead,' I ordered, and this time the helmsman, white-eyed, obeyed at once. The sails shook in protest, and from deep in the hull came the groaning of the masts in their steps.

'Brace up, brace up! Ready to tack ship!' I yelled across the waist.

Glancing upwards, I saw the sails and yards spread wide across the night sky, thrumming in the breeze as the ship lurched onwards. I risked a deal of broken gear aloft, or even a snapped topmast.

A looming figure appeared on the quarter-deck.

'What the bloody blazes is this?' It was the bellow from Pengarth that I dreaded. The sailing-master was hastily pulling up his slops. 'Stalbone, what in the name of Neptune's bollacks are you about? You've overstepped so far –'

'The water shoals, sir,' I said as calmly as I could. 'We are in great danger.'

'You're on a charge!' bellowed Pengarth in rage. 'Get those men off the braces. Steersman, resume your course.'

The fellow at the wheel looked nonplussed.

'Hold your course!' I barked. 'Youssef, the lead please.'

What had I brought on myself? It was too late to go back.

'By the mark – two fathom!' sang out the Barbar incredulously, as he hauled in the line. The ship drew one and half fathoms herself. There were just three feet of water under our keel.

'Two fathoms of water!' I said, whirling on the sailing master. 'Your orders, sir?'

Pengarth's mouth hung open. I did not wait for him to recover the power of speech.

'Up helm, tack ship!' I cried.

The bark pointed her bows towards the opposite tack. With a tremendous crashing of blocks and her mighty yards swinging in an arc across the night sky, the *Cornelius* came upright like a startled horse. She staggered through the eye of the wind and for an awful moment paused as if lost.

'Let go the braces!' I cried, and the lines streaked out under the power of the canvas. 'Brace up on steerboard tack!'

The seamen fell back to the capstan winch to sweat up on the other side. With a crack of canvas cloth, the sails filled with wind as the braces hardened and the sheets came home. She heeled onto her new tack and picked up her skirts to fly away eastwards. The *Cornelius*, heeling hard, began to dig her way out of the trap.

'Steersman, hold her to the wind,' I said. 'Full and bye.'

'Full and bye, sir,' called the steersman.

A hunched figure appeared at the companionway, and Captain Brogel tottered over to the wheel. Behind him appeared Gould and the Super, pulling their clothes on. Steadying himself by the mizen and clutching his chest, Brogel's voice shook.

'What is the meaning of this, Stalbone?'

'With respect, sir,' I said, going to him, 'we have run into two fathoms.'

He swayed and gripped me for support. 'The Lord save us, how can it be so?'

'Two fathom, by the mark!' came Youssef's cry, as he swung and hauled the lead-line.

The captain peered around the darkened quarter-deck. Everyone stood silent, stunned by our nearness to disaster.

'What is our heading?' asked the captain querulously.

The compass lamp glimmered in its binnacle by the wheel.

'East by south, sir,' I told him. 'I have brought her about in hopes of finding a safe course clear. The depth please, Youssef.'

'Two fathom and a half!' came the call.

'Beg pardon, sir,' I said, 'but we must take the speed off her.' I moved to the break of the poop and bellowed into the waist. 'All hands there, aloft and furl the courses!'

As the men moved to the ratlines and pulled themselves up, Gilly Pengarth went to the leeward rail and stared at the water, shaking his head.

'Pengarth,' cried Captain Brogel in a voice that cracked. 'How has this come about?'

The sailing-master came over slowly, glaring. 'Second mate Stalbone has steered off badly during the last watch.'

'It's a falsity, sir, and he knows it –'

'Silence.' The captain wheezed harshly and leant against the mast for support. 'Sailing-master, I cannot understand why we have closed the coast so recklessly.'

Suppressed rage infused Pengarth's voice. 'I – we – we are not near the land. Some fool's tampered with the log.'

'Nonsense – we are in shoal water!' raged Brogel. 'You have endangered the ship while I have lain indisposed.' He spun on me. 'Stalbone, what of your latitudes?'

'Sir, I have not been allowed below to plot my sights. They told me you were too ill.'

'More nonsense!' He whirled on Captain Gould and the Super, who looked shifty.

'By God, Gould – Pengarth – all of you,' the captain blazed. 'You have made an error of enormous proportions. I resume my full command on the quarter-deck from this moment onwards.' Panting, he put a hand on the mizenmast. 'Stalbone, what do you propose?'

'To make off the coast with the utmost caution.' Already, we could sense the ship slowing as the main and forecourses came off her. I called over my shoulder, 'The depth please!' and Youssef sang out three fathoms. 'Then we heave to till daylight while we establish our true position. So far off our reckoning, it'll not be easy. I may be able to shoot a star at dawn, and obtain a good latitude.'

'Can we make Charlestown on a board?'

'I do not know yet, sir.' I did not take my eye off the compass course or the set of the sails for a second.

'We must find that harbour,' muttered Brogel, as if to himself. He rubbed his chest absently and swung on the others. 'Did you hear? We do as Stalbone advises.'

The ship's movement was quicker now we were close-hauled, and as the *Cornelius* lurched into a wave, the captain fell against the rail. Instead of straightening, he sank down clutching his guts. As I ran over, he collapsed sideways and lay face up, eyeballs showing blankly.

'Get Neeta!' I cried.

The Super ran to the hatch and in a moment Neeta's startled face appeared. Sorenson helped her carry the captain below, while Pengarth stood rigid by the rail and I returned to the steering position.

'Youssef,' I called across, 'we must try to follow our own track back out. Let the leadsman carry on. You'd better tell the watches – they'll be short tacking all night but in the morning I shall stand them down for rest, bar lookouts.'

'Good plan!' he said and headed for the waist.

'Ready to tack ship!' I bawled. The men ran eagerly to the braces, a lively enough crew for any ship, I thought, even one in the hands of these commanders.

At a touch by my side, I found Neeta with me.

'Capitan very ill now – he sleep quiet. I think he dies soon.' Her eyes were full of tears.

'Care for him, Neeta. Find the surgeon and his draughts.'

She gripped my hand.

'Dutch man – fat, dead one – Capitan gave him gold for sending to Amsterdam. But he send all gold to Carolina – to Charlestown. All gold from Spanish

264

Main and Hispaniola. At first, just Capitan know, but Pengarth and Gould find out.'

'Waspik?' I said. 'He was entrusted to send the gold back to the owners – but he sent it to Charlestown instead?'

She nodded, crying softly. 'They want gold so bad, I think they kill my capitan now.'

So Hubert Waspik had tried to cheat the *Cornelius* and her owners of her spoils, miserable though they were. It began to make sense – Brogel's desperation to leave the Main and get to Charlestown, Pengarth's and Gould's blind dash for the coast.

'Stay by him, Neeta,' I said softly, giving her a squeeze. 'No harm shall come to him.'

She went to the companionway, casting around her like a wary animal.

I breathed deeply, welcoming the fresh night air. This was even more dangerous than I had bargained on. I reckoned I had to take the bark safe into Charlestown before Pengarth and Gould killed Brogel.

Then I swept my eye around the quarter-deck. There was a ship to be run, and for now I seemed be the only one fit to do it.

For two hours, I tacked the *Cornelius* one way, then tacked her back again, changing boards so often the seamen were exhausted. To relief all round, the marks rose steadily until at last, the leadsman sang out, 'Eight fathom!'

I let the ship run on another hour to give enough sea-room to heave-to till dawn. Gould and the Super reappeared and stood muttering, their heads together, Pengarth close by, hands on the taff-rail, glaring out over the sea.

'Furl main-topsail, back the course. Douse jibsails, let fore-topsail draw,' I ordered.

The men sweated the yards round and the maincourse snapped aback. The ship slowly lost way and settled herself to rest, barely forereaching.

'Helm amidships,' I commanded.

When the ship lay easy and quiet on the water, the Barbar came over with a quizzical look.

'Your watch, Youssef,' I told him briskly, ignoring the unspoken questions. 'Stand down the watches. I'm going to work out our position.'

Youssef blocked my way, and jerked his head in Pengarth's direction.

'They plan to take back the ship.' The Barbar's voice was low, and dark with intrigue.

'Let's not play their game, my friend,' I said. 'They want nothing better than a reason to kill me. Or you. All we have to do is get to Charlestown, and we can find Navy protection –'

'That is stupid!' he spat. 'Now is our best chance.'

'Out of my way,' I said angrily, 'we're going into Charlestown and that's an end of it.'

I shouldered past him and crossed to the companionway. To Hell with you all, I muttered, fight over the ship, squabble over the gold. I care tuppence for it as long as I get this ship to America.

In the Great Cabin, I found Neeta tending the captain with water and sponges. She sang a soothing song in Spanish, but Brogel lay motionless in the bunk, breathing lightly.

Fatigued, I sat down to work the calculations. Comparing the ship's noon latitudes with the log readings, I soon saw how the *Cornelius* had been borne relentlessly northwards by the Florida current, while Pengarth and Gould ignored the danger signs. After an hour's close work, there remained no doubt. We had closed the coast some forty leagues to the north of Charlestown. With the breeze from the south, we could no longer lay the harbour without a long and laborious beat back against the wind.

I studied the chart in a turmoil of conflicting desires. Youssef was probably right and the time to act was now, while Brogel lived and uncertainty reigned in the minds of Gould and Pengarth. Together, we could rally the watches and have the mutineers in irons before they drew a blade between them. But what I saw on the chart sent a thrill surging through me, and drove all else from my thoughts.

The nearest harbour was little more than ten or twelve leagues off, and with this wind we could lay it on a broad reach. It was the late Catholick King's settlement, tucked into the head of a series of channels that pierced fingers of water into the low coastal lands. I reached behind to the bookshelves and took down the volume marked *Harbours of the Coast of America, for Carolina, Georgia and Virginia*. According to this book, at the head of the channel was a safe, sheltered anchorage with swinging room for a large bark.

Pengarth and his fellows thought they were going to Charlestown to get their hands on the booty. But the gold could dam' well wait. Only I knew the ship's true position, and now we would go where I directed.

I reckoned off the compass course to my chosen harbour. The place was called Jamestown.

I jerked awake on hearing two bells of the dawn watch. Head pounding and mouth dry, I found myself sprawled half across the table in the Great Cabin, my every muscle stiff and aching. Pale light filtered through the framed windows, and I cursed my stupidity in having let myself fall asleep. I heard a grunt from behind and there was Neeta draped over Brogel, snoring softly, the long, jet-black hair cascading down her shoulders. The captain slept raggedly on, bereft of colour. Gently, I lifted the girl and laid her legs along the bunk beside him. She half woke and mumbled indistinctly, then fell asleep once more.

I straightened the charts, folded away the precious instruments and tables and, taking up the logbook, mounted the steps to the quarter-deck.

The sky was filled with the flat, grey light of dawn. As my head appeared from the hatchway, the sun burst from a low bank of cloud shrouding the eastern horizon and bathed the ship in its golden glow. The *Cornelius* lay hove-to on an easy Atlantic swell, foreyards backed, and the morning's rays glinting on the tops of the waves. The night had left a rime of damp saltiness on every surface, which the heat would burn off within an hour. I had missed any chance of a starshot at the dawn twilight, but on the instant I knew it no longer mattered.

Pengarth stood by the wheel, examining the compass. Captain Gould and Supernumerary Sorenson leaned at the taff-rail smoking their clays. Seeing me, they straightened up and beckoned.

'We allowed you the luxury of a rest, Stalbone,' said Gould. He was unshaven, and the eyes were shot with blood. From his dirty coat pocket protruded the black neck of a bottle of sugar-rum, and I saw poking out of his belt the handle of a pistol. 'You may now steer us into Charlestown with a clear head.'

I seethed inside, raging at having lost control of events almost as soon as I had gained it.

Sorenson wore an obsequious smile. 'Captain Gould has resumed command. We, the competent officers of the ship's committee, deem Captain Brogel's illness serious enough to prevent him from commanding us to our destination. Therefore – after much deliberation, as no doubt you appreciate – we appointed as captain our most experienced colleague, until such time as a proper vote may be conducted to confirm the correctness of that decision.'

Gould laughed, crinkling up at my obvious discomfort, and wiped the corner of his mouth on a sleeve.

'The Super here has even written it up in his blasted so-called log. Show him, Super, why don't you?'

Sorenson shot a black look at him, but nonetheless produced a leather-bound writing-book.

'I have indeed composed a record,' he said, 'of this – and certain other events – for the benefit of the owners on our return to our home port.' Sorenson held out the book. 'I should be grateful, Mister Stalbone, if you would examine my account and countersign beside the Barbar's mark.'

'Very well, Mister Sorenson,' I said, trying hard to steady my voice. I took up the book and went to the cuddy-box by the wheel, where Pengarth stood, and searched for the small quill and ink kept there.

The sailing-master scowled. 'Have you worked out where the entrance to Charlestown harbour is, Stallyboon?' He jabbed a finger on my breastbone. 'One smart word, and your neck goes like this.' He snapped his thick fingers together. 'You've lost your friend Brogel – he's as good as dead. You answer to me now.'

'Aye aye, sir,' I said, scratching a mark in the Super's book. 'I shall soon enough see us safe into the harbour. I have no wish to endanger our ship.'

Pengarth's eyes narrowed. 'Listen, my handsome,' he began, 'you better –'

'Stalbone!' It was Gould's shout. 'Quit your talk and come here. What's our course to be?'

Gratefully, I broke away from Pengarth and scanned all around. There was no sight of land from deck level.

'What do the lookouts say, sir?' I asked.

'Not a blamed thing, and no wonder,' said the Englishman, pulling out the half-empty bottle and extracting the stopper. 'You brought us so far offshore last night, it'll be all day before we spy the land.'

'Then steer west-northwest, sir,' I told him. 'It's not more than ten leagues into harbour.'

Gilly Pengarth sang out for the fore and main courses to be unfurled and the yards brought round, and the decks were suddenly alive with seamen running to their tasks. The *Cornelius* came reluctantly about, unwilling to find her groove until she carried a proper spread of canvas aloft. The breeze had fallen light, and every stitch of canvas was needed, but when the topgallants were set and drawing, she moved more purposefully through the sea. With the wind behind, Pengarth ordered the studding yards run out and the stunsails set outboard of the courses. When it was done, she answered the helm readily, spinning out a merry wake astern.

On the excuse that I needed to consult the seacharts, I managed to get below to the Great Cabin. From the charts and logs I obliterated the marks I had made in the night, then hid the coastal pilot volume behind several other tomes.

Glancing at Brogel and the sleeping Neeta, I stepped silently over and found a key-ring at the captain's belt. They had overlooked it. Hardly daring to breathe, I slipped it off and went to the gun locker. Opening the locker, I selected a pistol and a pouch, checked that it held six balls, tamps, wad and a filled powder horn. Swiftly, I loaded the pistol, tucked it into my waistband, slipped the pouch into my slops and drew my loose shirt down to cover it. I replaced the key-ring and, with a last look round, left the Great Cabin.

On the quarter-deck, Pengarth was occupied sailing the ship, and Youssef had gone off watch. Gould was getting drunker, while Sorenson had the

271

gullible look of a landsman about him. All's the way I want it for now, I thought.

At mid-morning, a cry came from the maintop lookout. 'Land ahoy – spy land on the bow!'

An hour later, the ship had fetched the dim outline closer and, squinting at the western horizon, I saw the low coast half hidden in a haze where the sea air met the warming land. It gave the place a mysterious and brooding atmosphere.

Gould came over. 'Mister Stalbone, where do we find the entrance?'

'I expect it off our steerboard bow, sir.' I was relieved to hear him ask, for clearly he had not touched at Jamestown before. 'Harden to the wind a touch and keep to the deeper water. There must be four or five fathom all the way in.'

Pengarth ordered the ship slowed, and called for the lead to be swung as the *Cornelius* made her second, more judicious, approach to the coast of America. The soundings showed the ground rising beneath the keel until the ship cruised along in six and seven fathoms of water.

Gould swigged more rum, and gave me a long stare. 'Don't you need your drawings in front of you?'

'There is no pilot's chart, sir. Once we find the entrance, we go in on soundings alone.'

Captain Gould smacked his lips thoughtfully, but seemed satisfied and went off to stand near Pengarth. I could not help fretting, for the time of discovery must be fast approaching. My only wish was to jump off the *Cornelius* before I was run through with a cutlass.

The ship nosed her way gingerly towards the unknown shore, the greater part of which lurked shrouded in a mist rising from the steaming swamp-grasses of Carolina. Half a glass later, the lookouts spotted what might have been an entrance and the *Cornelius* was steered in toward it. It was as uncertain an arrival as any bark could wish to make.

The coast was a pilot's nightmare, a low-lying and featureless plain of swamp-grass pierced by the sea into a maze of inlets. There were no rising landmarks to give us our bearings as we approached, and no way of telling which was the true entrance to the main channel. The *Cornelius* crept forward keeping four and five fathoms under her keel, until we came to what seemed a river's mouth. Then we were stemming a current flowing out to sea, and I knew we had found the way in. Still, I paid close attention to the soundings of the lead, for I had scant confidence now in our quarter-deck command.

Captain Gould slumped rum-sodden and sun-worn under the taff-rail. How I despised his callous disregard for men's lives and freedom, and I reckoned his sly ways and knowledge of men's weaknesses would yet catch us all out. Like the teredo worms that infested a bark's hull and weakened her frames, Gould's cunning might lie unregarded until every tie that bound us had rotted through.

Gilly Pengarth, striding proprietorially back and forth across the quarter-deck, glancing often over the steersman's shoulder, then marching to the break of the poop to give forth a stream of commands, changed course by the minute, now wearing ship, now tacking ship. The gear rattled aloft as our vessel turned this way and that like a horse without a rider, and I knew that the sailing-master, despite his confident tone of voice, was unnerved.

But what did I care now? At the first moment, I would be off. The *Cornelius* held nothing more for me and I longed to shrug her off my back and be away on my quest ashore. I was busy enough for now though, for the sailing-master's barked commands had us second mates, Youssef and myself, sending our watchmen scrambling from the belays to the braces, and aloft to the yards, now setting topsails, now furling courses. Worried that Gould or Pengarth might find reason to suspect my mis-Navigation, I ran to my tasks with one eye on the quarter-deck. Twice, three times or more, I tried to catch Youssef to let him know my intent, but each time we were called to our work before I could speak. My frustration mounted as I scanned the inscrutable landscape for signs of the settlement of Jamestown. Come what may, I had to be in the *Cornelius*'s first shore party, and make my break the moment her cutter's bow grazed the American shore.

A mumbled shout broke my train of thought. 'Stalbone – over here, man.'

It was Gould, clambering to his feet. Gazing blurry-eyed into the distance, he beckoned me over. 'This is Charlestown.'

'It appears so, sir,' I said guardedly, for I was unsure whether he had begun to suspect something might be amiss. 'Have you touched many of the harbours hereabouts, sir?'

'Snake-infested swamp Hell,' he said roughly, and fixed me with his eye. 'I know the Virginia and Georgia coasts a piece, but not the Carolina lands. Perhaps we have need of your nautical arts after all.'

I tried not to show my relief at this news.

'Aye, sir, the nautical arts indeed,' I breathed. 'The lead, the log, the lookout – and the latitude – that's the way I learned it.'

Gould's whiskered face crumpled up like an old canvas bag, and he began to laugh. 'By the Sovereign's bollacks, Stalbone, you give yourself airs. A brief taste of command has whetted you for more, I daresay.' He stopped laughing and seemed to sober up all at once. 'In Charlestown, the Navy is likely to keep a frigate on station. There must be a garrison of troops ashore, in all likelihood. Best not let them know we are mutineers,' he said evilly. 'I want no trouble from you, Mister Stalbone, when we hove in, nor from that damm'd hook-nosed Barbar friend of yours, neither. I trust you take my meaning?'

'Aye, sir,' I grunted, hoping for an order from Pengarth to let me break away.

'My, but that's a sore black look on your face, second mate,' Gould went on. 'It still bothers your mind, does it not, that a slaving captain has taken command of your proud bark?'

The man is insufferable, I thought, and all the

276

more so because he sees into me with such ease. Still I could not help responding to his taunt.

'It bothers me, sir,' I said hotly, 'that you endangered the vessel last night by running her full tilt onto a shoaling shore. It bothers me that you refused to let her Navigator reckon the latitude until it was almost too late. It bothers me that you confine our captain below without allowing the men to vote upon it. Furthermore, I protest –'

'Shut your pompous, blasted hatch, Stalbone.' Gould rested a hand on his sword. 'That is, if you want your neck to stay unbroke, and to keep your quarters whole to your carcass. I suggest you bottle your opinions and get on with your work.'

I felt an utter fool. What was I doing arguing with the man? Glad to make my escape, I sloped off to the rail, resolving to hold back my tongue.

Soon, we found we had worked far into a lead which looked promising, but now widened into a lake with no exit. We had no choice but to turn her back and look for another lead. Then came what I dreaded to hear.

'Stalbone – what about the pilot book?' It was Captain Gould again, advancing on me. 'I fancy I've seen one on Brogel's shelf, and I daresay you have consulted it, but I want to see it in case my loyal Navigator is intent on any trickery. For the whip hand, as it were. Get below and bring it up for me.'

I had to think fast here. Why had I not destroyed the pilot instead of merely hiding it?

'Sir, the pilot for this coast gives nothing on –' I

bit back the words a half-second before I blurted out the harbour's name. 'On this part of the coast.'

'What?' he shouted, red-faced. 'Why, Charlestown is by far the King's most established settlement hereabouts. The anchorage is the safest refuge for a hundred leagues. Don't tell me, Stalbone, that any pilot book would omit to –'

'Masts! Spy a vessel on the steerboard beam!'

The chorus of shouts from aloft stopped him short, and he whirled round to follow the lookouts' pointing arms, all thoughts of the pilot book forgotten.

'What is she?' he bellowed. 'What vessel – a frigate? A warship?' Agitated, he lurched off towards the rail, waving his arms and raising up a great noise. 'Lookouts aloft! Spy out her rig – how many guns is she – how stand her ports? What flags does she fly – name me the ensigns! Lively there!'

Pengarth grabbed the spy-glass from its place by the binnacle.

'English ensign at her truck,' he called with a worried look. 'Warship on Navy station duty, no doubt of it.'

Gould lurched over and took the instrument from the sailing-master. Holding it unsteadily, he examined the scene.

'Hoist the English ensign at the staff!' he called. 'Run up the friendly signals. Keep the ports closed, for the Lord's sake. No man is to show a musket.'

'We shall steer up to where she lies,' Pengarth called. 'It must be the main anchorage.'

By this time, everyone had left their stations and crowded to the rail, craning to see. A wave of relief broke over me as I sloped away towards the waist, for with Captain Gould's attention on the new matter, I had at least a momentary reprieve from my predicament. There would be no pleading with Gould and Pengarth when they found me out. I had the one shot in my pistol, then I could expect a savage thrust to the guts or pike-staff blade into my temple. Better to throw myself over the side now and swim for it. Yet they would be after me in a flash, and I knew only too well that no man can outswim a well-rowed boat. Caught in a trap of my own making, I waited and hoped.

The English warship's presence told us where the anchorage must be, so Pengarth had the *Cornelius* brought round to head up that way. She drifted on the gentlest breeze through the channels and entered a stretch of open water. Slowly we drew nearer as three masts, perhaps half a league distant and all but lost against the green-brown landscape, made their dim appearance, until at the head of the sea-lake we saw the great English bark, bristling with opened ports along her topsides, ready to run out her guns and loose off a broadside. At the shore's edge behind her, a broken-down wooden jetty poked out and a rough track led away into the hinterland. Beyond, where the swamp-grass ended and the scrubland began, rooftops were visible above the enveloping greenery, and wisps of smoke curled up from cooking fires. And there, I thought, must be the settlement.

'Lower the cutter,' said the sailing-master. 'Let's have a leadsman out to sound us to our anchor.'

Instantly, I knew that was my best chance – to

take out the cutter with the leadsman, scull as far off from the *Cornelius* as I could without arousing suspicion and then make a leap from her bows, out of musket range if I was lucky. I moved quickly towards the falls.

'Come on, lads,' I called briskly. 'Eli, Tosher, there! Help me with the cutter.'

'Ahoy, Stallyboon!' It was Pengarth. 'Not you – I want you on the quarter-deck up here alongside me. Where's the Barbar? He'll see to the cutter.'

Reluctantly, I let go the tackles and headed to the quarter. I passed Youssef on the way and tried to signal him by eye, but he only looked puzzled and went towards his task, preoccupied with his own thoughts.

I found Gould and Pengarth in a huddle with Sorenson, and some urgent parleying under way. With their attention off me, I went to the binnacle and took up the spy-glass from there, sweeping it briefly across the English warship's decks, then scanning away to study the terrain. The edges of the bay were fringed with meadows of tall swamp-grass, but beyond was a tangle of shrubs and trees. Far inland, many leagues from the shore, the plain rose towards a line of blue-tinged hills. I imagined a house, with enclosed fields and planted land, and wondered what I might find there – if ever I got away with my life.

My sweep of the horizon returned me to my starting point and, fiddling with the tube of the glass, I squinted at the great English bark. She was anchored right close in to the shore by the landing jetty. Even at a distance, I saw the warship was bearded at the waterline by a rime of thick green weed, as if she had lain too long tethered to her anchors without a sea patrol. Like the *Tryall*, she wore a hangdog air, her yards lowered and the second bower stowed crooked in the catheads. Yet unlike the slaver, she was no modest carrying ship built by merchants with their eye on her burthen rather than her sailing lines. This was a vessel of war, a full ship-rigged twin-decker with blazes of gold paint festooning her carved beak and lighting up her overhanging stern quarters with its beam-width open gallery. With two rows of gunports in her topsides, cannon at the weather-deck rails, and two pair of swivels fore and aft, I reckoned she boasted fifty guns.

As the *Cornelius* furled up her main-topsail and shed way to come to at the head of the bay, I focused on the warship's decorated stern. On it, carved in bold, gold-lined lettering, was her name. Suddenly, in the dancing image of the spy-glass, the letters came sharp. I gripped the instrument, my heart leaping. She was the *Success*.

A wave of shock thrilled into me, and my chest tightened. Quickly, my fingers fumbling with the tube, I brought the spy-glass to bear on the English ship's quarter-deck. Faces at the rail watched the *Cornelius*. At the poop, men in white tops and dark briches moved about, officers of the Navy, going by their dress. One figure stood a way off, clad in light colours. The figure was that of a woman.

I blinked, rubbed my eyes and squinted again through the glass. Could it be her? The *Success* must have hove in here many months ago, and surely Abigail would have gone ashore to the plantation, with her father. And with John Lynskill. Why would she still be aboard ship? Might she be confined there, unable to disembark? The more I peered through the dim spy-glass, the surer I became. Lord, I breathed, it is her, it must be her. She stood there on the deck, surrounded by all the paraphernalia of an English man-o'-war, looking lost and alone. I abandoned all thoughts of escaping to the shore. Somehow, I had to get on the *Success*.

A shout from Gould spun me round in angry surprise. 'Give up the spy-glass, blast you,' he said, coming towards me, 'you've no need of it.' He grabbed the tube. 'Go and see to the signalsmen, second mate – they're too slow.'

Furious, I did as I was bidden. The *Cornelius* had run up the red and white flag of England on her jack-staff off the taff-rail, and now we hoisted signals at the cross-trees to identify ourselves as friendly. After a delay, the *Success* signalled her reply.

'By the mark, seven!' sang the lead-swinger from the cutter going ahead, and the ship's company turned to the business of laying out an anchor. Youssef's watch broke out the main bower from its stow at the catheads and readied it to run out, while Pengarth fussed at them. Gould leant on the rail, studying the scene. Now, I thought, when the cutter returns I shall slip unnoticed over the side and be away in her while the officers are looking elsewhere. I shall have to row mightily to get beyond a shot. I furtively checked the butt of my pistol and cast around the quarter-deck. To my intense annoyance, Supernumerary Sorenson was approaching.

'It appears a desolate place, Mister Stalbone,' he said, grimacing.

I shrugged, trying to end the conversation before it began. Blast your eyes, I was thinking, get away from me, you superfluous landsman.

'A miracle, I think, that you found the entrance at all. Ah, the mysteries of the Navigator's art.'

'Aye, sir, a miracle, as you say,' I muttered. 'And it's remarkable that the Navigator is refused the means to do his work.'

He looked affronted, and moved a pace back. 'My advice to you, Mister Mate, or whatever shipboard name you go by, is to allow affairs that are no longer of any import whatsoever to you to fall from your mind.'

'Beg to dispute, Mister Sorenson,' I said sharply, 'but as a member of the ship's committee, I consider you to have endangered the vessel. The men are not pleased. We should have a vote and –'

'And what, sailor?' he said, backing away. His voice came out as a shrill cry. 'This sounds like a threat of mutiny!'

'Calm yourself, Mister Sorenson,' I said. 'I suggest you save your fears for what happens when the English Navy inquires about our purpose here. In Charlestown.'

'Why?' he said, fear and puzzlement in his voice. 'Why should the Navy take an interest?'

'Did you not hear in Sint Maarten, sir,' I said, moving close and whispering, 'that the King has commissioned certain English warships to claim spoils and prizes from Dutch-ventured barks where they find them? For all we know, the bark on station here may be one of them, but it's too late now. She'll have seen us.'

'No – I – I heard no such thing!' said the Supernumerary, his eyes darting about.

'I am surprised, Mister Sorenson, the rumours did not reach you, of all people. You may now understand why Captain Gould and Mister Pengarth are as jumpy as a frog in a bucket of hot broth.'

'O – by the Saints!' he stuttered, and I knew by the tremor in his voice he believed every word of it.

'Mister Sorenson?'

He backed away, one hand to his mouth, then crabbed off towards the far rail, glancing from side to side as if every crack in the deck-boards held an attacker. There was a bellow from Pengarth and the Super nearly leapt the rail in fright, but the sailing-master was only calling to let go the bower. From right forward came the rumble of the chain as it ran out, clattering through the hawse-hole. The chain ended after twenty fathoms and the rope-cable followed, raising a cloud of hempen dust from the beak. The Super stood trembling at the break, his confidence gone. At least he is away from me, I thought.

With a start, I spotted a longboat putting off from the *Success*. Two officers were perched in the sternsheets and a third at the bow, with six oarsmen in between. As it drew unhurriedly nearer, I knew only minutes remained before my subterfuge was revealed. I eyed the distance to the warship, judging that, in the warm water, I could surely swim across unless I got a musketball in my back. But perhaps there was a better way. I went swiftly to the break of the poop.

'Tosher,' I called. 'Bring a boarding ladder.'

The seaman came running over with a coiled rope ladder, and together we lowered it.

'That's all, Jakob,' I said, fastening the ladder at the rail.

The longboat closed. It was a matter of timing, and a mermaid's kiss of luck. I darted a quick glance round the quarter-deck. Everyone's eyes were on the approaching boat. Then a voice right by my ear made me jump.

'You watch the English warship – and I see the woman.' Youssef had crept noiselessly up on me from the weather-deck side. He held my arm in a bony grip. 'This girl possesses you.'

'In the name of Hell, Youssef, if –' I stopped dead as the Barbar drew aside his slop-shirt to reveal two pistol-handles poking up from the belt.

'These are fools who will lose their ship.' He was unsmiling as he jerked his head at Gould and Pengarth. 'You cannot leave – we act soon.'

I must have looked dumbfounded.

'Youssef, it's not the time – you're in too much haste and –' I trailed off. It came to me that I had thought of nothing beyond the prospect of finding Abigail. He might be right, but I was too close now to change my course. I looked the Barbar in the eye.

'I must go,' I said, 'but if you wait for me, I shall come back.' The sound of the English boat's oars splashed nearer, and I pulled Youssef close and

285

spoke urgently. 'Listen, my friend, we are all in danger. This is Jamestown, not Charlestown.'

The Barbar's mouth fell open.

'Do nothing, for the Lord's sake, till I return,' I hissed. 'Help me get clear – distract their minds for me. If you do that, I'll keep to my promise. I shall come back.'

'It is agreed,' he said, nodding solemnly. He gave me a brotherly jab in the waist and came into contact with the butt of my own hidden pistol. His face registered surprise, then he grinned. 'Go, and take with you the protection of Allah.'

The Barbar loped off to the chain-pump head, and a shadow of doubt fell over my spirits. Was I deserting Youssef and the *Cornelius* herself at the very hour of their need? Fervently, I wished it were not so, yet I knew that nothing – no mutiny, no danger aboard here – would alter my design of getting aboard the *Success*.

There were shouts as the longboat drew close under our topsides. Waiting by the rail, I did not turn but sensed Gould's stare boring into my back.

Looking down, I saw the officers of the King's Navy being rowed in alongside. They wore grubby white hose and dirt-stained shirts, and the handles of their swords were unpolished. Unkempt and unshaven, they showed the yellowing eyes of an enduring battle with the fevers. And the sugar-rum, I thought, seeing the senior man totter as the boat bumped the *Cornelius*'s hull.

This was the moment. I sprang over the rail and swarmed down the ladder.

'Take hold of my arm, sirs!' I cried enthusiastically. 'Welcome aboard the *Cornelius*.' The senior officer looked affronted and started to speak, but I got in first. 'Step right here and take hold of the ladder, sir. We shall have you safe aboard in no time.'

Drawing the Englishman to me and placing the Naval hand firmly on the ropes, I kept up a stream of chatter until both officers were clambering unsteadily up the topsides. The leading officer paused near the rail and turned round to speak to the young fellow seated in the longboat's sternsheets.

'Midshipman, I want you back aboard ship. Keep order – and stand by there for my signal.'

'Aye aye, sir!' the midshipman replied smartly. He was hardly more than a boy, in dirty white slops and his hair bleached from the sun. His superiors hauled themselves over the rail to make their salute to the *Cornelius*'s officers. I imagined Gould and Pengarth presenting themselves and warily returning the courtesy.

But I was already in the longboat.

'Scull me to your bark,' I said firmly to the midshipman. 'As Navigator of the *Cornelius*, I have business aboard.'

The young man looked astonished. 'I cannot do that, sir!'

I jangled the coins in my pouch to get the oarsmen's attention. Six weatherbeaten faces turned as one and fixed on me.

'A silver dollar for each of you if row me to your ship.'

Their faces broke into wide grins, revealing blackened teeth.

'Cast off there, lads – let's pull away,' said one of them.

'Marlowe,' said the midshipman. 'You'd best not –'

'Aw, come on, sir, I don't advise depriving us,' said Marlowe. 'Never stand between a sailor and a dollar.'

A great shout went up on deck and I heard Youssef's voice raised.

'All hands to the chain-pump! We are taking on water! All hands here!'

I cast off the line and shoved the cutter clear.

'Row, gentlemen, if you please,' I said, holding up bright coins. 'I have more of these, if you have the will to earn them.'

The boat was off, and the midshipman had to make the best of it.

'Very well, push off at the bow,' he ordered, too late. 'Oarsmen, unship sweeps, pull away lusty now, fellows. We are going there anyway, I suppose,' he said, glaring at me.

A string of white splashes trailed astern where the six oars bit the surface, and the longboat drew clear of the *Cornelius*'s shadow and into the hard sunlight. Now I could see on deck, where men ran about shouting while Gould and Pengarth stood by the English officers, bewildered by the sudden upset. Neither of them look over to see me in the longboat. Youssef's voice rang out in the still air, rising up a panic amongst the crew. He has been as good as his word, I thought gratefully.

At this commotion, the oarsmen faltered, their attention on the *Cornelius*.

'For a dollar a-piece, gentlemen,' I rasped from the stern, 'you may pull a touch faster.'

Marlowe grinned and dug his blade smartly into the water.

'Do like the officer says, lads. Pull away!'

'Pull away hard, men,' called the midshipman, scowling, and very soon we had opened the gap between us and the *Cornelius* to beyond the range of any long-musket shot.

Away at last, I leaned forward, urging the boat towards the *Success*, all my senses a-tingle with anticipation.

I gazed at the fast-receding *Cornelius*, sitting in serene repose on the smooth water, her sleek lines and clean rig a delight to a seaman's eye. Racked by doubts, I fretted over having left her when matters seemed on the cusp of resolution – by bloody means, I feared. Soon, we neared the giant, brooding hull of the *Success* squatting not far off, and I had little difficulty in turning my thoughts towards what I might find there.

I elbowed the young officer seated next me.

'I am Matthew Stalbone, second mate and Navigator aboard the *Cornelius*. What is your name?'

'Adam Pyne, sir. Midshipman, the *Success*.'

'How old are you, Midshipman?'

'Sixteen, sir, and four years in the King's Navy.'

He seemed to speak plain and honest enough, and his annoyance at my usurping command of the longboat was on the wane.

'By the condition of your bark, it seems you do not patrol,' I said, gesturing at the warship.

'The men refuse to go to sea. The post-captain –' Pyne twisted round nervously to see if we were being pursued. 'He's dead of the fever, and First Lieutenant Slush, who has gone aboard your bark with the Second Lieutenant, is somewhat – er, free with the lash.' His worried eyes met mine.

'Go on, Pyne, tell me the rest.'

'There is a great restlessness amongst the men, sir, but a relief is on the way. The *Abundance*, out from Spithead. She is overdue.' He glanced at the rowers and lowered his voice. 'There may be trouble when she hoves in.'

'And your landspeople – the English party?'

He brightened.

'O aye, sir, and a welcome to have them aboard. Not so much the merchant – a ratty fellow at best – but his daughter, Abigail, as she is called.'

The oars clicked in their sockets as the blades stroked the water. It was her. I held my eye fixed on the midshipman.

'Tell me about her.'

'A most elegant creature, sir. I and my fellow midshipmen wager and squabble to visit the quarter-deck. A woman may not leave the poop, sir, and a midshipman mostly stays before the mizen.'

'Why does she remain aboard at anchor?'

'There's disturbance ashore – it's dangerous for her there, though I daresay the *Success* may hardly be considered safe much longer. A plantation gentleman has caused great dissatisfaction amongst the poor settlers, and they are rebellious.'

Instantly I thought of John Lynskill. My features must have hardened as I leaned forward into the young man's face.

'What gentleman?' I almost shouted.

'Why, I – I – have not heard his name spoken, sir,' stuttered Pyne, taken aback.

Turning away in irritation, I scanned the warship's decks, until I caught sight of the figure in the white dress, standing apart. I wanted to leap the remaining distance and be with her in the next instant.

'What officers are aboard?' I asked, wrenching myself back to the matter in hand.

'The third lieutenant and my two fellow midshipmen, sir.'

'And guards? Lookouts?'

Pyne hesitated. 'I have to confess they are likely well drunk, sir.'

I was fishing six silver coins from my pouch when Pyne caught sight of the pistol butt.

'I do not know your purpose, sir,' he said, grabbing my sleeve, 'but I urge you – spare the bloodshed.'

'Pyne, may the Lord preserve your soul, but my purpose is peaceful – if I am left to it. Bring the boat to the break of the poop, by the boarding ladder.'

The midshipman's eyes were wide but he obeyed. As the longboat bumped alongside, I threw twelve glittering silver coins into the thwarts. The oarsmen let go their sweeps with a cry and scrabbled at each other's feet.

'Thank you, sirs!' I sang out, grabbing the rope and swarming up it, while Pyne glanced nervously about as if expecting a pistol shot. Swinging over the rail, I planted my feet on the *Success*'s decks and stood ready for a confrontation with a guard, but none came. Seamen sat or sprawled under awnings in pure indolence, unconcerned at the rotten gear and detritus lying strewn about. Apart from a sleepy eye opened here or there, they took no notice of their visitor, and I was glad of it.

A stout net was strung athwartships at the break, as if to prevent free access between the officers and the men. I went up the steps and sprang over, finding myself on a quarter-deck much larger than the *Cornelius*'s.

At the far side of the wheel, I saw the girl leaning at the rail, half-turned away. She was shaded under a deck awning strung from the cross-jack yard above. Planted at a forlorn angle on her hair was a cap, once fine with embroidered flowers at the band, but now dirty and torn. The cloth of her thin, worn dress, though dark with grime, failed to disguise her figure's fine structure. Her face was upturned, lids closed against the sun, as if she dreamt of flying away into the cloudless sky.

Beside her, head down as he leaned at the rail with an air of defeat, was Seth Jeffreys. But I barely registered him.

Stepping forward eagerly, I felt propelled towards the girl as if by an unseen hand. My arms seemed to go out before me unbidden, to sweep her up. But a pace off, I halted. Lightheaded, my chest tightening, I realised I had hardly drawn a free breath for a full minute. I sucked in a lungful of air, but my throat was dry and involuntarily I coughed.

She looked round. Her eyes widened, first in surprise, then in dawning recognition.

'Abigail,' I managed to croak.

Her hand flew up to her mouth and she shrank back, disbelieving. Her face betrayed months of anxiety and the rigours of shipboard life. Her skin, lined and drawn, was stretched tight over the cheekbones and an uncomely shade of brown from the Tropick sun.

'Matthew – is it you?' she said.

As she spoke, Mister Jeffreys straightened, and his brows shot up in startlement. He grabbed her.

'The Lord deliver us!' cried Jeffreys, tugging. He spotted my pistol. 'God above, he is armed – O, get away from my daughter!'

I took two rapid steps forward and grasped her hand.

The merchant fell on her arm and started pulling her roughly.

'Abigail, daughter, come away!' he cried, and I had to let her go. 'Lord, Matthew Stalbone! What can you want with us?'

I wrenched my gaze from Abigail's face and rounded fiercely on her father, my anger flaming. I gripped the merchant's collar and drew him close. So incensed was I by the sight of his weaselly face that, by the Lord, I had raised a hand to strike him before I knew it myself.

'Matthew!'

Abigail's cry stopped me short and I looked at her. Tears left glistening streaks as they coursed down the dry, browned skin of her cheeks. Years had passed and she was older now and sun-worn, a woman rather than the fresh flower of a girl I had left in Whitby. Trying to calm the chorus of questions singing in my head, I pushed Seth Jeffreys away and moved towards her.

'I have come for you, Abigail,' I said quietly.

She blinked the water from her eyes and smiled

in wonderment, shaking her head in disbelief. But before she could speak, her father set up such a commotion I half expected a Revenue Troop to arrive.

'Stalbone, I shall have you arrested!' he shouted, looking around the quarter-deck. 'Help, here! Help, I say – Ow!'

Abigail brought the heel of her shoe down hard on his shoe.

'Quiet, Father, for pity's sake,' she told him, as Jeffreys stared back in hurt and surprise. 'Will you let us talk? Matthew is not going to harm us.'

The flow of her tears was stemmed now, and coolly she scrutinised me. I became warm as she took in my open leather weskit, paper thin now in places, revealing my browned chest and tanned stomach. The slops around my lower half were roughly sewn with canvas patches and held up by the frayed leather strop which passed for a proper belt, where the pistol handle poked out. The baggy sailor's dress ended halfway down my calves and my bare feet were callused and darkened from years of running shoeless about the wooden decks. I stood there, hot with shame and passion while Abigail's gaze ran from my torso to my legs and back to my face.

She put her hand to her mouth and tried to hide her smile.

'Why, Matthew, you look almost a pirate!'

'Ah – Abigail – I –'

'Your hair – it has become paler than I thought possible. The sun has faded it perhaps. And your skin is beyond brown. It is uncommonly dark.'

'Abigail, the Tropick sun and – and you your-self –'

She put her head back and laughed. 'Yes, Matthew. Myself likewise, I daresay.'

I grinned. She was beautiful. Browned, worn, in her ragged clothes, she stood before me, a woman in a strong, tall body with a steady look in her eye. In that instant, I fell in love afresh, this time not with an artless girl but with a mature, composed woman. The blood coursed in my veins and, as I burned for her, she stopped laughing and we looked at each other. For a second, we were alone in the world.

Seth Jeffreys charmed away this spell.

'What do you claim of us, Stalbone?' he wailed, rubbing his damaged foot.

I swung on him, and all my fury returned.

'Claim? Can you only ever think of claims and payments – of property and commerce? As for me, I claim nothing. I come to pledge myself – to your daughter.' I glanced at her, then looked down sheepishly. 'To marry her, if she wishes it to be so.' I gently drew her towards me and to my great joy, she let me enfold her. 'We consider ourselves betrothed.'

'O no!' cried the merchant.

'Matthew, if only it could be so,' she said sadly. 'It is too late. Three months ago, I married John Lynskill.'

I held her away in despair.

'After so long, I had hoped that –' My imagination filled with the thoughts I had fought to suppress for years.

'Matthew, you must help us.' Abigail spoke

rapidly. 'We are trapped aboard here – we cannot go ashore. Lynskill has cheated and incensed all Jamestown and the settlers have risen –'

'Sweet Abigail, I understand,' I said, for a swift and complete answer to all our ills had come to my mind quite unbidden. Now her delicate face swam before me and a thick, distant voice spoke that I could not quite believe was my own. 'Tell me where to find Lynskill. I shall go and kill him, and we shall be rid –'

'Matthew, you must not add to the blood and misery!' she cried. 'What have you become?'

'I want you,' I said hotly. 'I intend to win you.'

The merchant instantly set up his wailing once more. I swung on him and prodded the silk-shirted chest.

'And now you remind me of claims and rights, Mister Jeffreys, I want my rightful dues – the money from the *Prosperous Anne*.'

'You don't understand!' cried the girl.

'O aye, I do. I want my money to make our life together.'

'You can't have it!' Jeffreys shouted. 'The money's gone.'

The muffled report of a pistol shot echoed across the stillness of the bay. For a second, we all wondered what was happening. There came a shout from Midshipman Pyne, hidden from our view in the longboat below.

'It's the signal from the First Lieutenant!' cried Pyne. 'Pull hard, lads, away to the *Cornelius*.'

The oars clacked as the seamen worked the boat briskly off, the midshipman sitting in the stern, intent on his task. I had no time to concern myself with the Navy's affairs, and wrenched Mister Jeffreys round to face me.

'What are you saying? Where is the money?' I demanded.

'Lynskill has it – go and find him!' he bawled, then perhaps remembering my threat, his face crumpled. 'No, don't go to him. O Lord, O Lord – what to do!'

'I know the truth, Mister Jeffreys,' I said, 'because the agent Waspik told me. He was ready to tell more, but the *Tryall* went down.'

Abigail gasped. 'What? The *Tryall* is gone?'

'Why, Abigail, do you know the bark?' I said, surprised. 'I met Waspik on board, but then she burned and sank. Hundreds of slaves were trapped below.'

'O how awful!' Abigail blanched. 'And what of Mijnheer Waspik?'

'He drowned. But he told me how your father took my money, Abigail.'

She stared. 'Matthew,' she said slowly. 'O my poor Matthew.'

I studied her face, puzzled, waiting for her to speak.

'There is no money for you now,' she said softly.

'What are you saying. What has happened?'

She took a long breath of air, and began. 'Lynskill took all our Whitby money,' she said, 'the money my father had saved for a dowry and brought with us to America. He put it all into the plantation here, for he had spent or lost the capital that Justice Lynskill afforded him, you see. But he wasted all of it, every farthing, on poor crops and unhealthy Negroes who would not work, and they all died. And he borrowed from the settlers here – O, it has been such a bad business, Matthew.'

'Abigail,' I said, taking her hand, 'what of my shares?'

'We argued, my father and I, over your shares, and the monies from the sale of the *Prosperous Anne*. I wanted it kept aside for you – until we departed Whitby, I still hoped and believed we might see you again – but he was determined to risk it into a Baltick venture, which he said would make a good profit. Before he had put it into a vessel to go across the North Sea, the Africk trade was opened up, and the profits were said to be beyond imagining. So he incorporated with some other merchants to raise up a larger sum, and invested it into a bark to go slaving.'

I gazed at Abigail, a sense of horror rising within me.

'Yes, Matthew,' she said, very quietly. 'Your money was invested in the *Tryall*.'

I blinked. I staggered a pace backward.

'That loathsome slaver?' I tried to gather my senses. 'Lord, all those poor Negro people – and I sat aboard with that vile fellow Gould. And – Lord, but it was my father's money. O, what a cruel thing!'

I buried my face in my hands. Despite my best attempts to resist it, a great sob heaved up.

Abigail held me tightly. 'My poor Matthew,' she murmured. 'My poor Matthew. You haven't lost everything.'

'I have!' I blurted. 'My money, my ship, my inheritance – all gone to that filthy trade.' I wiped the salty wetness away and focused on her face. 'But that is nothing, nothing at all, when I have lost you to John Lynskill.'

I pushed her gently aside and stumbled across the deck to the far rail. I wanted to be away from that place, even away from her. Then I heard Abigail call, and she came running over, distraught.

'Matthew! Matthew, he is not my husband – not until –' She faltered. 'You must listen to me, Matthew. I waited and waited for you. O, I delayed in any way I could think. I feigned illness, I pretended to be mortally afraid of going aboard an ocean ship. I said the airs would surely kill me. But you never came back, did you?'

I could not speak, for to be reminded of how I had failed to come back as I promised, and had left dear Abigail waiting and delaying, hoping I would return, distressed me beyond any words. But what could I tell her that made any difference? What use was it to say that I had been swept aboard a great Dutch flyer, and carried away across an ocean, never expecting ever to find her again?

'Matthew,' she said, 'I am only glad that you are alive and safe. And that you are here with me.'

In a while, I calmed a little.

'There is more I have to tell you, my love,' she said. 'When finally we had come to America yet I was not married, I could postpone it no longer. We were married aboard here, on the *Success*.'

I shook my head, wishing the words away.

'It was just to seal the commerce of the arrangement, Matthew!' she said. 'My father refused to assign the dowry unless a marriage was done. It was to ensure my future, he said, and bind the Lynskill family to the Jeffreys family in wedlock. And so we were bound in commerce too, and John Lynskill returned straightaway to the settlement and used the money to expand the plantation.' She lifted up my head and made me look at her. 'But the marriage was a commercial arrangement above all else, Matthew.'

I was miserable. To think of her married to that corpulent and overbearing bully – and after so much lost time between us, to have been reunited only to have her taken from me by this news.

'Matthew – can you understand this?' I heard her saying. 'Lynskill left me immediately the ceremony was done. We did not – the marriage is not – we are not man and wife under God!'

She cast her eyes down. The ship shifted in her chains as a breath of sea-breeze reached the inland anchorage, and the deck-boards trembled lightly. Slowly, I did understand. She was married, but she was not married, not until John Lynskill came back to claim her, to complete the union with his body. And that, I knew now above anything else in all the world, would never happen as long as I could draw a breath.

Understanding at last, sensing as sweet a relief as if I had been pardoned on the very gallows, I bent towards her face. We kissed, joining our lips for the first time since that fleeting moment in the old shipyard. When we parted, I could think of nothing to say that would not diminish what I felt.

Abigail's face shone with passion.

'In the eyes of the Lord, and the eyes of the law and in my own eyes,' she said, 'I am not married. I am free to go with you, Matthew.'

'Free – you are free,' I said, wonderingly. 'And you do want this – to go with me?' Who could wonder that I was slow to take in the import of it all? In less than half a glass's time, I had found Abigail, lost her, and now she had declared herself mine.

'We shall go away,' Abigail was saying. 'Leave at once and get away from this dreadful ship and this harbour. Can we go to your ship?'

I struggled to think. We had only to find somewhere to go, and some reason to go there.

'We cannot go to the *Cornelius*,' I said, my mind rapidly turning over the possibilities. 'It is far too dangerous. Yet I promised Youssef –'

'Matthew, wherever we go, we must take my father.' Her face had fallen, and she studied her father. He had gone to sit apart, huddling under the rail and muttering softly under his breath, all the while moving his hands is if he had a washbowl before him.

'Abigail – surely – I mean, he forced you to marry against your will, and he cheated me –'

'What do you think, that I can simply leave him? He is my father. I will not.'

She paused, and an expression came over her face, one I could not remember seeing since we were children together.

'Besides –' she began, and then gave me the flicker of a smile. There was nothing girlish now about her. She knew something more. Her look was not of complicity, as in the secret games we had once played, so much as pure conspiracy. When she spoke, it was in a low, urgent whisper, and her arm gripped mine fiercely.

'Father has a cache, Matthew – a secret store of coin in gold and silver pieces,' she said, holding her gaze on me. 'He has not told me where, but I think I know. It is at the Lynskill mansion, on the plantation. We must go into Jamestown and retrieve it. After all, in a way it is yours and mine.'

'Lord – that is our chance!' I cried, my heart lifting at the thought of our escape together. 'We must row ashore at once. How far to this plantation? Which way does it lie? Shall we find Lynskill there?'

There were two small launches hoisted by the warship's rail, safe from thieves but ready in the falls for lowering.

'We shall take a boat,' I said. 'Abigail, I have a few coin left – I must persuade these fellows to give up their launch to us.'

'He has coin, Matthew.' She nodded at her father.

I was on Jeffreys in flash, dragging him to his feet.

'Mister Jeffreys, we are leaving at once. Give me what coin you have about you.'

He stared at me, then began clawing at the air.

'Abigail – help, O tell him to leave me.'

'Give me your purse, Father,' she said calmly, reaching forward and slipping a pouch from his coat

303

pocket. I let him go and Abigail jingled several dollars and dubloons into my palm. They were damp and sticky from the merchant having kept them so close to him.

'You fellows! You there!' I strode towards the waist and pointed at a thick-set seaman who had raised his head at the sound of my voice. 'I am taking the small launch, steerboard side. Prepare to have it lowered away when we are aboard.'

Roused from his doze and probably thinking a Navy officer had given the command, the seaman levered himself to his feet and stumbled off to the ship's rail. I grasped Mister Jeffreys and pushed him forward, and the three of us stepped smartly off the poop and over to the launch. Three or four other sailors had gathered there and now stood eyeing us suspiciously. I helped Abigail over the rail and into the launch, which swung gently as she entered, and pushed the merchant after her.

'Now, fellows,' I said, turning to them with a smile and holding up a gold dubloon. 'I have the King's affairs ashore to deal with and I shall thank you to allow me the use of this boat, which shall be returned to you before dark. Lower away and the coin is yours.'

I leapt the rail and landed in the thwarts as the launch began its descent. When it touched the water I glanced up to see a row of faces at the rail, then I flung the coin upwards in a high curving arc. Their heads lifted as one, following its path, and they all disappeared inboard to grasp it as the coin rejoined the *Success*. How magnificent it is, I thought, to have the power of money rather than want it. I sat down opposite Abigail, planted one oar in the hand of my erstwhile benefactor and took up the other.

'Row away, Mister Jeffreys!' I called, and could not help but smile at his discomfort. As he reluctantly slotted his sweep in the lock on his side, Abigail and I, laughing together, kissed again, enjoying the sheer relief of getting away. We were off in a flash, not heading for the old jetty where I feared we might encounter Lynskill or the settlers, but instead for a narrow strand separating the lagoon waters from the vegetation crowding close to the foreshore. There, I had spotted a beaten path that led away into the hinterland.

In a minute, the bow of our launch grazed the sandy shore of America, and I sprang over the stem and, for the first time in my life, planted a foot in the New World. Abigail joined me and we put our arms round each other.

'Welcome to this new land,' I said, 'may it provide for us –'

I got no further with this sentiment, for a burst of distant firing crackled into the air, and pistol reports thudded across the still water of Jamestown Roads. Instinctively, I looked towards the *Success* and tensed ready to make a dash with Abigail for cover, for I thought the sailors there must be loosing off their muskets at us. But there was no musketry from the warship. The Navy sailors had scrambled to their feet and crowded to the rail, but their gaze was not towards us. All eyes were trained on the *Cornelius*, and I squinted beyond to see what the matter was.

Puffs of white smoke rose lazily from the flyer's

decks. I saw figures running about in disarray and heard a chorus of shouts drift across the bay. Cutlass blades flashed in the sun.

'Lord,' I breathed, my heart beginning to pump. 'There is a fight aboard her.'

'Look,' said Abigail, 'there's a boat coming off.'

I saw the *Cornelius*'s little cutter break clear from the privateer. It was packed to the gunnels with men, and they pulled like demons. More cotton balls of smoke appeared above the bark's side-decks, and I realised those on board were sending musket shots towards the cutter.

After a few minutes, as the boat neared and the crew of the *Success* urged it towards them, I discerned the faces of the rowers. The ancient, bent figure in the bows was unmistakable, and I knew they were friends. I began shouting and jumping in the air, waving my arms.

'Eli!' I shouted, and the old salt's face turned my way. 'Pull this way – over here! We are here!'

The cutter veered off from its course for the English ship and with renewed vigour the oarsmen stroked towards the shore.

'What the Devil's been happening?' I called as they neared.

'Sir, Gould has departed his sanity,' Eli panted from the bows. 'When they found out this is Jamestown, he shot the English officer. Captain Brogel came off his sick-bed and –' He trailed off as if it was too awful to recount.

'There was a terrible fight – a bloody thing, sir!' It was the Dutch boy Gaspar, looking haunted.

306

'Youssef led us – but we lost the ship. Now they're going to hang him – they'll hang the Barbar, sir!'

The news cut me like the slice of a half-pike. Lord, but I should have tried harder to put him off until the time was ripe. He had kept his promise to let me get away, and caused a disturbance aboard at great risk to his own life. I knew that now I had to fulfil my part of the bargain. Youssef would not hang, not even if it cost me my own life.

'By the grace of God, we'll fight!' I cried to the sailors as, seconds later, the bow of their cutter crunched into the sandy shore alongside our boat. I grasped the stem and surveyed the crew, a ragged and hangdog bunch, but loyal fellows if ever men were. They needed only to take new heart, and then I knew they could win any fight.

But what was I thinking? What had come over me, to abandon my Abigail? I twisted round and saw her puzzled countenance.

'No sooner do I find you,' I said, stepping close to her and only half-believing in my own speech, 'than I must leave you.'

I waited, hoping mightily that she would see the reason in my madness. At last, she gave a sad smile.

'You must save your ship – and your friend. Please –' She gripped my arm fiercely. 'Matthew, come back for me.'

'I shall, Abigail, I promise you.' I swallowed. 'This time, I shall come back. We'll fight for the ship and for Youssef, and I shall return for you.'

I took her by the waist and squeezed. Our lips touched once more.

'Wait here,' I told her. 'Stay hidden behind the

foreshore, clear of any sight from the ships.' Then I spoke harshly to Mister Jeffreys. 'I charge you with her life and her freedom, sir. Guard her and keep her safe for my return.'

Then I was off, shoving against the cutter's stem and pushing her keel free of the sand. I splashed half a dozen steps into the water before leaping for the boat, which rocked perilously as I hauled myself aboard. Eli and Gaspar leaned forward to steady me.

'Thank the Good Lord!' said the old salt, gripping my forearm. 'Pull steerboard side, my fellows!' he sang out, and the boat spun in the water until she came up straight, then took off as both ranks of oars bit the water in unison.

I sat dripping and panting in the boat, gazing back at Abigail, standing forlornly on the sandy shore, only her miserable father beside her. She waved. In dread of leaving her, I shut my eyes and prayed to be allowed to come back. Then I swiped the back of my arm across my eyes, for the salt sweat pricked at them, and turned to the company before me, grimly intent on the business in hand.

'How many are we here – eight, nine of us?' I said. The crew were all from steerboard watch. Close to them now, I noticed flecks of blood on their clothes. 'Are you all whole – any wounded?'

'Whole enough, sir!' they cried as one, but I saw the sabre cuts on their arms, and their cheer had little heart in it.

'Eli, how many fought with you?'

'Half or better, sir,' he said. 'But we were not rallied – it came on us too sudden.' He looked downcast. 'We had to get away for our lives.'

'Where are the rest?'

'Retreated to the foc'sle. The fight left them when Youssef was took.'

'Which officer did Gould shoot?'

'The First Lieutenant.'

'There's harm in that for us,' I said, worried. 'An English relief is due here, and she'll avenge that killing for sure. What weapons have we?'

'We have pistols, cutlasses and muskets a-plenty.'

Eli pointed down amongst our feet. Cutlasses were piled in a heap along with a dozen brace of pistols and half that number of long-muskets. There were dry powder pouches and horns, and bags of ball.

'Brave lads,' I said. 'Eli, who stood for Pengarth?'

'Much of larboard, and one or two of our watch, sir. Quaker John for one, the dirty traitor. It was steerboard fought best for Brogel.'

'And our dear captain? What of him?'

'Cut about in the fight, sir, and retired to his quarters hurt. Mortal or not, I cannot say.'

'Lads!' I stood up and balanced in the thwarts. 'You have showed yourselves brave and honourable. You fought for our captain and you followed Youssef – I salute you.'

They glanced up at me with haggard countenances.

'We are not beaten – we rally now to save our friends,' I told them. 'We have right on our side. And our strength and our courage too.'

They shifted about and straightened up a little.

309

'Here's my design. Quiet as water-rats, we shall get aboard under her stern, by the hawse-hole, then rally up the foc'sle fellows, arm them mightily and take the quarter-deck by storm.' I watched them lift their faces, and the light seemed to enter their eyes once more. 'We shall catch the traitors unawares – they'll be at the rum by now. Shall we let them have their spoils?'

This time a few pistols and cutlasses were waved aloft, and I heard half a cheer raised up.

'We shall be strong enough, lads. And we'll take our *Cornelius* back again!'

This time they shouted and drummed their feet, and I reckoned they were ready for anything. I picked up a pistol and began loading.

'Now, fellows, row back with a will,' I commanded.

The men pulled on the sweeps, stroking with vigour. The cutter lurched forward and I sat down with a thump. Eli banged me on the back.

'You've put the spirit back into us, sir!' he cried excitedly, and fell to loading pistols with me. For a while, we lapsed into quiet, busy at our work, and the *Cornelius* drew steadily nearer.

'Sir,' whispered Gaspar, puffing at the oars. 'Shall we truly take her back?'

The youngster's face was aglow with exertion.

'Yes, Gaspar,' I said. 'With loyal and good fellows like you, we shall take our *Cornelius* back.'

I squinted backwards across the five or six cables of water separating us from the shore of the great American lands. I was just able to make out a slender figure in white clothes. Did she raise in arm?

310

Had she seen me turn back to look? It was all too far away to tell, and I twisted round to face my men.

'We must,' I said, so low that Gaspar leaned forward to hear. 'We must have her back.'

# 17

# Settlement

We sculled in a wide circle to approach the *Cornelius* by the bow, unseen by the quarter-deck, where it appeared the entire complement had assembled. I noticed the *Success*'s longboat, which Midshipman Pyne and his men had returned in, tied astern near the break of the poop. It was empty.

There were figures moving about and a commotion on the quarter-deck as we slid under the beak of the ship, where the anchor cable dropped into the bay's murky water. By contrast with the activity aft, the fore parts of the ship were ominously still and silent as we came in under the shadow of the jutting bowsprit.

'Up!' I said, hoarsely. 'We have not a second to waste.'

We tied the cutter to the anchor rope, leaving it bumping gently against the ship's stem, and swarmed up the four-stranded cable, thicker than a man's forearm. We had loaded every pistol and each man had two stuck in his waistband, and a cutlass jammed awkwardly beside.

'Blood and bilgewater,' cursed old Eli, swinging himself feet first onto the beak. 'I dam' near lost my seaman's treasures there.' A dark red patch spread across his thigh where the whetted blade had nicked him as it swung.

After gaining the rail, and the nine of us were crouching hidden in the well by the anchors, I moved forward, bent low, but Eli whispered, 'Wait! Look.'

From the forehatch appeared a figure, his back towards us, staring towards the quarter-deck. It was Jakob Tosher. His shoulders drooped, he was weaponless, and it looked like the beginnings of a surrender.

'Jakob!' I called softly from my cover by the catheads.

Tosher spun round in surprise and his jaw fell open.

'Second mate!' he said. 'They have Youssef – we're coming up without our weapons.'

'How many are we, Jakob?'

'Fifteen in the foc'sle.'

'Call down to them. They are to show themselves as if they were quitting, but keep their weapons hidden.'

Jakob glanced warily aft to the stern parts, undecided. Come on, Jakob, come on fellows, I muttered.

Pengarth's voice boomed out. 'Out of there, you bastards! Show no weapons, or the Barbar dies.'

Tosher leaned down to the hatchway and spoke urgently to the men below. After what seemed an age, they emerged one by one, glancing at us, though I signalled them to keep their eyes directed aft. At last, they all stood facing the quarter-deck.

We could see the pistols and cutlasses up their shirtbacks. One or two kept looking nervously round, threatening to give the game away.

It was now or never.

I sprang from the well of the beak and in one leap was up onto the foc's'le.

'Now, fellows!' I cried, cutlass raised in one hand and a pistol in the other, and ran full tilt into the waist of the ship.

For an awful moment, I heard nothing behind and my instinct was to stop and turn to see why they were not following. Then I heard their roar of anger and the thud of many feet on the deck-boards and I knew they were up and charging.

On the quarter-deck, the figures froze, struck dumb by the sight of our mad onrush. Pengarth stood in his white clothes, red-banded at the waist, with Gould beside him and a dozen seamen gathered nearby, slouching and sprawling in a way forbidden under Brogel's command. The English warship party from the *Success* – officers and oarsmen alike – stood forlornly by, lashed to the rail. Adam Pyne, tall and willowy, hung his head in despair. At his feet, shot through the chest, lay the bloodied body of First Lieutenant Slush.

Standing on a box under the cross-jack yard was the Barbar Youssef, tightly gagged, hands bound awkwardly behind him. A rope slung from the yard ended in a noose around his neck. The box was too low to break his neck by the fall, for in true seamen's tradition a lingering end was meant, but Captain Gould stood next to him, ready to give the kick that would send Youssef into a goggle-eyed, gasping dance of strangulation.

My charge carried me clear across the waist and up the steps to the quarter before Pengarth gathered his wits. The mutinous seamen struggled to their feet unsteadily, as if they had plundered the rum stores. The sailing-master's face was blank with incomprehension but as understanding dawned, he cocked a pistol and levelled it at me.

'Hold your fire, Pengarth!' I bellowed in fury.

He discharged the gun not fifteen feet off. The pistol bucked as smoke and flames spurted from its muzzle, but the shot was wild and the ball buzzed angrily overboard. I dropped to one knee, raised my own pistol and released the trigger. The flash and acrid smoke momentarily blinded me, but I saw Pengarth go down with blood streaming from his shattered thigh.

All around were shots and cries as the foc'sle men clashed with the rebels, and the fight became a hand-to-hand struggle of death. The blades of cutlasses clanked as they struck, biting into flesh and wood alike.

Captain Gould lashed out with his foot at the box under Youssef, but it did not budge. He aimed a second kick at it. I dropped my empty pistol and, gripping the cutlass in both hands, stepped over Pengarth's writhing form and charged forward.

With Gould's second kick, the box fell away. The Barbar's legs jerked in desperation, a yard off the ground, and his eyes bulged as the rope strangled him. Gould saw me coming and raised a pistol. There was a flash from the pan but no smoke of discharge. Thanking my Creator for a poorly loaded gun or a spoonful of damp powder, I hurtled on with the cutlass levelled. Too late, Gould tried to twist away but the point pierced the fabric of his coat, and I bore in behind it with all my strength. Gould let out a groan of disbelief.

'Curse and dam' you – O God, my guts!' he said, clawing at the weapon.

His hands closed over mine and gripped the cutlass handle, pulling us both over. We stumbled and fell together, face to face. The rum on Gould's breath was noisome and, as we clung in this gruesome embrace, my cheek brushed the whiskers of his chin. He let his head drop to the deck, but when I withdrew the blade from amongst his innards, he suddenly lurched up at me anew. Aghast, I swiped the flat of the cutlass hard against his side. He reeled, sagged to his knees, blood streaming from a deep cut, and fumbled for a spare pistol. This time I grasped the cutlass with both hands and brought the heavy handle end down with all my might on his head. He slumped forwards and lay still. God, I've killed again, I thought dully.

Youssef's legs kicked in the air, but to my distress I found I could not reach far enough above his head to cut the rope. The only way was to get up on the yard. Ignoring the close hand fighting at every point around me, I launched myself in a fury towards the mizen ratline.

Quaker John stood in my way, pointing a pistol, his mouth pouring out a cascade of curses. From nowhere, Eli Savary stepped up with a cutlass raised high, and brought it down two-handed. The blade's chop severed the Quaker's wrist, and the hand fell away on the instant of pulling the trigger. The pan flashed and the pistol discharged, revolving in mid-air as the recoil sent it spinning and clattering into the scuppers. The ball smashed into the rail just by me, driving jagged wood splinters into my leg. John stood slack-jawed, gazing at his ragged wrist where the limb pumped thick blood in jerking arcs that spattered on the deck-boards. The hand twitched where it fell.

'Bind it, man!' called Eli above the noise and mayhem of battle.

In three paces, I was at the mizen shrouds and charging up the ratlines two at a time, somehow finding the footholds. A second later I was out along the cross-jack, above the maelstrom of wrestling figures and bloody combat.

Youssef's body jerked weakly on the end of the taut rope, and his face was turned upwards in a grimace of agony. The noose had forced up his jawbone and cut red weals round the neck. The stricture of the rope had squeezed his tongue out, which writhed like a landed fish. Panting with exertion, and fumbling like a fool, I pulled out my knife and sawed at the thick sisal. The fibres flew apart one by one until a single strand remained. With one last slice of the knife, I cut it clean through and Youssef dropped like a cannonball onto the deck. He stayed crumpled and still, and it was impossible to know if he were alive or dead.

Turning to make my way back along the yard, I caught sight of a Pengarth man stepping up behind Jakob Tosher. There was the flash of a knife blade.

With shaking hands, I pulled out my second pistol, cocked it and aimed for the seaman's chest. When I squeezed the trigger, the recoil threw me back and I grappled to keep my perch, but the ball found its mark and barrelled the man backwards with great force. As the sailor lurched against the rail, the knife fell from his hand and clanked at Tosher's feet. The Dutchman stared disbelievingly at the dying man and gazed around the decks, trying to figure where the shot had come from.

I clambered in the foot-ropes awkwardly along the yard to regain the ratlines, where I paused a second, breathless, and surveyed the battle. Stinging smoke from powder discharges billowed upwards in clouds, watering my eyes and catching my throat. The groans of the injured rose up all around in an awful refrain, while the *Cornelius*'s quarter-deck had taken on the look of a butcher's slab on a feast-day. But the blood-letting had reached its peak and now, from my vantage point, I knew the mutineers were beaten. A band of them cowered in the waist as Gaspar and the others advanced.

'Men of steerboard watch!' I called. 'Disarm them and tie the prisoners. Let the bloodshed end.'

Throwing myself down the ratlines, I ran to the Barbar. His head lolled brokenly, and his face was bloodless. I bent low over him to listen. He still breathed, thank the Lord.

'Jakob!' I shouted, straightening, and the seaman ran over. 'Tend him for me, will you?'

Tosher looked me up and down. 'Was it you on the cross-jack, sir?'

I nodded.

'Good shot, second mate,' he said, and turned to see to poor Youssef.

I went to find Eli, who was tying the arms and legs of the defeated men.

'Old salt,' I said, laying a hand on his shoulder. 'I want to thank you for saving my life.'

'The dam' turncoat!' spluttered the sailor in a show of outrage, but his voice was cracked with anguish. 'We should feed him to the sharks – they love a Quaker.'

'We've won back our ship, Eli,' I said, though I admit, gazing around at the aftermath of battle, I only half believed it.

Half a dozen injured men sat or slumped by the rails, while the hale and healthy brought pails of water to wash and soothe their wounds. The loyal foc'sle men corralled their prisoners in the waist of the ship, and the terrified seamen of the *Success* cowered right aft, still tied to the rail. Gould sprawled nearby in a pool of blood, and from the pocket of his torn coat poked the black neck of an unbroken rum bottle.

Then it dawned me who was missing from the tally.

'Jakob, Gaspar!' I shouted. 'Where's Pengarth?'

They shrugged. Unless the sailing-master had hurled himself over the side, I knew there was only one place he could be.

'Give me a couple of loaded pistols, Gaspar.'

The boy handed me a weapon.

'Sir – I have only this one left,' he said.

I checked the pan, cocked the flintlock and strode to the companion, passing Quaker John where he sat

319

under the rail holding, with the hand left to him, a dark, wet piece of shirt around the bloodied stump.

'Quaker, I shall have your pistol,' I said.

I bent over and snatched the weapon from its berth in his waistband. I checked the pan and hefted the gun, feeling for the weight of the ball and wad. It was loaded and dry. I cocked the lock back on its spring.

'Where's Pengarth, John?'

The Quaker gave a painful grin. 'Give me back my hand and I'll tell you.'

I went to the companionway and peered into the blackness below. There was no sign of movement, and I stepped quietly down facing forward in an unseamanlike way, but I needed to hold the pistols at the ready. I paused to get accustomed to the gloom. Going forward, I tripped on a sack-like object, lost my footing and stumbled forward, crashing heavily into the door of the Great Cabin. It burst open and I fell blindly into the room, dropping the pistols and landing on all fours.

Out of the corner of my eye, I could see Pengarth sprawled by the table with his shot leg twisted grotesquely underneath him. Opposite, Captain Brogel lay prostrate on his bunk.

For the second time in the half-hour, Pengarth, beads of sweat standing out from his face, raised a pistol for a shot at me.

'Well, well, my handsome,' he breathed heavily. 'I knew I should've left you in the sea.'

I threw myself sideways. An immense double explosion filled the confined cabin with a wall of noise, and the pressure pounded my ears. Pengarth's body was picked up and thrown like a child's doll against the cabin side by the sheer force of two balls striking his head and chest at close range. The big man's skull exploded in a mass of red and grey spray, and bone-shards from his cranium flew through the air as if they were pieces of smashed pottery.

Smoke writhed sinuously up to the deck-head, and the air cleared. Everything was eerily quiet. Cautiously, I raised my head. Pengarth lay still as a monument, the life blown clean out of him. Captain Brogel sat up half on and half off the bunk, as though transfixed by the sight of the sailing-master's body. He held two pistols, and wisps of white vapour curled from their barrels.

A woman's anguished cry broke the murderous silence. Shakily, I clambered upright and lifted the shattered, near headless Pengarth from Neeta, who lay sobbing and shocked beneath him. When I pulled her gently up and led her to Brogel, she fell on the bunk, covering her face with her hands. She was drenched in blood and brain from the captain's extinguishing of Pengarth.

Brogel's eyes were distended white orbs protruding above the sunken hollows of his cheeks. 'Dear Lord,' he said in a broken whisper, 'what death and carnage we have wreaked on my bark.'

I noticed how tightly the skin was drawn across his wasted features. Softly, he collapsed backwards, his breath ragged.

'Captain Brogel, we have the ship!' I said breathlessly, touching his arm. 'Your command is restored, sir.'

He gripped my hand with fierce strength and stared up.

'Stalbone – the Lord preserve you. If I do not live to see another day, the bark is yours. Take her – take the *Cornelius*.'

'But you shall live, sir – you must!'

There was a great sadness in his eyes now. 'Help me on deck, Matthew. I will speak to the men.'

'Sir, I protest it is impossible in your condition. You must remain here and rest awhile.' I saw Neeta gazing at Josua Brogel, her face wet with tears and blood. 'Neeta, come over here,' I said softly, 'and tend to our captain. He must keep here, safe by you.'

I gave her an encouraging squeeze on the arm, quickly collected up my pistols and left the Great Cabin, heading for the companionway steps. In the gloom of the passage, I stumbled again on the obstruction on the sole that moments before had caused me to fall helpless in front of Pengarth. Cursing, I gave it a vicious kick.

'Ooowww!' wailed the voice of the Supernumerary.

'For the Lord's sake, Sorenson,' I said in irritation, and partly relief. 'I dam' nearly shot you.'

'O save me, Mister Stalbone. They forced me, you know.' His fingers clutched at me like the tentacles of a squid. 'There's the gold too – we can share it if –'

'Up, man, rise up. You chose the wrong side,' I growled, heaving on the Super's arm. I pushed him unceremoniously up the steps and we burst into the sunlight once more.

Eli, Gaspar, Jakob and the others – all of steerboard watch and some from larboard too – stood on the quarter-deck and to my astonishment a ragged cheer arose from them. By contrast, the vanquished Pengarth men squatted in a line under the rail, hands tied behind their backs, defeat on their faces.

'Here's another for you, lads,' I cried, giving Sorenson a shove. Jakob caught him and tied him up.

'O sirs!' moaned the landsman. 'I had no part in this, please understand.'

Tosher gave a sharp tug on the bindings and forced him to squat.

'Quiet, Mister Sorenson,' said the tough Dutchman, 'or I'll rip out your treacherous guts and twist them up for a fishing line.'

I saw Youssef sitting at the base of the mizen, and went to him. The Barbar looked up with a wince of pain and tried to grin. Massive black bruises were appearing at the raw welts where the rope had nearly done for him.

'Youssef's not – ready – to die – yet, my friend,' he said, in a voice no stronger than a whisper. 'Maybe the Barbar – must listen to Mattoo. Next time – I wait – for you.'

I reproached myself bitterly, wishing I had been there to forestall the mistimed attack, or if not, at least to add my weight against the mutineers.

'Youssef, on this ship we must never fight amongst ourselves again,' I told him, smiling and giving a him pat on the shoulder. Then I cast my eye right round the decks. All was quiet after the mayhem of the fight.

'Fellows, we are the victors,' I called.

The loyal seamen cheered again.

'Eli, tell me, what's our state?' I asked.

'Three dead, sir, two on their side and one on ours. We have six more wounded but they'll live. Carpenter Sedgewick locked himself in with the sailmaker, and we found Surgeon Petty hiding by the galley furnace. We have put him to work with his pitch and saws.'

I shuddered at the thought.

'Where is Gould's body?' I said, looking around at the dead and wounded.

'O, you never killed him,' said Eli. 'He is below, and the surgeon says he shall heal in time.'

Uncertain whether to be relieved that I had not killed the man or alarmed at his living, I said, 'He must remain a prisoner. Keep him bound and confined.'

Then I caught sight of Adam Pyne and his men, entangled in our dispute, and who had suffered the fight helpless and bound, lashed to the rail.

'Free the men of the *Success*,' I ordered. 'Let them step up here.'

They were released and led forward by the midshipman, now the senior officer amongst them, for their First Lieutenant lay dead and the Second, who had taken a stray ball in the forearm, was half-delirious and in no state to speak.

'Midshipman Pyne, we of the *Cornelius* extend our apologies for the treatment you have endured. We wish you no further harm.' I put a hand on the

324

boy's shoulder. 'You're a good fellow, I believe, and we welcome you and any other man who wants to join us, as your own vessel seems a poor place for a seaman. Tell me, an English midshipman learns the Navigation aboard a warship, does he not?'

The young fellow brightened. 'Aye, sir – we are taught all the Methods.'

'After today, Adam,' I said, 'our ship needs a man like you.'

Silent on the blood-soaked boards of the quarter-deck, Midshipman Pyne studied me for a long moment, thinking perhaps of the life aboard a free privateer and what it might have in store for him. Then slowly he shook his head.

'My loyalty must be to the King and his Navy,' he said, his look steady.

'I understand. Take your fellows away in the longboat with the First Lieutenant's body.'

'Aye, sir,' said Adam, and led the way to the side of the ship.

There came a sound behind me, and Brogel appeared with Neeta at the head of the companion, his face grey with pain as he leant for support on the girl's arm. I stepped forward at once with Eli and we helped him across the quarter-deck to the break, where he stood looking out over his men assembled in the waist of the ship. A murmur rose from the seamen gathered there.

I felt Brogel's body quiver as he leant his weight against me and took up a long breath. 'Well fought, loyal men of the *Cornelius*.' His voice shook. 'I salute you and I honour you. But I speak now in some haste, as I fear – I fear the loss of my strength.

Before God, I believe I may not captain you tomorrow.'

There was silence, for none aboard could bear to give out a hollow denial of what we all could see was the plain truth.

'We cannot be without a leader,' he said at last, surveying the assembled men. 'In the tradition of a free ship, I propose we vote for a captain to succeed me.' He stopped short, and breathed painfully, clawing at his chest.

Jakob Tosher stepped out and stood before the assembly.

'Captain Brogel,' he said, 'we believe you are a brave man to speak so clear and strong to us. We wish you to continue as our captain, and that is what we fought for today. But –' He cleared his throat. 'If it comes to that pass, and we must have another as captain, then we know who our captain shall be.'

The dozen or more men in front of us exchanged looks, and muttered unintelligibly. As I leaned forward to hear, there must have been an anxious look about me.

Tosher caught my eye and gave an awkward grin.

'Say it more boldly, fellows. If we have a captain other than Captain Brogel, then it must be the one who led us to our recent victory. It must be Mister Stalbone!'

A great shout went up. The men waved their weapons in the air, calling out in support. I had hardly dared allow it, but now the truth of it was out, and I could see plain enough what they wanted.

Brogel's hand gripped my arm, and he gave a weak smile.

'Men – I honour your choice,' he said, and to my astonishment, the captain bowed low before them. 'In Mister Stalbone, you shall have a captain worthy of the title. From this moment I relinquish my active command to him, if he accepts the duty you have placed upon his shoulders.'

Of course I had dreamed of command of a vessel at sea. Yet in those dreams, the bark was a collier like the *Prosperous Anne*, or a Baltick trader, a bark of my own with perhaps a half-dozen in her crew and a hold full of wares for trade. How had it come about that I might captain a Dutch flyer, a privateer with forty or more men aboard, and one of the handiest fighting ships in the whole of the Main? I swallowed hard, touched by the show of loyalty from the men, deeply moved by Brogel's faith in me. Yet something disturbed me. I have lived barely twenty one years of life, I thought. Can I be master so young? I sensed a crushing weight settling on my shoulders, the burden of command and its dues of responsibility. It was as if I had been offered the wings of a magnificent bird in exchange for losing the use of my hands.

At last I managed to find my voice.

'This is what every man here wants – that I take command of the *Cornelius*?'

There was a chorus of 'ayes', strong and lusty, and I stood dazed, thinking how far the Dutch bark had brought me since the day I was plucked from the freezing seas off the Essex coast.

'You're good and brave fellows,' I said, aware of a crack in my voice. 'I pledge my life and my best endeavours to you, and to the *Cornelius*. She is the

327

finest vessel in the Main or the Americas. We shall work long and hard to be a crew worthy of her. Together, we shall keep her the fastest flyer on the high seas.'

The men banged their half-pikes and stamped their feet in a drumbeat of victory.

Then Captain Josua Brogel waved his arm in agitation and the noise subsided.

'Well spoken, fellows! He shall lead you well.' His voice rose into a quavering cry. 'He has full command, I say – let him propose the future of our ship. But first, bring forward the traitors. Bring me those who were for Pengarth and Gould.'

Jakob and the others pulled the uninjured men to their feet – the wounded could not rise – and roughly pushed them forward. They were eight, and stood with their eyes downcast.

The tars began a rhythmical chant. 'Hang them, hang them, hang the traitors!' they cried, and shuffled and stamped their bare feet on the warm deck-boards.

'No! They are defeated, but they shall not die,' Brogel said. He directed his gaze at each man, and each in turn diverted his eye.

'Face me,' he said.

The Pengarth fellows were prodded from behind with pistols and the points of half-pikes. Sullenly, they glared back at Brogel.

'Free them,' he said levelly.

Jakob and Gaspar and old Eli and all the rest of the sailors exchanged looks.

I was unable to hold my peace. 'Sir – Captain

Brogel, how can we free them? They are a canker amongst us.'

Brogel did not turn to meet my eye, but slowly said, 'And what would you have done by them?'

'I would –' I faltered. 'I would have them kept them in chains, sir. Or sent ashore to fend for themselves and –'

'And how many men,' said the captain, so low I barely heard him, 'are needed aboard to sail this bark, and to fight her?'

At once, I caught up with him. Of course – it was madness to think we could muster any firepower aboard the *Cornelius* if she were cornered or attacked. We needed those men, either aloft or at the braces or at the deck-pieces. Without them, we were a skeleton crew who could do no more than direct the ship's head to here or to there, but never fend off an enemy or put up an attack or fight off a prize-seeker. How could I be so dull as to have even thought it? What fist would I make of this command?

'They are beaten now, fellows!' Brogel's raised voice broke my thoughts. 'We shall make sailors of them again. Cut their bonds and let them stand free.'

The tars obeyed, slashing the ropes with their knives. The freed men rubbed their wrists, huddling close for safety.

'We need you,' Brogel went on. 'But weapons and drink are forbidden you. Off-watch, you shall remain below decks. Break our trust and you face the consequences. Tell me you accept these terms.'

The beaten men mumbled, and shifted nervously.

'Say "aye" to it – raise up your voices so I can hear,' said the captain.

'Aye,' they said at last, 'aye aye, sir.'

Behind them, the victorious seamen raised a shout of support. But the huge effort had done for Brogel's strength, and he slumped forward exhausted, bearing his full weight on my arms.

'Matthew – I have done all I can,' he whispered. 'I am so fatigued.'

To a further chorus of cheers, we – Eli, Neeta and myself – assisted our venerated captain to the companionway. He gave my arm a trembling squeeze and then he was gone. I returned to the break of the poop and stood before my men.

The bark was mine for now, but there was more to be done to make whole the wounds of the day. Everyone waited, and I supposed they were wondering what their new commander's first orders would be. I almost wondered at it myself, and even my own voice sounded detached.

'We must be ready to make for sea,' I declared, 'so I name Youssef the new sailing-master in place of Pengarth. Eli Savary and Jakob Tosher shall be the second mates, steerboard and larboard. Divide the watches as you will, but keep the traitors apart. Let's put sawdust on the boards and repair the ship's gear. We'll put to sea and bury the dead. When we're done, we'll break out small beer and sugar-rum. And kill fresh pork and make a feast.'

The crew of the *Cornelius* clapped heartily. Lord, I thought, if I have only learnt a hundredth of Josua Brogel's wisdom, it must help me now.

While everyone dispersed to their tasks, Eli came to me with a concerned look.

'Mister – er, Captain Stalbone, sir,' he said, pointing at my leg where wood splinters stuck out and the blood ran wet.

'In good time, second mate. First, care for those with worse than this. Pitch the Quaker's stump, cheer him with sugar-rum and tell him he can steer with one hand.'

With a worried shrug, he loped off to the rail where Quaker John sat in misery.

Now, I said to myself, I have good fellows with me, we have rescued the bark from the mutineers, and most of all, I have found my Abigail. What a day this has been! I went to the rail and looked out over the bay. The afternoon was sticky and close and the smell of drying blood lingered in my nostrils. Though my throat still rasped from the sharp tang of powder smoke, I breathed deeply, filling my lungs and exhaling at length, feeling exhaustion creep over me.

I watched as the Navy men loaded First Lieutenant Slush's body into their boat, clambered in and pushed off for the *Success*, with Pyne calling out the strokes. Wondering what they might find on their return, I let my eye rest a moment on the English warship lying quietly across the still water. Then my gaze stretched beyond and towards the sandy beach where I had left Abigail and her father only an hour before, though it seemed half a lifetime. At the sight of a movement there, I jerked bolt upright and squinted to see the better. A small launch was putting off from the shore and sculling towards the warship, rowed by a couple of burly fellows. It was the one we had taken from the *Success*. With a sudden fear, I went to the cuddy box by the wheel and snatched up the spy-glass. Twisting the tube, I brought it to bear on the shore and, raking back and forth, studied all around our landing place and the beaten track that led away from it. Amongst the tranquil vegetation, all was utterly quiet and still. Of Abigail and her father, there was not a sign.

They had gone, I had no doubt of it, to the Jamestown settlement. Jeffreys must have forced his daughter into the interior, to get her away from me – and back to John Lynskill, back to her husband.

Slamming the tube shut, I spun round and charged over to the rail, slipping on the wet patches and loose splinters lying about. Not more than a hundred strokes distant was the *Success*'s longboat, drawing sluggishly away, burdened with her men and their dead officer.

'Pyne!' I bellowed. 'Turn back, if you will.'

Half a cable off, the midshipman looked up puzzled, then had the longboat sculled round and brought back.

'Gaspar,' I called, spotting him passing into the waist. 'Bring me a pair of pistols and powder horns. Clean and load them for me, and let me have a cutlass.' Going to Youssef, I leaned over him. 'My friend, can you hold the ship for me?' He tried to struggle up, but I pressed him gently down, saying, 'Stay where you are – the men shall obey you. Make ready for sea, and if there's any trouble, take her out.'

He smiled lopsidedly. 'For that girl again, is it?'

'Not a girl, Youssef,' I snapped. 'Not the way you think.'

But then I softened. I was intensely glad the battle was done. We had saved the ship, Youssef had lived and the future seemed filled with promise. All doubt flew from me. I had only to deal with Lynskill, and she was mine.

'Wait for me till the sun goes down, Youssef, that's all I ask.'

As it sunk in to his numbed head, the Barbar began to show alarm. 'Mattoo cannot leave ship now.' He winced as he grasped my wrist, and the note of misgiving in his voice turned to anger. 'It is insult – contempt of those who fight for you.'

I was stunned. Did he think I was abandoning the *Cornelius* on a mere whim?

'Nonsense, I shall return immediately. I must find Abigail, and that's an end of it.'

'Mattoo still a fool, just like at Dartmouth.' With an effort, he twisted to one side and spat emphatically onto the deck-boards. 'What kind of a captain is it who can learn nothing? Nothing!'

I was riven by the vehemence of his feeling, and it came to me that I had not considered the greater jeopardy. But he was right, I was risking all – my command, the safety of our bark, everything. Unable to respond, I swept my gaze around the decks, only half-seeing the awful results of our bloody encounter – the wounded men slumped by the rail awaiting the surgeon's care, the broken cutlasses and spent pistols heaped in the scuppers, the sun-beaten decks patched with fresh sawdust soaking up red spatters of blood. A trace of burnt powder caught in the back of my throat as I turned back to Youssef, forcing a dry, rasping cough from me. I swallowed hard before speaking.

'To this ship,' I said thickly, 'and to those who sail her and fight upon her decks, I pledged my life.' My eyes watered and his features turned to no more than a blur. 'But not my soul, Youssef. That belongs to another, and I am driven to her above all else.'

'By Allah's mercy,' he breathed, his eyelids drooping in weariness.

My course was determined, and I stood up. 'If the English relief hoves in, you must put her to sea.' There came no reply, and I spoke more sharply. 'You'll hove up the anchor for sea, sailing-master. Agreed?'

The Barbar shrugged, then nodded. At once, I sprang away shouting, 'Gaspar – give me those pieces and a blade.'

The young sailor came running over, carrying two pistols and a pouch full of balls, wad and powder. Tucking the guns into my slops and the cutlass at my leather belt, I ran to the rail and vaulted it cleanly, landing with an almighty crash in the *Success*'s longboat. The oarsmen gaped.

'Midshipman Pyne, your pardon,' I said, and could not hide my relish at the very idea, 'but I beg the Navy's service one more time.'

He grinned, and gave the order. 'Pull away, lads, with a will!'

The oars dipped with regular strokes and, as the *Cornelius* grew more distant, the busy sounds of her crew at work receded into the humid afternoon air. She looks almost a toy, I thought, like the model a shipbuilder makes before the keel is laid or a plank sawn or a spar planed. But after the exhilaration of battle, the affairs of the ship seemed diminished now, its concerns minor. Even the thought of my captaincy evaporated like a morning sea-mist in the sun's glare. My present mission was beyond all such considerations.

# 18

# *Relief*

Midshipman Pyne, at my request, had the longboat steered to the landing place. I sprang from the bows with a shout of thanks and splashed the few steps to the beach, hearing him call the order to back off the strand even before I had properly gained a footing on the land. I stumbled ashore calling out her name, but in my bones I knew she would be gone.

Yards from the strand, the vegetation closed in around me except for the single foot-track that led off into the interior between tall clumps of swamp-grass and scraggy bushes. There was no sign of her or Jeffreys ever having been here.

'Abigail!' I called over and again. The thick planting absorbed my shout as if it were made of sponge. No sound returned but the receding clack of oarlocks as the longboat stroked away to the great hulk of the warship. Roundly, I cursed myself for ever having left her. If only I had better understood that Jeffreys would do anything to part us.

Hurriedly, I checked my pistols and, finding them dry, girded the cutlass belt around my waist and set off down the track towards the wisps of smoke rising from where I took the main settlement to lie. The track wound as if beaten out by drunkards, narrowing my view to nothing but the immediate ten yards ahead. So it was that the first settlement building I saw appeared of a sudden. It was a rough wooden arrangement of slatted boards, unpainted and crudely wrought, tilting where it had sunk some inches into the soft ground. If this was Jamestown, it was a mean place. But I knew from seamen's tales brought aboard that many shoreside ventures turned to the bad, for the country was wild, the soil diseased, the forests infested with savage animals and the plains thronged with fierce men native to the land.

I halted at the sight of the shack, and listened. Faint murmurings came to my ears, as of men talking in private. I crept forward with a pistol in my hand, cocked and ready. Peering round the corner, I found it was no more than eight feet long and half as wide, with a blank doorway in the side. I gained the opening in one stride and challenged whoever might be within.

'You there!' I called. 'What place is this?'

On the instant, the talk ceased. Silence reigned, except for the tremor of a breeze swishing the tall grasses. I gripped the butt of my pistol and took a pace forward into the doorway.

The gloom inside was deep. For a second I saw nothing, then a movement caused me to tense my arm and I almost discharged the piece without intending it. An instant later – thank the Lord – I realised the man squatting in the hut was unarmed and quite harmless to me. With widening surprise, I found myself staring at four such men, all Negroes, huddled into the interior of this box with their legs pulled up to their chins. None moved a limb to the tiniest degree as I moved carefully forward from the glare outside, the better to see them.

The men's eyes, the only patches of white against the dark walls and their black bodies, bore intently on me. I made out chains shackling their feet, manacles at their hands and neck-clamps of iron fixed to the boards behind each one. My mouth opened at the sight, and I tasted air that was close and stinking, a breath such as the one I remembered from the Godforsaken *Tryall*. So here, I thought as the sight revealed itself to me, were Africkan slaves at their destination, kept still in vile conditions, beyond endurance, beyond my imagination.

At last, I lowered my weapon, for I was safe from men who could barely move to scratch themselves, and gathered my senses enough to speak.

'Is this Jamestown?'

No one answered. Did they comprehend any tongue but their own?

'Jamestown?' I said again. Nothing. I tried a different tack. 'Lynskill?'

It was unmistakable. At the name, one of the Negroes flashed a look of anger at me.

'Where?' I said. 'Where is the Lynskill house?'

The moment was gone, and their eyes returned to the dull, withdrawn gaze of before, as if into an interior world. Yet is this their only means to resist, I thought, to keep the Africkan spirit unbroken even though their backs are put to labour and their hands shackled?

Quickly, I returned to the sunlight and took off at a pace along the path. A second slave-hut loomed from the enclosing swamp-grass, then a third, then two more. I glanced inside one and saw the scene of the first repeated exactly, four full-grown Africkan fellows cramped together in chains, and knew I had no need to see inside the next after that, or the dozen more that I stumbled on as I went. In a small open space, where the planting had been cut back, I found a stack of tools – picks, hoes, rakes, hooks and the like – an armoury of work implements for the ranks of softly singing Negroes at their labours and the overseers with their whips, as I had seen on the saltings of Sint Maarten. I quickened my pace, as much to distance myself from the conditions of slavery as to pursue my search.

At a run now, I sweated in the accursed heat, frothing saliva as I railed at the owners and slavers who profited by the trade and bought and sold black men as if they were less than sheep or cattle. Yet I knew in my heart from where my anger sprang. It was the thought of John Lynskill, and the others of his family, who had kept good Whitby men in hard labour and lived off their backs, and enclosed our land, and taxed us for no return. These were the Lynskills who had gone from Whitby with their spoils and invested it into yet more enslavement, a thousand leagues away in another land, yet rooted alike in tyranny and greed. And Lynskill was the man who had taken Abigail from me, who had married her.

Half insane with rage, I careered out of the dank vegetation into the open before I could arrest my run. Panting, I stood in the middle of a street of sorts, my two pistols raised and ready, my blood heated and my anger burning, sending me beyond all reason. If anything had moved in that instant, I would in my madness have shot it down in contempt.

But the street, a broad path of beaten earth and stones, lay empty and silent. Nothing moved or made a sound. Rough, clapboard houses were ranged along it either side, with raised boardwalks before them against the cloying filth of the wet months. Further off, the broadway disappeared into a shimmering wall of heat rising in rippling waves from the packed, flattened mud. The place wore a hangdog air, as if the builders of the dwellings had lost faith in their work and moved on long ago. Slowly, I calmed, and a measure of level-headedness returned. If this was Jamestown, I thought, it is a poor venture indeed, a far remove from the flourishing and prosperous New World I had had in my mind's eye when Abigail first told me of it.

I listened hard. Noises came from the distance, muffled by the thick air and unrelenting heat of the sun. Smoke rose from the very far end of the broadway. I discerned shouts and what might have been the clash of arms.

In a house to one side, a movement caught my eye, no more than a quickly withdrawn hand or the corner of a dress pulled back from sight. The town, it dawned on me, was peopled well enough, but whoever these faint-hearted souls were, they cowered behind their doors and breathed like animals gone to ground, fearful of discovery, in terror of attack. A hundred pairs of eyes, I realised with a prickle at my spine, were turned on me, yet I could not see a one.

I sloped off to the right hand where the movement had been, stepped like a cat onto the boardwalk, reached the first door and wrenched it back. It came clean off the hinge and clattered to the ground raising dust and, startled though I was, I was quicker than her.

'O sir!' cried the woman, struggling to free her hand from mine. 'No harm – I beg you – I have children here!'

She crouched under my grip, the skin of her face browned to a leather tan and creased by the sun, her countenance perhaps a decade beyond her true years.

'I'll not harm you,' I said, relinquishing her hand from my iron clasp, 'if you answer me this. Where is the Lynskill dwelling? Quickly, woman!'

'At the – the end of the broadway, sir,' she said fearfully. 'The Squire Lynskill's house lies beyond – before the grass plain begins.'

'Squire Lynskill?' My own voice sounded like another's, harsh and distant in my ears. 'What commotion is down there?'

'They're gone to – O sir, I want no trouble! Our men have gone to fire his house – they are angry. He has cheated them – all of us – he is a torment on us and – '

But I was gone, racing along the street between the buildings, which seemed ready to collapse on their footings, and mostly were closed up and abandoned. It looked an awful, desperate place, and I longed to be away from it and back at sea.

After a few minutes, I saw it up ahead. Set back from the tall grasses, on a smooth, green plain-sward, stood a fine white house of two storeys, with lattice-framed windows and a portico to its front door. The contrast with the neglected, mean air of the settlement was complete, and I had no need to speculate neither whose house this could be, nor why the settlers might take up in revolt against its occupier.

At the front of the Lynskill mansion was a band of thirty or forty men, mostly rough-clothed, waving pikes and farm tools and raising up a cry. One or two carried torch-brands, and were setting about firing the clapboard of the house at one corner. They were after John Lynskill, but all that mattered to me was that Abigail must be inside.

I broke away to the north and worked along behind the last of the broadway buildings towards a clump of trees at the rear of the big house. Approaching close in a crouch, I saw a young lad squatting nervously on the step of the kitchen door, a long-pike across his knee. He had not spied me. Shoving my pistols into my belt, I stepped boldly forward.

'Well done, lad – we are nearly through at the front,' I said.

He looked at me like a grouse startled in a bush. His mouth gaped open and he began to rise. I was on him before he spoke the first word, one hand smothering his face, the other behind his neck. I forced him down to his knees and the pike fell to the ground.

'Quiet, my lad, is all I ask of you, and you shall

come to no harm,' I said, pushing his face against the earth and planting a foot firmly on his neck. Ripping a strip of shirt off his back, I tied his wrists, then took another piece and gagged him. With the remains of the garment, I bound up his feet and drew them to his hands, knotting them together as if he were a hog at market. But I was careful not to hurt him, for he is only a farmer's lad, I thought, a virgin in battles and fighting, and surely wishes he could stay such.

Turning, I hefted the cutlass in my right hand and a pistol in my left, and stepped up to the kitchen door. I tested it and found it locked, but a sharp kick sprung it open with a crack. I squinted into the interior where a passage led off ahead with doorways to either side. All the shutters were drawn and little light illuminated the house, but my eyes soon became accustomed and the gloom lifted. The floorboards creaked under foot as I traversed the passage in a few steps, then put my head round the door-jamb to the left.

What greeted me was the sight of opulence without restraint. I saw tapestries hung from every wall, handsome highbacks, a mahogany dining-table of eight or nine feet length, chests, vases and lamps, ornaments lining the mantel – all the baubles and diversions of a rich man's house, what I considered now the booty of the Lynskills' plunder.

Though the ground floor was deserted, I knew I could not linger, for I heard the ominous crackle of flames and a multitude of shouts raised outside.

'Lay down your pistols, sir!' called a dignified

voice on the far side of the great front door. 'We come as farmers, not warriors. Our sole desire is to make peace and a bargain.'

There were muffled cries coming from above the ceiling. I went to the bottom of the stairs and took them two at a time to gain the turn, where I stopped again and listened. Surely, too, I heard a woman's voice raised. There was more light reaching the landing but a haze of smoke filled the upstairs passageway, so I crept to the nearest door and, hearing movements behind it, leaned closer to listen. To my surprise the unlatched door swung freely back revealing a high-ceilinged, double-windowed withdrawing room.

I immediately laid eyes on John Lynskill, standing at the window with half the shutter drawn back, pistol raised. Abigail was crouched next to him, holding spare pistols for defence against the mob. I had just time to spy Mister Jeffreys huddled by the window next along when Lynskill turned my way.

'Who the Devil is this?' he roared.

The sight of Abigail, whole and unharmed, left me off my guard. Lynskill levelled his weapon and fired. I raised my arm by instinct, and felt it buck bone-jarringly. My cutlass blade broke clean in two and the pieces flew away, clattering as they went. Then I crashed to the floor, stunned by the sledge-hammer shock, and felt my arm numbed from the hand to the shoulder, where I guessed the ball had struck. Unbidden, my left hand released its grip on the pistol, and I lay disarmed and helpless.

'Matthew – fly while you can!' screamed Abigail.

From a half-sitting position, dazed and disoriented, weaponless, I could do nothing to help myself.

Lynskill grabbed her wrists and held them as if they were kindling sticks, for the soft young man of Whitby days had become a fellow of formidable build and strength. Abigail let one pistol drop but clung determinedly to the second.

'Give me that,' Lynskill grunted, groping as she held it aloft.

I retrieved my fallen weapon and tried to bring it to bear with my left hand, but the two of them were twisting in a parody of a dance. With such a shaky aim, I could not risk a shot.

The crowd outside had fallen silent, but now they seemed to regain their spirits, and a voice boomed up from below.

'Squire Lynskill, we bear no pistols or muskets! Cease your firing and treat with us, I beg you, like the honourable man we know you to be.'

Lynskill, cursing the Lord to Hell and back again, ignored the plea. Mister Jeffreys, hunched by the sill, appeared utterly bewildered, moaning over and over, 'Let her go, let my daughter go.'

'You stupid girl,' cried John Lynskill, sweat pouring down his quivering face. 'Give me the dam' pistol.'

'Free her!' I shouted, half rising.

Lynskill narrowed his eyes. 'Just who in Hell's own name are you? Jeffreys, loose off your piece, you idiot. Put him down, can't you?'

'My daughter, my daughter,' bleated the merchant.

Smoke billowed in through the open window, momentarily distracting Lynskill.

'Look – these blasted fellows are torching my house,' he said. 'Jeffreys, you're not worth your pitiful dowry if you don't shoot.'

I struggled up with the intent of making a lunge, but it only served to make Lynskill grow more agitated towards Abigail.

'Miserable bitch – give me the dam' pistol!' he shouted. 'Blast it, she has the brains of a sheep.'

The merchant's face darkened. 'Do not say such things, sir!' he hissed. 'You may go too far, you know.'

'What's the point, merchant? There's nothing left save your daughter's company in my bed –'

A pistol shot discharged with a flash and an explosive crack. Taking the full force of the ball at close range, Lynskill sprawled backwards knocking Abigail over with him. A look of disbelief spread across his face, and he slid to the floor.

There was a moment of silence, then there came an anguished voice.

'By the Lord's great mercy, have I killed him? But the way he spoke – the Lord save us, save us O Lord!'

Seth Jeffreys, dazed, lowered his smoking weapon, not taking his eyes off Lynskill for an instant. The Squire lay brokenly, a small hole the size of a gold sovereign burnt through the loose shirt. Blood trickled from the ball's entry and his face registered pure surprise.

'Good God, Jeffreys,' was all he said.

Unsteadily, I crossed the room. The inside of my

mouth felt like cork, my shoulder throbbed, but I could think of only one thing. Using my left arm, and steadying it with the agonised right, I raised the pistol to Lynskill's head, two inches from the temple. The barrel shook. My finger closed around the trigger.

'We shall be rid of him,' I heard myself say.

Abigail put her hand on the pistol. 'There is no need, Matthew.'

Her voice was barely a whisper. I blinked. The effort of holding the pistol at arm's length grew intolerable. Then all of a sudden, my sense returned. Very slowly I lowered the weapon and looked at her. Thank the Lord, I thought, that she keeps her head when I lose mine.

Suddenly weary, I fell against the shutters and let the pistol drop, clutching my arm. It felt as though a hundred men had stamped upon it and beaten it with staves.

'Where has the ball struck?' I croaked.

Abigail ran her hands gently from my aching shoulder to the numbed wrist.

'There is no blood and no wound,' she said. 'You have suffered no more than a shock. Try to move the hand and fingers.'

I made a fist and released it. Shafts of pure pain ran up my arm and shot through my neck. My head reeled, but I knew at once she was right, and brought myself to examine the limb. It was quite whole, and I allowed a moment's relief to overcome me.

Below, the settlers were in tumult, having heard the shots. Even with Lynskill down, the danger remained great, for we had to make an escape and rejoin the *Cornelius* without delay.

'Quick, we must fly.' I tugged Abigail towards the door.

She resisted. 'My husband is not dead.'

I glared down at the bleeding Lynskill, and back at her. 'He's surely done for,' I told her, 'for the ball has passed into his chest.'

'It is a small wound. We cannot leave him.'

I gazed at her, disbelieving. 'Lord, Abigail, he was ready to kill us. And he has cheated and stolen and lied his way into riches. He deserves to die.' I gave a dismissive wave of my hand and poked a foot into the merchant's ribs. 'Get up, Mister Jeffreys. It's a wonder to me that you should be worth saving. You pledge your own daughter like a sack of grain for the highest bid.'

Abigail was incensed. 'I shall not hear it! My father has just saved your life – and mine. Think on it, Matthew.' She gripped my shoulders and shook me, making me wince in pain, but I was dazzled by the fierceness of her anger. 'You came for me, and you must take my faith and my loyalties too. I shall not leave this man to die.'

She went to Lynskill and tried vainly to lift him. He groaned and opened his dull and unseeing eyes.

'Help me with my husband,' she said quietly.

'Leave him,' I pleaded. 'He's as good as dead and he'll slow us down. Besides, the settlers will connect us with him.'

'Father, please help me,' she said, oddly calm.

Seth Jeffreys went cautiously over and together they dragged him upright. Clutching his reddening chest, Lynskill swayed like a drunken bear, leaning on Abigail. He gazed at me, glassy-eyed.

'Help me,' said John Lynskill.

His pleading tones disgusted me, and I clenched my teeth. 'I ought to have killed you in Whitby with my bare hands.'

His eyes were large with fear. 'Whitby? God – now I know you. It's Stalbone – the blasted rebel we should have hanged. Along with the rest of the rubbish.' He drew breath to a gurgling sound. Then his face clouded, perhaps in the shadow of death, and he sagged. 'Whatever – was in the past – I beg you to aid me now.'

I hesitated, sensing Abigail's eyes intent on me. I have too much to lose, I thought dully. Why risk it all to save the life of this unspeakable man? I would gladly watch him die. I want only to run away with Abigail, and regain my *Cornelius*, and escape from Jamestown altogether, and from Lynskill and the Hellish past.

But it was all too late. Even as I dallied with these workings of my mind, the settlers seized their chance. They smashed aside the front door to a chorus of victorious shouts and in seconds they were halfway up the stairs. For the briefest moment, I considered scooping up Abigail and making a leap to freedom from the window, but in my heart I knew that was a chance already lost to us. Hastily, I grabbed the spare pistols, but even the act of springing back the lock sent a thrill of fiery pain into my damaged arm. With a great commotion, the settlers advanced along the passage, the door burst open and they jammed themselves into the frame, a

349

dozen or more of them jostling with their staves and rakes and hoes braced at us.

'Stand where you are!' I said, a pistol quivering in each hand. 'The first two men to take a single step further shall die.'

'No violence!' called a voice from behind the throng. 'I pray to God, let here be no killing.'

I kept my aim as a stocky man of perhaps sixty years, in a long frock-coat and brimmed hat, elbowed his way to the front. He took in the scene with a horrified look, his eye lingering on Lynskill's bloodied form. Then he spoke in unhurried calm, spreading his palms wide in an unmistakable gesture of peace.

'Squire Lynskill, let there be no further blood-shed. It is all I can do to prevent the looting of your house, and the lynching of your goodself, no doubt. I beg you, command your fellow here to give up his weapons and abandon this violent cause.'

Lynskill leaned groggily against Abigail's slight figure. He must have been trying to speak but only a gurgle came, and a stream of blood and spittle ran down his chin.

'I do not know you, sir,' I said, swivelling my pistols to point at the speaker's chest, 'but I am not under Heaven's eye any fellow of this Lynskill. Neither have I any quarrel with you. The Squire's corpus is yours in exchange for safe passage for my party. Stand aside and let us pass.'

Abigail gave a sharp intake of breath, perhaps at the bargain I was laying down. But at the same instant, she was forced to quit the effort of keeping Lynskill's body upright. With a noisy sigh, his leaden bulk sagged to the ground and he lay spread-eagled face down, quite still and stone dead. For the first time, we saw in his back a bloody hole, four inches round, where on passing through the ball had carried away the bone, the flesh and now the life.

A gasp of excitement issued from the mob.

'Let no one move!' I said. 'There is your man, and all that you wish for is yours too. Take the house and its fancy furnishings and let that be a settlement to all your affairs. But stand aside for us.'

The settler's leader looked thoughtful, and his gaze travelled slowly from Lynskill's inert form and fixed on me.

'All the house and its contents?' he said evenly. 'For your free passage?'

I heard beside me Mister Jeffreys wailing softly.

'Indeed,' I replied, 'for none of us here believes any of it to be worth a poor candle against our lives and our freedom.'

'The Squire has not paid for our crops, nor provided Negroes, nor provisioned our pantries,' said the speaker. 'Nor has he given us the tools and seeds he promised, but instead extracted only bills, and hoarded the investment of our good faith. It seems an honourable bargain to take his property, for he shall enjoy no further use of it.' He swung round. 'What do we say, my fellows? Shall this house and all that's in it be our recompense?'

The mob shouted 'Aye' as one man.

'Then away, fellows, and clear a passage for these good people!'

They fell back down the stairs and with Abigail at my side and Jeffreys clinging to her frock, we passed freely out of the house, though I warily kept my weapons to the front. The speaker nodded and beamed as we went, his solemnity now replaced by a look of unbridled merriment, almost as if we had been guests who had graced his own house for an evening of innocent pleasure.

With great relief and thanks to the Lord, we sped off across the open, until at last I felt able to lower my guard and give relief to my arm. Distantly, we heard the sounds of the triumphant mob looting the house. Whoops of joy were quickly followed by the crash of breaking porcelain and valuables as the squabbling began for the choicest spoils.

The three of us dodged rapidly along the broadway and soon entered the narrow, twisting track where the tall swamp-grasses hemmed us in. The afternoon's bold light had softened into a slant and, realising how close it had grown to sunset, I spurred us onwards until we had passed by the brooding misery of the slave-huts and approached the shore.

Mister Jeffreys was beside himself with agitation, and kept up a constant refrain.

'All gone!' he repeated. 'All that we hoped for, gone from us.'

'Be silent, sir,' I rasped. 'Is it not enough that you thoughtlessly endangered your own daughter by taking her back there?'

'No, Matthew,' said Abigail, 'it was my own wish to go to the mansion, to retrieve what I could. Even so, it is little enough.' She put her hand on a cloth bag tied at her waist, which nestled into her belly in a way that betrayed its weight. 'The pity is we could not save Lynskill himself.'

352

I stopped and pulled her to me, a little roughly, I admit. But what was this now about her damn'd husband?

'What? Why did you wish him to live?' I almost bawled.

She was red-faced and quite as hot in temper as I was. 'He was a card to play, can't you see it? With his family, I mean to say. They are not to know the marriage was unconsummated. As my husband, he was more valuable to us alive.'

'I would take no money from that vile family!' I said, livid at the very thought.

'Then I trust you have gold enough aboard your bark,' she said, with a sweet look, 'to live well and honest upon your pedestal, though your appearance gives the lie to it, being more that of a common sailor.'

I was silenced, but boiling with anger none the less. Once again I had wrongly reckoned the quick mind and resolution of the girl. I let her arm fall from my grip and strode off.

More grimly now, we marched on until at last we broke clear of cover and came upon the sandy shore. Only then did I remember we had no boat to escape in, for I had seen the *Success*'s men take it back. I was on the point of hailing the warship – which rode at anchor not two cables from where we stood – in the hope of attracting Pyne when I saw Abigail force her way off into the thick growth behind the foreshore.

'Matthew!' she called. 'Help me with the boat.'

Dashing over, I found her with the small launch drawn right up and well-hidden, not forty paces from the open shore. It dawned on me that I must have seen the *Success*'s crew, out in their second launch, searching for but failing to find ours. Abigail had gone to great lengths to cover up the path it had made as she and her father dragged into hiding.

'Lord,' I said, in admiration, 'you did well to hide it.'

She straightened up and laughed. 'Why, what would you expect, that I left it in full sight for anyone to take?'

Abashed, I set to pulling the launch down to the shore, calling out to Mister Jeffreys to help me with the boat. Pain shot through my shoulder, but at last, panting hard, we reached the water's edge and pushed the boat out. Abigail got in the stern, and the merchant clambered in at the centre thwarts where he and I would row to balance the little craft. Then I shoved off, splashed into the water a few paces and levered myself aboard. It promised to be a desperately hard row, with my damaged arm and only the slight Mister Jeffreys on the other sweep, but pull away we did, and began to put a distance between our little vessel and the American shore.

Glancing over at the *Success*, which lay to her anchors between us and the *Cornelius*, I noticed a flurry of activity at her rail. Seamen ran about and an officer gesticulated. It looked as if a gunnery practice were under way, for I saw rammers raised alongside the big guns. Perhaps the officers had regained some order and were drilling her crew. It made me uneasy to think we had no choice but to row past her right under those mighty pieces.

The merchant stopped sculling and in some puzzlement watched the activity aboard.

'Let's row on!' I ordered, digging an elbow into him. His head jerked round and he drew back the sweep as if in a dream. Then we dipped our oars in unison and the launch lurched forward.

Now, I thought, for the *Cornelius* and our escape from this Hellish place.

355

# 19

# *Departure*

It was not many moments before we were passing under the great topsides of the English warship. Although her broad, rounded walls gave an appearance of outward calm, it was clear to me the *Success* was in turmoil. Through the open gunports, looking past the cannon, I saw men running about and heard the sounds of excitement drifting across the few yards of water separating us. Drawing back my oar for a stroke, I squinted up at the high rail and caught sight of Adam Pyne's anxious face leaning over. He was waving. I saw his mouth working, but could not distinguish the words.

A rumble like the thunder of a distant Tropick squall reached me. In the same instant, the world exploded in a shattering crash, the shock of which threw me backwards, knocking my ribs violently against the gunnels. What seemed a swarm of angry insects buzzed past, and choking smoke enveloped my face so that I gagged for air. Winded, mouth blocked with dry dust, a hundred bells clanging in my ears, I blinked my stinging eyes and saw a hole gaping in the topsides six feet above us, its jagged timber edges blackened and flaming.

The launch rocked like cradle in a tempest.

Jeffreys was gone. His daughter, thrown down like a child's doll, lay inert in the stern.

'Abigail!' I choked, scrambling back to her.

She opened her eyes. Flecks of blood covered her face, and a wood splinter protruded from her cheek. Sobbing in relief, I felt her coming to life again. She sat up, clinging to the gunnels, dazed but unharmed. I held her in my arms and picked splinters from her skin, dabbing the blood away.

She moved her head from side to side, as if not knowing where to look.

'Father,' she said slowly. 'Where is Father?'

He was nowhere to be seen. Wisps of smoke drifted from the gash in the *Success*'s sides, but nothing else moved. There came a splashing sound, and Adam Pyne's dripping head surfaced by the bows. He scrabbled one-handed at the gunnels and I grasped the boy's wrist, giving it the best heave I could manage.

'Take him first!' he cried.

Mister Jeffreys' pale face bobbed in the water alongside, and I realised Pyne had gone over the side to save him. I snatched at the merchant's collar and, with a deal of shoving from Pyne, dragged him bodily inboard, bundling him none too gently into the bottom of the boat. Then I extended my arm once more.

'Up, lad!'

The midshipman lifted a bloody arm and I hauled him over the gunnel. He sat, streaming wet, on the thwart. As his clothes drained, a pool of water six inches deep sloshed from side to side in the bottom ribs, and became tinged with red.

My head rang like a cathedral's carillon and my mouth felt as though it were carved from wood. It was with the greatest difficulty that I managed to speak.

'What in the Lord's name is happening, Adam?' I gasped.

He pointed to seaward.

'Look – the English relief!'

Across the fields of swamp-grass that lay between the bay and the open sea, I saw three tall masts, the sails clewed up and the yards squared off. The hull was hidden by the grassland, but by the height of her sticks she must be a mighty vessel. With no sails set, she glided along, plainly under tow by her launches. From the truck of her topmast there hung a four-yard colour, the red and white standard of the English Navy. There was no doubt about it, the *Abundance* had come to relieve her mutinous sister.

I grasped Adam's shoulders. 'Can you pull, midshipman?'

He nodded and bent to pick up a sweep. When we had rowed a few strokes clear of the *Success*, we could see the activity on deck. Seamen ran about in apparent disorder, yet I knew this random dance from the *Cornelius*'s own engagements. The gunports were blank now, but from within the ship came the rumble of heavy wheels and the clatter and jangle of the running-out tackles. One by one, at every gunport, appeared the black snout of a culverin. I saw an officer standing white-eyed, pistol raised as if to fire a warning shot.

'Everyone – down!' I bellowed, dropping the oars and pulling Abigail flat.

Orange tongues of flame spurted from the weather-deck guns all at once, followed by a deafening crash. A wave of heat washed over us, and an eerie wail passed above as the heavy balls shot in an arc over Jamestown Roads and disappeared to seaward where we had seen the *Abundance*. Moments after came the far-off crack and thud of heavy shot striking timber.

From the same distance, again the thunder rumbled, the air whistled, and a second massive single shot buried itself in the *Success*'s topsides, smashing through into the gun-decks and sending debris flying skywards. I saw a man's body flung up as high as the mainyard like a toy, only to drop back and catch in the larboard shrouds, where it hung broken-backed.

'By the blood of the Lord,' I croaked in amazement, 'does she fight her own Navy?'

'The *Abundance* – I saw her signal,' said Pyne. 'No quarter for mutineers, so the *Success* has chosen to make a battle of it.'

'Then we must stroke on. Pull hard, man!'

We rowed with all our might to get clear of another ragged discharge from the *Success*. But much the worse threat was from the English relief. The damage her two single balls had inflicted was as nothing to her full fire-power. If the Navy's gunners had the range, when the deadly weight of her broadside came over, the last place on earth I wanted to be was near the *Success* in an open boat. We stroked on with vigour.

I glanced round to spy the *Cornelius*. She lay two cables away, undamaged. Thank God, I muttered, they are not firing at her. Her ports were shut tight and she flew signals of friendship, making her intentions plain to the English Navy. But the Great Launch was out and I noticed movement at her bows, and men at the catheads. I knew at once that Youssef was obeying my orders. They were weighing the anchors to fly the danger, and it looked as though she would be gone before we reached her.

I rowed on in a fury, determined that with Lynskill's passing and the yoke of my past lifted, I would not lose the *Cornelius*. Adam pulled in unison, matching my every stroke with a vigorous effort, and my heart warmed to him as the cutter picked up speed.

A hand clutched at my waistband.

'Matthew – my dear boy,' said the merchant Jeffreys, in a wheedling tone. 'I still have a little gold – let me pay your captain to take us away on his ship.'

'Father, hush,' said Abigail, disgusted. 'We are in mortal danger, and you speak of money! Matthew shall see us safe.'

Mister Jeffreys seemed not to hear, as if his thoughts were only on saving himself. 'You shall have your money, my dear boy,' he went on, his sharp little features contorted into an ingratiating grimace. 'I know I did you wrong before, but please –'

'Do you hear, Abigail?' I bawled, pulling viciously on the sweep. 'He confesses it – do you not see what he truly is?'

'You judge me harshly,' he bleated. 'Everything I

ever did was done for my daughter, only for my
poor daughter –'

'You are an evil, treacherous man, Seth Jeffreys!'
I cried. I threw down my oar and made as if to grab
him by the throat. The merchant shrieked in fear.

'Leave him, leave him,' cried Abigail.

A jagged sound curtailed my revenge before it
began. It seemed as if the whole lagoon trembled
beneath us. The great roar sounded so close it tore
the air apart, and I sensed rather than saw the huge
cannonballs whistling overhead. There must have
been twenty shots loosed off at once and, in a volley
of thuds and cracks, the balls struck the *Success* at
her stern quarters, shattering the gilded decorations
and sending shards of splintered wood flying. As the
warship took the force of this salvo, I swear I saw
her masts whip like saplings. Debris was hurled a
hundred feet in the air – pieces of deck, parts of
guns and morsels of humanity. The shock of the
impacts sent rings rippling outwards from her hull
across the smooth water, rocking our boat as they
passed. I had never before witnessed what destruction a broadside of heavy shot could lay upon a
vessel when the gunners hit their mark with its full
weight.

I turned from the sight of this to see the
*Cornelius*. The Great Launch's tow-line from the
bow was pulled taut, her anchors were up and she
was moving ahead. Men scrambled aloft to the
topyards and began to loosen the bunt-lines. They
had not seen us.

Lord, I thought, why do I quarrel with the
merchant when we are about to lose our ship? In a

fury at myself, I got us back to the business of rowing. The oars clacked in the rowlocks but the distance to the ship seemed hardly to diminish, until at last we began to close on the flyer. Half a cable off, we all stood and shouted and bawled at her. Heads turned, shouts went up and the rowers in the Great Launch eased their strokes.

A minute later we bumped our bow alongside the bark's hull. Youssef's face appeared at the rail high above.

'Youssef pulls Mattoo from the sea again!' he called.

The Barbar laughed a mad cackle and called men over to help. I sent Abigail and her father safely up, then, still standing in the little boat, I looked across at Pyne.

'You came with us after all,' I said.

'Aye.' He smiled faintly, and nodded towards the smoking ruin of the *Success*. 'And this time, I've little choice but to stay.'

I remembered my own circumstance, when I too had come aboard the *Cornelius*, knowing nothing of what my future might be.

'You shall not regret it, Adam. But listen, do you know the channels? Will you pilot us out, Navigator?'

Suddenly he beamed broadly. 'Pilot her? Aye, sir, I shall. And with the greatest pleasure!'

I grasped his arm and squeezed. 'Then welcome aboard the *Cornelius*, Mister Navigator.' Glancing up, I caught the sailors gawping at Abigail. 'You men there! Jump down here and go with Mister Pyne to pull along with the Great Launch.'

When they dropped over the rail, Pyne took charge of the launch and I scrambled up the line, gratefully planting my feet on the *Cornelius*'s deck-boards. At once, I saw the Barbar, pale but seemingly restored to vigorous good spirits.

'We can't keep you down, Youssef,' I said, grasping his hand. But my joy at seeing him again was not matched by the hint of a smile on his part.

'This must be the last time our captain leaves ship,' he said, grim-faced. 'No good for privateer men. We need leader here.'

He spoke in the flat tone I remembered from the forecastle when he had failed to side openly for Brogel. Was Youssef put out at my return, then, having hoped perhaps to gain command himself? Or did he merely think my judgement poor and hot-blooded in going back for Abigail, a weakness in his captain that threatened the vessel's safety and success? Whatever the Barbar may hope or wish for, I told myself, I find no doubt in my resolve. Nor shall I ever find it, not for a second.

'You know why I went, sailing-master. She stands there, and I regret nothing.'

He looked from me – my torn and ragged weskit, grimed with mud and blood – to Abigail, who stood erect, her dress filthy and ripped, and her father leaning on her for support. His brown features began to crinkle.

'Thanks be to Allah for your return,' said the Barbar, clapping me across the shoulders and grinning at last. 'The captain is allowed to have wife in his cabin.'

'Youssef, my friend, lay your doubts aside. Your

loyalty and good sense are my sheet anchor. And now you've got to get us clear. Keep both launches pulling and loose out some canvas. Let's hope for a wind with the last of the light.'

'Aye, captain,' said Youssef, and ran off forward.

The launches kept their tow-lines taut, dragging the ship bodily through the water. Then, as the sun dipped towards the western horizon, a light breeze sprang up off the land, its cooling air pouring towards the sea. Youssef sang out for topsails, and at the yards the men obeyed. Soon we shall sail her out, I thought, feeling the air brush my cheek.

I caught sight of Abigail, cradling her father's head in her hands as the merchant sat by the rail, a picture of wounded dignity. He shrank away fearfully as I approached.

'Abigail, go below with him,' I said. 'Find the girl Neeta.'

Seth Jeffreys called out weakly, 'Matthew, I – I wish to speak with the commander of this vessel. I can offer him –'

'You are speaking to him, Mister Jeffreys,' I said, 'but I am busy with my ship.'

Abigail straightened in surprise.

'Aye, you heard me right,' I said briskly. 'I am master of the *Cornelius*. Now, let's have you two below so I can take her out to sea.'

I steered the merchant and his daughter purposefully to the companionway and went back to the wheel to instruct the helmsman. Out of the corner of my eye, I watched Abigail. She waved, then disappeared down the steps, leaving me with the image of her smiling face. What must she think, I wondered, when she has discovered, in the midst of such turmoil, that I have become commander of this flyer?

On the quarter-deck, I studied the *Abundance* as she passed by on the far side of the anchorage. She approached her quarry, fully engaged in her work, as fearsome a vessel as any seaman could cast his eye upon. Her stern quarters, lavishly decorated with carvings and heraldry, were all picked out in golden paint. Her rig was a thicket of tackles and lines, and the mainmast at its base was wider than a man's armspan. The decks were alive with men loading and firing the guns, and along her yards were ranged musketmen preparing to release their volley. As she turned to close the *Success*, which seemed so much smaller and in poor trim by comparison, it was apparent she planned to grapple alongside and board the mutinous warship.

Thank the Lord she is intent on the *Success*, I said to myself in sheer wonderment at the sight of the mighty warships in action. It was the strangest thing, to see these two great barks of the English Navy fighting. But I understood they fought for the right to command, just as we had done this day. I believed it laudable to command, but supposed I had often aimed high and struck low. Now it seemed to me that duty, honour and justice must be of less import to a captain than authority, power and might.

The breeze ruffled my hair and I swung round, spotting Youssef in the waist.

'Let's make our flyer fly, sailing-master!' I sang out.

With a grin, the Barbar dashed off, calling out the orders. 'Unloose courses!' I heard him cry, and the command sent men running aloft. Soon, with her big lower sails filled and drawing, the *Cornelius* began to outrun the rowing of the launches and I ordered them hauled up and stowed for sea. Just as I was thinking she could benefit from some high canvas, for the channel had broadened now and gave us a cleaner wind, I heard Youssef's voice again.

'Aloft and unfurl topgallants!' came my sailing-master's order.

Then we were safely past, and I knew no one – not even the *Abundance*, though she had no mind to – could catch us once we gained the open waters. At last, the breeze filled in and the flyer sped free of the confining channels of the Carolina coast, dashing towards the unbroken reaches of the Atlantic.

'Run due east,' I called to my helmsman, hoping that when we cleared the shore, we would find an ocean wind.

The sun dropped below the horizon as if a lamp wick had been turned down, plunging land and sea into darkness, save for a lingering glow in the western sky. Standing on the quarter-deck watching the compass over the steersman's shoulder, I breathed the night air, smelling the warm, grassy lands at my back. There was a whiff of smoke in it once or twice, perhaps from the fighting ships. Then I remembered the torching of the Lynskill mansion, and I fell to imagining his house ablaze, with sparks shooting into the black sky, and the settlers carrying off the failed plantation man's treasures. It seemed an apt end, brimful as it was of rich men's trinkets, some of them perhaps acquired with money from the sale of the old collier, the *Prosperous Anne*. For a moment, I forgot myself and welcomed that tangy smoke as a just revenge. I even revelled in how deeply the Lynskill family would have suffered that loss, for I had learnt that the more men crave gold and its petty rewards, the harder to bear its going from them.

The *Cornelius* shuddered beneath my feet, and soon enough we would lose all scent of the land and fill our lungs with the clean ocean airs, and see the fish flying between the wave-tops and watch the sea-hogs jump in the curling wave at our stem. Even as I thought it, the bark launched her bows along the Atlantic swells, lifting her fine prow to ride them with ease.

I caught Youssef's enquiring eye. He looked up at the mizenmast and I gave a nod in reply.

'Set mizen staysail!' he ordered. 'Square off on cross-jack yard.'

Wanting the wind brought on her quarter, I told the helmsman to come two points to larboard. At once, the Barbar called up from the waist of the ship.

'Where do we go, captain? To the north, to the cold lands? Youssef hopes not.' He gave out a ripe cackle and sent men to harden the braces.

I smiled back at him, but it set me wondering. I had not thought beyond my first instinct of escaping to sea, where the *Cornelius* could recover, unmolested by pursuers. But where then? Not to Charlestown to recover the Waspik gold, for it would be dangerously full of English warships. No, I thought, the greed for gold has poisoned enough men's minds, not least my own. Could I take the ship home to Amsterdam? With the coffers empty, and a mutiny behind us, the owners would have us all hanged for pirates. To a place, then, where the *Cornelius* could ply an honest trade, perhaps in furs and skins and timbers and horns. But how would I keep these fellows of mine from their want of an easy prize? Plain dealing and noble cargoes might prove a harder business even than bloody raiding and piracy.

The black Atlantic night, pricked with stars, enveloped the bark as she put the leagues between her stern and the turmoil ashore. How I loved the way the sounds of the ship became attuned to the rhythms of the sea, with the frothing bow wave, the creak of blocks, the rustle of canvas. I murmured commands to the helm, and listened as Youssef called for the trim of a sheet here or the touch of a brace there. I cast my eye over the spread of ghostly white sails above, and sensed the power of the wind as once more the gods of the air took the ship in their hands.

Her stern rose to the building seas as we worked offshore. The rollers passed under her keel and her beak plunged into the troughs, throwing aside arcs of spray at either side. I stood beside the helmsman, sensing his quick response to every movement of the *Cornelius*, and found myself transported back across the years to my last hours aboard the *Prosperous Anne* when, all through that desperate night, we had struggled to keep her off the shoals. Yet with time those terrors had faded in my memory. Instead, I remembered the joy of sailing the collier-bark, the thrill of sending her dashing down the swells, gripping the long tiller-bar as it trembled in my hand and I drove the tough little vessel to the limits of her speed.

This night, in command aboard a bark twice her length and four times her burthen, a sleek flyer built for speed and handiness, I would no longer hold the vessel's course so completely in the palm of my hand, nor move my body with hers like a rider on a horse. I gazed out over the long weather-deck stretching before me, and listened to the creak of the blocks as she rolled, and heard the groaning boards when she lifted her head to a larger sea. She is a mighty bark like no Whitby collier, I mused, but fast and powerful, built not to haul back-breaking loads of cole but to fly across the waves. She can be sailed only by a band of men working in harmony. I must steer her and sail her and direct her course through my fellows, through my spoken orders to them, and through their obedience to my command. And I knew this held the prospect of adventure greater than any prentice boy aboard a worn-out collier-bark had ever dreamed possible.

My reverie continued thus a while, until I became aware of a slender figure at my side in the darkness. It was Abigail, and she moved close and touched my arm. Her skin was warm against mine, and I pressed her hand between my palms. In the faint starlight, I watched her face and thought how I had the chance of a life now in which to love her. But when she spoke, I was quickly cast down.

'Matthew,' she said in a quiet voice, 'you did not tell me the poor captain was dead.'

I had known he could not live more than a few days or hours longer, yet the wave of sadness that invaded me was overwhelming. This was the captain who had hove up and stopped the *Cornelius* for me when Pengarth would have left me to die frozen on the Essex shoals. It was with Josua Brogel that I had learnt the nautical arts to a degree far beyond any years of book studying. Brogel it was who gave me practice in the Navigation on the quarter-deck as we rolled down the Atlantic trades towards Sint Maarten and shot the noontime sun. Josua Brogel it was whose eye had gleamed with passion as we discussed the worlds of Science and Reason and Astronomy, the ways of God and His Universe and the celestial mysteries.

I bowed my head. 'We shall bury him with honour in the first light of morning,' I said quietly.

'Yes, Matthew, and let us hope it marks an end of the blood and the death.'

Abigail's voice was gently calming, and my heart went to her as she held me close, knowing that I needed her comfort. We stayed like that for a long time, no words passing between us, while the *Cornelius* heaved her deck-boards more lively under our feet and briskly swung her stern to the following seas. Then she spoke again.

'Matthew, shall we be safe on your ship?'

'She is a fine ship, my love, and there are good

370

men here, loyal and true.' I trusted she would understand that the future was not without danger. 'They have been set against each other, but we must hope that is past.'

'Poor Neeta, she told me – the fighting aboard here.'

'I wish I had never seen it,' I said, with a heavy heart. 'We have killed for greed. We have shown terrible injustice to brave and honest people. We have been worse than the Lynskills, worse than –'

She stopped me with a kiss.

Holding her close, I felt as if a part of my life had become complete. When we separated, I spoke tenderly.

'I respect you, Abigail, for standing by your father. He does not deserve you.'

'Respect, Matthew?' Teasing, she pretended to be downcast. 'Only that? In Whitby, you spoke of nothing but love.'

I held her, pressing the length of my body against hers. I wanted to stay with her forever.

'We shall make a new life now – we shall make an honest trading ship of the *Cornelius*,' I said. 'We shall redeem ourselves and our seamen. We shall return with honour.'

She laughed and squeezed me.

'All this at once, Matthew!' Then she fell solemn, as though a burden weighed on her. 'I have lost much, in property and money and position. But they seem to signify so little.' She looked at me for reassurance.

'Everything is changed,' I said, 'and we have enough – this ship, each other.' I watched her mobile, pretty face, shining with love. 'Do you remember my father, when we were so small? He hung for his honour.' I stroked her cheek, thinking of what I had longed to say for years. 'I am the son of Robert Loftus of Whitby. I am not a Stalbone, but a Loftus.'

I waited. She was the only person in the world I could truly open my heart to. She was smiling.

'I am Matthew Loftus,' I told her.

'Then,' she said slowly, 'I am Abigail Loftus.'

Who could not love her for that? Hardly daring to breathe, I held her slender waist and caressed the curve of her hip. Our eyes did not leave each other's faces for a long minute, and we kissed again.

There came a rattle from above. I sighed and tore myself away to cast my eye aloft to the great spread of flaxen canvas that swelled above, filling with the American breeze and carrying us away to the ocean.

'The ship, Abigail,' I said, with what I hoped was a rueful smile. 'She needs me too.'

She nodded. 'See to your ship, Matthew.'

I went to the break of the poop. 'Trim sheets, there, Youssef. It's not like you to be dreaming.'

The Barbar was leaning on the rail at the waist with young Adam Pyne, deep in conversation, gazing at the sea foaming past at the water-line.

'Aye, captain!' said Youssef, startled out of his reverie.

I could see the grin on his narrow face as he crossed the weather-deck to rouse Gaspar and old Eli, the Dutchman Jakob Tosher and the others from where they rested under the rail, singing or murmuring in low tones. Even the one-handed Quaker was with them, though silent and brooding. When the sailing-master's voice rang out clear, the watchmen sprang to the belays as one, and trimmed her to the breeze.

Instantly, the *Cornelius* responded, dipping her beak to meet the rising swells of the deep ocean. Her bows parted the seas, spraying out broken waters that gleamed and hissed along her sides and sparkled with jewels of green phosphorescence. The flyer plunged on into the velvety night, where the stars hung suspended above the ocean like markers on the celestial way and looked to me for all the world as though they were beckoning her onward.

*Marcus Palliser's new novel will be available in hardback from William Heinemann in April 2000.*

# DEVIL OF A FIX

It is 1702, and in the lawless Caribbean sea young Matthew Loftus determines to captain his ship by honest trade rather than piracy and plunder. But his crew lust after the spoils that the fast, well-armed *Cornelius* can win, and even his love, Abigail, doubts him.

Encountering an old man who chants endless numbers and incantations, he learns of a secret almanac that advances the science of navigation. Falsly accused of mutiny and seeking pardon, Matthew embarks on the cause of solving the Longitude, the lack of which wrecks hundreds of ships and drowns thousands of seamen. But is the almanac what it seems? Can it really give a position fix at sea by sighting the moon against the stars?

Pursued by unprincipled merchants, duplicitous privateers and the English Navy through the battles on the high seas and sinister perils on deserted tropical shores, Matthew struggles not only with navigational uncertainties but also with the venal motives fuelling commerce and the war in the Caribbean.

The passage is strewn with the reefs and shoals of treachery and falsehood, and beset by clashing currents of political trickery, patronage and ambition. Despite loss and injustice, through gales and sea battles, he sails his beloved schooner towards the great goal he has set himself.

## ALSO AVAILABLE IN PAPERBACK

ALL ARROW BOOKS ARE AVAILABLE THROUGH MAIL ORDER OR FROM YOUR LOCAL BOOKSHOP AND NEWSAGENT.
PLEASE SEND CHEQUE/EUROCHEQUE/POSTAL ORDER (STERLING ONLY) ACCESS, VISA, MASTERCARD, DINERS CARD, SWITCH OR AMEX.

EXPIRY DATE ............. SIGNATURE ...................................
PLEASE ALLOW 75 PENCE PER BOOK FOR POST AND PACKING U.K.
OVERSEAS CUSTOMERS PLEASE ALLOW £1.00 PER COPY FOR POST AND PACKING.
ALL ORDERS TO:
ARROW BOOKS, BOOKS BY POST, TBS LIMITED, THE BOOK SERVICE, COLCHESTER ROAD, FRATING GREEN, COLCHESTER, ESSEX CO7 7DW.
TELEPHONE: (01206) 256 000
FAX: (01206) 255 914

NAME: ........................................................................

ADDRESS ...................................................................

........................................................................

Please allow 28 days for delivery. Please tick box if you do not wish to receive any additional information ❑
Prices and availability subject to change without notice.